BUELL HAMPTON

By

WILLIS GEORGE EMERSON

First published in 1902

British Library Cataloguing-in-Publication Data
A catalogue record for this book is available
from the British Library

CONTENTS

Willis George Emerson.................................5

THEME...7

DEDICATED TO MY OLD SWEETHEART............9

AT LAKE GENEVA 11

A CHANCE MEETING............................16

A DECLARATION................................22

THE DEPARTURE................................28

A FRONTIER BANKER............................35

MAJOR BUELL HAMPTON 41

THE CATTLE KING 49

A COMMITTEE OF FIVE..........................56

AN AFTERNOON DRIVE 62

HOME OF THE HORTONS 68

DADDY'. CONSENT 73

KANSAS PROHIBITION 78

MAJOR HAMPTON'. LIBRARY 88

THE SONG..92

THE RETRACTION................................96

THE OLD VIOLIN 101

LENOX AVONDALE'. ARRIVAL 105

A LOVE SONG 112

AN INVITATION TO JOIN 118

3

A DINNER AT THE HORTONS 126

THE FOOT-RACE. 132

THE ELECTION 139

A FORGED LETTER 146

REVERSING THE HIGHER COURTS. 153

ALMOST A TRAGEDY 158

REACHING A DECISION 163

THE HOT WINDS 167

"THY WILL BE DONE". 172

JACK REDFIELD ARRIVES. 179

THE QUARREL. 190

THE PASSING OF LORD AVONDALE 194

THE SILENCING OF GOSSIP 200

A RIDE AMONG SUNFLOWERS. 204

THE PRAIRIE-FIRE. 214

A BUCKING BRONCO 221

A STARTLING REVELATION 228

TRYING TO REMEMBER 233

TRUTH STRANGER THAN FICTION 239

JUDGE LYNN HAS AN IDEA 244

THE CATTLE THIEF CAUGHT .255

A ROSICRUCIAN 263

A NEW-MADE GRAVE. 271

UNDER THE QUIET STARS 279

WILLIS GEORGE EMERSON

Willis George Emerson was born in 1856, and spent his early education at Knox College, Illinois, USA. He later attended *Northern Ohio University*, after which he was admitted to the bar in 1886. Emerson quickly lost interest in the legal profession however, and moved to Kansas where he became heavily involved in politics; actively campaigning on behalf of the Republican Party in both the 1888 and 1900 elections. Emerson is best known as a prominent American novelist though, and is famed for his evocative tales of the Mid-West. Among his better-known novels are *Buell Hampton* (1902), *The Builders* (1906), *Smoky God vs. Voyage in the Inner World* (1908), *The Treasure of Hidden Valley* (1915) and *The Man Who Discovered Himself* (1919). *Smoky God vs. Voyage in the Inner World* is particularly notable for its unusual plotline; the protagonist discovers an Eden like civilisation in in the centre of the earth, where a scientifically advanced race of long-lived giants is discovered worshipping a 'smoky God' – the interior sun. This was the first literary work to bring Emerson widespread acclaim. A man of many talents and interests, Emerson also worked as a newspaperman, lawyer, politician and promoter, forming the North American Copper Company in Wyoming. Emerson is also credited with founding the town of Grand Encampment, a municipality in Carbon County, Wyoming. With Emerson's Copper Company based there, it became a booming centre of copper mining and smelting. A sixteen-mile tramway was built to carry copper ore from the mountains into the town for smelting; a tramway which was, at the time, the longest in the world. He died on 11 December, 1918.

THEME

Once an American mother, with the wealth of a Croesus and a lovely daughter, longed for titled distinction.

In her net she caught an adventurer, clothed in a frayed-out remnant of a former nobility—and an eyeglass.

They bartered and came to terms,—dollars, title,—while an innocent girl was thrown in as an incident.

> "And what is writ is writ,—
> Would it were worthier."

Childe Harold's Pilgrimage.

Every author who, early or late, finds it his delightful, yet dangerous, privilege to "get under cover" owes something to Pliny the Younger for recording the fact that Pliny the Elder used to say that "no book was so bad but that some good might be got out of it."

With this delightful assurance as an incentive, the author of "Buell Hampton" began, some twelve years ago, to construct the story herewith presented.

There is so much in the following tale of the great Southwest that is based upon facts and actual happenings that I hardly know where history ceases and fiction begins.

I know the grain-bags of promise were torn open and found to be filled with the tare seeds of disappointment, which were blown carelessly about by the wind-puffs of adversity.

The Osborns, the Hortons, queenly Ethel, and Marie,—the singing girl,—Lord Avondale, Jack Redfield, and Hugh Stanton are still in the land of the living, and will doubtless peruse these pages with varying degrees of approval. Judge Lynn died about one year ago, but will long be remembered in the Southwest for his oddities and grotesque sayings. I was present when a shadow fell between the old banker and his beautiful young wife, and, with the days, it deepened, until it was obliterated by the clods of Graceland Cemetery.

The prairie-fire, the foot-race, and the pitiless hot winds were actual occurrences, while the fields of sunflowers are, in season, still to be seen in all their gorgeous splendor.

Major Buell Hampton is a flesh and blood personality, with whom I spent many an enjoyable evening, and whom I learned to love for his wealth of wisdom and kindness of heart. His rise and fall, the tragedy on the red banks of the Cimarron River, and his strange disappearance, are a part of the tragic history of the cattle-range of the Great Southwest. The music of the old violin still lingers with me, and is inseparable from the strange character and complex destiny of this wonderful man.

W. G. E.

DEDICATED TO
MY OLD SWEETHEART

My sweetheart of the long ago—
With rosy cheeks and raven hair—
Sang lullabies so soft and low,
All joyous was the rhythmic air.
Though other links with luckless fate
Have brought me bruises bathed in tears,
From childhood up to man's estate
Her love has held me all the years.
Our ties grow fonder, day by day,
While graces, all, in her combine.
Oh, love! make good and glad the way
Where walks this sweetheart—Mother mine.

CHAPTER I.

AT LAKE GENEVA

IT was only a game of tennis that brought on this affair of love's entanglement.

Ethel Horton, with rich, maidenly flushes on her soft cheeks, played as she had never played before—played and won.

Athletic suppleness and vivacious buoyancy were emphasized in every movement of this intense American girl.

With heightened color, she contested the game, point by point.

It was thrilling sport, and her clever opponent was Lenox Avondale, an Englishman.

And while this exciting neck and neck game was in progress, her mother, Mrs. J. Bruce-Horton, was idly conversing with Mrs. Lyman Osborn on a wide veranda of the hotel that overlooked the blue waters of the lake.

"Really," she observed, leaning back in her easy chair, "Lake Geneva is not such a bad place, after all. One can get on here very well for a few days."

"Oh, yes," said Mrs. Lyman Osborn, as she seated herself languidly, and gazed across the blue waters, "yet I fancy that in time it would become quite dull for us, it is so thoroughly American. Let me push the cushions under your shoulder a little farther, dear."

"Thank you," replied Mrs. Horton, "that is more comfortable. What does Doctor Redfield say of my illness?"

"That in a week's time we can continue our journey to the Southwest."

"My dear husband," murmured Mrs. Horton, reflectively,

"how glad he will be to see Ethel! It has been four years since the child was placed in that fashionable London school; she was then only fifteen. Her dear father will hardly know her."

"The thanks of all are due to you, my dear Mrs. Horton, for the educational advantages that Ethel has enjoyed."

"Yes, my husband is so determined in his ideas; but I manage to spend as little of my time on the frontier, you know, as possible, and I certainly shall see to it that Ethel does not deteriorate under the influence of our stupid American ways. She is certainly a girl of rare gifts, and I could never have forgiven myself had she been educated in the States."

"Quite right," assented Mrs. Osborn, "your husband may stay with his herds of cattle, and my husband may stand at his bank counter, year in and year out, if it pleases them to do so, but you and I will take our annual trip to merry England," and Mrs. Osborn laughed a ripple of indifference at the crude taste of their respective husbands.

Mrs. J. Bruce-Horton was a woman in her early forties. Her features were regular, and her complexion had a youthfulness not in keeping with her age. Her heavy brown hair was most becomingly arranged. Her neatly fitting suit of tweed,—a production of Redfern,—in keeping with the latest London style, admirably set off her rather stately figure. Her companion, Mrs. Lyman Osborn, was probably thirty-five, although in appearance she seemed much younger. A pink and white skin, fair hair, and blue eyes combined in giving her a bewitching appearance.

They were returning from a trip to England, whither they had gone to bring home with them Ethel Horton, who had recently finished her education in a London school. At Chicago Mrs. J. Bruce-Horton had been taken suddenly ill; and Doctor Redfield had been recommended and summoned. On his advice they had come to Lake Geneva until Mrs. Horton sufficiently recovered to continue their journey to southwestern Kansas.

Mr. John B. Horton was known in the West as a great cattle baron. Soon after the war he married in Baltimore, and moved

West to engage in the cattle business. His lonely dugout of frontier days had given way to one of the most palatial residences in the West. This beautiful home had been erected on the site of the dugout, near the line between Kansas and No-Man's-Land, and not far from the Cimarron River. Horton's Grove was known far and wide. Indeed, it was practically the only timber in that section of the country. In this grove two mammoth springs burst forth from the hillside, and formed a beautiful stream named Manaroya. Here, near the edge of the grove, and on the banks of the gurgling brook, less than three miles from Meade, Kansas, John Horton had erected his home.

With their accumulation of wealth had come an ambition on the part of Mrs. J. Bruce-Horton—as she inscribed her cards— to give her daughter Ethel all the advantages of a thorough education. Vassar had been thought of; but the banker's wife, Mrs. Lyman Osborn, had suggested that foreign travel was indispensable in reaching a correct decision.

Captain Lyman Osborn was a veteran of the Union army, and was many years his wife's senior. He was engaged in the banking business at Meade, and divided his time between his duties at the bank, and his son, Harry, who was not more than five years of age. The father fairly idolized the boy, and, while he was with him, was quite content that his young wife should travel abroad—if that were her pleasure.

Against her husband's wishes and advice, Mrs. J. Bruce-Horton had selected a London school for their daughter, and since Ethel had been placed therein, she had spent a portion of each year in England, accompanied by her bosom friend, Mrs. Lyman Osborn. In many ways these two women were dissimilar, but their very dissimilarity seemed to bind them more closely together. They had both become tinctured with the weakness of title-worship, and perhaps the most cherished wish of Mrs. J. Bruce-Horton was that Ethel should marry into some titled English family.

"I do wonder," she sighed, "if there are any people desirable for one to know stopping at the hotel."

"Very doubtful," lamented Mrs. Osborn. "The fewer Americans we know the better for us when among our friends on the other side."

"Quite true," assented the other, devoutly.

"It is so embarrassing, when one is among one's English friends, to have American acquaintances intruding themselves. Oh, here comes Ethel!" observed Mrs. Horton.

"Oh, mamma!" cried Ethel, as she came running toward them, all out of breath, "our side won."

"Why, Ethel, what have you been doing?" exclaimed her mother, as she held up her hands in amazement.

"I have just finished the jolliest game of tennis I ever played in my life; and my! did n't we do them up!"

"Such language, Ethel; do you know—"

"Why, mamma, if you could have seen how we Americans vanquished two rum Englishmen you would have shouted 'Hail Columbia' and 'The Star Spangled Banner' forever!"

"Ethel, Ethel, such language is so unbecoming!"

"I know, mamma, but I am in America once more, and I feel in a 'Hail Columbia' sort of mood. There," said she, "and there," as she stooped and kissed her mother affectionately. "Now don't scold me any more. My, but I am having lots of fun."

Mrs. J. Bruce-Horton adjusted her glasses, which had been displaced by Ethel's impetuous embrace, and inquired, "Did you say that there were some English families stopping at the hotel, Ethel?"

"Yes, mamma, the Countess Berwyn and Lady Somebody—I don't remember her name—and her son and an English friend of his."

"Not such an undesirable place to stop, after all," remarked Mrs. Lyman Osborn.

"No, indeed!" exclaimed Mrs. J. Bruce-Horton. "But really, Ethel, you must be more particular. You must not speak so disrespectfully of our English friends. You know we have so many across the water."

"Why, mamma, I am not disrespectful; I am only happy, and so glad that I am home again in my own country. Well, bye-bye, I must go and dress for dinner—Oh, yes, will Doctor Redfield be here this evening?"

"I presume so," answered her mother, inquiringly, "but why do you ask?"

"Oh, nothing," replied Ethel, and she hurried away—with her young face all aglow with happiness.

"Brimming over with animation!" said Mrs. Osborn, as she looked at the retreating form of the girl. "Together we must control spirited Ethel until she is safely anchored in the harbor of English nobility."

"Yes, indeed, we must," acquiesced Mrs. Horton; "and it is very kind of you to take so much interest in helping me."

Ethel Horton was a tall and stately girl. She had laughing eyes, pouting red lips, and teeth that resembled the delicate tints of the conch-shell. Her intellectual forehead, slightly aquiline nose, radiantly youthful complexion, and wealth of dark brown hair, made her a creature beautiful to look upon.

"I wonder why Ethel inquired about Doctor Redfield," mused Mrs. Horton, thoughtfully.

"Oh, it was nothing," rejoined Mrs. Osborn, "still we must beware of these broad-shouldered men with blond mustaches. He really is quite attractive; however, Ethel is not sentimental, is she?"

"Good gracious, no!" responded Mrs. Horton, emphatically, "not in the least."

"So much the better, then," affirmed her companion; "it will be a great deal easier to work out a destiny that will be for her own good. We should be able to make a great match for her, my dear. I will help you, and we shall not fail. Now we must find out about these English people."

CHAPTER II.

A CHANCE MEETING

WHEN Ethel returned to her mother after dressing for dinner, her tennis suit had been exchanged for an airy lace dress of soft material and such complete simplicity that it set off her youthful form to the very best advantage.

"By the way, mamma, Lady Avondale is the other Englishwoman stopping at the hotel. She and the Countess Berwyn are traveling together."

"Lady Avondale!" exclaimed the mother, "did you say Lady Avondale? My dear friend, Lady Avondale!"

"How charmingly fortunate," lisped Mrs. Lyman Osborn.

"Yes, indeed," agreed Mrs. Horton, with unmistakable complacency, "how kind they were to us a year ago! You know, Ethel, we were entertained at Lady Avondale's country-house a year ago, and oh, what a lovely estate they have, and how delightfully kind they were to us. We must send our cards at once."

"Oh, here comes Doctor Redfield!" exclaimed Mrs. Osborn; and the three ladies turned toward a tall, broad-shouldered man of about thirty, who bowed politely as he approached them.

Dr. Jack Redfield, as he was familiarly called by his friends, although young in years, had nevertheless "won his spurs" in the medical profession. He had a lucrative practice in Chicago, and occupied a chair in one of the leading medical colleges. His head was of a Napoleonic cast. He had deep-set, expressive blue eyes, short brown hair, a rather heavy blond mustache, and a square chin indicative of great strength of character. In physical proportions he seemed an athlete. His neatly fitting attire proved that he kept abreast with the conventionalities.

"How are you feeling this evening?" he asked, addressing Mrs. J. Bruce-Horton.

"Oh, much better, thank you."

"I fear it is almost too cool for you here on the veranda, and I suggest the wisdom of your retiring to the parlors."

"Oh, do you really think so, doctor? It is so very pleasant here, and yet it is very thoughtful of you to mention it. Perhaps," continued Mrs. Horton, turning to Mrs. Osborn, "we had better go in."

"I will accompany you," said Doctor Redfield. "I think it best to change the medicine."

"Will you come, Ethel?" asked Mrs. Horton, as they arose.

"No, mamma, it is so very pleasant out here, and you know that I am not ill."

As the invalid and her companion moved away, Doctor Redfield turned to Ethel and said, "I trust you are enjoying your temporary sojourn at Lake Geneva."

"Oh, very much, indeed," replied Ethel, with a smile, "I think the rowing is simply grand, and the shady walks and drives are superb."

"Of course as a summer resort," said Doctor Redfield, "it may not compare with Bath or Brighton, but I doubt if the Lakes of Killarney or the scenery surrounding them surpass, in point of beauty, Lake Geneva."

"You are quite an American, aren't you?" said Ethel, laughingly.

"Intensely so," replied Doctor Redfield.

"Well, we can't quarrel on that point, for I am more in love with my own country than before I went abroad."

"I beg pardon," interrupted Mrs. Osborn, who had returned from escorting her companion to the parlors, "but Mrs. Horton is waiting for you, doctor."

"Very well, I shall come at once," he answered, while a flush of embarrassment overspread his face; then, turning to Ethel, he said, "I trust that Lake Geneva may continue to be as interesting during the next few days as it has thus far proved."

"Thank you," replied Ethel, and the doctor was led away by Mrs. Osborn.

In the meantime, Mrs. J. Bruce-Horton had sent her own and Mrs. Osborn's card to Lady Avondale. Soon after Doctor Redfield concluded his professional call, Lady Avondale presented herself, and the titled Englishwoman and her American friends were profuse in their protestations of pleasure at the meeting.

After the dinner-hour, when Dr. Jack Redfield was leaving the hotel, he looked wistfully along the veranda in the hope of again seeing Ethel, but she had disappeared.

He was not only a skilful practitioner, but he knew the value of a patient like Mrs. J. Bruce-Horton, and when he had such an one on the road to recovery he was willing to humor her whims as much as the occasion permitted. As he walked toward the lake, down the graveled path so exquisitely bordered on either side with fragrant flowers, which were watered by frequent whirlabout fountains, each throwing its refreshing spray far over the lawn, a feeling of satisfaction at his professional success, and of complete contentment with the whole world, elated him. This feeling might have been continued indefinitely but for a single incident—a fate-like incident—that changed the story of his life.

As he came to a turn in the path he found Ethel reclining on a rustic seat and looking out over the blue waters of the lake.

"I am not a highwayman," said Ethel, jestingly, "but nevertheless I mean to waylay you."

"Indeed!" said Jack, inquiringly.

"Yes, I wanted to ask you about dear mamma. You do not think she is dangerously ill, do you?"

"By no means," replied Doctor Redfield, reassuringly, "her indisposition is rapidly giving way to my treatment, and I think that within a week she will have quite recovered."

"Oh, thank you, doctor, I have been so worried about her."

"With the assurance that I have given, you may cease worrying entirely," said Jack as he turned to leave her.

"Why are you in such haste to go?" asked Ethel, coquettishly.

"I am not particularly in haste," replied Jack, "but perhaps I interrupt your reverie."

"Yes, but I want to be interrupted," returned Ethel, laughingly.

"Very well," said Jack, seating himself near her.

Jack Redfield was anything but a Beau Brummel. The idea of yielding himself to maiden sovereignty had never occurred to him. Indeed, his lack of homage to woman might almost have been interpreted as a poverty of gallantry. Nevertheless, in the few days that he had been making professional calls on her mother, he had awakened to a knowledge of the feet that Miss Ethel interested him, to say the least. There was a wild dash of independence and of frankness about her that possessed a charm for him which he was unable to analyze.

As Jack looked out over the lake he was conscious that Ethel was studying him closely. Presently she said, "I cannot make myself believe that you are a physician."

"Indeed, why not?" interrogated Jack, much amused by her frankness. "You evidently expected me to perform a miracle in your mother's case, and, as I have failed to do so, you judge me harshly."

"Oh, no! not that," protested Ethel, "but then, I always fancied that doctors, who give bitter medicine, cut up people and saw bones, should be old and grim. Now, you don't look like a doctor at all to me."

"Well, as I have to make my living in the uncanny way that you have described, I must say that I am glad every one does not share your hasty judgment of me."

"Oh, thank you," said Ethel, "that's very well put. I know you think I am not very kind."

"No, I would hardly go as far as that," said Jack, "but I doubt my ability to hold my own in a conversation with you, much more than I would my skill in a surgical operation or a bad case of measles. I have faith that my treatment would be successful, but I have no faith that you would not vanquish me very quickly with your repartee and your direct way of putting things."

"Oh, what a refreshing compliment," laughed Ethel. "I thought because you were a doctor that you were stoical and grim, but you really seem quite the reverse."

"I am indeed surprised," said Jack, "not at you, but rather at your impression of me. I did n't know that I possessed the gift of being complimentary to ladies; in fact, the social side of my life has been very much neglected. My time has been so taken up with my studies and profession, that I have cultivated but little the ways and customs of the social world."

"Well, you are different from some people I know—Dr. Lenox Avondale for instance—but then he is English and you are an American."

"I am quite content to be an American, with all my stupidity in regard to social matters. He doubtless was reared among a titled aristocracy, and society is a second nature to him. I believe—pardon my frankness—that your life has been much the same, and that you will continue to dwell in a social atmosphere. From remarks made by your mother and her friend I doubt not that they have mapped out a great career for you."

"I trust I am too loyal an American," returned Ethel, proudly, "to take part in any career that is not entirely congenial to my own tastes, and your deductions as to yourself are quite incorrect. For my part, I think more of one who is noble and manly than I do of those English or American idlers, who think only of the latest fashions and who change their attire half a dozen times a day and are, even then, at a loss to know just what to do to kill time."

Jack looked at Ethel as she was speaking, and he was conscious of a budding admiration for her that was quite a new feeling to him.

"Bravo," said he, applaudingly, "those are grand sentiments. No one can say that they are un-American; but I fear that you are surrounded by conditions that may force you to change your views."

"Oh, I assure you," said Ethel, very earnestly, "I have the

greatest admiration for workers, whether with the brain or with the hand. It is hardly fashionable, I suppose, to admit such views, but I can't help my convictions."

"I hope," said Jack, "that you may have the courage of your convictions, but I am not blind. I have already discovered that which is marked out for you. If your mother and Mrs. Osborn were not occupied with Lady Avondale, this accidental meeting of ours would not have taken place."

"A destiny marked out for me?" inquired Ethel, in surprise.

"Yes," said Jack, and his voice shook a little as he spoke, "a destiny that does not lie along the line of brain-workers. It is along a highway burnished with titles, on the one side, and with wrecked hopes, broken hearts, and much unhappiness on the other."

A silence followed. Presently he arose and quietly clasped her proffered hand. Over it he bowed in deepest respect. She was conscious that a strange, intense earnestness was moving this strong man. His every emotion said goodbye, but his lips spoke no word. He turned quickly from her and disappeared in the gathering twilight, and still, without knowing why, she remained where he had left her—watching, wondering, waiting.

CHAPTER III.

A DECLARATION

LADY AVONDALE was very gracious to the Americans, flattering their vanity by presenting them to the Countess of Berwyn. On the Following day, much to their gratification, she introduced them to her son, Dr. Lenox Avondale.

Doctor Avondale was, in fact, a rather distinguished personage. He was perhaps forty years of age, and while not an especially brilliant conversationalist, he talked quite fluently of the race-track, the chase, and kindred topics. Of the English army he knew much, having been appointed surgeon therein by Her Majesty. There he gained a wide reputation for skill in his profession. He was, however, decidedly blasi, and not even the usually alluring subject of out-door sports was sufficient to arouse in him more than a passing interest. He had a tendency to yawn at the dinner-table, and exhibited but little consideration for those occupying less exalted positions than himself. He cultivated a bored expression and complained a great deal about the "beastly American customs." He had obtained an indefinite leave of absence from the Army and was thoroughly "doing the States." His elder brother, Lord Avondale, had contracted an intermittent fever the year before, while in Australia. This fever had developed into serious complications, and his death was considered to be a question of only a short time, whereupon Dr. Lenox Avondale would succeed to the titles and estates, which are among the oldest in England. The estates, however, were so heavily encumbered with debts that it had been considered necessary to cast about for some American heiress, who, in consideration of sharing the titles, would bring with her enough American dollars to relieve the property of its indebtedness; indeed, Lady Avondale's mission to America was to assist her son in this undertaking.

Mrs. J. Bruce-Horton, in conversation with Lady Avondale, had assured her that if Ethel married a suitable person she should receive three million dollars on her wedding-day, and perhaps twice that much at the death of her parents.

Lady Avondale explained about the sickness of Lord Avondale, her eldest son, and that she was daily expecting to hear of his death, at which time her dear son, Lenox, would succeed to his brother's titles and estates. To all appearances she was very frank and confiding with Mrs. J. Bruce-Horton; but she failed to say anything about the multitude of debts.

Mrs. Lyman Osborn seemed particularly to fancy Dr. Lenox Avondale, and he paid much attention to her. She assured her bosom friend, Mrs. Horton, that she was very proud of his attentions—not for herself, but because of the opportunity it gave to pave the way for "a most desirable match for dear Ethel."

"You are a sweet, good creature; you are indeed," said Mrs. J. Bruce-Horton, when in the privacy of their room. "I could not manage. it, I certainly could not, without your assistance."

"I don't believe we had better be in too great a hurry about starting home," concluded Mrs. Osborn.

"Yes, I understand," agreed Mrs. Horton, nodding significantly, "I think that my health will not permit me to start for a couple of weeks. But, really, have n't you noticed, Lucy, what a deliciously wholesome foreign air there is about this place? With Lady Avondale and the charming countess here I could almost fancy that we were again in dear old England."

"On, it is perfectly lovely," rejoined Mrs. Osborn. "Dr. Lenox Avondale has invited me to go rowing this evening, and I certainly shall not miss the opportunity of pressing upon him the superiority of dear Ethel."

"It is so good of you," lisped Mrs. J. Bruce-Horton, "to take such a deep interest in the child. She is inclined to be rather wilful, and perhaps a little headstrong, but, by judicious management, I am sure that we can overcome her silly, girlish ideas."

That afternoon Doctor Redfield called and found that Mrs. J. Bruce-Horton was very desirous that he should advise their remaining longer at the lake. He was not slow in making the suggestion. He wondered a little at the peculiar turn that affairs had taken, and the sudden attachment of his patient for Lake Geneva. However, he rightly attributed it to the presence of the English guests. When he left Ethel on the evening before, a strange feeling had come to him. He longed to see her, and he wondered if an hour of tender confidences would ever again be theirs. He remembered the pressure of the girl's warm hand. It had thrilled him. Leaving the hotel in the afternoon, he hesitated a moment on the veranda in an uncertain frame of mind. Then he walked briskly down a path leading through a dense wood that shaded the shore of the lake. An hour afterward he returned to the hotel, he having seen nothing of Ethel. On taking his leave, he saw Dr. Lenox Avondale, accompanied by Mrs. Lyman Osborn and Ethel, going toward the boat-house. Ethel recognized him, and he fancied that there was a warmth in her smile as she bowed.

Thus matters went on, day after day, for several weeks, until Mrs. Horton was pronounced entirely recovered. "We shall be leaving in a day or two," she observed to Doctor Redfield, "and, thanks to your skill, I am quite myself again."

When Jack had gone, Mrs. Osborn looked knowingly at Mrs. Horton, and said, "I think it is just as well that Doctor Redfield is not coming any more. Ethel has spoken several times of him, and has really exhibited more interest in him than I like."

"There is certainly no sentiment in Ethel," replied Mrs. J. Bruce-Horton, "and I feel sure, from what I have said to her, that she is favorably impressed with Dr. Lenox Avondale—still, one cannot be too careful."

While these two friends were thus plotting together, Dr. Jack Redfield was strolling along the beach with Ethel. His daily professional visits had been brightened with the anticipation of seeing her, and his heart had been gladdened by the belief that she, too, had looked forward, with more than passing interest, to his coming.

There are natures that blend and harmonize instantly. Friends are discovered—not manufactured or purchased, and congenial souls recognize one another by the restful influence that each imparts to the other. Ethel Horton and Dr. Jack Redfield each felt this kindred bond of sympathy and mutual discovery. When such souls meet, they defy all social customs.

"I don't know," Ethel was saying, naively, "why your visits give me so much pleasure. Am I too frank in saying this?"

"Oh, no," answered Jack, "I presume it is because you are so deeply interested in your mother's recovery, but I should like to believe that this is not the only reason. I should like to feel that you entertain an interest in me personally, although you must repent of it after we separate to-day, for doubtless I shall drift entirely out of your life. Perhaps that is your wish, and perhaps it is best that it be so."

A blush came to Ethel's face. She walked on silently at his side.

"Don't talk like that," she finally said, in girlish reprimand, "it makes me think that you are disagreeable. I shall always remember you." She laughed a little as she said this, and looked archly up at Jack.

"Remember me!" said Jack, as he turned toward her under the shading branches of an elm that stood near the shore of the lake. "Yes, I should like to believe that you would remember me, but you cannot. Not only is your destiny marked out for you, but even your friends have been chosen for you, and I am not on the list. No difference what your personal wishes may be at this time, you will soon forget me."

There was an earnestness approaching sternness in his voice.

"You are very cross to-day," said Ethel, sadly, "very cross, indeed. I could not forget you, even if I were to try, and I do not think it kind of you to say so."

"Are you quite sure?" inquired Jack, half rapturously.

She raised her eyes to his, and after a moment said, "I am sure. But what difference can it make to you? I shall never see you again."

Jack could not reply at once. He turned partly away and looked out across the waters. As Ethel glanced at him she saw that his face was ashen. She feared that he was vexed and would again say something cross to her. She remembered the feeling that had come over her once before when she was with him. At the sight of his sad face her thoughts became those of pity; and she fell to wondering why friends have to part. She came close to his side, and, laying a hand on his arm, said, pleadingly, "You must not be angry with me to-day; indeed you must not. Why, your arm is shaking as if you were cold."

"Yes," replied Jack, in a low, trembling voice. "Oh, Ethel, Ethel, can you not see—can you not understand that I love you? My heart is beating for you with fierce hammer strokes through every fibre of my being. I have no words to express myself, but I know, yes, before God, I know that I love you better than my own life."

Tears stood in Ethel's eyes, and in their startled surprise Jack read that his impassioned declaration had been too sudden.

"Oh," sobbed Ethel, as she bowed her head to hide her tears, "if daddy were only here."

"Forgive me—forgive me for speaking, if I have offended you, but the thought of your going away from me, perhaps forever, quite unmanned me." Lifting one of her trembling hands, he kissed it passionately. "Forget me, Ethel, forget me to-morrow, if you will, but only tell me before we part that I am forgiven."

"No, no," said Ethel, between her sobs, "I am sure there is nothing to forgive. Oh, I cannot understand this strange feeling that has taken possession of me. If daddy were only here so I could talk to him. I am afraid to speak to mamma."

"Well, do not speak to her," said Jack, soothingly, "but when you reach your home tell your father, if you will, and, if you can give me your love, write me and I will come to you at once."

"It is good of you to say that," said Ethel, still sobbing, "I really believe I love you now."

Jack was about to throw to the winds all his good resolution of giving her time to decide, and he would have taken her in his arms then and there, and claimed her for his own forever, had not a colored boy from the hotel interrupted them.

"Beg your pardon, miss," said he, "but Mrs. J. Bruce-Horton wished me to say would you please come to her."

Jack dropped a piece of silver in the boy's hand, and said, "Please say to Mrs. Horton that Miss Ethel will come very soon."

They turned and walked slowly, side by side, along the path, in the now uncertain light, toward the hotel, enjoying love's first awakening. Presently Jack spoke.

"You will not forget me, Ethel, but you will write for me to come, will you not?" The soft pressure of the girl's small hand, which was resting contentedly in his, and her sweet, low words of assurance made Jack happy, and yet he was conscious of the sadness of parting. As they neared the hotel he lifted her hand to his lips again and murmured, "Good-bye, Ethel, God bless you."

"Good-bye," she whispered; and her eyes were brimming with tears. "I shall not forget my promise, and I am sure daddy will be on our side."

Jack hurried down the walk, and Ethel stood on the veranda, looking after his retreating figure. A soft mist of awakened love overflowed her young heart and enveloped her.

She turned and went into the hotel—a woman; her girlhood had vanished with the awakening.

CHAPTER IV.

THE DEPARTURE

WHEN Mrs. Horton and Mrs. Osborn learned from the messenger boy that Ethel was with Doctor Redfield their agitation became apparent. They agreed that the best thing to be done was to hasten their departure from Lake Geneva. They wisely decided not to mention the affair to Ethel; but they determined to be more careful and observant of her in the future. Before retiring, they determined to start for the Southwest on the following day.

Lady Avondale was blandly polite, and she assured Mrs. Horton that already she had learned to love Ethel, the dear child, as if she were her own daughter. "Lenox," she said, assuringly, "is taken with her, really he is quite attentive; have n't you noticed it, Mrs. Osborn?"

"I must admit," replied the intriguing Mrs. Osborn, "that he has expressed his admiration for her quite freely, while the dear boy's eyes betray an eloquence of feeling that cannot be doubted."

Had Mrs. Horton tried to give an explanation why she desired such an alliance, she would perhaps have floundered hopelessly in a sea of interrogation-points. Until she met Mrs. Osborn this Anglomania idea had never even been thought of by this otherwise sensible American mother. There are natures that influence us, unconsciously to ourselves, in strange and mysterious ways. We meet a person, and instinctively we are impressed with some peculiarity that he or she possesses. We hardly know just what it is, nor do we even stop to analyze our feelings. This one peculiarity might outweigh, in our minds, a hundred glaring defects—defects which in others would be not only quickly noticed by us, but severely condemned. Hence, in our newly formed fondness, friendship, or whatever it may be, we practically become blind to faults.

Mrs. Horton had formed a strong attachment for this very clever woman. This power was not an unconscious one to Lucy Osborn. She had quickly discovered it, and she meant to profit by it,—not in a mercenary way, no, she would have scorned even the thought of such a thing, but in a social way; through an alliance for Ethel she would in some way build an altar for herself.

She experienced little love or sentiment for either Mrs. Horton or her daughter, but she determined to use them as a means to an end. In most things Mrs. Osborn would have been considered an average woman—no better, no worse. Her desire, her ambition, her mania, however, to enter into English social circles was paramount to all other considerations. It was the gaunt tigress of her nature, famishing with desire, ready with hidden tooth and claw to pounce upon every opposition.

"I can assure you, Lady Avondale," said Mrs. J. Bruce-Horton, and she flushed deeply as she spoke, "that a marriage between my daughter and your son, when he shall have succeeded to his family title, will be most agreeable to me."

"So nice of you to say that, I am sure," lisped her Ladyship, while in her heart she was saying, "Why, this silly American woman is extremely amusing."

"I trust," continued she aloud, "that your worthy husband will also approve of the contemplated alliance of our families."

Mrs. J. Bruce-Horton shrugged her stately shoulders in an affected manner and looked bored. Mrs. Lyman Osborn came to her rescue.

"I promise you, Lady Avondale," she observed, "that when Mrs. J. Bruce-Horton speaks, she does so for her entire family. Mr. John B. Horton is, perhaps—well, a little stupid, as American men of business so often are, you know. He is perfectly at home with his vast herds of cattle, mavericks, brands, and all that sort of thing, but when it comes to social questions, or to a family alliance like this, my dear friend, Mrs. J. Bruce-Horton, is in full authority."

"Ah, just so," replied Lady Avondale, as she adjusted her eye-glass and nodded her head wisely, "I understand."

In the meantime Ethel had retired to her room; but not to sleep. She had a good cry all to herself, after which she bathed her flushed face and, after the manner of women, felt much relieved. She sat down and gave herself up to thoughtful reverie. She remained thus far into the night; but, finally, arousing herself, she said aloud, "Yes, he is a brain-worker, and oh! how I love brain-workers! Bah, I hate idlers!"

In the morning she awoke from the refreshing sleep of youth. She had scarcely finished her toilet when there came a knock at her door. It proved to be the colored bell-boy who had interrupted them on the evening before.

"Please, miss," said he, with great obeisance, as she opened the door, "the gemman said I was to give you this letter in pusson."

"Thank you," said Ethel as she took the missive. Hastily tearing away the envelope she read:

"My darling Ethel:—It is now after midnight. I have walked along the path and stood under the old elm in the mad belief that I might see you again, although I must have known that it was impossible. I am sustained by the abiding hope of seeing you after you have spoken to your father. I trust it will not be long. I believe in you. The honesty of the soul that shines out through your eyes cannot be doubted. I am thrilled with deepest reverence, when I think of you,—a reverence such as one might feel when standing before a snow-white sacred shrine of peace, purity, and innocence. Know that my love is immortal—it cannot die.

"Affectionately,

"Jack."

30

It was no shame to the noble heart of Ethel Horton that she kissed Jack's hurriedly written note over and over, and bathed it with her tears. On the impulse of the moment she rang for pen and paper, and wrote:

> *"Dear Jack:—Your note has made me very happy. We leave to-day for the Southwest. I have thought it all over, and I know that I like you awfully well. I am conscious of a strange sensation that may be—well, I don't know what it is. Do not give up hope, but share my faith in daddy. Yours,*
>
> *"Ethel."*

Before leaving Lake Geneva, it was understood between Mrs. Horton and Lady Avondale that her son was to visit them at their ranch in southwestern Kansas. He intended spending about two months, later in the fall, hunting in the mountains of Colorado. Dr. Lenox Avondale looked upon an alliance with the American heiress as necessary for the preservation of the estates in England, and he accepted his mother's arrangements as a matter of course. The flirtation which he had secretly begun with Mrs. Osborn promised a recreation within itself when he should visit the Hortons.

As for Dr. Jack Redfield, he was impatient to see Ethel once more, and in the hope that she had not yet gone from Lake Geneva he boarded a train, and at noon was at the lake, only to find that the Hortons and Mrs. Osborn had taken their departure an hour before. He had not yet received Ethel's letter. He returned to the city, determined to bury himself in the multiplicity of his professional duties and study until his summons should come from Ethel Horton.

That evening on returning to his apartments on Dearborn Avenue he found among his letters the note from Ethel. His other mail he left unopened, while he read and re-read this message of hope. It was so sacred to him—it meant so much.

This great, strong fellow who, heretofore, had been proof against love's tender passion, had awakened to find himself thoroughly ensnared in its silken meshes. No, he did not wish to be' free. As he walked to and fro in his room, he idealized Ethel with an ardent chivalry that might have become a knight of old.

The door-bell rang and Hugh Stanton was announced.

"Admit him," said Jack. "I wonder what he wants. No, I will not tell him of my happiness."

A moment later Hugh Stanton was ushered into Jack Redfield's presence. They greeted as the warmest of friends. Between these two it was always "Jack" on the one side and "Hugh" on the other. They had been classmates at Princeton. After graduation Hugh had turned his attention to commercial pursuits, and had gradually worked his way up to the cashiership of one of Chicago's most conservative banking institutions.

Hugh Stanton presented a striking contrast to his friend, Doctor Redfield. He was slightly below medium height, and rather stout. He had a handsome, good-natured face, black eyes, fair skin, and a silky, dark mustache. His thick, dark hair was inclined to be wavy, while his rather small hands and feet suggested a patrician ancestry.

After their greeting Jack produced a box of Havanas, and settling themselves in comfortable chairs, he observed, "Well, old boy, what's the news?"

"I am about to leave Chicago," replied Hugh, with an interrogative smile as much as to say, "What do you think of that?"

"Leave Chicago!" exclaimed Jack, in amazement. "Why, man, you have one of the best positions in the city."

"Yes, but you know that my father's estate, which has been tied up so long in the courts, is at last settled; and I find myself with fifty thousand dollars in ready money at my command. That amount does not mean much in a city like this, but on the frontier, where rates of interest are high, I can soon double it several times; and then, too, I am tired of city life. One is too much of an atom in a great throbbing centre like Chicago."

"Well, you astonish me," said Jack, "you almost take my breath away. I thought you were permanently settled and thoroughly in love with your surroundings."

"Well, you know there is an old saying," said Hugh, smiling, "that it is better to be a big fish in a small pond than a small fish in an ocean. I have been in correspondence with the captain of my father's old company, who is now on the frontier, and am offered the cashiership and an opportunity to purchase half the stock in the national bank of which he is the president."

"It is rather strange that your father's estate was so long in being settled," said Jack, reflectively.

"Yes," said Hugh, "more than twenty years from the time of his supposed death. He fought in the battle of Bethel Church and was numbered among the missing, but we were unable to establish the fact of his death. My mother died when I was a mere child, and then I lived with an uncle, who has had charge of my affairs; but at last everything is settled, and the money is now to my credit in the bank."

"And so you are going to the frontier. I fear you will soon grow tired of it," said Jack, "the contrast will be so great. What sort of man is he with whom you are going to associate yourself?"

"I cannot say," replied Hugh, as he knocked the ashes from his cigar, "I have never met him. He was captain of the company in which my father was first lieutenant, and I have had considerable correspondence with him in trying to obtain information in regard to my father's death. This correspondence has, strangely enough, led to the present contemplated business arrangement."

"Well, we must see much of each other between now and the time you start."

"My dear Jack," replied Hugh, "I have already resigned my position and I shall leave to-morrow for my new home. I have called to-night to have an old-time chat, and to say farewell."

Jack looked at his friend incredulously, and said, half indignantly, "Well, why have n't you called before?"

"I have called nearly every evening for the past two weeks,"

33

replied Hugh, "but you were never at home."

"Oh, yes," said Jack, looking up at the tiers of books on the shelves, and plucking his mustache, reflectively. "Yes, that's so, I have been away—professional calls, you know."

Soon Hugh Stanton took leave of his friend and the following day found him en route for Meade, Kansas.

After crossing the "Big Muddy" at Kansas City, Hugh began to realize, for the first time, that he was entering the "Great Plains"—that he was, indeed, in the West. He gazed meditatively from the car windows and beheld, in rapturous anticipation, the vast, rolling, monotonous prairies. He was coming to a land of promise, a land of hopes and of disappointments, a land of vast herds and of writhing winds, a land of struggling farmers and of princely cattle barons, a land of wild flowers and of sunshine. Here, Hugh Stanton was soon to become an actor on the realistic stage of the Southwest. He was to become, first, an actor in melodrama, then tragedy, and finally he was to play a part in a mighty orchestral avalanche of mystery.

CHAPTER V.

A FRONTIER BANKER

MEADE, Kansas, was at that time almost a typical western frontier town, situated some forty miles southwest of Dodge City—the nearest railroad station—and on the western bank of a small stream known as Crooked Creek. It had then a population of three or four thousand people, and was an important commercial centre for ranchmen and cattlemen. When Hugh Stanton arrived on the old four-horse stage-coach from Dodge City, late one afternoon, he found himself covered with dust and almost exhausted from the tiresome ride. The leading hotel was the Osborn House, where he found convenient and pleasant quarters. The hotel property belonged to Captain Lyman Osborn, who also owned several brick business blocks at Meade.

That evening he met Captain Osborn, who gave him a hearty welcome to Meade and expressed sincere pleasure at his decision to join him in the banking business.

On the following day, after carefully looking over the books of the Meade National Bank, Hugh made arrangements to purchase one-half of the capital stock of the institution and was duly elected and installed cashier.

Those were halcyon days in southwestern Kansas. Hugh, to his amazement, found that deposits in the bank amounted to over half a million dollars and that a semi-annual dividend of fifteen per cent, was regularly declared.

Captain Osborn was a man of perhaps sixty years, military in bearing and possessing a flowing iron gray mustache and an imperial mien that gave him a distinguished appearance.

"Sir, you remind me very much of your father, Lieutenant Stanton," observed the captain one day after Hugh had become his partner in the banking business. "There was not a braver man in the company. We were bosom friends for many years before the war with the South, and we enlisted at the same time. I feel very proud, Stanton, my boy, that we have become associated in business. I know that I can trust you implicitly, and I have need of some friend to lean upon."

The rich, deep voice of the old captain quivered a little as he spoke, and a shadow of melancholy flitted across his face.

"You will not be disappointed with the profits," he continued,— "they are certainly enormous compared with returns on money in the middle or eastern States."

"I am quite sure," replied Hugh, "that I shall like the change to the frontier, although it differs vastly from the busy metropolis that I have just left."

"Doubtless," said the captain, "the contrast is very marked. There are many reasons why I like southwestern Kansas. The climate is superb; then there are so many old soldiers here, and you know between the veterans there is a sort of unspoken friendship. Scattered throughout our valleys and across our prairies you will find the boys who wore the blue and those who wore the gray dwelling on adjoining farms, and the best of neighbors. There are many old soldiers of the late war living among us; one of the most prominent of whom is Major Buell Hampton, editor of the *Patriot*. While he and I differ materially in politics, yet, withal, he is a most cultured and entertaining gentleman. I have understood in a vague way that he won his title fighting for the Southern cause. Then, there's Mr. John Horton,— perhaps the most extensive cattle owner in the Southwest. His herds cover not only his own vast range, but also the plains of No-Man's-Land and northern Texas. Before the recent rush of settlers into this part of Kansas it was a great range for his cattle."

"Has the settlement of the country inconvenienced the cattlemen?" inquired Hugh.

"Considerably," replied the captain. "You see the cattlemen have a theory that this is not a farming country. The settlers know better. Now last year and the year before there were no finer crops anywhere in the world than were grown on the farms in this part of the State. The old earth was recklessly improvident in her generosity; every farm was an overflowing granary of plenty. However, we have no quarrel with John Horton. He is one of our largest depositors, and a very manly fellow. His millions have not turned his head, although I cannot say as much for all members of his family. Ah, here comes a young scapegrace that I want you to know."

As the captain spoke, a little boy came bounding toward him through the open door of his private office, and nestled on his knee. The captain caressed him tenderly. The boy slipped one arm coaxingly about his father's neck, and received the introduction to Hugh very bashfully.

"This is my boy Harry," said the captain.

The little fellow was perhaps not more than five years old, but his face beamed with an older intelligence.

"We are great companions," said the captain, "and he takes more liberties with me than he has any right to—that's what you do, you little rascal," said he, addressing the boy and giving him an affectionate hug.

"Won't you come to me, Harry?" said Hugh, in a coaxing voice.

"No, sir, 'cause we're not 'kainted yet—when we is 'kainted I will."

"This gentleman is my friend, Harry," said the father, "and therefore he is your friend, too."

"All 'ite, then," said the boy, "I's your fwend, too," and he held out his hand, which Hugh clasped as a bond of good-fellowship between them.

Hugh Stanton very early discovered that Captain Osborn's life was centred in his young son. That evening, by invitation of the captain, Hugh dined at the Osborn home. He was very much surprised at the youthful appearance of the captain's lovely wife. She made no efforts to conceal her feelings of superiority and indifference toward the captain, but she was very gracious toward Hugh, and chatted away incessantly about her travels and her English friends. It seemed that the iron will of the captain, which he was noted for exercising in the business world, was changed to all forbearance and courtly respect toward his wife; although one could readily discover a sad lack of sympathy between them. Indeed, there was but little in common between Captain Osborn and his wife. During dinner the captain made some remark relative to the superiority of American institutions, when his wife quickly interposed:

"Captain, you know nothing about it. You will do far better to discuss matters of business, bank stocks, and that sort of thing. They seem to suit your particular style of intellect; but of society and what constitutes the best taste, why, really, you are not an authority."

The captain reddened a little, and replied, quietly, "Very well, Lucy, I freely acknowledge your superior judgment in such matters—perhaps I ought not to have spoken; but I know one thing," said he, chucking little Harry under the chin, "this boy and I are in love with each other, is n't that so, Harry?"

"Yes, we's made a barg'in, mamma," cried the little fellow, "papa and I is lovers, and when I dets big I's doin' to be his par'ner."

"Indeed!" said his mother, as she elevated her eyebrows. "You and your papa have delightful times together. Well, I am glad of the attachment," said she, turning toward Hugh with a wearied expression, as much as to say, "Let them go their way, and I will go mine."

"I hope to see much of you, Mr. Stanton," she said, with her most bewitching smile. "Are you fond of society?"

Hugh confessed that he knew but little of the social world, having led a rather busy and secluded life.

"Well, you will not see much society in southwestern Kansas," observed Mrs. Osborn.

"My dear, you must introduce him to the Hortons," ventured

the captain.

"With pleasure," replied his wife. "Mrs. J. Bruce-Horton and I are very close friends. We but recently returned from England, where her daughter, Ethel, was graduated last June. We have many friends across the water."

The old captain looked deep into his cup of tea, while an ironical smile played across his face. "Our English cousins," he remarked, "are very partial to American dollars."

"Oh, Captain," exclaimed his wife, while her smiles disappeared and a look of displeasure replaced them, "I have before observed on numerous occasions that you know nothing of England, her customs or her people, and light remarks about my English friends are not relished, I assure you."

The captain laughed good-naturedly, as he winked at Hugh, and said, "I beg your pardon, Lucy, my dear, I was only quoting a view I saw expressed recently in the *Financial Gazetteer.*"

"Yes, in the *Financial Gazetteer,*" repeated his wife, contemptuously, "you are competent to judge things only from a strictly commercial standpoint, and it would be much better for you not to speak than to make such stupid remarks."

She again relaxed and turned toward Hugh with a charming graciousness. "Yes, I shall be pleased, Mr. Stanton, to introduce you to the Hortons. Miss Ethel is a delightful young lady; but mind," said she, coquettishly shaking her finger at him, "you must not lose your heart, as she is already spoken for."

"Oh, indeed!" replied Hugh, "how unfortunate for me!"

"What," said the captain, "is Miss Ethel to be married?"

"Now, Captain," and the tiger's claw protruded just a little as she spoke, "you must not ask direct questions. At present it is quite a secret; but as a friend I was only warning Mr. Stanton, and 'forewarned is forearmed,' you know."

"Very well," said Hugh, "I know I shall be delighted to meet them, as they are such friends of yours."

"Oh, thank you," replied Mrs. Osborn, bowing at the compliment.

"Friends of ours, too," remarked the captain. "Think of John Horton's fat bank account."

"Oh, Captain," cried his wife, with an exasperated expression of countenance, "won't you—can't you divorce, for one short evening, the coarseness of business from the refinements of social intercourse? It seems impossible for the captain to rise above his bank counter," said she, apologetically, to Hugh.

"Not a bad level to maintain," replied the husband, "and a good many people would feel quite content if they were on a level with the Meade National Bank counter."

"I do not say anything against your business, Captain, but please do not try to step outside the beaten path with which you are familiar. It is unbecoming in you, and makes you appear quite ridiculous, I assure you." The captain winced, in silence.

Shortly after they had arisen from the table, Mrs. Osborn went driving, and the captain and Hugh sat on the broad veranda and smoked their cigars, while the veteran told reminiscences of the war. The infinite tenderness with which the captain held his boy was touching to Hugh. The little fellow nestled contentedly on his father's knee, where he soon fell asleep. When the captain finally arose to carry him within, the child murmured in his dreams, "Papa an' I is lovers—is lovers."

"Did you hear that?" exclaimed the old captain to Hugh, and a tear fell from the bronzed face of the father, and rested like a benediction on the soft cheek of the sleeping boy.

CHAPTER VI.

MAJOR BUELL HAMPTON

MAJ. BUELL HAMPTON, editor and proprietor of the *Patriot*, called at the bank one morning and was introduced to Hugh by Captain Osborn.

"I am indeed delighted," said the major, as he extended his hand, "to meet any one who is Captain Osborn's friend. The captain and I were both for humanity during the late unpleasantness, acting our parts, however, in different ways; and now we are neighbors and friends, both believing in the same government and respecting the same flag, although I must say we offer up our devotions at different political shrines."

The major laughed good-naturedly, when Captain Osborn said, "Yes, we believe in the same government, but we have different professions of faith."

The major was an exceptional specimen of manhood. He was six feet two inches tall, straight as an Indian, splendidly proportioned, and weighed, perhaps, two hundred and forty pounds. His broad-brimmed slouch hat was suggestive at once of the South.

On the silk lapel of his Prince Albert coat was a dainty carnation *boutonnihre*. This little flower was in keeping with the tenderness of the man's heart. A heavy gold chain, with many a link, encircled his neck as a watch-guard. To those who knew him best, this chain was symbolic of his endless donations to the poor. Like the chain, his charities seemed linked together—without a beginning, without an end. His carefully polished shoes and neatly arranged necktie denoted refinement and good taste. These outward evidences of genteel breeding were not offensive to the poor, but, rather, inspired them with confidence and courage to accept alms from this man. His long, dark hair and flowing mustache were streaked with gray, his nose was large, his forehead knotted, and the wrinkled lines of his face were noticeable,—strong, deep-cut. There was a thoughtfulness, a gentleness, a kindness beaming from his gray eyes and from every lineament of his rugged face, and, indeed, from every motion of his powerful frame, that forced a conviction into the heart that here was one upon whom God had set his seal of greatness—of goodness.

There were times, however, when in deep meditation, that his eyes seemed resting afar off on some unraveled future. An observer might fancy that a cloud had obscured the radiance of his soul, leaving in its stead only dissolving shadows of sadness. Then the lines of his face would deepen and his soul would seem far away on some errand of mercy. It was in such moods that he became patriarchal in appearance, and the observer might well have exclaimed, "Here is one over whom an hundred winters have blown their fierce north winds," but, when he turned again, with his inspiring smile of benevolence, to answer perhaps the simplest question of the simplest questioner, few would have judged him to have seen more than half a century. At such times the soul-light seemed illuminating his classic yet gentle race with kindly interest for the little things of earth, and his years would then have been reckoned by summers and south winds—not by hoary winters.

"By the way," said the major, turning to Hugh, "what is your political belief?"

"I am a Republican," replied Hugh, "but I trust, though differing politically, that our social relations may be most pleasant."

"Thank you," replied the major, with urbane courtliness, "I share your wishes, but I may as well tell you now, as later, that the Republican party is bound to be snowed under, root and branch, in our local election this fall."

"That remains to be seen," interposed Captain Osborn, smiling. "The game of politics is never out until the returns are all in."

"That's all true, Captain," replied the major, "but if your Republican soul does not languish in utter despair when the returns are all in, then I shall have labored in vain. The *Patriot* goes to every nook and corner of the county, and I fancy it is like 'bread cast upon the waters,' or 'sowing seeds of wisdom'—results of a satisfactory nature are sure to follow."

"I presume," said Hugh, "that Captain Osborn is a Republican because he believes that the better class of Northerners adhere to that party, and on the other hand, Major, you are a Democrat because no respectable Southerner could live in the South and not be a Democrat."

"That's well put, young man," said the major, looking kindly at Hugh, "the only fallacy in your deduction is that I am not a Democrat, although I voted that ticket for many years in Kentucky. Politically, I am supposed to be a Populist; in truth I am a Reformist. However, Mr. Stanton, I will not intrude my political faith upon you at our first meeting. I am sincerely delighted to have met you; and in some way I have an impression that we shall become great frends. Do you love music?"

"Passionately fond of it," replied Hugh, "but, unfortunately, I cannot play even a Jew's-harp."

"A soul without a language," said the major, as he looked benignly at Hugh. "Internal rhythm and melody that move us with their invisible touch, and then die away like a song on the night wind—into silence—when one is unable to express the emotions that stir the inmost soul. Yes, I believe I understand you."

Hugh looked at the major in amazed surprise. "Yes," said he, "I believe you do. I believe you understand my feelings even better than I do myself."

"Now I am sure we are to be friends," said the major, laughing. "Come and see me often. The latch-string hangs on the outside of my house, while my den at the *Patriot* office has an easy chair awaiting you at all times."

When Major Hampton had taken his departure Captain Osborn observed, "Well, Hugh, did I not tell you that he was a cultured gentleman? How do you like him?"

"Why, Captain," replied Hugh, "he is a revelation to me. I am drawn to him as steel to a magnet. What a physique! What a noble, face, so full of rare intelligence, sympathy, and tenderness! Really, Captain, the major is one of the most perfect specimens of physical and intellectual manhood that it has ever been my pleasure to meet."

"Very true," replied Captain Osborn. "Yet, in one way, he is quite an enigma. Formerly a Kentucky Democrat—now a Populist of the most ultra type, an organizer of the Farmers' Alliance, and the founder of a secret society among them known as the 'Barley Hullers.' It seems incongruous to me that he should entertain and champion such political heresies."

"You may be unduly prejudiced, Captain," said Hugh.

"Well, possibly I am," replied the captain, "one thing is certain, however, I am not a politician, and I manage, on account of our banking interests, to keep my views pretty close at home. At the same time, Stanton, an old, grizzled veteran like myself, who fought for four years for the preservation of the Union, is liable to be rather set in his political opinions."

"While I do not agree with Major Hampton, politically," observed Hugh, "yet otherwise I am very favorably impressed with him."

"That's right," said Captain Osborn, "so am I. He is an amiable gentleman, always dresses immaculately, as you saw him this morning, and is noted far and wide for his deeds of charity and his kindness among the poor. If any are sick within twenty miles of Meade, Major Hampton knows all about it. He visits them, and takes care that they are properly provided with medical aid. He is a warm supporter of the Ladies' Aid Society, and contributes most liberally to the different churches, although he evinces no preference for any particular creed. Indeed, he is quite popular, and, between ourselves, Hugh, I should not be a bit surprised if he told the truth about snowing us under at the polls this fall. You see the 'Barley Hullers' is a secret organization, and, therefore, an unknown quantity, and I have no doubt that the major will control it at the coming election, to a man."

After banking hours that evening, Hugh called at the *Patriot* office. "Come in, Mr. Stanton," cried the major, in most hospitable tones, as he ushered him into his own private "den." Its moquette carpet, easy chairs, Turkish divan, beautiful pictures, and shelves well filled with books—all combined to make this little editorial "den" one of surprising elegance. The major had laid aside his Prince Albert coat for a smoking jacket.

"These are Congressional Records and works on political economy," said he, waving his hand toward the book shelves, as he noticed Hugh looking at them. He lounged negligently on the divan, and threw one arm back carelessly over his head.

"You have quite an extensive library, Major," observed Hugh, as he seated himself.

"My library is at my home," replied the major, "these are but a few statistical volumes which I find necessary in writing editorials for the Patriot. There is hardly a recent work of a political nature published that is not represented on these shelves. By the way, Stanton, there are some pretty fair cigars in that box—help yourself."

"Thank you," said Hugh, as he lighted one.

Presendy the major arose from the divan, and, after lighting a cigar, observed, "By the way, Mr. Stanton, are you fond of books?"

"I certainly am," replied Hugh, "they have been my best friends. Many hours of solitude have been beguiled by their pleasant and profitable companionship."

"Of course you read novels?" said the major, inquiringly.

"I presume you regard it as a weakness," replied Hugh, "but I must admit that a good novel has a great charm for me."

"On the contrary," replied the major, "I regard a good novel as healthful reading. The works of Scott, Thackeray, Dickens,

Lytton, Victor Hugo, Hawthorne, J. Fenimore Cooper, and of many other novelists, may be read with profit. Some of our greatest historians have been novel readers, and some of our greatest novelists have clothed history with romance and made it immortal, thus diffusing historical facts far more widely than could have been done in any other manner."

"I agree with you," replied Hugh, "though I must admit that fiction has a general tendency to cultivate a dislike for more solid reading."

They were interrupted by a knock at the door, and the major called out, "Come in!" The door opened and a tall, gaunt, rough-looking fellow came stalking in. The major, nastily rising from the divan, said:

"Why, hello, Dan, how do you do! Come right in. Mr. Stanton, allow me to introduce to you my friend Dan Spencer. Dan, this is Mr. Stanton, the new cashier of Captain Osborn's bank. My friend, Spencer," continued the major, "is one of our 'horny handed sons of toil.' He belongs to the big frontier army that is noted for having seen better days.'.rdquo;

The newcomer was, indeed, a study. He had exceedingly large feet and hands. Huge Mexican spurs were buckled to the heels of his high-topped boots. His small, restless, gray eyes and sandy hair were in keeping with his stubby red beard, large mouth, and sunburnt nose. It required no second introduction to discover that Dan Spencer regarded the major with reverential homage. Whenever he spoke, Dan had a habit of wambling and grinning, thereby disclosing his tobacco-colored teeth, and quivering like a creature in convulsions. The one noticeable feature about Dan Spencer was an abnormally long fanglike tooth, almost directly in front. This tooth protruded from the lower jaw, and when Dan spoke it wobbled about like a drunken man. Hugh fell to watching this tooth, and he fancied that every heavy breath on the part of its owner caused it to sway about like a willow buffeted by the wind.

After the introduction he said, addressing Hugh, "Waal, how

do you like this 'ere country?"

"Quite well, what I have seen of it," replied Hugh.

"Don't reckon you've seed much yit. You'll find lots uv pore corn-juice, canned goods, ig'nance, and side-meat. I 'spect the ig'nance, though, will nachally give way afore better brands of red liquor."

Before Hugh could reply, Dan turned his wobbling tooth toward the major, and said:

"Hell is poppin' agin, Major. I jist came in from No-Man's-Land and I heerd that two hundred head uv old Horton's fat beeves hed been stampeded, cut outer his herd an' run off."

"Great God!" exclaimed the major. "Stealing Horton's cattle again? You don't mean it!"

"You bet I surely do. The beeves are sure 'nuff gone," replied Dan. The major walked back and forth in an agitated way for several minutes, as if he were in deep thought. Presently, turning to Spencer, he said:

"Go down to the pasture and cut out the roan pony; also select a fresh one for yourself and be ready to start with me in a couple of hours." Turning to Hugh he said, "My dear Mr. Stanton, you will have to excuse me. We go to press early to-morrow morning and I must write up this cattle robbery for the *Patriot*. You may not be acquainted with the conditions that exist on the frontier, but there are a lot of cattle thieves in this locality that must and shall, by the Eternal, be torn out root and branch. I must also ride over and see Mr. Horton this evening. Well, good-bye, Stanton, come to see me often."

Hugh was profoundly impressed by the troubled look of the major, and, as he walked along the street toward the hotel, he shuddered as he thought of the vengeance that would be meted out to the cattle thieves if Major Buell Hampton should have the passing of judgment upon them.

He soon, however, dismissed all thought of the cattlemen and of their troubles, and, while softly humming an air from "Robin Hood," began writing a letter.

CHAPTER VII.

THE CATTLE KING

HUGH STANTON had now been in Meade about a month, and was well pleased with his new position. Money poured in from the East for investment, and seemed as free as water among the people. Deposits continually increased in the bank, while the ruling rates of interest were very high. Investments were quickly turned and immense dividends declared and sent on to the Eastern capitalists, who in turn became intoxicated with the desire for more of these large profits, and consequently sent back their money for reinvestment. Not content with this, they borrowed to the full extent of their credit, at a low rate of interest, and sent on the funds for Western investment and speculation. Barley, wheat, and other cereals yielded enormously, and lands that had been purchased from the government at a dollar and a quarter per acre changed hands—within a year—at from thirty to forty dollars per acre in favored localities. Real estate in Meade that had cost original purchasers from fifty to one hundred dollars per lot sold readily at from one thousand to five thousand dollars each.

During all the progress and prosperity there was one class— the cattlemen—who were firm disbelievers in the agricultural permanency of the Southwest. Prominent among these disbelievers was John B. Horton, the cattle king. Major Hampton said, in the columns of the that the cattle barons wanted these rich, nutritious buffalo grass lands for their vast herds of cattle, and that in their selfishness they were willing to prevent their settlement by the actual tillers of the soil.

49

One afternoon Hugh went horseback riding down the Crooked Creek valley. He was exploring territory new to him, and presently he came to the banks of the Manaroya, a beautiful stream that had its rise in Horton's Grove. The cool, refreshing waters of this rapid, pebble-bottomed brook were, indeed, a welcome sight. It presented a striking contrast to the dreary stretch of gray and brown prairie lands that lay monotonously level for miles in every direction; save a large elm-tree and Horton's Grove, perhaps a mile away to the westward, which were like coral islands in a vast inland sea. Hugh had dismounted and was standing idly at its brink watching the restless, rippling waters in their flight from the gushing springs in the lichened woods above, on and on, even to the boundless ocean. Here the waters sparkled in all their purity—filtered dewdrops.

"How restful," mused Hugh, "what a fairyland for dreams—for day-dreams."

There, before him, the tiny bubbles in the eddies seemed to dance and laugh and chase each other round and round in romping play. Now they paused as if to rest—or to whisper great secrets—or, perhaps, it was to warn each other of the dread future in the mighty ocean beyond. Just below, the channel widened, and the noisy waters of the riffles changed into a miniature lake—calm, peaceful. The lone elm-tree, with its spreading branches, grew upon the brink; its gnarled and twisted roots reached far out into the bed that held the placid waters. This cool retreat was the summer home of the lazy turtle, of sunfish and of "mud-cat." Out from coverlets of rock and root peeped many an unseen, blinking eye in wonderment at Hugh.

Here, in this tranquil pool, nature had fashioned, with her magic brush, a picture framed about with countless wild flowers. In this realistic dream every fluttering leaf on every limb and branch trembled in rhythm. Here the shadows sifted, the sunbeams danced, the birds flew. Here the butterflies floated lazily in holiday attire, as if on wings of pleasure. Here the gaudy-winged "snake feeder" skipped from side to side, across the waters, as if he were abroad in search of trade and barter.

Again, this embryonic lake was a mirror for sky and cloud—for each nodding flower and grass blade that craned its little neck, in vanity, over the margin, that it, too, might see itself reflected in this looking-glass of nature. Higher than Jacob's Ladder appeared the bending sky and floating clouds, and yet, inverted, they seemed deeper than lie buried the broken images of a life.

Suddenly Hugh's reverie was broken in upon by the calling of a brusque "Hello, there, pard-ner! Are you looking for mavericks?"

Hugh found himself face to face with a rather heavy-set man, with a full gray beard and soft dark eyes. The stranger had dismounted from his mustang, and stood eyeing Hugh critically from the opposite bank.

"I have lost no mavericks, that I know of," replied Hugh, stiffly. "May I ask what you are doing and what you are looking for?"

"I am attending to my own affairs," replied the man. "I am on my own land, which, perhaps, is more than you can say for yourself."

"I may not be on my own land," answered Hugh, half angrily, "but I am attending to my own business. Am I breaking any law by taking a gallop across the valley, or resting by this stream of water?"

The stranger laughed good-naturedly at Hugh's irritation. "Hot blood of youth," said he; "come, don't be so touchy. There's only a small thing between us—a narrow stream of spring water. You look like a manly fellow, and I suppose you are all right, although you are a stranger to me."

"I am a resident of Meade," said Hugh, "and the cashier of one of its banks."

"Is that so?" asked the man, in surprise. "You are Mr. Stanton, I reckon, Captain Osborn's friend from Chicago."

"Exactly," replied Hugh. "May I inquire your name?"

The stranger threw himself again into his saddle, touched spurs to his horse, and, at a single leap, cleared the brook. Dismounting at Hugh's side, he said, "My name is Horton. My home is about a mile from here, in Horton's Grove."

Hugh's breath was almost taken away. Here before him stood the great cattle king, John B. Horton, whose estimated wealth was ten million dollars; and yet a man as free from affectation as a cowboy.

"Give us your hand, young man," said he. "It is well that we should be acquainted. I have been intending to come in and see you, but am kept so exceedingly busy, looking after my cattle, that I have but little time for social matters. Through the machinations of a band of cattle thieves, during the last year I have lost over a thousand head of beeves that were ready for the market."

"Why, that is a terrible loss, Mr. Horton," observed Hugh. "Is it not possible to catch the thieves?"

"Easier said than done, young man," replied the cattle baron. "I would n't care much for the thirty or forty thousand dollars' worth of cattle they have already taken, if I could only break up the gang. However, I do not wish to bore you with a ranchman's troubles. How do you like our country?"

"Oh, very much," replied Hugh. "I am well pleased with it so far. It seems to be settled with a thrifty class of farmers, and their crops are certainly looking well."

John Horton laughed derisively. "Farmers!" he ejaculated. "Why, young man, in five years there will not be a so-called farmer within one hundred miles of where you are now standing. The influx of self-styled settlers and farmers is a spasmodic farce, transitory in the extreme. You doubtless regard Meade as a growing, healthy town; yet, within five years from to-day, I shall pasture my cattle on the grass that will be growing in her streets."

"You astonish me," said Hugh. "With such a calamity confronting us there can be left but little hope."

"I am aware," said John Horton, "that Captain Osborn has a different belief. My old friend, Major Buell Hampton, also takes occasion to brand me as a 'cattle baron' in the columns of his paper. Nevertheless, Mr. Stanton, they are both my friends, and

I esteem them both as royal good fellows. I assure you, however, that they are sadly mistaken in regard to this being a farmer's paradise. Wait until the hot winds come. Now hot winds don't hurt the buffalo grass a particle, for it is indigenous to this soil and climate; but there's nothing grown by the farmer that can stand before the hot winds."

"Major Hampton was telling me the other day," said Hugh, "that the cattle thieves had just stolen two hundred head of your fattest cattle."

"Yes, that is the latest outrage; but they have been stealing my cattle for the last year. Before the settlers came here we had no cattle thieves to speak of in this country. Major Hampton is a true Southerner, and is doing nis utmost to run down the thieves. I contend that the thieves are none other than the so-called farmers. The major, however, insists that the gang is made up of lawless cowboys."

"The major seemed very much provoked when he heard of the theft," said Hugh, "and from the article that appeared in the *Patriot* the following morning, I imagine that he would be a very severe judge."

"The major's personal assistance and the influence of his paper are both on the side of law and order," replied Mr. Horton. "I have no doubt that sooner or later we shall be successful in running down the thieves."

The cattle king removed his sombrero, and, leaning against his horse, fanned himself with its broad brim, as he continued:

"The major is a little weak up here," tapping his forehead, "or else I am when it comes to the matter of politics. I served in a Georgia regiment through the last years of the war, and fought for the cause that was lost. When the war was over, I accepted the conditions of our surrender by respecting the stars and stripes, and have voted a straight Democratic ticket without a scratch ever since. I cannot understand how the major could give up his democracy for populistic doctrines. However, he is withal a noble fellow."

As the cattle king bared his head, Hugh noticed that it was quite bald, and that it had a great red scar near the crown.

"It is very gratifying," said Hugh, with his eyes on the scar, "to see those who fought for the lost cause and those who fought to subdue the rebellion living here, side by side, in peace."

"Yes," replied Horton, "the wounds are all healed, but the scars are left. Hello! there comes Bill Kinneman, one of my most trustworthy cowboys. Hello, Bill, what's the news?" Bill Kinneman was short and stoop-shouldered. He had a low forehead, thick black hair, cut square around, a small nose, a protruding chin, and a scraggy beard. A pair of squinting, bloodshot eyes combined with his other facial make-up to give him the appearance of a brute.

"Oh, nothin' much to tell," replied Bill. "I foller'd 'em five days, an' they clean got away from me."

"Could n't you pick up their trail?"

"Yass, we found whure they crossed the Cimarron down in the Strip."

"Well, why did n't you follow them?" asked Horton, impatiently.

"We foller'd 'em as fur as we could, but somehow we wuz jist strugglin' round in the coils uv error, fur we dun lost the trail— we did fur sure."

"Well, Bill, I am disgusted with you," said Mr. Horton. "I used to think you were a nervy fellow and sleuth-hound to track down a thief, but of late you always disappoint me."

"I know I'm a pore cuss, but don't unbosom yourself too malignant agin me. Don't be too hard on me, Mr. Horton. I would n't wonder a mite if he'd overtake 'em," said Kinneman.

"Who the devil do you mean?" asked Horton, angrily.

"Major Hampton; he's quite a stayer. He's at least a mighty sight thet ere way. He'll whup the hull danged outfit if he comes up with 'em, thet's what he'll do. A shootin' is likely to ensoo if he finds the thieves. Anyway, suthin' mighty thrillin' will occur on the landscape thereabouts, for the major will sure 'nuff use his artillery."

"Where did you see the major?"

"Way down on the Cimarron, below the red bluffs, jist whure I turned back. I was assoomin' you'd want me to come an' make a report. The major sent word to ye thet he was purposin' to foller 'em, an' he'd go clar to the Missoury if he had to."

"All right, Bill. You may go on to the ranch, put up your pony, and get something to eat."

The cowboy touched his spurs to the jaded bronco and galloped away up the valley.

"Major Hampton," said Horton, turning to Hugh, "has good blood in him. I have an impression that he will overtake the thieves."

Soon after this Hugh took leave of Mr. Horton, who gave him a pressing invitation to call at his ranch. Hugh accepted this invitation by promising to visit Mr. Horton at no distant day.

CHAPTER VIII.

A COMMITTEE OF FIVE

THE Barley Hullers' Association was a secret society made up principally of tried and true members of the Farmers' Alliance. It had been founded by Maj. Buell Hampton, who was district organizer of the Farmers' Alliance in southwestern Kansas. It was said that the primary incentive of the farmers thus associating themselves together was to prevent the excessive prices which they were compelled to pay for articles purchased, and to raise the ruling prices which they had been forced to accept for the products of their farms.

About a mile northeast of Meade, in an old deserted building that had formerly been used as a sugar mill, were the secret lodge-rooms of the organization. This dilapidated building was provided with a spacious reception-room, an anteroom, and a hall of deliberation, and was indifferently illuminated throughout with green and red lights.

The written work of the order was said to be very literary in tone and was based upon the great principle that in union there is strength. Its professed object was to exact justice from the contending forces of the commercial world. Indeed, it was an organization founded on the principles of the brotherhood of man and of fair dealing toward all classes.

Maj. Buell Hampton enjoyed, perhaps, a pardonable pride in this organization, which was strictly a child of his own making. The members had passwords, grips, and everything of that sort, whereby one brother Barley Huller might know another, whether in the dark or in the light. It was a custom, among the members of the organization, to turn out in force on the Fourth of July and other holidays. On such occasions they paraded the streets to the tat-tat-too music of a snare drum and the shrill whistle of a fife. Their badge was a cluster of barley heads, worn as a *boutonnihre*.

When crops were good the Farmers' Alliance organization usually languished, but when they were poor a marked revival invariably sprang up. It was the highest ambition of the young farmer who was a member of the local Farmers' Alliance to show, by his zealous work and adherence to the principles of that organization, that he was worthy and eligible to membership in the Barley Hullers.

There was a system of procedure in these secret meetings which gave a better idea of the aims and accomplishments of the order than anything disclosed in its written by-laws or professions of faith. At these secret meetings one might find two or three dozen stalwart farmers seated on broken chairs and benches, while their chief presided. The exercises consisted of a general exchange of confidences, which were usually made in speeches intended for the general good of the order.

A few evenings after Hugh had made the acquaintance of John Horton, the Barley Hullers had a meeting, at which Bill Kinneman, a prominent yet rather inflammable member, was present. Several members made spirited speeches and finally Kinneman got the floor.

"Mr. President," said he, "I'm no corn-field sailor ner exhortin' evangelist, but I'm 'lowin' if anybody crosses my trail, why, we'll jist try a tussle an' see who's locoed fust. Fur the las' ten years I've bin ridin' the range, workin' like a nigger fur other people, an' durin' all this time I hev never hed a single ray uv hope 'til I jined the Barley Hullers."

The twenty-five or thirty members sitting around cheered him lustily at this convincing confession.

Bill continued: "There's a lot uv us laborin' fellers thet hasn't hed no privileges up to the present time, an' now we air proposin' to hev a little fairer divide. Fur my part, I'm tired uv bankers, cattle kings, middlemen, an' all the other blood-suckers who air feastin' in luxury on our hard labor."

"Hear! hear!" shouted the crowd. Thus encouraged, Kinneman continued:

"Speakin' wide open and onrestrained like, I want to say it's mighty nigh time we wuz provin' a man's better 'n money. It's time our brotherhood wuz banded together tighter 'n ever an' thet we stop bein' slaves fur these 'ere money kings who hev got their iron heels on our necks an' air grindin' us down in the dust like as we wuz a pack of Russian serfs. We ask fur bread an' they giv' us a stun; we ask fur meat an' they give us a serpent, an' by an' by we'll hev to ask permission to breathe the pure air uv heaven, as we take a gallop acrosst the range."

Wild huzzas and more hand-clapping greeted this, and the speaker continued:

"I'm liable to git hostile in the extreem an' somebody's goin' to git hurt on this 'ere range afore long onless a change sets in. The question is, hev n't us workin' fellers got to thet pint uv life whure money is more respected than the genuine pure artickle uv manhood? Thet's the question, feller citizens, fur us to settle. Pussonally I'm feelin' a heap careless."

Cries of "Good!"

"That's right!"

"Come again!" were heard on every side.

"Lets us," continued Kinneman, "take our cue from these 'ere money fellers. Ev'ry cussed one uv 'em is in a pool or a trust uv some kind an' hang together jist like so many cockle-burrs, an' we, my br'thers, mus' do the same. We're the fellers thet's workin' like dogs an' they're the fellers thet's hevin' all the big dinners. Now, I say, is the time to stop. It's no longer a question uv capital an' labor, it's a question uv life, an' jestice on one side an' death an' injestice on t'other. There's liable to be a select assortment uv guns doin' onusual permiscus work in these 'ere diggins if some people don't quit assoomin' sooperior airs over us laborin' men. My doctrine is to hustle an' git what b'longs to us, peace'ble if we

58

can; if not, git it anyway.'.rsquo;

"That's right!"

"Now you're talking!" was heard from the open-mouthed auditors.

"Now, gen'lemen," concluded Kinneman, "I don't b'lieve in a feller screechin' round too much. Talk's mighty cheap. I b'lieve in bein' plenty p'lite; same time I want to be doin' suthin'. An election is clus to hand, an' the fellers thet git the support uv the Barley Hullers in this 'ere county air dead sure to be elected, and I onbosom myself enuff to say that they've got to pay fur it an' pay fur it han'some, an' no misunderstandin', an' don't yer furgit it, an'—"

"Hold on!"

"Hold on!" cried several voices. "We must not go into politics."

"Major Buell Hampton," said one member, "has expressly provided that politics shall not be mixed up in this organization. Now, while I am with Brother Kinneman in much that he has said, yet I draw the line on violating any of the rules of the order."

Bill Kinneman was about to reply, when a greasy-looking member stealthily took him by the coat sleeve and whispered a few words to him.

"All right, Mr. President," said Bill, "p'rhaps I wuz actooally a leetle too fast, an' I 'poligize fur whoopin' it up in so ondefensible an' hostile fashion." Other members spoke, but in a less fiery manner. Most of them were moderate in their expressions, and urged that in union there was sufficient strength to accomplish all the aims in a peaceful and friendly manner.

Soon after the meeting broke up, the lodge-room became a lobby, thick with smoke from numerous pipes. Kinneman was praised on every hand for his fiery speech. A little later the farmers wended their way in different directions toward their respective homes, while Kinneman and his four associates skulked back into the old mill building, and sought the privacy of the room of deliberations, taking special care that the window curtains were well drawn.

"You mighty nigh upset our game, Brother Bill," said Dan Spencer.

"Well, I 'poligize. I clar furgot myself, sure," replied Kinneman, good-naturedly. "Now, if it's agreed, I'll act as chairman, an' we'll state briefly the objec' of this 'ere conference. You fellers nachally know thet most uv the Barley Hullers in the county air opposed to mixin' up in pol'tics 'cause Major Hampton has said they mus' n't. Now, boys, I reckon us five fellers know er thing or two thet beats a bob-tail flush all holler. There's five offices to be filled in this 'ere county this fall. The Democrats hev nominated a man fur each office, an' the Republicans hev dun the same, an' so hev the Populists. Now, I ain't pluckin' brands from the burnin' fur nuthin', an' I move thet we be a committee—a committee uv five—to see each uv these candidates an' collect as much as we kin fur influencin' the Barley Hullers in this 'ere county. We're a secret society an' they don't know we ain't 'lowed to mix up in pol'tics. I hev a theery we can harvest each uv 'em fur a couple uv hundred, an' thet would make a mighty neat 'jack-pot' to divide 'tween us five, an' make things kind er gay an' genial like."

"That's right," cried his associates. "I second the motion," said another, and soon it was agreed and carried that these five stalwart "lights" of the Barley Hullers, who for self-aggrandizement were thus willing to bring reproach upon their society, should sally forth and secretly pounce upon the various political candidates, and, under the promise of giving to each the support of the Barley Hullers—of the county,—intimidate them into paying certain sums of money.

It should not be imagined that these five members constituting the committee were fair representatives of the organization. Indeed, most of the Barley Hullers were honorable, well-meaning, hard-working men, who had joined the society in the hope that it might better their condition both socially and financially. There was an air of mysticism surrounding the order, as there is surrounding all secret societies; and while nothing was positively known of its inside workings, except by its own members, yet the Barley Hullers was at this time held in high regard by the Farmers' Alliance societies throughout the country. As usual, however, the rank and file became only tools in the hands of a few demagogues who managed to gain and hold control for the sole purpose of pelf and plunder.

CHAPTER IX.

AN AFTERNOON DRIVE

HUGH STANTON was not only a successful, hard-working young man of affairs, but he possessed innate refinement and gentleness. Scrupulously honorable himself, he frequently gave others credit for higher and more manly attributes than they really possessed. His unusually dark hair and fair skin would cause the most casual observer to turn and look at him a second time. His small feet and hands and tapering fingers suggested effeminacy; but Hugh Stanton was not effeminate, for his heart was strong and manly. In appearance he was an ideal society man—a veritable Beau Brummel. As a matter of fact, however, he had scarcely any knowledge of society or of its ways.

His father had fought in the battle of Bull Run, and later at Bethel Church. Hugh was then an infant in his mother's arms. The young mother was heartbroken when she learned that her husband was numbered among the missing. She died a year later. The son was christened with his father's name and was given a home with his uncle and guardian. He possessed a studious turn of mind, and, even as a boy, had been noted for his success at school. Later, he led his classes with distinction at Princeton. Dr. Jack Redfield was Hugh's ideal of true manliness, and, to the credit of Jack, his measure of sterling manhood was Hugh Stanton.

After their college days they had kept up, in an intermittent way, their social relations, but, as year after year went by, each became more and more absorbed in his own special pursuits, and gradually they drifted away from their old chum-day relations. Although Hugh had lived at Meade for a month, he had never thought of writing to Jack Redfield, and if Jack had been asked Hugh's address, he could not have given it, for the very good reason that Hugh had neglected naming his objective point in the West.

One morning when Captain Osborn came to the bank he handed Hugh a daintily perfumed, monogrammed note. Opening it, Hugh found an invitation from Mrs. Osborn to drive with her that afternoon to the Hortons, where they were expected to dine.

Hugh offered the note to the captain, who asked, "Well, what is it?" looking at Hugh over his glasses.

"A letter from Mrs. Osborn," replied Hugh.

"Well, is it not for you?" inquired the old captain.

"Certainly," said Hugh, "but then—"

"If it is for you, it is not for me," said the captain, "and, Hugh, my boy, understand for now and for all time that I have no curiosity as to any arrangements my wife may make or any letters she may choose to write. I trust her without question."

"I hardly know why," said Hugh, "but some way your words chill me." He waited a moment in silence, and then went on, "I wish I were nearer to you, Captain, for ever since I saw that tear fall on little Harry's sleeping face I have longed to be as close to you as a son." The captain noticeably softened, and said, huskily, "There, there, Hugh, my boy, sit down and let me tell you something. You know I am much older than Mrs. Osborn. We have been married twelve years. She was about to enter a convent when I met her pretty girlish face and fell desperately in love with it; and, notwithstanding my almost fifty years of life, it was my first and only love-affair. She finds pleasure in society, and I despise it most cordially—regard it as a hollow mockery. It is not right to object to that in which she finds innocent pleasure. I am a sort of turned-down back number, while she is in the zenith of life. I have thought it all over, and here are my deductions: Mrs. Osborn must have an opportunity of pursuing those innocent paths of amusement in which she finds her greatest pleasure. She has given to me our little Harry, God bless the boy! She is Harry's mother, and therefore she can do no wrong. When you are older you will learn that love is a looking-glass sort of an affair, framed about with a gossamer network of illusions, easily broken and impossible to mend."

There was a pathetic tenderness in the old captain's words as he uttered the last sentences, and it struck Hugh, at the time, as being odd.

"Now, my boy," continued the captain, as he looked kindly at Hugh, "I have spoken to you as to no other person on earth. If you were my own son I could not have spoken more freely."

"Thank you," said Hugh, as he took the captain's outstretched hand, "I shall strive earnestly to prove myself worthy of your confidence."

"Not only on account of your father, whose memory I certainly revere, but also on account of yourself, I shall try to be all that a father should be to such a son; and, Hugh, if anything should ever happen to me, do as much for little Harry, and the account will be more than balanced."

Hugh gave his promise, and soon after he turned to his desk, but the captain's words kept ringing in his ears. The promise that he had made impressed him strangely, and he was conscious of a disturbed, rather than an uncomfortable, feeling. He sent a reply to Mrs. Osborn, accepting her invitation, but was not at all sure that he had acted wisely. During the afternoon, Mrs. Osborn called at the bank, and Hugh was driven away in her elegant carriage. It was a lovely Indian summer afternoon, with scarcely a breath of air stirring. As they turned from the street into the country road, Mrs. Osborn, who had kept up an animated yet light conversation, said:

"For one afternoon, Mr. Stanton, you are my captive."

"A most willing one, I assure you," replied Hugh, laughingly. She threw herself gracefully back among the soft upholsterings of the carriage seat, and jestingly replied:

"Indeed, is that so? Had I known your willingness, I certainly would have called you away from the bank counter long before this."

"We have been very busy of late," replied Hugh. "It is not often we can get away."

"You must not serve the god of business too faithfully," said Mrs. Osborn, "but rather make him serve you."

"Very well expressed," replied Hugh, as he looked at Mrs. Osborn, and realized more than ever before that she was, indeed, a most beautiful woman. Her azure eyes were bewitching in their languid softness. Her shapely mouth and full red lips might have suggested danger, yet, withal, there seemed something sincere in her fascinating ways and in the sweetness of her smiles.

"For my part," said she, "I think travel affords a recreation that is doubly enjoyable, because there is no such thing as business to disturb one. Have you ever been in England, Mr. Stanton?" she asked, sweetly.

"Never," replied Hugh, "but I have promised myself a thorough European tour when some convenient opportunity presents itself."

"Oh, how lovely that will be, and how laudable the ambition. It would be so pleasant if you could get away next year and go with us—I mean Mrs. Horton and myself. Our practical husbands stay at home, you know," said she, laughingly, "and we do the traveling for our families."

"Still, it would be more pleasant," replied Hugh, "if your husbands could arrange their business affairs and accompany you."

"I am not so sure about that," said Mrs. Osborn, and she gave her pretty shoulders a shrug and looked at Hugh so intently that, in sheer embarrassment, he looked away. It began to dawn upon him that she loved adoration and adorers alike. Presently Mrs. Osborn laughed softly, and said:

"Why, what a silly one! You are either the most ingeniously clever man or else the most intensely innocent one I ever met."

"I fear," said Hugh, confusedly, "that I am not very clever, and I am quite sure that I am not worthy to be called innocent."

"You are a contradiction," went on Mrs. Osborn, as if Hugh had not spoken, "and yet—well, really you interest me. We must see more of each other—but here we are at the Grove, and there is my dear friend, Mrs. Horton, on the veranda."

Hugh was soon presented to Mrs. J. Bruce-Horton, who received him with unfeigned cordiality. "My husband," said she, "has spoken so much of you since your chance meeting the other day, that I have been quite impatient to meet you."

"Well, I like that," said Mrs. Osborn, with a haughty air and elevated eyebrows, addressing her hostess. "Indeed, have you only heard of Mr. Stanton through your husband? Does all I have said go for nothing?"

"Oh, I beg your pardon, my dear Lucy," replied Mrs. Horton. "Of course you were the first to tell us about him." Then, addressing Hugh, she continued, "My friend Mrs. Osborn, I assure you, has been most profuse in complimentary remarks."

"I am powerless to express my gratitude," said Hugh, gallantly.

"Mr. Stanton," said stately Mrs. Horton, bowing, "my daughter, Miss Ethel." With true frontier hospitality Ethel advanced and, extending both her hands to Hugh, said:

"You are, indeed, most welcome, Mr. Stanton. It was daddy's wish that we make you feel at home when you called, and it will not be my fault if we fail in doing so."

Hugh stammered out his thanks, as he accepted a chair. Ethel was a revelation to him. She was the same girl on her father's ranch that she had been at Lake Geneva, when she completely captivated Jack Redfield. To Hugh she seemed a budding rose just opening into a greater beauty; and yet, what could add to her loveliness! She seemed a queen just stepping from a canvas. Her eyes, her mouth, her nose, her hair, her smile, her voice—these were among the entrancing glories of Ethel Horton.

Hugh Stanton did not believe that he loved her—no, not that— he simply longed to know her better, to give her his confidence and to receive hers in return—a generous, platonic regard, actuated by, well—only respect, he told himself.

The day marked an epoch in Hugh Stanton's life. The seeds of a mysterious ambition had been planted—what of the harvest?

CHAPTER X.

HOME OF THE HORTONS

JOHN HORTON had erected his home upon a little hill overlooking a lake that had been made by damming the Manaroya. More than twenty acres of placid water were within its shores. Rising back of the house—which, of itself, was palatial—was a picturesque hill, much higher than the one upon which had been built the residence. This hill was covered with heavy forest trees that stretched away to the north. The grounds about the Horton country home were laid out as artistically as a city park. A wide, terraced green sward stretched away from the house to the very edge of the lake. Ornamental shrubbery and fruit-trees were growing here and there, and numerous fountains played their vapory waters over fragrant flower-beds. A veranda, southern in its appearance, extended along the front and one side of the house.

The interior of the Horton house was richly elegant. There was one room in which Mrs. J. Bruce-Horton had assembled the art treasures which she had picked up in her travels. Rare old china and Dresden ware, bowls from Corea, mounted buffalo-horns and deer-antlers—were all arranged together in complete harmony as if they had been lifelong friends instead of strangers gathered from the antipodes. Indeed, this palace home of the Occident had been enriched by some of the choicest treasures of the Orient. Paintings from masters and rich tapestries and hangings suggested, at once, refinement and a lavish expenditure of money. And still there was a warmth of welcome pervading the Horton home that robbed it of stiffness and formality.

While the hostess and her daughter were entertaining Mrs. Osborn and Hugh on the veranda, Mr. Horton joined them and assured Hugh that he felt honored by his presence. He hoped that his visit was but the beginning of an acquaintance that would ripen into lasting friendship.

"I cannot understand it," John Horton had said to his wife, when telling her of his meeting with Hugh, "but I feel interested in that young man in an inexplicable manner. I like the spirit he displayed when I was chaffing him about being on other people's land."

The dinner-hour passed pleasantly. Hugh quite forgot all thought of embarrassment and joined heartily in the informal conversation. During the dinner, Mrs. Horton mentioned, incidentally, that Dr. Lenox Avondale would probably visit them during the fall.

"We shall give him a hearty welcome," observed Mr. Horton, "and even though we live on the frontier, we are nevertheless whole-souled fellows, Mr. Stanton."

Hugh could not understand it, but he was conscious of displeasure and resentment at the mere mention of the Englishman's name. An invisible thorn pierced a half-formed ambition. Ethel sat at his right, and until now he had quite forgotten Mrs. Osborn's warning in regard to Ethel's betrothal.

"I am just wild to show him how we American girls can ride," said Ethel, enthusiastically. "Would n't it be great sport, daddy, if Doctor Lenox Avondale, by mistake, should try to ride one of our bucking broncos? Oh, it would be glorious!" she laughed.

"I believe it would test his horsemanship most thoroughly," replied Mr. Horton, much amused.

"Ethel," said her mother, chidingly, "you must not think of playing any jokes on Doctor Lenox Avondale." Then, addressing Hugh, she continued, "He is quite a distinguished surgeon, late of the English army. He has been traveling in America for over a year. All last winter he was in the Southern States. He belongs to one of the oldest families in England."

"He is so intellectual," observed Mrs. Osborn, "and just blasé enough to be interesting. He does not pretend to possess great goodness or innocence, but I daresay he is quite as good as many who do."

As Mrs. Osborn made this remark she cast a furtive glance at Hugh; and he, remembering their conversation during the drive, colored perceptibly. After dinner they returned to the veranda, where Hugh found himself near Ethel.

"Are you a good horseman, Mr. Stanton?" she asked.

"I can't say that I am a good horseman," said Hugh, emphasizing the word "good," "though I am very fond of riding."

"It seems so strange that one like yourself should come away out here on the frontier to live," said the girl, as her eyes rested inquiringly on his face.

"My coming here," replied Hugh, "happened in a most natural way. I do not see anything strange about it. Thousands of people are immigrating to the West."

"Yes, but you had to leave your home and your people," said she.

"Almost every one does that when he comes to a new country," replied Hugh, "but, unfortunately, I had no people to leave."

"No people!" exclaimed Ethel. "Why, how odd! You must have an interesting history."

"On the contrary," replied Hugh, "it is a very uninteresting one. I am an only child. My father lost his life in the war, and my mother died while I was yet very young—so there you have my genealogy in a nutshell."

"And have you traveled abroad?"

"No, I have not as yet treated myself to that pleasure. I have been somewhat of a student. My earlier years were spent with books. After leaving college I engaged in business, and have really had no time for travel."

"Oh, then you are a brain-worker," said Ethel, smiling. "I like brain-workers," and her eyes wandered afar down the valley. She was thinking of Jack Redfield.

Hugh interpreted her words as a compliment, and he marveled

at the mysteries of women. He was sure that Dr. Lenox Avondale was unworthy of this beautiful girl. He mentally determined to question Mrs. Osborn in regard to Ethel's betrothal on their way home that evening.

"Come often and without formality," was the pressing invitation extended to Hugh as he prepared to go.

"Just drop in at any time," said John Horton, "and you will always find a welcome."

Hugh assured them that he would take advantage of their kind invitation, and when he and Mrs. Osborn started away down the country road he told her that he had never spent a more pleasant evening in his life.

"You must not forget what I told you," said she, looking volumes at him with her expressive eyes.

"Oh, you mean in regard to Miss Ethel," said Hugh, innocently.

"That is exactly what I mean," replied Mrs. Osborn, laughing. "I told you that she was spoken for, and, now mind, you must behave or I shall not take you to the Hortons again."

Hugh laughed good-naturedly, and presently said: "Mrs. Osborn, is there no way to break that Englishman's head? I hardly think it's fair to lose such a jewel as Miss Ethel from the Southwest."

"I knew it," said Mrs. Osborn, looking archly at Hugh. "I knew you were a silly fellow who would fall in love at the slightest provocation. I know of no way you could break Doctor Lenox Avondale's head, but I have an idea that he is a sufficiently determined Englishman to play sad havoc with yours, should you interfere with Miss Ethel."

"Do you call Miss Ethel a 'slight provocation'." inquired Hugh.

"Well, perhaps not so slight as some others might be," replied Mrs. Osborn, condescendingly.

"Put your mind at rest," Hugh continued, "for I did not lose my heart irretrievably, as you seem to suppose. The young lady appeals to my chivalry and respect, and I am sure I would be quite satisfied if she were my friend and I had the right to ward off a danger if I saw it approaching her."

Mrs. Osborn laughed softly to herself, and looked incredulously at Hugh.

"I presume you think that I am modest in my wishes," said Hugh, "or, possibly, you quite disbelieve me, but I assure you I state truthfully my position."

"That may be your position to-night," said Mrs. Osborn, "but what will it be to-morrow or next week or next month? Ah, I know you men too well to believe in your platonic friendships. A woman may successfully maintain such a feeling,—a man, never."

Hugh made no reply, and for awhile they drove on in silence. As they alighted from the carriage at the Osborn door, she laid a hand on Hugh's arm, and, bending toward him, she asked, in a soft, pleading voice:

"What would you give—what would you do for a friend who would tell you how to supplant Doctor Lenox Avondale?"

Hugh drew himself away in surprise and answered, "Nothing, Mrs. Osborn, absolutely, nothing. If the Englishman is Miss Ethel's choice, then he is my choice."

The intense and passionate expression on her face gave way to an assumed one of listless drollery, and she smiled. "How charming—what a valiant knight you are. I admire such men, I do indeed. Of course you know I was only jesting, for I assure you no one could supplant Doctor Lenox Avondale. He is quite secure—quite secure indeed."

CHAPTER XI.

DADDY'. CONSENT

ETHEL HORTON remained on the veranda watching Mrs. Osborn's carriage as it disappeared in the gathering darkness. Her mother complained of fatigue and retired to her room. In reply to an inquiry from her father, Ethel said:

"Oh, yes, daddy, I like Mr. Stanton very much. He is quite interesting. I think your tastes and mine are much alike anyway, don't you?"

"I think they are," replied the cattle king, gallantly, "although it is a compliment to me, rather than to you, my little girl."

Ethel laughed. "I say, daddy, you can make as fine speeches as any of them. I don't think you are a bit stupid," and the girl crossed over to her father and, nestling up close to him, was soon seated on his knee.

"This is something like old times," said her father, as he clasped her closer to him. The moon was climbing over the eastern horizon, causing the waters of the little lake below to appear like a sheet of silver, while the rough edges of the rippling waves were as golden as the sunflowers that grew at the margin. It was an hour for girlish confidences, and one that Ethel determined to improve.

"Did you ever think," inquired her father, teasingly, "that I was especially stupid?"

"No, daddy, I really never did; but, do you know, in England they boast a great deal, in quiet ways, about Englishmen, and all that sort of thing, and if you are an American they make you feel fidgety, as if having been born in America were a calamity."

"That's all nonsense," replied her father, "don't let your little head be turned by that sort of rubbish. To be an American, Ethel, in my mind, is a greater good fortune than to have been born a member of the most distinguished of England's titled aristocracy. Understand me, daughter," he continued, "the English are a great nation, but titles, of which some boast so much, had a beginning, and the conditions that surrounded their forefathers, and gave them an opportunity to do deeds of valor, are also here in America, developing the sterling qualities of manhood in their highest perfection."

"Bravo!" cried Ethel. "That's good, daddy; it makes my American blood just tingle. It's better than a feast to hear you talk. I wish," she continued, half petulantly, "I had never gone away to that London school."

"No, Ethel," replied her father, as he gently stroked her heavy, dark tresses, "no, you must not say that. It was your mother's best judgement that you should go; and her ideas and tastes are of a very high order. I have been lonely during the four years of your absence. But life again seems complete now that you are at home."

"Do you believe, daddy, that the best class of Americans care for titles, royalty, or anything of that sort?"

"My dear child, many wearers of English titles nowadays are but twaddling idlers—frayed remnants of a former illustrious ancestry. Whatever other views you may entertain, never believe that there is anything in a mere title. True manliness tells; and titled or not, a man is a man if he possess the sterling qualities of manhood. I would not disparage any man simply because he bore a title, neither would I give him a hair's-breadth of preference. This, my little girl, is a plain statement of your old father's views."

Ethel nestled still closer to him, and with her head resting against his breast remained silent for awhile. He fancied she shivered a little, as if a sob were struggling for mastery. Presently she said, with a slight tremor, "I want to talk to you, daddy; I want to tell you something no one else knows. Do you think, daddy, if some great English lord should come over here for me that you would give me up to him, and let me be carried back to England and, perhaps, never see you again?"

"Why, Ethel, my darling child," replied her father, hesitatingly, "I presume that if your heart were set upon it, I would give my consent. Your mother has intimated what we might expect, but it will be a great trial to me, Ethel."

"Oh, mamma has intimated, has she?" mused Ethel, half to herself. "Listen, daddy—what if a brain-worker, a real American brain-worker, should want—want me—you know, and I should care for him—for this poor brain-worker—care more for him than for all the money in the Bank of England and the titles of all the nobility thrown in—what then, daddy? What then would you do? Would you be on my side, or against me? Tell me, daddy, dear, how would it be?"

The girl's breath came short and quick, and the last part of her question was uttered in a rapid, jerky fashion. John Horton felt her tremble with suppressed excitement, and a light began to dawn upon him. He imagined, and rightly, that the girl was half-afraid of her mother.

"In such a case as that, Ethel, can you doubt the stand I would take?"

"No, but let me hear you say it, daddy; let me hear you say it—just what you would do."

"On your side, my daughter, on your side forever, and we would fight to a finish on that line, if it took all the beeves and mavericks on the range."

"Oh, daddy, daddy," cried the girl, as she threw her other arm around his neck and gave way to a flood of tears, "I—I love you so—so much!"

Tears sprang to the cattle king's eyes. Ethel's soft sobs stole out along the veranda into the calm moonlight and away on the shadows into the woods where they lost themselves among the tall trees and on the wandering night winds. When she reached her own room that night, she wrote a letter to Jack Redfield, which read as follows:

"Dearest Jack:—Daddy is on our side. I am almost too happy to write. I know now what that feeling was,—love, Jack, love for you. Come and see me as soon as you can, and meet the grandest daddy in the whole world. Yes, I love you, love you, love you.

"All your own,

"Ethel."

Mrs. Lyman Osborn called the next day, and in her neighborly kindness she consented to carry this letter, with others, from the Horton ranch to the post-office.

On the following day Mrs. J. Bruce-Horton called at the Osborn home.

"My dear Lucy," said she, sinking into a chair in Mrs. Osborn's exquisite boudoir, "I felt that I must see you. You attended to the letter properly, I suppose?"

"Trust me for that, my dear Mrs. Horton," replied Mrs. Osborn, meaningly.

"How good of you," murmured Mrs. Horton. "I really could not hope to get on at all in this matter if it were not for you."

"You see my fears in regard to Doctor Redfield were well founded," replied Mrs. Osborn.

"Indeed, I realize it," said Mrs. Horton, emphatically, "and now we are confronted by this Mr. Stanton. My husband is really quite charmed with him. I don't see why Doctor Avondale is so dilatory about coming. I certainly wish he would hasten."

"My dear Mrs. Horton," replied her friend, "trust me to guard off this Mr. Stanton. I have already assured him that Miss Ethel is spoken for, and I feel sure that he is too honorable to intrude himself when he regards Ethel as already engaged."

"But she is not engaged yet—that is the trouble," exclaimed Mrs. Horton, who at heart was really an estimable woman, although worldly and ambitious to gain a foothold in English aristocracy. Perhaps if she had never met Mrs. Osborn, Ethel might not have been sent to London. In her intercourse with English acquaintances, however, Mrs. Horton herself had become a devotee of the nobility.

"How delightfully innocent you are," laughed Mrs. Osborn. "Why, my dear Mrs. Horton, of course she is not engaged, but that does not prevent our saying she is, when it will protect the girl."

"Perhaps you are right," replied Mrs. Horton, with a sigh, "but I do dislike duplicity, and really, Lucy, I feel worried about that letter. I fear we are hardly doing right, and yet it seems to me that one is forced to questionable measures in a case like this. Why Ethel can't see the advantage to be derived from a marriage into such an old family as the Avondales is quite past my comprehension."

"It takes time to cultivate the taste," replied Mrs. Osborn. "Americans, as a rule, are naturally very stupid, and we American women are especially headstrong; but we, my dear Mrs. Horton, have mixed with the purple, and our eyes have been opened. I doubt not," she continued, "that either Doctor Redfield or Mr. Stanton would be quite eligible, but then they would develop into men of affairs and, like your husband and mine, would be wedded to their money-making schemes rather than to their wives."

"My husband," replied Mrs. Horton, "is certainly a good man, very indulgent and devoted; but some way he does not appreciate the nobility. He even argues with me and sometimes almost convinces me, against my own knowledge, when the question is raised. Still, I am much attached to him; I really am, Lucy."

"Oh, don't be sentimental, Mrs. Horton," laughed her companion. "Come, it's very bad form for a wife to pretend to be in love with her husband. Don't try to talk to him about the advantages of a suitable English alliance for Ethel. He does not understand, as you and I do, and it's only a waste of words. Wait until Ethel is Lady Avondale, and you and I will quite desert the frontier for merry old England."

CHAPTER XII.

KANSAS PROHIBITION

ONE evening, not very many days after Hugh's visit to the Horton family, he happened to meet Linus Lynn, the justice of the peace. Linus Lynn not only discharged the duties of village squire, but he was also engaged in the land, loan, and insurance business. He introduced himself to Hugh in the most matter-of-fact way, by saying that he had been intending, for some time, to do himself the honor of calling at the bank and getting acquainted.

"But business, you know, Mr. Stanton, is a very jealous master." A Falstaff smile overspread his chubby, side-whiskered face as he spoke.

"Quite true," replied Hugh, "and it's my misfortune not to have met you before. I hope soon to form the acquaintance of every business man in Meade."

"That's where you're wrong," said Judge Lynn, as he shut one eye knowingly.

The judge was in many respects an odd-looking individual, with his round face and straggling side-whiskers, and Hugh instinctively said, at first sight, "Here is a character."

In the first place and chiefly, his appearance gave evidence that Kansas prohibition did not prohibit. His bloated face attested to this—his immensity of waist measurement added proof—his whiskey-dwindled legs were argument eloquent, while his alcoholic breath was conviction itself.

This was Judge Lynn,—good-natured, frank, easy-going, improvident, in debt to everybody, and still willing to borrow. Unendowed with wisdom—and yet ignorant as a child of the

78

fact—a man whom everybody liked simply because there was no reason why he should be hated.

He knew every resident of Meade—in fact he knew every soul in the county and for miles beyond its borders—he also, in turn, was known. He was a pioneer of Kansas—came out from Indiana when very young, and in his years of residence in the Southwest had told people of his boyhood exploits on the banks of the Wabash. According to his own story he had been a great foot-racer—in fact, had never been beaten. The only evidence, however, of such athletic feats, came from his oft-repeated—even proverbial—assertions in regard to them.

He was a fixture on the streets of Meade, and had industriously whittled every dry-goods box in front of every store. He entered into political discussions, harmlessly; and there were even those who believed that he had convictions of his own.

He was a philanthropist in the way of giving good advice. Without solicitation he told the merchant how to conduct his business in order to reap the greatest results. He told the banker, in the same generous way, in whose hands it was safe to place loans. He would walk as far as a mile to inform cattlemen when to sell their herds.

Above all, Judge Lynn posed as the consulting oracle of the farmer, and the farmer—let it be understood—generally listened while he talked. Then, too, he was a weather prophet. He frequently prophesied as to a scourge of grasshoppers,—of chinch-bugs,—of hot winds, but seldom foretold a rain, of which the farmer stood in the greatest need. His prognostications as to "dry spells" really made him his reputation. In fact, it was his own normal condition to be "dry" and it had passed into a byword that when the judge suggested a "dry spell" it meant that he was short on change and "long on thirst." Usually, out of courtesy, the farmer, thus advised, would invite him "round the corner" to take a drink. On returning again to the street, the judge would immediately commence repeating the prophecy of a "dry spell," while his alert eyes would search the faces of his listeners, in an eager endeavor to pick out the one who would next invite him to take a walk "round the corner." Indeed, it may be stated as well here as later, that in drinking matters Judge Lynn, according to his own statement, was a "repeater."

In a professional way, Lynn recognized to a very high degree his own ability. In fact, on several occasions, he had taken issues with and attempted to reverse decisions of the higher courts.

The peculiarities of his appearance were augmented by a tall silk hat. This hat the people declared he had always had, and they reverenced it for its years of service.

The younger generation, in their thoughtlessness, if not their rudeness, had nicknamed Judge Lynn the "town spinning-top." Now, while this was an evident lack of courtesy on their part, it was nevertheless suggested by his appearance. Indeed, he did slope from the waist line up to his number six hat, and down to his number six boots, as abruptly as a top tapers. And then, too, he was always spinning yarns. The more daring boys went so far as to discuss among themselves, in caucus secrecy, the great time they could have if, by some means, they could wind a cord around the judge's spindle-legs, and on up to his mighty waist, and then, by some device, jerk the cord and send him into revolutions. Then they said that he would actually be a spinning-top and the greatest attraction in the town.

"There's where you're wrong, Mr. Stanton," repeated Judge Lynn, "plenty of fellows around here that you're better off not to know. It's expensive to know them."

"Why, how is that?" inquired Hugh.

"Well, let's walk around here," said Lynn, "where we can sit down, and I'll give you some p'inters that won't come amiss for you to know."

Hugh accompanied his new-found acquaintance, who led him around a corner and down a paved alley. A little farther on, the judge knocked; a door was quickly opened. Hugh's curiosity was soon satisfied. He found himself in the back room of one of the many drug stores of Meade. The place was provided with deal tables, chairs, and lounges. On the walls were hung pictures of the race-track and the prize-ring. The two seated themselves at one or the numerous small tables.

"Well, what'll you have, Stanton?" asked the judge. "It's my treat."

"Seltzer," replied Hugh.

"Hey, there! seltzer and a beer," called out the judge to the "druggist" in attendance. "Seltzer may suit you, but beer is good enough for me," said Judge Lynn. "Fact is I never drink anythin' stronger 'n beer until nine o'clock, and then take it straight. My life is guarded 'round with well-defined rules, and I'm a stickler on rules, and never break 'em unless the occasion is a little out er the ordinary."

"I was not aware," observed Hugh, when the seltzer and a foaming glass of beer had been placed on the table before them, "that we had saloons in Meade. You know Kansas has the reputation of being a great prohibition State."

"That's our boast—no open saloons," said the judge, as he blew the foam from his glass of beer, "we Kansans are mighty particular 'bout appearances. Now, there's twenty odd drug stores in this 'ere town and every one of 'em has a back door."

"What!" exclaimed Hugh, "do all the drug stores have a saloon in the rear?"

"Not a saloon, Mr. Stanton," replied the judge, suavely, "but they all have a restin'-place—a gentleman's parlor, so to speak, like this, where you can have anythin' you call for, from a plain seltzer to a Manhattan cocktail, and I might add they're all doin' a devilish brisk business."

"Hey, there!" cried the judge, knocking on the table with his cane, "fill 'em up again. You see, Mr. Stanton, I was the first representative in the legislature from this county, and, as a true Kansan, am proud of the reputation the State enjoys. We legislate for the people and drink for ourselves, askin' no questions. Why, there's Ike Palmer and Bill Young, the editors of the roarin'est temperance organ you ever saw. They are great patrons of these restin'-places on life's highway. We all meet here on an equal footin', and no serious jar threatens to interrupt our customs. These temperance editors, in flamin' editorials, proclaim, week in and week out, the fact that not an open saloon mars or disgraces the fair name of Meade. We all take pride, as a matter of course, in sendin' these papers to our Eastern friends."

"I knew all about the theory of prohibition before I came to Kansas," said Hugh, "but I have received to-day my first actual knowledge of its practice."

The judge, shutting one eye, looked benignly at Hugh and said, "Your conclusions are pre-matoor, howsomever, I expect, Mr. Stanton. I'm the gol darndest 'cyclopedia of knowledge that you ever run ag'inst. Say, hold on a minute; my nacheral impulse is to drink, so I guess I'll have another beer."

"Beg pardon," said Hugh, "please drink with me," and he motioned to the attendant.

"Oh, all right," acquiesced the judge, "just as you say. I promised to give you some p'inters. This 'ere expose; as it were, of practical temperance in the Sunflower State is p'inter number one. Now, there's the professional claim-prover—know anythin' about him?"

"Nothing whatever," replied Hugh, as he sipped his seltzer.

"Well, you see I allows it's my dooty to tell you," said the judge. "The professional claim-prover started in the eastern part of the State, proved up a quarter-section, sold it out to a mortgage loan company, moved on west to the next county, changed his name, proved up another quarter-section and sold it out to a mortgage company, and so on. These professional provers-up of land are a distinct class. They emigrate from the older counties to the newer ones in swarms, like grasshoppers. Did n't know about 'em, did you?"

"I did not," replied Hugh, "I am very much interested. How do they sell out to the mortgage companies?"

By this time the judge was beginning to feel the influence of drink, and gradually grew more bold and more talkative than ever.

"Well, gee whillikens, Stanton, I must say you're tender. Don't know much, do you?"

Hugh admitted that he did not, while secretly finding much amusement at the odd character he had discovered.

"Well, I do; bet yer life I do. 'Bout these 'ere claim-pro vers is p'inter number two, and sellin' out to the mortgage companies is p'inter number three. Here, waiter, by the great horn spoon, I've got to have another drink!" said the loquacious judge, rapping on the table. "Wonder if they expect a man's goin' to sit 'round here all night and drink nothin'. I'm hot; hotter'n a burnt boot. Got to have somethin' cool an' refreshin' or I'll be locoed."

"What will it be, gentlemen?" asked the attendant.

"Seltzer for me," said Hugh.

"Seltzer be hanged!" cried the judge, and then recollecting himself, he said, "Beg pardon, Mr. Stanton, what time is it? I left my watch on the piano this mornin'."

"Just nine o'clock," replied Hugh, looking at his timepiece.

"Bring me a straight," said the judge, and then, turning to Hugh, he observed, "I have an idee I can tell the time within ten seconds when nine o' clock comes 'round. Habit, you know; habit is everythin' to a sensitive man. Bet yer life it is. You wanted to know somethin' about sellin' out land to mortgage companies. Well, this is the way it's done: all the big farm mortgage companies in the United States are represented by local agents throughout these new counties in southwestern Kansas. They started out makin' mighty conservative loans, but at enormous rates of interest. After awhile the loan companies got to competin' with one another for business. Instead of lowerin' the rate of interest, as they should have done, they offered to take bigger loans; so, instead of loanin' a man three hundred dollars on a quarter-section of land that he has just proved up and paid the government a dollar and a quarter an acre for, they 're loanin' one thousand to fifteen hundred dollars on every one hundred and sixty acre tract that is offered. If you'll consult the records you'll find that from ten to fifteen thousand dollars is loaned daily on land in

83

this 'ere county alone. It's a mighty big county, but they'll have the last quarter-section mortgaged, by and by; the last link in the elephant's chain 'll be broken sooner or later, and then look out for squalls. The mortgage business is what makes money so plenty on the range now, but mark the words of Judge Lynn and profit by 'em—the time to make hay is when the sun's a-shinin'. One of these fine days the bottom 'll jest nacherally drop out, and there'll be a wailin' and gnashin' of teeth. Do I know anythin' more worth tellin'. Well, I should say I did. Have n't begun to uncork yet. Mighty lucky you met me. Bet yer life."

"You amaze me," said Hugh, "I don't understand why so much confidence is manifested on every hand if your pessimistic views are correct."

"Mighty easy to explain that," said the judge, as he ordered another cocktail, "jest as easy as failin' off a log. You see, ninety per cent, of the people in Meade have come here durin' the last three years. They're all tenderfeet and never have experienced a hot wind. Well, for a wonder, this is the third year of roarin' good crops, but the buffalo-grass is here yet, and as long as it's in the country these dangnation hot winds are liable to blow. When they come—" and here the judge drained another glass. "As I was sayin'," he went on, wiping his mouth with his coat sleeve, "when these hot winds do come, they'll sizzle things up 'round here into a burnt crisp, like a hot skillet does thin slices of bacon. Bet yer life. Yes, sir! you'll think it's a breath from the lower regions for sure, and the hull kit and bilin' of 'em will be dumped into a seethin' sea of bankruptcy, and don't yer forget it."

Hugh was greatly interested in the judge's prophecies. He attributed the judge's glibness to the liquor he had drunk, but, nevertheless, his words had a ring of prophecy about them. He determined to speak to Captain Osborn the next day in regard to the matter.

"No one 'round here believes me," said the judge, "they're all holdin' bobtail flushes and tryin' to bluff nachure; but I'm assoomin' they'll be called good an' plenty. You may speak to

Captain Osborn if you like; it won't do no harm—won't do no good, nuther. Of course you'll believe him and go right on as if you'd never heard me talk. Reckon I can tell thoughts when I see 'em squirmin' all over a man's race. Bet yer life I can."

Hugh arose. "Hold on, Stanton," said the judge, "not yet; not until I've treated the noomerous departed to a whiskey straight. Here, fill 'em up again," he called to the attendant. Hugh sat down, and Judge Lynn began again: "Say, have you ever met my old friend, Major Buell Hampton?" Hugh replied that he had. "Well, he's brainy," said the judge, "he's way up—a nacheral born leader. You bet. Ever since he was nominated for the legislature, and refused to run, he's been regarded by his political associates as the Bismarck of southwestern Kansas. Fact is, he won't take no office. His editorials are hummers; they keeps a-breedin' trouble a heap for the Republicans. They're what converted me to the faith. Bet yer life, I know a political truth when I find it blowin' 'round loose."

"Oh, you're a Populist, too, are you?" inquired Hugh.

"Bet yer life I am," replied the judge, enthusiastically, "though I'm not a Barley Huller. Fact is, the Barley Hullers is a great organization, sort o' select, you know,—the 'four hundred' of southwestern Kansas, as it were."

"That being the case I should suppose you would join them," said Hugh, with a tinge of irony in his words.

"No, sir!" said the judge, emphatically. "I've political aspirations, and if I j'ined, it might be said by designin', malicious, an' malignant political enemies that I'd done it to further my political ambitions; and a sensitive man like me, Stanton, could n't stand that kind of talk and whisperin' 'round. Bet yer life I could n't You look sorter supercilious and disbelievin', Stanton, but I'm statin' solid facts; yes, sirree."

Hugh was about to make a remark, when the judge went on, in a low, confidential tone: "Between us, Stanton, I once put in my application for membership with the Barley Hullers. Never been able to learn definitely what the investigatin' committee reported, but I do know they were short of oil that night at their lodge-room, and those condemnedly awkward farmers balloted on my application in a practically dark room. Course they could n't see what colored balls they were droppin' into the jedgment box. Well, would you believe it—it's a coincidence, sir, without a parallel—every cussed ball was as black as Egyptian night; yes, sir."

"Well, that was strange," replied Hugh, laughing. The judge did not even smile, but said, "Strange! Why, it was devilish strange, and I felt really crushed all one evenin', but I was too keen a politician to let 'em see it. Oh, I know two or three legerdemain tricks when it comes to pullin' wires. Bet yer life I do! I'm a heap too permiscus for any of 'em."

They arose from the table, and the judge asked the white-aproned druggist for the bill.

"Remember, a part of it is mine," said Hugh, taking from his pocket a roll of money.

"Not if the court knows herself," said the judge, waving Hugh aside with one hand, while he plowed deep into his trousers pocket with the other.

"But I insist," said Hugh.

A look of dismay and astonishment came over the judge's face, as he dived first into one pocket, and then into the other. Presently he said, "Stanton, loan me ten dollars. Thanks. Will hand it to you in the mornin'. Here," said he, turning to the druggist, "take it all out of this. No, Stanton, no, sir! you sha'n'. pay a cent—not a copper. I invited you to take a social glass, and unless you wish to offend me, you'll say nothin' more 'bout payin'. I want you to know you're coastin' 'round town with a highflyer when you're hobnobbin' with me, you bet."

The druggist handed the judge the change, which he put into his pocket, as they went out along the alleyway into the street.

"Well, Judge," said Hugh, "I am delighted to have met you."

"Well, sir," replied the judge, "them's my sentiments to a dot. Bet yer life. I can give you lots of good p'inters 'bout this 'ere country, and don't you forget it; an' while my conclusions are sorter pesterin' idees to Captain Osborn an' others, still they're not as raveled and frayed idees as some people will want to make believe. Howsomever, time will stampede 'em a heap, and don't you forget it. By the way, Stanton, do you ever finger the pasteboards—play a social game, you know, once in awhile?"

"No, thank you, I never play any game of chance," replied Hugh.

"Well, I do," replied the judge; "fact is, I'm a sort of sociable animal, any way you take me. Buck Truax runs a little game over in the back end of his furniture store. I promised to drop in durin' the evenin'. Politics, Stanton," said the judge, nudging him with his elbow, "politics, you know. Oh, you bet I know a thing or two. I know how to break eggs with the boys. Well, good night, will see you in the mornin'."

"Good night, Judge," said Hugh, accepting his outstretched hand.

As Hugh turned down the street toward the hotel, the moon was shining brightly. When he reached his rooms, he sat by a window which commanded a view of Crooked Creek valley. The coyotes were howling in dismal cadences away to the north, beyond the old mill. Presently he saw a red and green light, and wondered if the Barley Hullers were holding a meeting.

CHAPTER XIII.

MAJOR HAMPTON'. LIBRARY

WHEN Hugh told Captain Osborn of his conversation with Judge Lynn, the captain laughed.

"And so he told you the country was going to the dogs, did he? Well, my boy, when Judge Lynn, as he is called, imbibes a few drinks of whiskey, he is fond of uttering prophecies of the nature you describe. He owes everybody in town. I would not be surprised if he would ask you for a loan of five or ten dollars before a week."

"Well, if he should," asked Hugh, looking up, "would I be safe in letting him have it? Would he not return it?"

"Never," returned the captain; "he was never known to pay even the most trivial debt unless compelled to do so; yet he is a rather good fellow for all that—does no one any particular harm. He served one term in the legislature, and ever since has had an idea that he is a great political factor. As to the hot wind part of his story, that is the stereotyped cry of the cattlemen. I presume Lynn is getting ready to make a speech to a cowboy audience. I have lived here for five years. There was little or no farming attempted during the first and second years, but for the last three years the agricultural yield has been enormous. I have never yet experienced the hot winds. The rain belt is, year by year, creeping westward, and the so-called arid region is giving way before the farmer's plow."

"I suppose," said Hugh, "that it is simply a war between the cattlemen on the one hand and the farmers on the other. The elements are not taking sides."

"I should say," replied the captain, "from the crops we are raising, that the elements are taking the farmers' side. By the way," he continued, "Major Hampton called this morning, and asked me to present his compliments to you. He wishes you to call at his home this evening, and I promised him that you would do so."

"Thank you," said Hugh. "The major has been away almost two weeks. I wonder if he found anything of the cattle thieves."

"No," replied the captain; "he got on their supposed trail, and followed it to St. Louis, only to learn he was mistaken after reaching there. The major is certainly a most persistent man." That evening Hugh called at Major Hampton's home. His house was a cottage in design, although large and roomy. There were little porches here and there, and a wide veranda in front. The yard was enclosed by a neatly-painted fence. A green, velvety lawn evinced much care. The major met Hugh at the door.

"Come in, come right in," said he, cheerily, as he ushered Hugh into his library. Low, richly-carved bookcases occupied the walls. Every shelf was filled with tawny-colored volumes. Above one of the bookcases was a large mounted buffalo head, and across the room, as a foil for the buffalo trophy, was a pair of mounted Texas steer horns, measuring almost six feet from tip to tip. A few bronzes and choice paintings, artistically arranged, set off the room. The ceiling was delicately frescoed in blue and gold, while a deep frieze of red suggested warmth.

"Thank you," said Hugh, as he seated himself in a chair pushed toward him by the major.

"Well, I am glad to see you again, Stanton, I am indeed," said the major. "I have been looking forward to a visit from you with the keenest pleasure."

"It is very good of you to say so," answered Hugh, "but I am quite sure that I have reason to be congratulated more than yourself!"

"As to that—ah!" exclaimed the major, hastily arising from a leather couch, where he had thrown himself, "Mr. Stanton, permit me." Some one had entered the room through a side door directly back of Hugh's chair. He arose and turned as the major spoke.

"My daughter, Miss Marie, Mr. Stanton." The girl appeared to be about eighteen years of age. She bowed rather coldly, and turned toward her father, asking, "How soon will you want me to sing, papa?"

"Oh, ho!" laughed the major, "that was a little surprise I had in store for Mr. Stanton. You have robbed my program of part of its interest."

"I beg your pardon, papa," said the girl, her lips parting in a sweet smile, "now that Mr. Stanton is advised of it, he will have ample time to prepare his nerves for the ordeal. You see, papa," she went on, "Ethel Horton has invited me to go driving with her. We will not be gone long—perhaps an hour."

"All right, daughter, that will be soon enough," replied the major.

As the girl turned to go, Hugh noticed her wealth of bronzed hair. She was just budding into womanhood, and her soul shone out through her deep blue eyes, as if challenging one to doubt her. Hugh's glance was half critical, although not the glance of personal interest.

There was a time to come, however, when he would wonder how it had been possible for him to look upon this girl with other than feelings of personal interest. Little did he dream, on that first evening at Major Hampton's, of the great sorrow that was to come—a sorrow in which this light-hearted, innocent girl would awaken to a grief that could not be comforted—a grief that he, himself, was destined to share with her.

"She is a wonderful girl," said the major, after Marie had gone. "I doubt if her equal can be found in the Sunflower State."

"Very prepossessing," replied Hugh. "Her face is a most intellectual one."

The major opened a fresh box of cigars. "Have a cigar, Stanton," said he. "I feel in a humor to talk, and nothing aids more in conversation than smoking a good cigar."

After the cigars were lighted, the major returned to his former reclining position on the lounge.

"My dear Stanton," said he, "are you at all interested in politics?"

"I can't say that I am," returned Hugh. "I usually vote, and that's about all."

"I, perhaps, am not claiming too much when I say that in politics I am a philosopher. If I had the power, I would try the experiment of setting aside this so-called political economy, and these financial heresies, substituting therefor a little common sense in conducting the affairs of state. In a great country like ours, whose mountains are fairly bursting open with tons of unmined precious mineral, a country whose credit is unlimited, we should be able to furnish employment to a million men, in building better roads, in constructing dikes, in making canals for waterway transportation, and in reclaiming arid lands. Instead, our present limited population is congested into inactivity; our highways are lined with the unemployed, and, while surrounded by plenty, our people are actually dying of starvation."

"I am aware," replied Hugh, "that there are many unemployed, especially in large cities like Chicago and New York. The poor people are usually provided with free soup-houses, however, and need not starve."

"My dear Stanton," said the major, with great earnestness, "patriotism cannot and will not survive on charity soup. The plan that I have in mind would set in motion the wheels of our paralyzed industries. It would do away with idleness, and elevate the starving man to a position of self-support and self-respect. Benevolent soup-kitchens destroy self-respect, and loyalty grows lean on such a diet."

Hugh was about to reply, when the bell rang. The major hastily arose, knocked the ashes from his cigar, and opened the door.

CHAPTER XIV.

THE SONG

THREE men stood on the veranda. "Why, how do you do?" said the major, "come in. I am very glad to see you."

Judge Linus Lynn, with his weather-beaten tile, Bill Kinneman, with his red eyes, and Dan Spencer, with his wobbling tooth, all stalked into the room.

"Why, hello, pardner," said Dan Spencer, as he caught sight of Hugh, "how d' ye do?" They all shook hands.

"We jist drapped in fur a minit, Major," said Bill Kinneman, "to say hello. Did n't know yer hed company, or we would n't hev cum. Heerd you'd got back. Did n't see nuthin' of the cattle thieves, I reckon?"

"Nothing," responded the major, thoughtfully. "I failed. Tell Mr. Horton that I struck the wrong trail, and followed it down through Oklahoma, and on east to the Missouri River, and then to St. Louis, only to be disappointed in the end."

"Purty danged good nerve, I can tell ye," said Dan Spencer, "to foller them cussed cattle thieves like the major did. I'm thinkin' I'd be purty hostill if I had to do it;" his tooth wobbled like the side motion of a fanning-mill.

"Don't care if I do," said Judge Lynn, greedily, as he reached over, and helped himself to a cigar.

"Why, certainly, gendemen," said the major, and, eagerly rising, he passed around the box of cigars.

"Jist about the time o' day I smoke," said Dan Spencer, as he threw an enormous quid of tobacco toward the cuspidor. Bill Kinneman expectorated a sounding pit-tew of tobacco juice at the receptacle just as Judge Lynn threw a burnt match in the same direction.

"Waal, boys," said Dan Spencer, when their cigars were going, "we've got toomultuous dooties to perform, an' I guess we may as well move on. Jist drapped in fur a minit, yer know, Major."

"That's right, boys," replied Major Hampton, shaking hands most cordially with them as they started away, "come often and be in no hurry about going, is the standing invitation you each have." They all shook hands with Hugh, and soon after crept out along the veranda and down the steps into the street. When they were gone, the major said:

"They represent the masses. We cannot ignore them. Rightly guided, they are a power for good morals and good government; otherwise they are liable to menace the very foundations of our society." Presently they heard some one singing.

"Hello!" said the major, "Marie has returned. Well, Stanton, let us quit the library and our cigars. By the way, I am a student of men, and I am surprised that you are not a musician, for you certainly have a soul full of it. I want you to hear my daughter sing. I fancy," he continued, hesitatingly, "that she has a fairly good voice."

They adjourned to an adjoining room. From a musician's standpoint this room was a veritable dream. It was furnished with a "baby grand," a complete musical library, containing some rare volumes; also with busts of Beethoven, Haydn, Bach, Handel, Mendelssohn, Chopin, Liszt, Schumann, Wagner, and other famous composers. On the walls were well-selected paintings, each in itself a study pertaining to music.

"This, Mr. Stanton," said the major, "is my daughter's studio. You are the first stranger ever invited into this room."

"And who is her instructor, may I inquire?"

"I direct my daughter's education in all her studies," modestly replied the major.

"I am sure I feel highly honored," returned Hugh.

Marie glanced innocently at him over her shoulder. She was

standing before a music-case, with one foot slightly advanced, and as she turned to look at Hugh her gracefully poised figure seemed to him a perfect model.

"You are most welcome," said the girl, smiling, "or we would not have asked you here."

Hugh was wondering why he had been invited into the sacredness of this musical retreat, from which others were excluded, but his reverie was interrupted by the major's seating himself at the piano. He struck a few chords on the keys, and, after running through several modulations, he glided into Mendelssohn's Symphony in C Minor. The major's great body swayed back and forth as the music moved him with its entrancing power. Someway, the spirit of the melody stirred Hugh in a manner strangely new.

The music suddenly ceased with a few jagged, broken notes, mixed together in a wailing discord, and the major turned sharply around toward their guest.

"Oh, papa," cried Marie, "why did you do that?"

"All right, Stanton, my boy," said the major, laughing, as he tossed his long, gray locks back from his forehead. "I see I am not mistaken; you have a soul filled with harmony, although you may not be able to play, as you say, even a jew's-harp."

Marie sang a selection from the "Bohemian Girl," while her father played the accompaniment. Her rich, deep tones, silvery in their sweetness, vibrated and filled the room with a melody almost divine. She breathed into the song the fullness of her intensely musical soul. Her flutelike tones budded and then crescendoed into full-grown fragrant flowers, which gradually died away, like the falling petals—one by one—of an over-ripe rose. An impalpable sense of mystery and majesty seemed to envelop the singing girl to the now exalted and thrilled senses of Hugh Stanton. What subtle power was this that thrilled him through and through? It was unfathomable—he could not understand the genius of the invisible that swelled up about his exalted brain and filled him with a spirit not his own, while his soul throbbed in ecstatic delight. She ceased singing, and Hugh sank back into his chair, exhausted. The music had exhilarated him with new and wonderful thoughts—devout thoughts, divine ideas. The major turned from the piano, and discovered Hugh in the mysterious struggles that come to a traveler when his soul has been swept away on the surging deep of song.

Hugh soon took his leave of Major Hampton and his daughter, gratefully accepting their cordial invitations to call again at an early day. That night he dreamed of dwelling in some sacred and mystical retreat surrounded with music and poetry. Then the scene changed, and he saw a wide waste of desolate prairie stretching away in every direction. Presently Marie Hampton stood before him, weeping bitterly. Her fair cheeks and amethyst eyes were bathed in tears, while near her was Ethel Horton, speaking words of consolation. Between them was a mound of earth, and, looking closer, he saw it was a new-made grave.

CHAPTER XV.

THE RETRACTION

IN addition to the *Patriot* there were two other newspapers published at Meade. One of these, the *Mascot*, advocated Republican politics. The other was a mongrel sheet, promulgating uncertain political views. This publication left the press under the high-sounding name of the *World*.

The editor and proprietor of the *World* was a Mr. Frank Fewer. His enemies said the "fewer" the better of such unprincipled knaves. Politically, he favored the candidate who bought him last. The influence of his paper was a commodity for barter and sale.

On the day after Hugh's visit at Major Hampton's, the *World* made its weekly appearance, and contained in its columns the following article.

"HOME AGAIN."

"His Excellency, Maj. Buell Hampton, an old played-out politician, who edits a little five-by-nine sheet around the corner, known as the Patriot, has returned to the city. The editor of the World is not advised as to whether the old boodler has been away organizing a society of Farmers' Alliance in some remote township, or a lodge of Barley Hullers. It is only a question of a short time until this illiterate decoy duck will slink from southwestern Kansas to pastures that are new."

During the forenoon the major called at the bank and asked

Hugh to accompany him to the *World* office.

"Certainly," said Hugh, "I will go with pleasure." Captain Osborn opened the door of his private office, and invited Major Hampton and Hugh into his room.

"Major," said the captain, "why are you going down to the *World* office?"

"To kill the dog who penned and published this calumny," replied the major, as he handed the captain a marked copy of the *World*.

The old captain laughed heartily and tried to infuse the major with a jovial spirit, but he would not be infused. His face was very white, and the lines about his mouth had a hard, set expression, like a tiger ready to spring. "I would n't pay any attention to it at all," said the captain, soothingly.

"Fewer's blood, sir," hissed the major, "alone can blot out this contemptible insult. He has defamed my character, and, by the Eternal, he shall pay the price."

"Hold on, Major," said Captain Osborn, "I am your friend in this matter, and I cannot permit you to make a mistake. Suppose now that we force the *World* to run off another edition containing an '*amende honorable*,' or something of that sort—what then?"

"I do not believe," said the major, reflectively, "that he will do it; but if he will, and bring out the issue to-day—a full issue, mind—I will then let him off with a horsewhipping."

"Well, now, that's better," said the captain, shaking hands with him, as if the affair were settled. "You stay right here, Major, until I come back."

When Captain Osborn arrived at the *World* office, he found Frank Fewer, Esq., seated in a rickety old chair, engaged in wrapping bundles of papers preparatory to sending them away.

"Good morning, Captain," said Fewer, while an idiotic grin covered his face.

"Good morning," returned the captain, "have n't sent away this week's papers yet, have you?"

"No," replied Fewer, "only a few around town; but why?"

The iron will of the old captain arose to the emergency. "Fewer," said he, "but for my friendly interference in your behalf, you would now be a dead man."

"What!" shrieked the editor.

"A dead man, I say!" reaffirmed the captain, in a quiet, determined voice. "Here," said he, opening a paper, "this libelous article—why did you print such a contemptible thing?"

Fewer was at heart a groveling coward. He whined and begged, and protested that Lem Webb, a misanthropic lawyer, had written the article, and that he, Webb, had agreed to pay him five dollars for its publication.

"It will cost you your life, sir," said the captain, with a stern military ring in his voice. "There is but one way to avert the calamity in which your corpse must necessarily figure as the principal attraction."

"How, Captain? For God's sake tell me," begged the now trembling editor.

The captain explained the conditions. "Suppress all of the present issue possible, run off another issue of the paper, containing an *amende honorable*, and take a horsewhipping. Otherwise, death."

The terms were agreed upon instantly, and the captain hurried back to inform the major of the "unconditional surrender," and to prepare a copy of an amende honorable, while the frightened editor commenced making preparations for a special edition.

That afternoon the World again made its appearance, and contained the following retraction:

"AMENDE HONORABLE."

"At the solicitation of Lem. Webb, Esq., and on account of a promise of five dollars, I maliciously and wilfully permitted a libelous and untruthful item to appear in the columns of the World this morning, derogatory to the character of Maj. Buell Hampton.

"This open letter is a public acknowledgment on the part of the editor of the World that he knew the item in question to be a malicious lie, at the time it was published, and he hereby publicly apologizes to Major Hampton. The editor further desires to state that he personally knows Major Hampton to be a cultured gentleman of unquestionable moral character,—a man whose high sense of honor and integrity is above reproach. Respectfully,

"Frank Fewer,

"Editor of the World."

That evening Bill Kinneman and Dan Spencer waited upon Editor Fewer at his home.

"Hello! gentlemen," said Fewer as he came down the walk in front of his house to meet his callers.

"Hello! yourself," replied Dan Spencer. "We only called jist fur a minit. We's in a pow'rful big hurry. We've got Major Hampton's proxy to hosswhup ye."

"Oh, come, gentlemen," whined Fewer, "after the retraction I published, the major can't really mean to subject me to so great a humiliation."

"I reckon that's about the size of it," said Spencer, trembling with a wrath that made his fang-like tooth wobble from one side to the other as if it were trying to dodge a calamity. "We're not a-bustin' with perliteness," said Spencer, "in projectin' 'round over the range this 'ere way, I suppose, but I'm assoomin' dooty is dooty an' jestice knows no fav'rites."

Frank Fewer turned, and fled with all the speed that he could command. Bill Kinneman sprang into his saddle and, touching spurs to his horse, galloped madly after him. The cowboy loosened his lariat as he rode, and swung the coil dexterously over his head several times. Then, with a quick, powerful twitch, the rope shot out like an arrow after the sprinting editor. The loop fell over his head and shoulders, then tightened, binding his arms to his sides. A few minutes later Frank Fewer was a horsewhipped editor.

Smarting with pain and humiliation, Fewer called on Attorney Webb, determined to bring suit for the outrage perpetrated upon him. The lawyer was just reading the *amende honorable* article, in which he discovered that Fewer had sacrificed him most shamefully, in attempting to save himself. A little later the editor picked himself up from the sidewalk, a badly thrashed and a thoroughly kicked man. Thereafter the *World* was known as a journal that attended strictly to its own business.

CHAPTER XVI.

THE OLD VIOLIN

HUGH called at the *Patriot* office to congratulate the major on Fewer's retraction. He found him in his den dictating an editorial to his daughter. Hugh was made welcome, not only by the major's words, but also by Marie's smile.

"You see that my daughter is my amanuensis," said the major. "She has mastered the pothooks of shorthand so thoroughly that she is able to report the speeches of our public men, although some of them are very rapid talkers. In addition to this she is the 'typo' of the *Patriot*. She has worked in the printing-office for four years, and during the last year has read and corrected her own proof. I maintain that an experience in a country printing-office is a liberal education in itself."

Hugh was very much surprised to find that one so young as Marie possessed so much practical knowledge. These accomplishments, added to her rare musical talents, increased the interest that he was beginning to feel in her.

Marie soon returned to her type-setting case in the back room, and the major, taking up some copy that was lying on the table, said, "We are enjoying good times in southwestern Kansas, but the metropolitan dailies of our larger cities constantly remind us that something is wrong in our economic system. While one class surfeits itself with feasting, another class in the same locality is starving. Has it ever struck you, Mr. Stanton, that something is radically wrong and unfair in the distribution of wealth?"

"Really, Major," replied Hugh, "I am not sufficiently versed in political economy to discuss the subject intelligently. I believe that there is an improvident class of laborers in this country, who, when out of employment, are immediately out of money—a people who signally fail in the obligations that they owe to the general government and to themselves."

"The obligations of the government and of its citizens," said the major, warmly, "are mutual. A government that demands defense from its citizens in the hour of peril, and fails to provide work for them in the time of peace, is cowardly and lame in solving the simplest elementary problems of human existence and comfort."

"But is there so much want and misery abroad in the land?" asked Hugh. "Thanksgiving proclamations from the various States disclose the fact that prosperity and plenty abound. I fear, Major, that you are pessimistic on this subject."

"My dear Stanton," replied the major, earnestly, "a Thanksgiving proclamation, nine times out of ten, is a burlesque on our civilization. If the same amount of energy were expended in encouraging enterprises that increase the riches and happiness of communities, as is put forth in enacting laws that encourage and protect individual riches, much more good would result. A selfish law begets and encourages selfishness, and smothers every altruistic virtue. The result is, that robbery and jobbery are alike legalized; not by the consent of the governed, but by bribed legislatures. The rich grow richer, and, under the legal protection of bristling bayonets, they enforce oppressive and unjust laws; while the poor continually grow poorer and more miserable. I cannot blame the masses for not tolerating the licentious luxury of the rich. All just laws derive their legitimate power from the consent of the governed."

"Would you not consider, Major, that he would indeed be a bold man who would take issue with Ruskin on this subject?" asked Hugh.

"He might be rather a very foolish man," replied the major. "What does Ruskin say?"

"He says," replied Hugh, "that none but the dissolute among

the poor look upon the rich as their natural enemies, or desire to pillage their homes and divide their property. None but the dissolute among the rich speak in opprobrious terms of the vices and follies of the poor."

"That's all right, Stanton," said the major, but there was an irritable ring in his voice, as he arose and walked back and forth with his hands clasped behind his back. "That's all right," he repeated; "the trouble is, however, that too many of the rich are dissolute."

"How about the poor?" asked Hugh. "Isn't there a considerable number of them who would like to divide up property?"

"Hold on, Stanton," said the major; "stop right there. You and I must not talk politics. My convictions are so strong that I find myself irritated by your words. I am beginning to feel ugly toward you."

"Questions of social or political reform, at best, are usually unsatisfactory," replied Hugh, "and I quite agree with you that nothing can be gained by heated discussions."

The major made no reply, but soon afterward, at his request, they walked down the street toward his home. On reaching the privacy of the library, the major turned to Hugh and said, "Stanton, I have something to say to you. I feel like taking you into my confidence more than I have ever done, and still—well, I don't know,—some other time, perhaps, might be better." Hugh observed an earnestness in the words of the major, and in the expression of his face, that he had never noticed before. There was a soft intonation in his musical Southern voice that was most convincing. This, together with his dignity and refinement of manners, elevated him in Hugh's eyes almost to the height of sublimity. He turned away from Hugh in apparent half indecision, and went into another room; but soon returned with a violin.

"What, are you master of all musical instruments?" asked Hugh, looking up in pleased surprise.

"Master is a strong word," replied the major, as he gently

tuned the aged Stradivarius, and softly thumbed the strings. Then, tenderly embracing the violin with his chin, as he placed it in position, he brought his bow at right angles, and Schumann's "Trbumerei" trembled from the strings in soft and plaintive melody, filling every corner of the room with echoing and reechoing notes of sweetness. Other airs followed one after another in quick succession, and, as he played, the pleading tones seemed to grow richer and deeper in their harmonic cadences.

The gathering twilight deepened into night, but still the major went on caressing and winning from the violin selections and improvisations that would have charmed the most cultured ear. Sometimes the strings would cry out like the pleading wail of a lost soul, and float away through the window, charging the night wind with quivering melody. Again the notes seemed glints of moonbeams falling aslant through the gloaming, and lighting up the face of the old man as if with a halo of glory. Then the music changed, and it seemed no longer to be the work of mortal hands, but, rather, the soulful touch of some rare and heavenly spirit that was sweeping over the strings with sublime inspiration—with divine outpourings of a soul.

The elevation running through the harmony was devoutly exalting. The notes were brought together in full, rich strength, deftly caught back again, then bursting forth like a raging storm on the boundless ocean. Presently a single note rang out like a warning of danger. It was a wild, surging tone, and cried piteously, as if pierced and torn. Then the music ceased, and the silence of night throbbed with countless echoing notes that floated away on the invisible air. Tears were in the strings of the old violin, in the trembling zephyrs that were wafted in at the open window, and in Hugh Stanton's eyes. It was music never again to be heard, yet never to be forgotten.

CHAPTER XVII.

LENOX AVONDALE'. ARRIVAL

AS the weeks wore into months, Hugh Stanton saw a great deal of the Hortons. The cattle king seemed drawn to Hugh by some strange attachment which he could not explain. Even Mrs. Horton began to feel a sense of security about Hugh's presence at their home that she could not have believed possible a few months before. Perhaps she relied on Mrs. Osborn's assurance that she would be responsible for Mr. Stanton's non-interference with their plans for Ethel.

Hugh had been thrown much in Ethel's society, and his admiration and platonic regard for the girl had strengthened at each succeeding meeting. He fancied that he noticed a shade of sadness on Ethel's face, and once or twice he was sure that he discovered traces of tears. They frequently went horseback riding together down the valley, and he found her to be an expert equestrienne.

It was a bright autumnal day, and Hugh and Ethel were returning to the Horton home after a long ride. She had been telling him of Lake Geneva; and he confessed that, notwithstanding his long residence in Chicago, he had never visited that beautiful resort. Once Ethel was tempted to ask him if he were acquainted with Doctor Redfield, but her letter had never been answered, and she refrained from doing so. She had not given up hope, however; but lived on from day to day in the belief that, sooner or later, the man to whom she had completely given her heart would come and claim her.

On entering the house, Ethel uttered an exclamation of

surprise, as she went forward to welcome a stranger whom her mother was entertaining. Then, turning, she introduced Dr. Lenox Avondale to Hugh. The Englishman bowed indifferently to Stanton, and turned again to Mrs. Horton to finish some remark he had been making. There was a supercilious air about the man which Hugh instinctively disliked.

As Hugh took his departure, Ethel followed him to the veranda and insisted that they must have their ride together the next afternoon. Hugh believed her solicitude to be an effort to make amends for the haughty indifference of the Englishman.

"Miss Ethel," said he, "I surrender unconditionally. No, I'll not say that—it is with this condition; if you are sure that you want me, let me know; but I fancy your time will be entirely taken up during the stay of your English friend."

As Hugh rode thoughtfully homeward, he saw a carriage coming toward him. It was Mrs. Osborn driving over to the Grove. At her salutation he dismounted and stood beside the carriage.

"Did you meet Doctor Avondale?" she asked, with an air of triumph playing about her pretty face.

"I had that honor," replied Hugh.

Then followed some light conversation, in which Mrs. Osborn tried to be most captivating in her quick repartee.

"Are you sure, quite sure, you do not want to ask me a single question?" she interrogated.

"Well, I should like to know how long the Englishman is going to remain?" said Hugh, hesitatingly.

Mrs. Osborn broke into a silvery laugh, as she replied, "What difference can it make to you? Your regard for Miss Ethel is only of a platonic nature, don't you know?"

"That is very true," replied Hugh, "I have not changed my mind a particle; nevertheless, a platonic regard may be strong enough to cause one to take a deep interest in one's friends."

"You are quite clever to put it that way," said Mrs. Osborn. "I shall try to ascertain, and will let you know just how long Doctor

Avondale expects to remain, although you are such a naughty boy I ought not to favor you a particle."

"What have I done?" asked Hugh.

"Oh, you neglect your friends so,—unless, perchance, it is your platonic friend, Miss Ethel," she said, looking archly at him. "I was telling the captain only the other day that we invited you at least a dozen times to our house for every one time you honored it with your presence."

"One does not like to wear out one's welcome," replied Hugh, evasively, "however, I shall be delighted to call to-morrow evening if agreeable."

"Very well," said Mrs. Osborn. "No," said she, after a moment's hesitation, "come to dinner this evening. I think, perhaps, I shall entertain Doctor Avondale to-morrow evening."

"Oh, very well," replied Hugh, and with this arrangement he bade her good day.

When Hugh arrived at Captain Osborn's that evening, he found the captain with his little son, Harry, on a shady grass-plot, which was screened from the street by twining honeysuckles.

"Hello, Hugh, my boy," cried the captain, as he saw him coming through the gate, "come out here, and make yourself at home."

"How do, Untile Hoo," said Harry, as he advanced to shake hands with his father's friend, "don't 'ou fink dis is a nice p'ace?" asked the little fellow, waving his small hand around the enclosed nook.

"Indeed, it is, Harry," replied Hugh, "one of the most delightful places I ever saw."

"Dis is where papa an' I turns a tourtin'," said he, innocently. "We's failin' more an' more in love wiv each uv'er ever' time we turns out here, is n't we, papa?"

"That's what we are, you little rogue," laughed the captain, beaming tenderly at the child.

Soon after, Mrs. Osborn drove up, and they all went in to dinner. As the meal progressed, Hugh was satisfied that the relations between Mrs. Osborn and her husband had not materially improved.

"I presume," remarked the captain, "that this distinguished surgeon, Dr. Lenox Avondale, will take up his quarters at the Grove, and stay indefinitely. It's a great deal cheaper than stopping at a public hotel."

"Captain," said Mrs. Osborn, coldly, "your inference is very unbecoming. You may speak disrespectfully in a general way about the English people, if it pleases you, but I cannot allow thoughtless remarks about my own particular English friends to pass unnoticed."

"I beg your pardon, Lucy, I thought Doctor Avondale was the particular friend of Mrs. Horton and Miss Ethel."

"And why not mine also?" she inquired, rather testily.

"Oh, I did n't know that," said the captain.

"Well, that's it, Captain; there is so much that you don't know, and your remarks are so careless that you quite provoke me."

"There's one thing I do know," said the captain, as usual taking refuge in his boy. "I have a young gentleman at my right, here, who is the worst little rascal in southwestern Kansas."

"Oh, don't tell on me, papa; don't 'ou tell!"

"What's that, Harry?" inquired his mother, curiously.

"Oh, dat's a se'tret 'tween papa an' me."

The captain laughed heartily. "'Ou see, mamma, I p'a'.d a big joke on papa an' it turn out to be a joke on me; dat's why I wants to teep it a se'tret."

"Well, I'll not tell, Harry; I'll be true to you."

"Dat's wight, papa, I did n't fink 'ou'd tell."

"Doctor Avondale will be a fellow lodger of yours at the hotel," observed Mrs. Osborn, addressing Hugh.

"Indeed?" said Hugh, inquiringly.

"Yes, I have discussed the matter with him, and he has decided, much against the wishes of Mrs. Horton, that it would, perhaps, be more pleasant for him to stop in town."

"Well, why did n't you say so at once, Lucy?" asked the captain.

"Because I was kept so busy defending my friends against

your unwarranted attacks."

"Oh, come, my dear," said the captain, "you know I would not offend any of your friends intentionally under any circumstances. You also know, I believe, that my greatest happiness is to see you happy."

"Why, Captain," laughed his wife, "this new rtle is quite becoming to you; it is, indeed. How charmed I am to hear you say such nice things, and, as a test of your sincerity, I shall ask you to be more careful of your remarks in the future."

She then turned away indifferently, and told Hugh that Doctor Avondale would probably remain three or four weeks at Meade.

As Hugh walked down the street toward the hotel, after leaving the Osborns, he wondered what the next year would bring forth. He was conscious of an interest in Ethel Horton that he could not quite understand. He believed that he could far more easily analyze his feelings toward little Marie Hampton, with her rich contralto voice, than he could his friendship for the queenly Ethel. "My life," mused Hugh, "is like a vast, leafy forest, tormented by strange winds. It abounds with sighs and laughter, songs and murmurings and half-spoken whisperings, while all is a labyrinth of mystery."

In the meantime, Dr. Lenox Avondale had dined with the Hortons, and had succeeded in making himself quite agreeable. Ethel felt his searching eyes upon her, and they filled her with a certain dread—an uneasiness. She did not interpret his look as one of impudence—no, but, rather, the critical scrutiny in which a buyer of fine stock might indulge at a horse fair, especially if the proposed buyer were looking for blooded fillies with which to replenish his stables.

The coming of Lenox Avondale, his reception at their home, her mother's special efforts to entertain him, a half-overheard conversation of Lucy Osborn with her mother, had all conspired to awaken Ethel to the seriousness of the situation. Her secret resentment was all the more keen because there was no open warfare, neither would there be. She was expected, simply, to drift into a net, from which escape would be impossible. Her troubles would have changed to the merest schoolgirl sport, if she were only fortified with even one word from Jack Redfield, but her letter was unanswered.

She was indeed glad when Avondale pleaded weariness, and started on his return to Meade soon after dinner. When he had gone, Ethel strolled down toward the lake, and paused at the little summer-house. She was no longer the freehearted and happy girl who once gamboled over the prairie, but had become as a bird that is caged, and its wild spirit broken. Her heart beat a dirge of regret. She was, indeed, an object of pity.

The intrigues of Lucy Osborn, seconded by the negative assistance of a well-meaning and yet a weak and influenced mother, had subjected her to grief and humiliation.

"Oh, Jack," she sighed, half aloud, "Jack, why have you broken my heart? Why have you not come to me, and loved me? You taught me the lesson of life—how to love—and now it must be you have forgotten me; but the love—my love—is still as fragrant as a full-blown rose, and, like the rose stem, it has many thorns, but I cannot give up the rose because of the thorns on the stem; neither can I give up this great love, nor forget it, nor put it away from me. Yes, I will hold it close to my aching breast, and let the cruel thorns pierce my sorrowing heart."

A brown thrush flew from the summer-house and alighted in front of her. It was the mate of the constant mother bird, who, during the summer, had warmed the little speckled eggs of anticipation into winged life; and Ethel knew it well. She had brought it crumbs for many a day. She loved it. Taking from a pocket of her apron a handful of crumbs, she motioned as if to toss them, and the thrush hopped nearer to her, down the path, for it was not afraid. "Now, look out," she said:

"One's for the money,
Two's for the show,

Three's to make ready,
And four's to go."

She tossed the crumbs to the bird, and it seemed to thank her with many a chirp. She called this thrush her little poem of the air.

"Oh, bright-winged thrush," she said, with girlish superstition, "I beg you to tell of him who won my heart so long—so very long—ago. Is he true? Tell me, thrush, tell me, tell."

The thrush winked his knowing eyes, and, turning his head sideways, seemed to consider the weighty question put to him. Then he chirped,—not in dirge-like tones, but in notes of hope.

"Oh," said Ethel, "who knows, who knows?"

She sighed as she looked fondly at the bird. "How little, fair thrush of the woods, do you know of the human heart! How little you know of the intrigues of the wicked, wicked world! How little you know of hopes deferred and of the sorrow that kills! Your song is one of hope. You answer me with cheery chirps, but still I believe you not—I believe you not."

CHAPTER XVIII.

A LOVE SONG

DOCTOR AVONDALE was comfortably lodged at the Osborn House. His haughty indifference and condescending politeness had undergone a marked change. He sought to cultivate an acquaintance with the townspeople, and his efforts were generously rewarded, for very soon he was on friendly terms with the best people of the town. He persistently sought to identify himself with the Hortons. It became generally understood that he was Ethel's accepted suitor. They frequently went driving or horseback riding together, and he was much in her society. Many of her acquaintances looked with displeasure upon the turn that affairs had taken. Before the advent of the doctor, they had allowed themselves to believe that the destinies of Ethel Horton and Hugh Stanton were one! Prejudice against the Englishman, however, gave way before his forced geniality. He was certainly assuming a new rtle. He exhibited marked consideration toward every one, and confined himself to inquiring and learning, rather than to parading his own personal knowledge and experience. His pride and sense of superiority exhibited themselves, however, when he discussed medicine and surgery. In one of his trunks he carried leather cases containing a complete outfit of the finest surgical instruments manufactured. The local physicians, with one accord, acknowledged that Dr. Lenox Avondale was certainly a great surgeon. Medical publications mentioned delicate surgical cases in which this Englishman had successfully operated, and it was not long until he had quite a reputation in the frontier town.

He was a frequent guest of Mrs. Osborn, and, as the weeks

went on, whisperings and knowing looks began to be exchanged among the people. Captain Osborn appeared to grow more silent as Doctor Avondale's attentions to his wife increased. He applied himself closely to his banking affaire during business hours, and every morning and every evening he gave himself up to the companionship of his boy.

One day in speaking of his son to Hugh, he said, "That little fellow was born to be great. He daily gives evidence of his wonderful innate scope of mind. When he grows up he will plan what other men dare not do, and he will execute what other men dare not even plan."

"He is a remarkable boy," Hugh replied, and mentally concluded the boy's greatness would be inherited from his father.

"He may have vices as dazzling as his virtues," continued his father, "and, doubtless, far more picturesque; but if it should be so, I shall forgive him, for truly great characters are seldom found without some thread of weakness. The weakness, however, may be overcome by gentleness and good advice—never by harshness." They were seated in Captain Osborn's private office at the bank during this conversation.

"I dare say he will be a great comfort to you when he reaches manhood's years," replied Hugh.

"He is now," said the father, "and I tremble sometimes at the thought of his ever growing away from me." Somehow, the old captain's voice always became husky when he spoke of his boy, and Hugh determined to change the subject of conversation.

"By the way, Captain," said he, "I called on Major Hampton last evening, and was delightfully entertained."

"How does it come that you do not call at the Hortons' any more?" asked the captain, turning around in his chair and facing Hugh.

Hugh reddened a little. "Oh, I fancy they are kept busy entertaining Doctor Avondale," replied Hugh.

"Lord Avondale," corrected the captain. "My wife tells me that he received a cablegram, forwarded by mail from Dodge City, advising him of his brother's death, and thus the doctor succeeds to the family titles and estates. Better be careful, Hugh," he went on, jestingly, "or you will let this English lord carry away—not only an heiress, but one of the loveliest girls in the world. I have never known any one who could even play with Cupid without receiving a scratch on the heart—or inflicting one."

"I hardly believe, Captain," Hugh replied, slowly, "that we have much to do with the shaping of our own destinies, for we are but barks on an open sea, tossed and driven about by every wind of chance. The harbor that we expect to make is seldom reached. I am but little acquainted with love's tender passion. I hardly know that I should recognize it, if it were to come to me. Miss Horton's wishes and preference must be considered above all else."

"Ah, Hugh," said the captain, gravely, "she is too sensible a girl not to prefer a man like you to a 'fungus of nobility,' such as Lord Avondale. My advice to you, my boy, is to go in and win. The sooner the question is settled, and this Englishman takes his departure, the better. There are two duties which you owe in this affair. One, of simple justice to yourself, if you care for the girl, and I believe you do; the other, protection to her. The environments that are closing around Ethel Horton, and the influences that are being brought to bear to crowd her into a marriage with this fortune-hunter, are damnable—yes, sir, damnable!" The captain fairly shouted, as he made this last remark, while his usually calm face flushed with excitement and anger.

"Why, Captain," exclaimed Hugh, "you cannot mean that Miss Ethel is being unduly influenced in this affair—that she is not acting of her own free will."

"That is exactly what I mean," replied the captain, "and if you were not as blind as a bat, you would have seen it long ago."

"Yes," replied Hugh, "but she was betrothed to Lord Avondale before I met her. You remember what Mrs. Osborn said?"

The captain was about to reply, but changed his mind, and turned to his desk. Presently he said, in a subdued voice: "Hugh, in great confidence I will say that I believe Mrs. Osborn was mistaken. They are not betrothed even yet, but soon will be unless you step to the front, like a man, and save the girl from the inevitable fate that otherwise awaits her."

That evening Hugh sat thoughtfully at his window. He had told Ethel Horton that he would come to her if she sent for him, but he had received no word. The weeks that had intervened since he had seen her last seemed like as many months, or even years; and, yet, his interest was only one of solicitude, he told himself, rather than one of love. He was half inclined to ride over to the Hortons, in the old, informal way. He left the hotel with this intention, but changed his mind before he had walked very far, and, turning down a side street, he sauntered aimlessly along. Presently Mrs. Osborn's carriage whirled past him. He saw that Lord Avondale was with her. They were so much interested in conversation that they did not see him. The road that they were following led away into the country, in an opposite direction from Horton's Grove. Hugh paused, and considered whether he had not better return to the hotel, and order his horse, and gallop out to the Grove. In his indecision he walked on down the street, toward Major Hampton's house.

As he neared the house, he heard Marie singing. There was a wild, pleading pathos in her voice, and a passionate earnestness, often sinking into a dreamy melody, so low and plaintive that Hugh almost held his breath for fear he might lose a single syllable of her words. She was singing a love song, with music even sweeter than the sentiment:

"By waters deep, in my lonely dreaming,
Come visions fair of a fancied seeming,
While other nights are wafted back to me;
Nights so fleeting, when our hearts were beating
With tender love and sweetest rhapsody.
On ebbing waters of languid river,
Where the moonbeams play and lances quiver,
Reflecting stars, from bending arch of blue,

I watch them glisten, and wait and listen
To the night bird's song, while I dream of you.
The mist clouds rise, then fall apart,
Yet still I dream of you, sweetheart."

When the music of the song had died away, Hugh walked meditatively along the graveled walk toward the house, and up the broad steps to the veranda. Marie answered the bell.

"Why, how do you do, Mr. Stanton?" said she, extending her hand in greeting. She led him into the major's library, and invited him to be seated. "I am glad you've called," she said, "for I am so lonely. I fear you will be disappointed, however, for papa is not at home."

"The major not at home?" repeated Hugh, with surprise in his voice.

"No," replied the girl, the light in her face fading. Hugh saw her sudden change of expression, and he felt that he had been rather uncomplimentary.

"In that event," said he, by way of atonement, "I shall have the still greater pleasure of a visit with you."

"Me?" she exclaimed, while the light rekindled in her face. "I am not nearly so clever as Ethel."

"You underestimate yourself," replied Hugh, gallantly.

"Ethel says you do not come to see them any more. Are you afraid of the Englishman?" There was a suppressed merriment in the girl's voice as she asked this question.

"No," replied Hugh, "I am not afraid of him, but I dislike him very much."

"You are very frank," said Marie, laughingly. "As Ethel is my dearest friend, I will tell you something—she does n't like him either. There, is n't that good news?"

"I have not seen as much of you as I have of Miss Ethel, but it is my misfortune."

"Yes," said Hugh, reflectively, "but tell me, do not girls sometimes marry men whom they very much dislike?"

"I don't believe so," replied Marie, with girlish frankness, as she looked at Hugh with her innocent blue eyes. "I wouldn't, I'm quite sure."

"Oh, would n't you?" quizzed Hugh, jestingly. "That is because you are a genius, and gifted people may do as they like."

"You must not speak that way," said the girl, chidingly. "It is not candid, and I want to believe everything you say." There was a message unconsciously sent from Marie's eyes as she spoke.

"Perhaps I was partially jesting," said Hugh.

"Do you know why I told you about Ethel?" asked Marie, later in the evening, when Hugh was preparing to go.

"No, why did you?"

"Because," she stammered, while a blush tinged her face, "because, Mr. Stanton, I want to make you happy."

As Hugh went down the path, wondering at Marie's words and at the mystery of women, he met Bill Kinneman. The cowboy's face wore a foreboding scowl.

"Hello, pardner," said he. Hugh responded cordially.

"Look'e 'ere," said the cowboy, "you highfalutin fellers better keep away from this 'ere part of the range when the major ain't home. I'm liable to spread you 'round profuse-like, an' sort o' decorate the landscape with yer nachalness."

"I learned that he was away from home after I called," replied Hugh, rather stiffly. "Where I choose to go, however, is nothing to you." Saying this, he turned down the street, leaving Bill Kinneman muttering in suppressed anger.

CHAPTER XIX.

AN INVITATION TO JOIN

AS Hugh Stanton walked along the street toward the hotel, after his call at Major Hampton's house, he tried to analyze his feelings toward Ethel Horton. His conversation with Captain Osborn had filled him with a sense of responsibility and uneasiness. The assurance of Marie that Ethel did not take kindly to Lord Avondale was a confirmation of the captain's assertion that she was not yet betrothed to the Englishman. Was it his duty and within his power to save Ethel Horton from a life of unhappiness? For such he believed would be her lot should she marry Lord Avondale. His interest may have been seasoned with a semblance of selfishness, for he did not, at the time, entertain a doubt in regard to his own ability to make her happy. Thus the days went on.

The Hortons and Captain Osborn seemed to be the only ones in the entire community who did not know of the relations existing between Mrs. Osborn and Lord Avondale. Of late, the Englishman had even neglected Ethel Horton in his mad passion for this fascinating woman. They set all discretion at defiance; and mutter-ings of a great scandal were whispered on every side among the lovers of gossip. In her skilfulness, Mrs. Osborn had entirely blinded Mrs. Horton into the belief that it was her personal interest in helping to make a match for dear Ethel that prompted her to take such deep solicitude in Lord Avondale.

The marriage between Lord Avondale and Ethel had been agreed upon, as far as Mrs. J. Bruce-Horton and the Englishman were concerned. Ethel, however, did not take kindly to the woonings of his lordship, and she repulsed all his advances of a sentimental nature. His attempts at sentiment had a harsh, metallic sound to Ethel, as compared to the divine melody that murmured forever in her heart,—a heavenly refrain as sweet as the oriole's song in primeval forests,—telling of a deathless love for Jack Redfield. Lord Avondale regarded the matter, however, as practically settled, since he had received word of the death of his brother. The family titles were now his, and he determined to barter them for American dollars.

"All American girls," said he, "have to be subdued—their spirits have to be broken—before they make good wives."

Hugh tried to persuade himself that he had the courage to declare his love to Ethel, and to ask her hand in marriage. His regard for her was certainly very great, while her marked friendship and consideration for him had caused him to believe that she reciprocated his feelings. The more he thought it over, the stronger became his convictions that delay was dangerous. In proposing marriage he would be asserting his right, as an American gentleman, and, at the same time, discharging his duty, as Captain Osborn had put it, in saving her from a misalliance.

One evening when he returned to his hotel he found Judge Linus Lynn awaiting him.

"Good evenin', Mr. Stanton," said the judge, extending his hand in such a friendly way that it admitted of no refusal, "been waitin' for you several minutes. Major Hampton wants to see you. He's at the *Patriot* office."

"Very well," replied Hugh, and together they started down the street. Major Hampton admitted them and at once locked the door.

"My dear Stanton," said he, "I am, indeed, delighted to see you. First of all let me apologize for locking the door and pulling down the curtains. The town is full of Barley Hullers to-night, and callers will besiege my office unless I take this precaution. There are potent reasons why I wish to talk with you. We want to bind you more closely to us by indissoluble bonds. This is why I have sent for you."

All three seated themselves, while the major was yet speaking. Hugh observed that Judge Lynn's eyes wore a particularly glassy expression, while the odor of liquor seemed completely to envelope his rotund figure. The judge frequently smacked his lips, as if he were tasting something, and affectionately caressed his side whiskers in an attempt to wear an expression of sobriety.

"Gentlemen, help yourselves to cigars," said the major, waving his hand toward a well-filled box that occupied a prominent place on the table. "I find great pleasure in the soothing effect of a good cigar."

Hugh and his host lighted cigars. Judge Lynn tipped over the box in his clumsy effort to lift one out.

"Gee whillikens!" exclaimed the judge, in self-derision, "I'm the tarnalest awkward man in the Southwest. Worse'n a bovine in a china-shop, bet yer life I am. Fact is, my nerves are clean knocked out. Overwork, Mr. Stanton, overwork! Say, Major, will you 'scuse me a minit? I want ter see a feller 'round the corner. Did n't think of it till jest now."

"Certainly," said the major, as if he were glad of the judge's desertion.

"Mr. Stanton, I have sought this interview for the purpose of making a suggestion, which, if you consider favorably, will result, I feel sure, for the good of the many."

"I certainly feel honored," replied Hugh, "that you take so deep an interest in me."

A little later, Judge Lynn returned through the back door. "Bet yer life," he interposed, "I settled that feller mighty quick; don't take me long to do business; no sirree."

"The condition of the times," the major went on, paying no attention to Judge Lynn's interruption, "suggests the necessity of better organization among the masses. It is the old doctrine taught by the bundle of sticks. The interests of the poor and lowly can be advanced only by teaching them that in union there is strength. This has been made necessary to the world's progress, because of greed and selfishness, which grow like tares, choking out the wheat of altruism."

"Bet yer life," interposed Judge Lynn, in a hobbled, thick voice, "bet yer life, the major knows what he's talkin' 'bout. Gosh all fishhooks! Think I don't know facts when I hear 'em gurglin' down 'round me like water. Oh, I'm gay an' genial-like to-night, I am."

"Lynn, will you keep silent!" said the major, sternly.

"Jest remin's me," said the judge, getting on his feet in a rather uncertain manner, "I've got to pay a bill to Buck Truax that's over a day past due. 'Scuse me, gentlemen, fur 'bout five minits. Will I be back? Well, I should say I would. Course I will. You can't lose me. Bet yer life you can't."

"As district organizer of the Farmers' Alliance," continued the major, "I am brought into contact with the bone and sinew of the country. I frequently meet progressive spirits—the advance-guards, as it were, of a higher development—who will lose nothing when the progress of civilization overtakes them. To meet the requirements of the hour, and with the hope of bettering the condition of mankind, I conceived the idea of organizing a secret society, where these advance-guards might meet and deliberate upon all live, progressive topics of the day, and especially upon the problems most vitally affecting the welfare of humanity—an organization free from political influences. One of its objects is the diffusion of knowledge, which surely will be followed by a general advancement of the human race. Now, I wish to ask you, Mr. Stanton, if its conception and its objects are not most worthy?"

"Without question," replied Hugh, "to diffuse knowledge and to better the conditions of the human race are most important motives, underlying the superstructure of all good government."

"It is not the government as set forth by the laws of a nation, so much as it is, my dear Stanton, obedience to the unwritten laws emanating from the first Great Cause. The hope of humanity is happiness, and happiness consists of a great love, and much service and sacrifice to the children of men and to the Omnipotent Ruler of the universe, who will hold us responsible if we are derelict in our duties to those who are helpless and incapable of self-protection. This work approaches holiness, which might be defined as an infinite compassion for others."

"Bet yer life," said Judge Lynn, as he staggered into the room. "When the major speaks, it's nachral we want to lis'n, that's what I say—golden thoughts are droppin' 'round here from lips of wisdom—reckon I know."

"Judge Lynn, will you please be quiet?" said the major..

"Course I will; gimme a cigar. Maybe I don't know brains when I hear 'em workin'."

"Our organization," continued the major, "embodying these great principles, is known as the Barley Hullers. Its principles and the intricacy of its beneficent workings partake somewhat of the accumulated wisdom of the centuries. In the secret haunts of earth, far removed from the busy marts of commerce, lives are being dedicated to the work of solving the mighty problems of humanity. The leaching out of selfishness, through the sieve of much suffering and self-denial, is having its effect. The world is to become better through the practical advocates of these mighty principles. Mr. Stanton, you are needed in the vineyard. We want our deliberations enriched by your words of wisdom. You certainly owe some of your time to this great work of human advancement."

"I do not see," replied Hugh, hesitatingly, "how I could benefit your organization. Besides, I am a banker, and most of the members of the Barley Hullers, I take it, are directly engaged in agricultural pursuits."

Judge Lynn here interrupted, shutting one eye in a knowing way. "Great Scott! man, that's where you, as a member of the Barley Hullers, would have a special lead-pipe cinch on these other bankers. Yes, sirree! Jine the Barley Hullers, and you'll scuttle your contemporaries in the seethin' sea of desperation. Gee, that's easy."

"Yes, there would doubtless be a personal gain," said Hugh. "In a business way I can readily see the advantages, but, if there were no other reasons, that in itself is sufficient to decide me against permitting my name to be offered as a candidate for membership."

"Judge Lynn," said the major, sternly, "will you confine yourself to your cigar and let me discuss this subject with Mr. Stanton!"

"Well, why not?" said the judge, as he blinked and looked with an intoxicated blankness at the major. "Bet yer life; course I will; I'm not hankerin' after any man's job. Not a Barley Huller no way. But I can tell, on short acquaintance, a good article of barley juice when I taste it, bet yer life I kin."

Major Hampton's face wore a look of irritation, but, as he turned from the judge to Hugh, the latter noticed that an expression of kindly sympathy had gained the mastery.

"The unwritten manual of the Barley Hullers," said the major, "aims at the betterment of the human race, and advancement must surely mark its onward course. The organization is destined to be a power for good. Its influence will be felt, both in the state and in the nation."

"Bet yer life," interposed Judge Lynn, in maudlin tones. "There's Mrs. Fleece, the blue-stockin' catamount of the Sunflower State; she's in this 'ere great work heart an' soul, while her henpecked husband runs a drug store. Hully gee! how I wish I owned a drug store. By the way, that reminds me," and here the judge staggered to his feet again, and said he had to see a man "'round the corner." He, however, soon returned. His intoxication was becoming more noticeable, and his interruptions increased with each trip "'round the corner."

The major contained himself with fortitude, and went on addressing Hugh with great energy. "New lodges are daily being organized in different parts of our State; indeed, the influence of the Barley Hullers is beginning to be felt even beyond the borders of the Sunflower Commonwealth. Assistance, my dear Stanton, of which you know not, will help to scatter the seeds, looking toward the equality of the people in every neighborhood throughout this nation; and I prophesy that in the very near future the members of this society will rise in Herculean might, and sweep the Augean stables of plutocracy and of plutocrats, and will never stop until they organize a lodge of Barley Hullers in the Green Room of the White House. The rich must contribute to the needs of the poor, and an equalization of wealth must conform to the equality of men, as foreordained by the Supreme Ruler."

"How can you accomplish all this," asked Hugh, "if the Barley Hullers is a non-political organization?"

"A general uprising of the people," said Major Hampton, "an uprising of advanced thinkers and their proselyted followers who, with one accord, will rise like the high-capped waves on the limitless deep, and, in a phalanx that cannot be stayed, will march against the strongholds of capital, financial conspiracies, and legalized robbery. Of course many things may conspire to blind the people. Gifts by millionaires to so-called 'charitable institutions,' such as churches, hospitals, and asylums, have a tendency to lull the people into inaction. These pretended philanthropies, given to be seen of the world, are but hollow mockeries, and will prove, instead of robes of spotless white for the donors, only worthless rags of shame and disgrace."

"Your earnestness and sincerity, Major," said Hugh, "I cannot doubt or question, but I do believe that it is not proper for me to join the Barley Hullers."

The major looked grieved. "Well, Stanton, think it over," said he, "think it over, and after awhile you may decide differently."

"Give it to my way farin' frien', Major, them's my sentiments to a dot; bet yer life they are."

"Judge Lynn," said the major, "keep quiet; you're drunk."

"A' right, Major," replied the judge, hazily. "Heerd some'un shay speech wazn only silver-plated anyhow, an' silence wazh golden. I know two or three legerdemain tricks, bet yer life I do. Gimme 'nother drink."

"Major Hampton," said Hugh, when the judge had subsided,

"your words have made a great impression upon me. Do you know that sometimes I am filled with a vague sense of mystery when listening to your impassioned words in behalf of the multitude? Your charities have also caused me to marvel. It matters not in what part of the country I travel, I find where your secret charities have blessed the poor and needy, and then—"

"That's all right, Stanton, it is not I to whom thanks are due. There is a higher power that is responsible for every benevolent act of my life. I am but an instrument—a missionary—doing the work that has been assigned to me, and I am far from being satisfied with the results of my labor. It is growing late, and perhaps we had better go."

In the meantime Judge Lynn had ceased his interruptions. He had fallen into a drunken stupor.

"Assist me, Stanton," said the major, sorrowfully, "and we will let him rest here for the night."

Soon Hugh and the major were walking thoughtfully homeward along the deserted streets beneath a myriad of twinkling stars, while Judge Lynn was snoring lustily in drunken stupor on a large, leather-covered lounge, muttering incoherently the while, "Bet yer life! Bet yer life!"

CHAPTER XX.

A DINNER AT THE HORTONS

BARLEY HULLERS," mused Hugh, when he awoke the next morning, "composed of chosen spirits, with *boutonnihres* of barley heads as an insignia of rank. I doubt not that if I were engaged in agricultural pursuits I should join them. But why, I wonder, did Major Hampton solicit me to identify myself with the order? The more I see of the old major the more I admire him, notwithstanding the half mystery that seems a part of him, and the contradictory elements in nis nature. Let me see—I have decided to ask Ethel Horton to be my wife."

As he made his toilet he saw a reflection of his face in the mirror, and blushed as if he had been caught in the very act of preparing a declaration of love to Ethel. "Yes, it is a privilege and a duty. I can do no more than try; and then conscience urges me on."

Arriving at the bank, he found a letter from Mrs. J. Bruce-Horton inviting him to the Grove for dinner that evening.

"I also received one," said Captain Osborn, approaching Hugh's desk. "I presume that the Hortons are giving a spread in honor of Lord Avondale."

"Do you think it has any significance?" asked Hugh.

"Well, I am a little worried about it," replied the captain. "They may announce Ethel's engagement for all one knows, but, sir, I don't believe it! No, sir, she is too sensible a girl and has too much American blood in her to be caught by an English title."

"I hope you are right," observed Hugh, sighing secretly, as he went on with his work.

That evening, on arriving at the Grove a little late, Hugh found not only the Osborns and Lord Avondale, but also Major Hampton and his daughter Marie.

Ethel Horton was all animation in helping her mother entertain, but Hugh's quick eye detected a shade of sadness in her face. The light-hearted girl whom he had known in the first months of his residence in Kansas had to him now more the appearance of a conventional young woman of the world. Formalities had banished much of the girlish frankness of earlier days, leaving, indeed, only a trace.

Marie Hampton was attired in a beautiful evening gown of white silk, with a knot of La France roses at her corsage. Her beauty struck Hugh as never before. It aroused in him a sincere admiration. Her heavy bronzed tresses reflected the various shades of gold. As their eyes met a rich color flushed her cheeks. Hugh could not decide which outrivaled the other,—Ethel, the stately brunette, or Marie, the ideal blonde.

Mrs. Horton, in an elegant creation of Red-fern, was graciousness to every guest, while coquettish Mrs. Osborn appeared more youthful and girlish than ever. She smiled compassionately upon the captain and knowingly at Lord Avondale. She had a word of compliment for every one, and in many ways proved herself a most agreeable woman in the art of entertaining.

Lord Avondale, in his regulation black, roused himself above his usually dominating peculiarities, and seemed to be quite charmed with Ethel's beauty, and to be genuinely interested in her.

Major Hampton had been discussing a painting when Hugh was announced, and, as he turned to receive him, Hugh was more than ever impressed with the grandeur of the man.

"What a rare specimen," said he to himself, "of an American nobleman, both physically and intellectually."

After the greetings, Hugh's eyes sought Ethel's with a hope that he might find some message in them, but they gave no response, and he was conscious of a chilled feeling at his heart.

John B. Horton, cattle king, was at his best. In his hearty frontier way he was the very prince of hosts. His black eyes beamed with good nature and hospitality.

"My friend Stanton," said he, as he waved his hand toward the ladies, "lovelier specimens of the fair sex can't be found. As for my daughter, you know, I am hardly an impartial judge—am so prejudiced in her favor. But look at Miss Marie,—why, her development completely astonishes me. I remember her as a little girl in short dresses, Stanton. It was only a little while ago, but now where can a young woman be found more queenly than she?"

Soon dinner was announced, and all seated themselves around a table both elegant and sumptuous. The conversation became animated. Ethel was especially vivacious, and won laurels in the repartee of the hour. Sometimes her laughing eyes would rest pointblank upon Hugh, and then again upon Lord Avondale.

As the dinner progressed, the Englishman turned his attention from Mrs. Osborn, much to her chagrin, and entered into a spirited conversation with Marie Hampton. The young woman proved herself a most brilliant conversationalist. Major Hampton looked beamingly upon his daughter, and smiled at her quick repartee, as if it were a personal compliment to himself and his instructions. Indeed, there was not a book in her father's library with which she was not familiar. Her passion for study was gratified whenever she was not called to other employment. Before the dinner was half over the keen eyes of Mrs. Osborn had discovered what Hugh had never dreamed of,—that Marie Hampton was in love with him.

"The silly goose," said Mrs. Osborn to herself, "he knows as little about affairs of the heart as a babe in swaddling-clothes."

In Marie's eyes Hugh was all that was noble, strong, and grand. She imagined that her secret was wholly hers; and she loved to pay him homage in silent girlish adoration. To Mrs. Osborn's quick, experienced eyes, however, the rosebud was opening, and the warm, red petals were showing through the calyx of concealment which Marie was trying to throw around her adoration.

Lord Avondale announced that he expected to leave on the following day for Colorado, where, according to previous arrangements, he was to meet a party of English friends at Colorado Springs, and from there go hunting for Rocky Mountain sheep. Hugh fancied that he saw a pleased expression come to the face of his old friend, Captain Osborn; and a sigh of relief escaped his own heart at the thought of Lord Avondale really going away. He was glad not only on Ethel's account, but also on account of the captain. He felt that the absence of this man might prevent complications in which Mrs. Lyman Osborn would be implicated.

"I am a little surprised," observed Lord Avondale, "that you Americans don't take the time to go shooting, when your mountains are so full of such excellent game. I regard shooting as rare sport—I do, indeed."

"Our lives are rather busy ones," replied Mrs. Horton, "but doubtless we would do well to imitate our English cousins and give ourselves more holidays. We Americans have seemingly fallen into the custom of sticking rather close to our business affairs, and you know it's a hard thing to get out of a rut."

"Quite true," replied his lordship, "but all work, you know, and no play, makes Jack a dull boy."

"Sometimes Jack is not so dull as he seems to be," put in Captain Osborn.

"Of course, I meant nothing personal, you know," said Lord Avondale, "for we are all aware that Americans are decidedly good business men,—quite sharp and thrifty, you know."

"Some of them are," observed Major Hampton, "but the masses are poor,—kept so by the sharpness of the few. Indeed, they are sadly in need of a protection which, at the present time, our laws do not afford."

"It is not," said Mrs. Osborn, "because our men cannot, but rather because they will not advise themselves of English ways and customs, and profit by the example."

"Thank you," said Lord Avondale, "that was a very clever speech, my dear Mrs. Osborn. I regard it as a compliment, I do indeed."

"Habit and education," said Mrs. Horton, "have much to do with our lives. Before I commenced visiting England, I entertained entirely different views from those I do to-day. At best, we Americans are but an offspring from the mother country, and the child should never cease to love and reverence the parent. I should have been greatly dissatisfied with myself had I permitted Ethel to be educated in the States."

"My dear Mrs. Horton," said Marie, looking up with a flushed face, "what text-books did Ethel study in England that cannot be found in America?"

"It's not that!" exclaimed Lord Avondale, "it's the surroundings, you know,—the absorbing of ideas peculiar to the English people, to which Mrs. Horton refers."

"Thank you," said Mrs. Horton, with her blandest smile, as she bowed to his lordship.

"I will not ask in what way they differ," said Marie, "but I will ask in what way they are superior to the influences to be found in America?"

"Quite clever," replied Lord Avondale, "quite clever, indeed. I could hardly answer the question you ask without also answering the one you say you will not ask."

"Well," persisted Marie, "I am waiting for the answer;" and a haughty expression came into her deep blue eyes.

"Ah! they're so civil, don't you know; the people in England are educated to respect their superiors, while the better class and the nobility are educated to be gentle toward inferiors."

"But," said Marie, "what if there were no class distinctions? Then may not Americans act toward each other the same as the better class and the nobility act toward one another? Are not Americans as civil as Englishmen?"

"Really, Miss Hampton," said Lord Avondale, "I regret having been drawn into this discussion. I am quite willing to admit that in many parts of America the people are quite civil. Last winter I was in New Orleans. I found the people of the South remarkably civil,—much more so than the people of the Northern States."

"And do you know the reason?" asked Marie with flashing eyes.

"No, really, Miss Hampton, I do not. I would be charmed if you would enlighten me, I really would—you know." A supercilious smile overspread the face of Lord Avondale, while Marie's handsome countenance glowed with an increased beauty in defending her country.

"That part of our country," replied she, "New Orleans especially, was settled principally by the French, and the North by the English."

"Ah! ah!—is that so?" stammered Lord Avondale. "I admit I am somewhat deficient in history, don't you know."

Captain Osborn laughed outright, much to the chagrin of his wife.

After they had returned to the parlors, both Mrs. Horton and Mrs. Osborn agreed that Marie had been shockingly rude to Lord Avondale. While they were talking of the affair in one corner, Ethel—*sotto voce*—was telling Marie that she was the dearest girl in the world, and that she loved her more than ever for having vanquished Lord Avondale.

Soon after, the guests took their departure, and the next day Lord Avondale left Meade on the stage-coach, to enjoy a few months' shooting in Colorado.

CHAPTER XXI.

THE FOOT-RACE

THE Saturday afternoon following the dinner at the Hortons' and Lord Avondale's departure, several ranchmen, cattlemen, and townspeople were seated on the veranda of the hotel. They had been discussing local politics and venturing opinions as to the probable result of the coming election.

"I'm assoomin' the only big money I've got to bet on the 'lection," said Bill Kinneman, "is on the proposition thet nobody kin tell fur sure jist how 't will come out. Mos' every one's jist guessin' and strugglin' in the coils uv error."

This truism seemed to strike the humorous side of those present, and they guffawed their approval.

"I reckon," said Dan Spencer, "a feller kin onbosom hisself an' tell purty nigh as much 'bout 'lection, as they kin when Lord Avondale will be hoofin' back inter these 'ere diggin's. Don't like the English nohow."

"What do you know about the English people, Dan Spencer?" asked Bill Mounce, the blacksmith, rather tartly. "Let me say to you the English are all right. My mother was born in England and I'll fight for my mother and her people as quickly as I would for my father's side of the family."

"Bravo! Bravo!" shouted those listening.

"The facts are," said Len Follick, a sturdy-looking farmer, "nearly every one of us can trace our lineage back to old England in one or the other branches of our family, and the idea of us condemning England because of a few Lord Avondales—more or less—is quite ridiculous." Dan Spencer's tooth was shaking

132

around like a weathercock in a wind-storm, but before he could make reply the blacksmith said:

"Why, boys, look for instance at Seaton Cornwall. You all know him. He is one of the best citizens in the country. He's English all over, but none of you ever heard him say a slighting word of this country or its flag."

"Guess, Dan, you'll hev to cave in; you're sure'nuff locoed," laughed Kinneman, "everybody knows Seaton Cornwall is one of the whitest fellers thet ever galloped over the range."

"Say, what you fellers talkin' 'bout anyway?" asked Judge Lynn, coming up on the veranda.

"What's we all talkin' 'bout?" said Dan Spencer, glad to turn the conversation, "why, we's jist talkin' 'bout hoss-racin', foot-racin,' an' 'lections, wonderin' who'd git the offices, an' gen'rally stampedin' our brains 'round a whole lot. B'lieve you used to be a foot-racer, did n't you, Judge? Can you run now?"

"Can I run? Well, I should say I could. Why, look 'ere, Dan Spencer, jist you write to Ed Reimond back in Indiana, and ask him 'bout the greatest foot-race ever pulled off on the banks of the Wabash. Hully gee, but in them days I had wings when there was a sprintin' match on the boards. Course I hain't run for many a year. I know how, though, bet yer life I do. Why, what's the matter with you anyway, Dan? What are you snickerin' that way for? Maybe you don't believe I used to be a record breaker? Who can beat me? You say Bill Mounce can? Not on yer life. Mounce, you can't touch one side o' me on a foot-race—no, sirree."

"No use gettin' hostile, but I jist heerd him say he could," rejoined Dan, grinning aggravatingly.

"Look 'ere, Dan," said the judge, with evident irritation, "our friend Mounce here may be a good blacksmith—guess he is—but he has n't the p'ints for good speed. Now, I have, bet yer life I have; you jist ask Louis Boehler."

The result of this conversation was a foot-race at four o'clock that afternoon, between the judge and the blacksmith, down in the valley of the Crooked Creek. From the enthusiasm of the spectators one might well have mistaken the affair for a Derby day race.

Bill Mounce was even more unfavorably proportioned for a sprinter than was Lynn. Mounce was short and stocky, and tipped the scales at 225 pounds; Lynn at 175 pounds. Judge Lynn, barring his great stomach, his little toy balloon-shaped face, pipestem legs, and a few other defective points, might possibly have possessed some of the characteristics of speed.

There were fully two hundred spectators lined up to see the race. These were divided about evenly between the farmers and cattlemen.

The cowboys began betting on Lynn. Even Dan Spencer "hedged" and then doubled. The farmers picked on Mounce as the winner, and the price for their wheat and barley was accordingly up for all takers.

When all was in readiness, the horse-shoer and the legal servant clasped hands and bent well over, each with an extended foot on the line. At the crack of a revolver away they sped, running, side by side, like two ice-wagons drawn by oxen— but stampeded.

It must not be supposed this race was any "ten second" affair. The timekeeper needed no stop-watch. Any old-fashioned clock, with wooden wheels, could have kept track of the seconds that passed in that hundred yard dash. Some said that the affair reminded them of a geological description of the movement of the glaciers. In time the race was ended, however—the blacksmith winning by about two feet. Mounce was greeted with huzzas. Lynn was broken-hearted—got drunk immediately and was hauled home in a farmer's wagon.

This race was but a preliminary to greater things. It was simply a practice run compared with another sprinting contest between Mounce and Lynn, which took place some two weeks later—a contest still memorable in the annals of foot-racing in the Southwest.

Judge Lynn sent word to his cowboy backers that he was

training nightly, and would put up the race of his life. While the judge was thus living in seclusion by day and practising by night, an evil report became noised about, that the judge had thrown the former race for the price of a gallon of whiskey. Few, however, believed the rumor.

Now, as the time for the second race drew near, interest became very great, and all the people interested in racing contests were on the tiptoe of expectation.

The place selected for the affair was in the valley, some two miles south of Meade, on the banks of the Manaroya. Here the sod had been removed and an ideal race-course made.

The day came on and was a perfect one. The valley lay like a basin, with its borders yellowed with countless sunflowers; a large drove of fatted cattle were peacefully grazing just below the racetrack, while the winding waters of the Manaroya cut the valley like a restless ribbon. Not less than two thousand people were present to witness the greatly advertised race. The interest may have been somewhat farcical with many, for, in truth, it could be little more, at best, than a "fat man's race."

Lynn himself had arrived early and had gone over the track carefully, surveying, apparently, every inch of it with all the critical acumen of a veteran in the business. He was clad in a long robe—a Cardinal Richelieu affair—that swept the ground. He was silent, even stoical, and this unnatural phase gave him an unusually wise appearance.

Seaton Cornwall, an Englishman loved by everybody who knew him, had been selected judge of the race. He, in turn, appointed a score or more of time-keepers, as if fearful that some error might occur in obtaining a new record in Western sprinting.

When all was apparently in readiness for the dash, some of the cowboys called Judge Lynn to one side for a conference. His backers withdrew and surrounded him. To the great throngs of spectators it was evident that the cattlemen had some special instructions for the judge, and so they had. One wild-looking fellow, Orth Hudson by name, with leather leggins, spurs, sombrero, and a brace of revolvers, acted as spokesman. "Judge Lynn," he said, "on the other race, which ye pretendid to run, most of us fellers bet heavy and lost a month's wages on ye. Some say as how ye throwed that race fur a gallon of whiskey. If ye did, you'se ought to be killed. Now, we're still b'lievin' in ye—money talks—an' we're goin' to back ye agin an' put up our last dollar on ye. We're proposin' to git every cent these 'ere farmers hev got; but, Judge, it's up to you—do ye savey? it's up to you. We're not lustin' fur trouble, Judge, and I don't like much to say it, but I has to, 'cause I's been picked out by the fellers to spechully tell ye plain that ye'll win this 'ere race or be shot. I tell ye this so there'll be no mis-onderstandin'. We're proposin' to be ca'm, but if ye lose this 'ere race, there'll be a stampede ensue, an' you'll not last long to pester the landscape with yer explainin' o' things."

Judge Lynn turned pale. "Gentlemen," said he, "I'll win this race or die."

"Yes," said the cowboys in chorus, "that's what we've 'greed on," and they carelessly laid their drawn revolvers across the pommels of their saddles.

"Judge," continued the spokesman, "we're predictin' if ye cross that 'ere tape line behind Bill Mounce, we'll fill ye fuller o' holes than the top end of an old-fashioned tin pepper-box. Do you see?"

The judge saw. He was easily the worst scared man in the big Southwest at that very minute.

The cowboys wheeled their ponies around and galloped for position, and the judge, unattended, walked thoughtfully back to the starting-place, still retaining his distinguished robe.

Now, when time was called, the people were treated to a number not on the program—a sight that must ever remain vividly fixed in the recollection of every man who witnessed the incident. It was the judge. He stepped out from under his huge cloak, and behold "the little man in red"—he underwent, as if by magic, a strange metamorphosis. He was clad in a skin-tight suit of flaming red material, and looked a veritable Mephistopheles.

The people saw the grotesqueness of his make-up, and sent up deafening yells.

The blacksmith looked upon his athletic rival and trembled. The fantastic attire of the judge was evidently driving terror into his heart.

Judge Linus Lynn had come to win, even if it took blood, or the appearance of it, to encompass his adversary's defeat.

Now, the burly horse-shoer was attired in his usual clothing, save his leathern apron used at the forge had been laid aside. His feet were bare and his trousers rolled up to his knees.

Seaton Cornwall shouted, "Ready!" The contestants lined up. Lynn crouched so low for the start that his round head seemed to be on a line with his knees.

"Ready!" repeated Cornwall, and then a pistol-shot started the men away over the course. The report of the pistol silenced every tongue. Even the lazy cattle looked up in mild-eyed wonderment at the pranks of men.

Both sides of the track were patrolled by mounted cowboys with drawn revolvers. The rolling ball in red understood the meaning,—his eyes bulged out in awful effort.

At the end of twenty-five yards Lynn was leading Mounce by about seven feet—at fifty yards their relative positions were unchanged. The muscles of the blacksmith's legs, below the knees, were knotted in terrible tension, and his teeth were clinched in desperation. At the end of seventy-five yards he was running nearly abreast with the figure in red. Both men were puffing like hedgehogs. Then the people shouted, each to his favorite, "Lay to," "Lay to," "Get there,"—and so they did—with a last mighty effort; but the horse-shoer "laid to" the better and won the race.

Lynn went madly on—nor looked back. Fifty shots were fired in the air. Visions of pepper-boxes floated before him. He was headed into the herd of cattle. Presendy he stopped and whirled about like magic. A bull, maddened by his fiery red attire, accepted the challenge like a Spanish bovine, and rushed toward him with fire in his eyes. The judge yelled in terror, and bounded away in awful fright, running as he had never run before. The bull was not a half dozen feet behind him, lunging in mad leaps, and bellowing a hoarse murderous roar, while his sharp horns were almost scraping the earth.

The people trembled with fear. The cowboys plunged their spurs deep into their ponies' sides and galloped frantically to the rescue. They came alongside of the maddened bull and, quick as a flash, a score of bullets were buried in the bull's heart, and he fell to the earth in the throes of sudden death.

It was all over in an instant, and then Lynn, seeing the danger was past, shouted, "Say, maybe you fellers think I was throwin' that race with the bull, but I wasn't. No, sirree. I was jist doing my level best and don't you forget it."

So ended the much talked of foot-race,—a contest that forever silenced Judge Lynn from talking of great sprinting exploits on the banks of the Wabash—or anywhere else.

CHAPTER XXII.

THE ELECTION

THE Tuesday following the incident of the foot-race was election day. The *Patriot* prophesied that, out of the three thousand probable votes cast in the county, fully sixteen hundred would be for the Populist ticket.

In private conversation Major Hampton confessed to Hugh that he really had no idea how the election would go. "You see, Stanton," said he, "I am not a politician, although many believe me to be one. No, I am simply trying to use a political organization as a vehicle to carry into practice certain ideas emanating from truth, and which, practically applied, would better the condition of the masses. Politics with me is only a means to an end."

They were in Hugh's room at the hotel when this conversation occurred. The major walked back and forth across the room, as he talked in confidence with Hugh about the probable result of the election.

Hugh noticed that the lines in his old friend's face would deepen at times like veritable hillside gullies that had been plowed deep by the waters of a mountain torrent. Then, again, when he approached his one absorbing, altruistic idea of helping the poor, lifting up the suffering and benefiting mankind by surrounding them with conditions that would enable them to help themselves,—at such times the deep lines and furrows would almost wholly disappear from his face, and it seemed illuminated from some great light within, a phosphorescent reflection from some mighty reservoir of molten gold—perhaps from the old major's heart.

Election day came, and Democrats, Republicans, and Populists all turned out in force to try to elect their different candidates. Crops of all kinds had been remarkably good in every township of the county, and both the Democrats and Republicans said that good crops argued well for their success. They contended that hot winds and poor crops were necessary adjuncts to a triumph of Populism at the polls. Each of the three parties, as is usual at election time, claimed that it would elect its own candidates by rousing pluralities.

The day after election, when the returns were all in, the astonishing fact was developed that the Democrats and Republicans had divided the elective offices about equally, while the Populists had polled in the entire county only fifty-five votes.

The *Patriot* came out the next day with a double-leaded editorial, in which Major Hampton scathed pretending Populists in unsparing terms. The article was as follows:

"FIFTY-FIVE TRUE MEN."

"The remnant of the Spartan band numbers, all told, fifty-five souls. These do not glory in saying, 'There are only a few of us left,' but are bowed down in abject humiliation at the thought of the Pharisees and hypocrites, with whom, in the past, they have been associated. These traitors pledged their support at yesterday's election. They sold out to the enemy—they have bartered their votes, their manhood, and their honor, like Judas of old, for a few pieces of silver. The bloated bondholder and coupon-clipper—even the millionaire, with his ill-gotten gains—are as princes compared with these Ishmaelites who have bartered away their very souls with their votes. Benedict Arnold, who attempted to betray his country, was not more despicable than the low, groveling traitor who sells his vote. The "Patriot" boldly proclaims the fact that if every one in the county who professed to believe in the doctrine of purity and progress had voted his avowed

sentiments, the Populist ticket would have received a majority of the votes in the county. Instead, however, but fifty-five
loyal men had the courage to cast ballots that upheld the
ticket and platform of the people.

"The editor of the "Patriot" desires to announce that he is
about to embark in the ship "Argo" for a trip up Salt River;
and like Jason, of heathen mythology, with his fifty-four
companions, he expects to sail away, not in quest of a 'golden
fleece,' but simply with a desire to breathe the pure air of
self-respect. His good ship "Argo" shall be anchored where
minorities are frequency stranded, away from the turbulent
vicissitudes of political warfare.

"LATER."

"Since writing the above, the editor of the "Patriot" has been
confronted with a condition that may seriously interfere
with his contemplated trip in the ship "Argo", as the bark is
limited in its capacity. Over twelve hundred subscribers of
the "Patriot" have called, each one solemnly assuring the
editor, in strictest confidence, that he was of the immortal
fifty-five. The facts conflict somewhat with the statements
made by this cloud of witnesses, but as most of our callers
have renewed their subscriptions to the "Patriot" for another
year, we have concluded to go on making a valiant fight on
the side of right, with a hope and a prayer that the returns of
next year's election may show a different result."

A few evenings after the election, Bill Kinne-man and Dan
Spencer and their three committeemen associates met in the old
mill to divide their booty. As it was not the regular night for the
Barley Hullers' meeting, they had no fear of being molested.

"Say, Bill," said one of the committeemen, "did you see the
major's editorial?"

"See it," replied Kinneman, in a surly tone, "I surely did. Waal, Spencer, speekin' wide-open like," he continued, "it's dang near time we hed thet report made."

"All right," replied he of the wabbling tooth, as he expectorated a vigorous pit-tew of tobacco juice toward a dark corner of the room, and stroked his short, stubby red beard with a greasy hand. "All right, boys. You see me an' Bill onbosomed ourselves an' whooped it up purty lively, an' teched all the candidates as hard as we dared. All the Republican candidates an' all the Democratic fellers snorted an' cavorted 'round an' actooally threatened to stampede, but they fin'lly got genial an' coughed up, or agreed to if they wuz 'lected. When we come to the Populist candidates, nary a danged one of 'em would give a cent, but some of 'em talked mighty malignant like. You see they thought they had a spechul lead-pipe cinch, anyway, on the Barley Hullers' votes, an' put on superior airs, but that's where they reckoned some porely an' got left, see?" Whereupon all five of these stalwart committeemen laughed immoderately.

"Waal," continued the tooth wabbler, "as soon as the returns of the 'lection wuz in, me an' Bill started out an', bustin' all over with p'liteness, tackled the fellers that wuz 'lected,—part of 'em Republicans an' part of 'em Democrats. You see we surely held a paper with their names to it, an' they nach'ally had to cough up the money, 'cause they's afeard we'd blow on 'em—leastways that's what we told 'em we'd do fur sure. Course we knowed too much to dun the fellers that wuz defeated. So here's a thousan' dollars fur you-alls, in long greens, to dervide up,—two hundred dollars apiece,—not so bad, eh?" The division was soon made, to the apparent satisfaction of all, and the conference broke up. When the other committeemen had gone, and Bill Kinneman and Dan Spencer were alone, Bill said:

"Look'e 'ere, Dan, you reported a thousan' dollars; how much did you sure'nuff git, now, on the squar? Be straight with yer pard, or somethin' will happen. Yer personal'ty is liable to be scattered over the landscape. I've dun got the drap on you, an' am feelin' plenty hostile." As he said this, he carelessly fingered his revolver.

"Course, Bill," said Dan. "You see I collected sixteen hundred dollars. That leaves me an' you three hundred dollars apiece more."

"Waal, that's more like it, an' certainly prevents a misonderstandin'," said Bill. "Course I nach'ally knew you wuz givin' them jays a razzle-dazzle, but you cain't razzle-dazzle me. I wish we could 'a' got along 'thout 'em, but as they usually do most of the kitchen work, an' you an' me git the big end of the boodle, I guess we've got no kick comin'."

Presently they mounted their mustangs and started down the valley toward Meade.

"Say, Dan," said Bill, "can you fur sure keep a secret?"

"Waal, if the court knows herself, I kin. What's roamin' 'round permiscus-like on yer mind, Bill?"

"Waal, I ain't got no partic'lar use fur thet Stanton feller. If I don't miss my guess, he's snoopin' 'round Major Hampton's ranch."

"What's that to you, Bill?"

"Waal, speakin' wide-open like, it's a mighty sight to me, pard," replied Bill. "I don't intend Marie Hampton shall fall in love with thet highfalutin cuss, even if I's got to scatter his nachalness over the landscape."

"Put 'er thar, Bill," said Dan, extending his hand, and breathing hard on his restless tooth. "I don't hev to hev a meetin'-house fall on me afore I see which way the wind's a-blowin'. Thet Hugh Stanton is a kind o' soopercilious, high-steppin' chap, an' if he goes to interferin' with you, we'll fix him as easy as rollin' off a log. No use gettin' peevish, Bill, but if his attitood is sort o' pesterin' you, jist say the word, an' he'll not be lustin' fur trouble very long on this 'ere range."

"Do you mean it, pardner?"

"I surely do," replied Dan.

"I don't mind onbosomin' myself," said Kin-neman, "an' sayin' she's the purtiest woman in the hull world, an' I b'lieve the major 'ill be favorable."

"Course, Bill," said Dan, "I'm married an' hev nuthin' to say, but if I wuz n't you'd hev to speak up in meetin' or you'd surely git left. Oh, I know a purty face when I sees it, an' there ain't nary a one on the range that compares with the major's daughter."

Kinneman's swarthy face flushed with the greedy desire which he had long felt to possess Marie Hampton for his wife. Presently he said:

"Do you think I kin make it, Dan? I'm feelin' a heap careless toward that 'air Stanton feller."

"Make it?" repeated Dan, "Course you kin. I'm assoomin' you need n't be afeerd of any man when it comes to sprucin' up to a gal. If he's got money an' you ain't, then it's different agin," and Dan Spencer leered at his companion with a wicked eye.

"Say, Dan," Said Bill, "what would be yer attitood in a case of this 'ere kind? Is moneybags to be respected more 'n a man?"

"I'll be hanged if I know fur sure," replied Dan, as he scratched his chin, shut one eye, and breathed heavily against his big tooth. "If a man hangs 'round an' gits in the way betwixt you an' sumthin' you want, why, you've got to git him off the face of the airth, I reckon, even if an accidental shootin' ensues."

"Say, Dan," said Bill, in a subdued voice, "I'll bet big money you're the nerviest feller I ever run agin' on the range."

"Waal," said Dan, rather pleased at the compliment, "if there's any money in it, jist try me."

"Is that solid, Dan? Are you givin' it to me straight?"

"Solid an' straight, Bill, sure. Course it's a heap o' pressure to assoom; still, if the inducements are toomultuous 'niff, I can sure git action on my artill'ry."

"All right, I'll not furgit yer promise. I may need you pow'rful suddin some o' these 'ere dark nights."

"Waal, jist bring yer roll along when yer lookin' fur me, an' you'll fin' me dead game. Listen, what's thet? Guess the major's home sure 'nuff, an' playin' on his fiddle."

The two cowboys reined their ponies, and in silence listened to the melodious strains of the major's violin. They were far down the valley from the major's home, and the music seemed mellowed in the soft moonlight, and sweetened by the distance. He was playing "Home, Sweet Home," with countless variations. The melody traveled lazily on the night currents, and, when it finally died away, trembled and rested like a benediction on the peace and quietude of the sleeping valley.

Soon Dan Spencer was galloping for his dug-out, east of Meade, and Bill Kinneman was heading his bronco across the prairie toward Horton's ranch.

CHAPTER XXIII.

A FORGED LETTER

ALMOST a month had passed since Lord Avondale's departure, and yet Hugh had not visited the Grove. He thought a great deal about Ethel, and he was conscious of a sense of relief now that the Englishman was gone.

One evening, about this time, he determined to pay the Hortons a visit. His reception was most cordial, and he fancied that there was more than usual of the old-time animation in Ethel's eyes. An opportunity came during the evening, when they were alone, but he did not improve it as he had intended. He did not declare his love in words, though he felt confident that Ethel read his heart in his flushed face. Thus he procrastinated, day after day, until the weeks hastened into months, and the springtime of the year had come again.

During this time he saw much of the Hortons. The bond of friendship between the cattle king and himself had materially strengthened. Mr. Horton frequently warned him of the collapse, which he believed to be inevitable, of the hopes of all engaged in or dependent upon agricultural pursuits in Southwestern Kansas. At such times Hugh would listen patiently until the cattleman had finished, and then he would adroitly change the subject.

Both Major Hampton and Captain Osborn assured him that, while John Horton was doubtless perfectly sincere, yet the abundant yield of crops during the preceding years, and the entire absence of the hot winds, was proof, irrefragable, that the cattleman's theory was wrong. They also believed that John Horton was sadly mistaken regarding the cattle thieves, who still continued their untiring and fearless raids. The claim of the cattlemen was that a coterie of farmers had banded themselves together for the profitable and yet dangerous business of cattle-stealing. John Horton was the heaviest loser, because his herds were so extensive. Captain Osborn's views coincided with those expressed in the *Patriot*,—that the thieves were a band of cowboys acting under the direction of some able leader. Both these theories were freely discussed, while the cattle-stealing continued without interruption, and not the slightest clue was obtainable as to who did the lawless work.

The thieves knew, all too well, the punishment awaiting them if they should ever be captured, and its severity caused them to exercise the greatest caution.

There is an unwritten code on the frontier that a man may engage in a quarrel, and shoot and kill his adversary, provided both parties are armed and no unfair advantage is taken. If one has a number of such quarrels and each time "kills his man," he then becomes a most formidable candidate for sheriff in his county. On the other hand, if two men quarrel and one comes upon the other stealthily and, without warning, shoots him in the back, the act is construed by this unwritten code of the West as being a cowardly murder. The assassin is usually taken to some "Dead Man's Hollow" and shot to death. There is hardly a community on the frontier but has its "Dead Man's Hollow," where the "law" is administered at the hands of the vigilantes.

While this code prevents outside interference in a so-called "fair fight," even though death may result to one of the parties, yet, if a cattle thief is caught, he must, without exception, pay the penalty with his life. Indeed, a thief is looked upon with less commiseration, if possible, than a cowardly murderer.

In the meantime, the winter months were gone, and spring was paying another visit to sunny Kansas. The boundless brown prairie was once more changed to a world of brightest green, and, far and wide, over the landscape were myriads of simple dandelions and modest daisies that danced to the wind like a vast constellation of twinkling stars.

The meadow-lark and the brown thrush had again returned to their summer home to herald the approach of another mating-time, but still Hugh Stanton had not declared his love to Ethel Horton, nor had Lord Avondale returned to pursue his wooing of the American heiress.

Hugh Stanton fancied that he detected a shadow of sorrow in the girl's face, and in her voice; and a fear arose in his heart. Was she grieving because of Lord Avondale's absence? His unselfish regard for Ethel was so keen that it caused him much pain. Over and over he assured himself that he would willingly surrender his own slight claim if in doing so he might add to her happiness.

One afternoon Mrs. J. Bruce-Horton came up from the Grove to see Mrs. Osborn. Even a casual observer could have told that the stately wife of the cattle king was unusually agitated. She mounted the Osborn steps and rang the bell in a nervous manner.

Soon after, these two friends were seated in Mrs. Osborn's private room, engaged in earnest conversation.

"What shall I do, Lucy? What can I do? What ought I to do under the circumstances?"

"My dear Mrs. Horton," replied her friend, suavely, "do not agitate yourself. It is the easiest thing in the world, I assure you, to arrange this seemingly unfortunate affair."

"Oh, I don't know, Lucy, whether it is easy or not. No one knows the half a mother endures with a marriageable daughter to look after."

"Oh, fie!" Mrs. Osborn laughed, as she rang for her maid. The door opened, and, turning to the girl, she ordered a small bottle of Tokay, which was soon set before them. "Now, my dear, drink a glass of wine. It will strengthen your nerves."

"You see, Lucy," said Mrs. Horton, as she sipped her wine nervously, "this is the third letter Doctor Redfield has written. He seems so persistent."

"You have it with you?" asked Mrs Osborn, as if she were asserting a fact.

"Yes," replied Mrs. Horton, as she took the letter from her bag and handed it to Mrs. Osborn, "I want you to put this with the others. Oh, dear! I feel so worked up over this affair; and to think of Lord Avondale's misfortune! How long do you suppose it will be before he can again travel?"

Mrs. Osborn carefully scrutinized the handwriting on the letter. A diplomatic expression came over her beautiful face. "Yes, it is Doctor Redfield's writing," she affirmed, half to herself. "Oh, how long, did you ask, before Lenox dare travel? Perhaps a month; his physician tells me he has had a narrow escape. His broken arm—the result of his hunting trip in the mountains—was the least of his sufferings, poor fellow. A fever set in, he writes me, and for a while he was quite delirious. He will be here as soon as he can safely travel,—within a month, I am quite sure."

"I shall be so glad when he returns," sighed Mrs. Horton. "Ethel seems much more reconciled of late."

"Indeed?" replied Mrs. Osborn.

"Oh, yes," continued Mrs. Horton. "I was urging the advantage of a marriage with Lord Avondale the other day, and she replied, in a most indifferent manner, 'Very well, mamma, I have ceased to care one way or the other, if it pleases you, I presume it ought to be acceptable to me.' She then said something about being tired of life, and broke down in tears. Of course I consoled her as only a mother can."

"Subdued at last!" cried Mrs. Osborn, triumphantly. "We may now hope to see merry old England again. Away!" she went on, exultingly, "away with American stupidity! We have outwitted her blond-mustached 'brain-worker.'.rdquo; Mrs. Horton seemed to catch the spirit of her friend's confidence. "Yes," she ejaculated, "see England and our many friends; and, oh, to think how proud I am, Lucy, that my daughter is to be Lady Avondale. Why, it is quite enough to make the heart of any mother throb with ecstasy."

"Indeed it is," replied the designing Mrs. Osborn, "and you are entitled to so much credit for the clever ways in which you have managed it."

"No, Lucy, you are deserving of the praise in this affair far more than myself," replied Mrs. Horton. "Indeed, I could not have gotten on at all without you."

"I certainly have done my utmost to serve you," said Mrs. Osborn, in a sycophantic tone. "I feel sure you will always be grateful—and Ethel, too, won't she?"

"Indeed, we shall," replied Mrs. Horton, unhesitatingly.

"And I shall always be a welcome guest at Ethel's English home?" Mrs. Osborn went on.

"Always!" replied Mrs. Horton. "Of course you will. Why ask such a question?"

"Oh, I know I shall be, I assure you," she replied, demurely, "but then I wanted to hear you say so, don't you know? Now there is only one serious phase in our program—Doctor Redfield." She still held his letter addressed to Ethel.

"What would you advise, Lucy? You are so clever, and know so much better than I what is best to be done."

"My dear Mrs. Horton, will you be guided by what I say, entirely?" She was standing near an elegantly carved escritoire as she spoke.

"Entirely, Lucy, I will do as you say," replied Mrs. Horton. Quick as a flash Mrs. Osborn caught up an ivory paper-knife and tore away the envelope.

"Oh, Lucy!" cried Mrs. Horton, excitedly. "Don't! don't—I feel so guilty."

"My dear, there is no turning back," replied the cool and calculating Mrs. Osborn. "A title for Ethel is at stake. We must burn every bridge behind us." Then, glancing at the letter, she read aloud:

"My own dear Ethel:—I lift up my voice for the third time, and call to you. Will you not answer? I am as one in a wilderness of doubt and sorrow. My heart tells me that you have not forgotten your promise—a promise that has

stimulated me with sweetest hope all these weary months of waiting. One word, Ethel,—only one word; even if it is to say that you have forgotten me. With my heart's tenderest love, I am all your own,

"Affectionately,

"Jack."

"His devotion is quite amusing," laughed Mrs. Osborn, as she seated herself before her escritoire and began writing. Presently, turning to Mrs. Horton, she said: "Here is your reply:"

"Dr. Jack Redfield,

"Sir:—My daughter has referred your several rather amusing and absurd letters to me for reply, and desires me to say that your communications annoy her very much. As she is already betrothed to Lord Avondale, and will be married in a short time, you certainly cannot, if you possess any gentlemanly breeding, wish to intrude further upon her your unreciprocated attentions.

"Respectfully."

"Oh, Lucy," cried Mrs. Horton, half-hysterically, "I cannot sign such a letter; I cannot indeed. Let it go unanswered."

"Just as you say," she replied, while a tigerish look of hatred and disdain arose to her usually pretty face. "Perhaps," she went on, in a low purring voice that required an effort to modulate, "it will be as well to dismiss all thought of Doctor Redfield. I am quite sure we shall never hear of him again."

Soon after, Mrs. Horton took her leave and, as she drove slowly homeward, she was glad that she had not signed that awful letter. She sighed a little, as if a weight rested on her conscience. "I am truly glad," she said to herself, "that Lord Avondale will soon be with us."

Mrs. Osborn was provoked at her friend's lack of courage in grappling with and crushing all possible danger. After the departure of Mrs. Horton, she read Jack Redfield's letter again. Then she read the reply which she had prepared for Mrs. Horton to sign. "This letter ought to be sent," she observed, "or I am no general." Dipping her pen in the ink, she addressed an envelope to Dr. Jack Redfield, then—turning to the letter—she paused a moment. Her courage failed her, and she laid down the pen. Unlocking a small drawer of her escritoire, she took out a bundle of letters, and, selecting the topmost one, commenced reading. As she read one after another, a passionate light animated her beautiful face and eyes. "Lenox, dear Lenox!" she murmured. "Yes, I will do it."

Taking up the pen, she hastily signed the name of Mrs. J. Bruce-Horton to the letter, then carefully enclosing it in the envelope, she went quickly out and posted it.

Thus, at the expense of conscience, she made an instalment payment on a title for Ethel Horton.

CHAPTER XXIV.

REVERSING THE HIGHER COURTS

THE evening after the mailing of that fatal letter to Dr. Jack Redfield, some one rapped on Hugh Stanton's door.

"Come in," said Hugh, as he went on with his toilet. The door opened, and Judge Lynn walked in. The judge's facial appearance gave evidence that he had just come from a barber shop. He frequently passed one hand over his smooth-shaven chin, as if to call attention to it.

"Hello, Mr. Stanton," said he, as he helped himself to a chair. "You're dressin' up like you might be goin' somewhere."

"I have been invited to dine with the Osborns."

"Jist so; danged good place to get a square meal; bet yer life it is."

"The Osborns are very hospitable people," observed Hugh, as he went on with his toilet.

"Look 'e here, Stanton," said Judge Lynn, "did you think I was drunk the other evenin' when you and Major Hampton and myself were discussin' the Barley Hullers?"

"I don't know," replied Hugh, evasively, "were you?"

"No, sir," said the judge, emphatically, "don't you believe it; not for your life. I jist got to thinkin' about a case I'd decided in my court that day. A complex, tryin' question of law, sir, always exhausts me, as it did the other night, and I fell asleep." Hugh turned his face away to conceal his amusement.

"What's the matter with you, anyhow, Stanton; you're gettin' mighty disbelievin' it 'pears to me; what are you grinnin' 'bout? Can't a feller go to sleep if he feels like it?" asked the judge.

"How is business in your court, Judge?" asked Hugh, paying no attention to his irritation.

"Oh, she's poppin' these days, and don't you forget it," replied the judge. "You see, we've had no rain since last fall, and here it's the first of May. Dry weather nachally makes our people irritable and brittle. Fellers 'round here can't pay their interest, and the Eastern capitalists are gettin' down on 'em. Mortgages are bein' foreclosed, right and left; bet yer life, law business with me is hummin'."

"We certainly need rain," said Hugh. "The farmers, however, tell me that the barley, wheat, corn, and other crops are looking fairly well, notwithstanding the dry weather."

"That's a fact," replied the judge, "crops are lookin' devilish good, considerin'. Fact is, there's lots of water in the ground from last year's rains, but she's oozin' out danged fast lately, and within a week or two more, unless we have rain, things'll be dryer 'n powder dust. Yes, sir, loan companies are already gettin' skittish, and sendin' back applications for farm loans, unfilled."

"Oh, come," said Hugh, "you are a pessimist. We shall have a good rain before many days, and then you will change your mind."

"Don't you believe it, sir," remarked the judge, with emphasis. "Now let me tell you,—but gosh almighty, what's the use of talkin' to you, Stanton; I can't convince you, though I am right. It's only a waste of words. You 're lariated with the balance of 'em, and held in the iron grip of error. You go on believin' jist as you please, anyway. Say, I called for a little favor. I want to borrow five dollars."

"Want to borrow five dollars?" repeated Hugh.

"Yes, sirree, I do," answered the judge, "and see here, Stanton, you must n't refuse me. You see I had a case in my court the other day, and sort of attempted to interfere with a decision of the Supreme Court of the Sunflower State. It has resulted in the attorney-general's gettin' gay and frisky like, and sendin' me the most contemptible and impudent telegram I ever read. I want the five dollars to telegraph back my defense. Fact is, I have jist got to have it; bet yer life I have. Oh, I can mighty near tell by the way my neck itches that somebody is makin' a halter for it, bet yer life."

"Why don't you send it collect?" asked Hugh.

"Why, dangnation, man, I tried it, and the fool of an operator down here someway don't have the right idee about the importance, dignity, and responsibility of my court, and he would n't send it unless the shekels were put up in advance."

Hugh handed the judge five dollars, and asked him if he did not think he had exceeded his authority in interfering with a decision of the Supreme Court.

"Law, my dear Stanton," replied the judge, blandly, as he put the five dollars in his pocket, "law is my hobby. Speakin' unreserved-like, they can't down me on the statutes, no, sir; and if I had that low-down varmin of an attorney-general here, why, I'd fine him for contempt of court; bet yer life I would. Oh, I know a whole lot when it comes to law. Well, I must be goin'."

"Good day," said Hugh, as the judge started toward the door; "call again."

"Good day," responded Judge Lynn. "I'll hand you back this special accommodation tomorrow."

A little later Hugh hurried along the street toward Captain Osborn's, laughing softly to himself at the oddities of Judge Lynn. When he reached the Osborn home, to his surprise he found Miss Marie Hampton there.

"I intended to surprise you," said Mrs. Osborn, coquettishly, "by having Major Hampton and Marie with us, but have succeeded only partially. The major is away from home, but I carried Marie away with me this afternoon, and have persuaded her to remain with us for dinner."

"I am truly delighted with your thoughtfulness," replied Hugh, bowing deferentially to Marie, "but, really, Mrs. Osborn, you have no need of adding to the attractions of your lovely home to induce me to come."

"I am not so sure of that," replied Mrs. Osborn, as her musical laugh rang out merrily, "the captain and I are beginning to believe that you are incorrigible in your habit of neglecting your friends."

"Hugh is a most excellent man of business," replied the captain, "but he throws social obligations to the winds, unless his frequent visits to the Hortons prove an exception."

"Don't jest about impossibilities, Captain," said Mrs. Osborn. "Lord Avondale will soon return, and—well, we all know what that means."

Hugh's face reddened at Mrs. Osborn's words. He was not at all sure about the correctness of her inference.

"My calls at Major Hampton's are quite as frequent as at Mr. Horton's," replied Hugh.

"You could come oftener and still be welcome," observed Marie, while her heart beat fast with admiration for Hugh, an admiration she could not entirely conceal.

"Oh, thank you," said Hugh, "that is a compliment I shall not soon forget," and, as he spoke, caution beat a hasty tattoo on the drumhead of conscience.

Hugh could not help noticing that Marie was growing more and more beautiful. She was attired in an evening dress of black lace, which was admirably becoming to her graceful figure. Her heavy tresses shone like burnished gold and the softer shades of copper, while the rose hue of perfect health tinted her cheeks. The animated way in which she conversed with Hugh confirmed Mrs. Osborn's suspicions that she was in love with him, while he was too stupid, she told herself, even to suspect it.

The dinner-hour passed pleasantly, Mrs. Osborn giving the captain but few of her tiger-claw scratches. The veteran invariably took refuge in the snug harbor of little Harry, whenever a serious break seemed imminent, and thus warded off all collisions with the war-cruiser of his domestic life. As they arose from the table, Hugh turned to Mrs. Osborn and asked her rather abruptly when Lord Avondale was expected.

"Why, what is that to you?" replied the wily

Mrs. Osborn, as she looked rather exultingly at him.

"I am interested in knowing," replied Hugh.

"Well, but your interest is only platonic, you know."

"Perhaps," answered Hugh.

"Oh, perhaps," repeated Mrs. Osborn, as she elevated her eyebrows and smiled bewitchingly at him. Hugh, however, made no reply, and Mrs. Osborn's nerves received a shock by his silence as well as by the turn affairs were taking. She mentally resolved to wire Lord Avondale, on the next day, to hasten his coming.

Returning to the drawing-room, Captain Osborn pushed aside the heavy hangings that separated it from Mrs. Osborn's music-room.

"Lucy, my dear," said he, "I am sure Miss Marie and Mr. Stanton would enjoy some music."

"By all means," said Marie, "I have often wished to hear you play, Mrs. Osborn."

"Captain, what shall I play?" asked his wife, seating herself languidly at the piano.

"Oh, anything," replied the jovial old captain, "anything from 'Old Dan Tucker' to the 'Fisher's Hornpipe.'.rdquo;

"You will observe," said Mrs. Osborn, looking back at Hugh over her shoulder, and smiling, "that my husband is quite primitive in his musical tastes."

Then followed several selections. She played mechanically, however, and with little expression. There was no soul to rebound from the strings of the instrument. In the very middle of a classical piece, which was beyond her, she suddenly stopped playing, and, turning to Hugh, said:

"Excuse me, but did you not, on one occasion, speak of Miss Hampton's playing?"

"I doubtless have mentioned it," replied Hugh.

"Ah, you naughty girl!" exclaimed Mrs. Osborn, laughing, "why did you not tell me? Come, Marie, you must help me entertain these American financiers—these men of affairs. I promise you," she went on, patronizingly, "that they will not know whether you play excellently or otherwise."

CHAPTER XXV.

ALMOST A TRAGEDY

"ICAN'. speak for Captain Osborn," said Marie, as she seated herself before the piano, "but I fear, Mrs. Osborn, that you misjudge Mr. Stanton."

"Oh, thank you," said Hugh, bowing at the compliment.

"Papa insists," Marie went on, as she looked at Hugh with her laughing eyes, "that you are wonderfully appreciative, and, doubtless, critical."

"Indeed," interposed Mrs. Osborn, with some surprise, "well, had I known that, I would have been more careful in the selections I played." Marie turned to the instrument, softly fingering the keys and striking a chord here and there until finally she drifted into Chopin's Fifth Nocturne. Her interpretation was that of a born artist. The music fairly rippled from her deft fingers, as she glided on and on from one beautiful cadence to another, until at last—note by note—as if sobbing a farewell, the melody died away. Then striking a few chords sharply, she took up a lively refrain, which gradually materialized into Rubinstein's Melody in F. There was a wild abandon and rare power in her playing that appealed to Hugh Stanton's soul like the wild sweep and rush of sighing winds in a primeval forest.

Again the music melted away to a single note, which quivered like an echo that would not cease its reverberations. Then, gathering the notes in her masterful hands, she played

Beethoven's exquisite Moonlight Sonata. As the rich tones
came in answer to her wonderfully magic touch, Marie seemed
oblivious of time or of place, and conscious only of the music
which swayed and lifted her. She astonished Hugh, Mrs. Osborn,
and the captain as well, in her wonderful interpretation of
the grand old master. Presently she glided skilfully into the
first movement, sustaining and making each melodious note
sing out like a thing of life; then, with a genius bordering on
the infinite, she masterfully executed the allegretto movement
with vivaciousness, and the agitato movement with a hurried,
standing effect, and concluded the adagio with an indolent,
romance melody of whispers. There was something almost
divine in the rich harmonies that filled the room with rapturous
ecstasy, while the languorous air trembled with renascent song.

Hugh Stanton had arisen and gradually approached the
player as the music went on. When it ceased, he seemed
suddenly to awaken. Mrs. Osborn was noticeably moved by
Marie's renditions, and yet her admiration was for the execution
rather than for the music itself. She observed Hugh's agitation,
and mentally resolved that Marie Hampton's music should
prove the solution of keeping Hugh Stanton from declaring
himself to Ethel Horton. To Hugh she spoke, in a low voice,
of Marie's wonderful gift and of her lovable character. Hugh,
however, answered only in monosyllables, for he had been
strangely moved.

Mrs. Osborn interpreted his silence differently; and rejoiced
at her clever planning in bringing them together in her own
home, that she might read what was written.

Hugh escorted Marie to her home that evening. As they
walked along he was conscious of a wonderful power in the girl,
which he could not understand. In the uncertain darkness her
beautiful face was forgotten, and he thought of her only as a
materialized genius, whose musical skill had enthralled him.
Naturally reserved in the presence of women, he felt more
awkward than ever when they were alone, and he was not sure

that he answered intelligently Marie's questions and vivacious girlish talk.

At the door, their hands touched for a moment, as Hugh bade her good night. He could not quite understand his feelings, but he concluded that it was only the remembrance of the music that thrilled him.

Looking back, as he walked along the street, he saw the dim outline of a man following him. So deeply absorbed was Hugh in his own thoughts that he did not hear the footsteps gradually gaining on him. When he reached a darker portion of the street, and not far from the hotel, his pursuer tapped him lightly on the shoulder and said:

"Look 'e here, Stanton; I propose bein' plenty p'lite, but I think we'd better hev a talk. I'm not assoomin' to be much on chin music, but what I say goes." Hugh turned and found himself face to face with Bill Kinneman, the cowboy. Kinneman was noticeably under the influence of liquor.

"What do you want?" asked Hugh, rather brusquely.

"I want you to browse on a different part of the range an' quit hangin' 'round Major Hampton's; thet's what I want, an' you'll do as I say, or by the Eternal I'll give you a dose uv this," and quicker than a flash he pushed a revolver into Hugh's face.

The streets were deserted and they were quite alone. Hugh realized his imminent danger. Kinneman held a cocked revolver in his face, and it would be folly to do other than try to effect a compromise. Presently he said: "Kinneman, I thought you had some sense."

"Waal, hain't I?" asked the cowboy, still holding his revolver in close proximity to Hugh's face.

"You are certainly not a good judge of human nature," replied Hugh.

"Waal, now look 'e here, my wayfarin' frien', I'm no corn-field sailor, an' I want you to know it," said Kinneman. "The old major's daughter possesses sooperier rectitood, and is not fur you. She don't step in yer class, but she does step in mine, see? An' you're flounderin' in the quicksands uv error if you think different."

"Oh," said Hugh, "I am beginning to understand what you mean. You are in love with Miss Hampton, and you fancy that I am also."

"Thet's 'bout what I'd say if I wuz unbosomin' myself," replied Kinneman, as he pressed a little closer to Hugh.

"Your fears are groundless," replied Hugh, emphatically. Kinneman dropped his revolver to his side and exclaimed, "Pardner, is thet squar'."

"My dear sir," replied Hugh, "I do not know what love is. I have made no untruthful statement, if that is what you mean by asking, 'Is that square?'.rdquo;

"Thet's all I wanted to hear you say," said Kinneman; "but somethin' mighty thrillin' is liable to happen if you reach fur yer artill'ry, so jist keep yer hands away from yer belt." With this, he turned on his heel. He walked a few steps and then stopped.

"Look 'e here, Stanton," said he, "speakin' wide-open like, there's only one special thing on earth thet I've set my heart on, an' if I find thet you've lied to me, I'm 'lowin' I'll push you off the face uv the earth, an' fill you so full uv holes that St. Peter won't know you. I'll take my chances on the major bein' favorable, an' thet girl's goin' to be mine if I hev to kill a baker's dozen to git her." With this he walked away in the darkness.

Hugh hastened to the hotel. Whether from the exaltation occasioned by Marie's playing, or from the counteracting influence of Bill Kinne-man's wicked threat, or from both, he knew not, but nevertheless he felt strangely disturbed, as if a soul chord had suddenly been unkeyed in his life's harp.

He sat by the window far into the night, endeavoring to choose a course to pursue. Lord Avondale would soon return. A sense of duty forced itself upon him when he thought of Ethel Horton, and he determined to declare himself to her without further delay. He tried in vain to analyze his feelings toward the beautiful and accomplished Marie. A mist rose up before him and he seemed to hear once more the Moonlight Sonata. Then he felt that his interest in Marie was embodied solely in the one word, music. He longed for a confiding hour with his old boyhood friend, Jack Redfield. "If he were only here," he mused, "I would talk it all over with him and be guided by his advice." Seating himself at his table, he determined to write to him. Then he fell to musing again, and left the letter unwritten.

CHAPTER XXVI.

REACHING A DECISION

TWO weeks had passed since the Osborn dinner. One morning the captain observed to Hugh, "My boy, have you been idling your time away, or can't you decide?"

"I don't quite catch your meaning," said Hugh, pleasantly.

"Well, to be more explicit," replied Captain Osborn, "you haven't yet asked Ethel Horton to become your wife, have you?"

Hugh's face reddened, and he answered, slowly,' "No, I have not."

"Perhaps you have changed your mind," the captain went on. "Mrs. Osborn says you are desperately in love with Miss Hampton, but I don't rely on second-hand evidence, and that is why I ask you pointblank. Of course, follow your heart, my boy, wherever it leads you, and you'll not make any great mistake, provided your affection is reciprocated. Reason cannot be depended on in such matters, for usually it spreads its wings and flies away when we become thoroughly inoculated with the illusion of love."

"My dear Captain," replied Hugh, "I feel it to be both a duty and a privilege to declare my love to Ethel Horton. I believe I love her, and I am ashamed of myself for having procrastinated as I have."

"Are n't you sure that it is love, my boy?" asked the captain.

"No," replied Hugh. "I am impressed, however, that my interest in Ethel Horton is genuine, and I know that whatever I say to her will be sincere."

"Well, you had better say it pretty quick," observed the captain, gravely. "My wife tells me that the Englishman will be here to-morrow."

"To-morrow," repeated Hugh, looking at the captain in surprise.

"To-morrow," repeated the captain, "and I fancy that, with all his English traits, bad manners, and poor taste, he will not dilly-dally as you have about asking a girl like Ethel Horton to become his wife."

Hugh made no reply, but all day long he kept thinking of Ethel Horton. Sometimes Marie Hampton's deep blue eyes would look at him from under their long lashes, and he would fancy that in their pleading sweetness he beheld a fascination that lost itself in mystery. He put it away from him, however, and went on thinking of Ethel.

That evening found him at the Grove. Ethel's greeting was all that a hesitating lover could desire. She was seated in an easy chair on the wide veranda overlooking the terraced lawn and the lake. The cool breezes from the far-away foothills came gently down, gladdening the landscape with their refreshing breath.

Hugh seated himself near her, and they soon fell into a pleasant conversation. He fancied that there was less restraint in her manner and voice than usual, but in her soft brown eyes there was still a look of sadness. The fun-loving girl he had first known was now a subdued and saddened woman.

"I have something that I have long wanted to say to you," said Hugh.

"Indeed?" she asked, listlessly, raising her eyes to his face.

"Yes, something I wanted to say long ago. I can hardly believe," he went on, "that we have known each other only a year." The flush had gone from his face as he spoke, and in its place had come an expression of uncertainty. Ethel moved uneasily in her chair. Her heart cried out, "Oh, Jack! Jack!" while her better judgment prompted her to look upon Hugh Stanton as a welcome avenue of escape.

"Ethel," said he, and his voice was low and earnest, as he bent toward her, "I have come to-night to ask you to become my wife. I

164

do not say that my feelings are those that are pictured sometimes in fiction; but, Ethel, the deep respect I have felt for you from our first meeting has ripened into a warm and intense feeling. I cannot pay you a higher compliment than I have in asking you to Become my wife. I am filled with a chivalrous sentiment that will not be satisfied unless the right is given me to protect and care for you." He raised her hand to his lips, and kissed it deferentially. She did not seek to withdraw it, but remained silent.

When Hugh looked at her face, he saw that her eyes were full of tears. She was gazing far away across the brown prairie.

"Yes, Hugh," she finally faltered, "you have, indeed, paid me a compliment—the greatest that man can pay to woman, but I fear that you would not be satisfied with what I have to give."

"Satisfied!" cried Hugh, in the excitement of the moment, "satisfied? Why, Ethel, tell me that you care for me, and it will make me the happiest man in the world."

There was a pitiful look in her eyes as they rested on his face.

"Hugh," she said very slowly, "it is a woman's heart that an earnest man desires when he asks a woman to become his wife. My heart is like the worm-eaten rosebud,—it is the semblance of what you seek, not the reality."

Hugh imagined that she referred to Lord Avondale, and, again, he told himself that it could not be true,—that she surely was not grieving for him.

"Listen, Hugh," she went on, "listen, while I tell you of a great love which grew up in my heart almost in a day, and which flourishes and grows stronger with each passing hour. The fear that my love is unreciprocated has grown almost to certainty. The love still remains,—but hear my story, and then,—then, Hugh, if you still wish me to be your wife, after you have had time to think it over, my answer shall be as you wish." She then told him briefly of Jack Redfield, and of the great love that had come to her on the shores of Lake Geneva,—a love for him that must abide forever,—although he, perhaps, had already forgotten, as he had so long left her letter unanswered. Hugh's astonishment was very great,—he was stunned,—but he did not mention the fact that he even knew Jack Redfield.

When she had finished her narration, he asked: "What of Lord Avondale?"

"Oh, Hugh," she replied, "I shall marry you, if at all, to escape that calamity. Do you not feel honored," she said, smiling through her tears, "at the use I may make of your devotion?"

"My devotion is very great; it is eternal, Ethel," replied Hugh, huskily.

"Understand, Hugh," said Ethel, "my respect and confidence in you are almost limitless. Indeed, I have come to look upon you as a tower of strength. It is my desire that you should deliberate long and earnestly before you arrive at a conclusion. When you have done this, Hugh, know that your wishes shall be mine."

They had arisen from their chairs, and were standing near the edge of the veranda. When Ethel ceased speaking, Hugh remained silent for a long time. He finally said:

"Ethel, my little girl, I feel more than ever that I have a duty to perform, and that duty is to protect you." He lifted her hand again to his lips, and then hurried away. A little later he was galloping madly across the prairie toward Meade, where he was soon in the privacy of his own room.

For the first time in his life, he believed Jack Redfield to be a scoundrel. All his chivalrous manhood had been aroused by Ethel's story, and he determined to protect her—though it cost him his life.

Through the long, weary hours of the night he paced restlessly back and forth in his room, nor did he seek his pillow until the gray of another day had dawned—the day that brought Lord Avondale again to Meade.

CHAPTER XXVII.

THE HOT WINDS

LORD AVONDALE took up his residence, as before, at the Osborn Hotel. He called frequently at the Hortons', and was also much in Mrs. Osborn's society. The tongue of gossip was again beginning to wag. She and the Englishman renewed their relations afresh, and went on with a boldness that might almost cause one to doubt the truthfulness of the rumors.

Lord Avondale's self-conceit and audacity were more apparent than on his former visit. He felt sure that Ethel Horton would soon become his wife; and he not only entreated, but commanded Lucy Osborn to hasten the affair along, as he was impatient to return to England.

Hugh, in the meantime, was following Ethel's advice, and deliberating most earnestly as to what was best to do. He could not understand why his old friend, Jack Redfield, whom he had always regarded as the personification of honor, had acted in such an inexplicable manner toward Ethel Horton. If Ethel had not told him of her love for Jack Redfield, the way out of the dilemma might have been very simple. In that event, he would have married her at once, and sent the English lord about his business.

It was nearing the last days of June. The cool night breeze, so exhilarating in the Southwest, died away each morning as the dawn streaked the east, and the sun climbed above the horizon. The limitless sky bent above the earth in silence and grandeur. No breath of air stirred leaf, or flower, or grass-blade. It was but one of a hundred such quiet, perfect days, on any one of which you might have searched the heavens from horizon to horizon and found neither cloud nor the semblance of one; silent, hazy Indian summer days. The bountiful fields of wheat and barley were beginning to yellow with golden promise. The farmers said that the wheat and arley were almost out of "the milk," and in the "dough," and, while the dry weather would prevent the kernels from filling as in former years, yet, after all, there would be a fair yield. The cattlemen laughed and said, "Wait, and you'll see whether the Southwest is an agricultural paradise or a cattle range."

The farmers, however, were not easily discouraged. They pointed with pride to the thousands of acres of growing corn, and said, "See how rapidly it is growing. It is not firing, even at the roots, to speak of, and its color is such a dark healthy green; it is so luxuriant and tall, with its broad bending blades,—so stately, indeed that a squadron of cavalry might ride a few rods into the edge of the field and be hidden from view." The farmers expressed a firm belief that the corn, which was beginning to "tassel" and "silk," would have plenty of rain to make it "ear" well, and that an abundant yield would reward their labors, even though the small grain should happen to prove a light crop.

It was, perhaps, ten o'clock one morning when Hugh walked down the street from the hotel to the bank. Major Buell Hampton and Captain Osborn were discussing the weather. They were standing on the sidewalk in front of the banking-house, and several townspeople, cattlemen, and farmers had congregated around them; and the discussion of a possible crop failure became general.

"'Pears to be mighty sultry on the range these 'ere days," said Dan Spencer, as he borrowed a chew of tobacco from his neighbor. "Speakin' careless-like, I don't reckon this dog-goned dry weather kin loaf 'round much longer. I'm 'lowin' the water's sure 'nuff all dried up in Crooked Creek; dang my buttons if it ain't."

"Mighty sorry fur you farmer fellers," observed Bill Kinneman, patronizingly. "I'm not hankerin' to be onpop'lar, but you jist wait an' you-alls 'll see what kind uv a farmin' country this is."

"It is either a farming country," said Hugh to Captain Osborn, "or else our bank is located in the wrong part of the world."

"Country's all right, my boy," replied Captain Osborn. "Don't get disheartened. We'll have rain before many days."

"Now, look 'e 'ere, boys," said Judge Linus Lynn, who had joined the group a few minutes before and caught the drift of their conversation. "Let me tell you what's goin' to happen. I am no tenderfoot—say, what's all you fellers laughin' at, anyway? Can't a graduate of a jagcure make a few sober remarks without bein' giggled at, I'd like to know. If you fellers had just a little wit—but you hain't got it—to put with yer giggles, you'd have sarcasm. You bet!"

"Hain't you tasted no corn-juice yit, Jedge, fur sure?" asked Dan Spencer, laughing.

"Not a dangnation swallow!" replied Judge Lynn, emphatically. "I took my friend Major Hampton's advice, availed myself of the gold cure at his expense, an' by the great horn spoon, I'll never drink nary another drop; no, sirree. Bin shakin' hands with the back end of drug stores, partin' company with my good cash, an' bein' bit with the same old snake long enough. Oh, I know when I've got enough of even a bad thing. Bet yer life I do. Now as I was goin' to say, I'm no tenderfoot. I've lived in Kansas twenty years. Uster gather up buffalo-bones from these prairies with a yoke of oxen, haul 'em two hundred miles an' sell 'em at ten dollars a load. Yes, sir; think I don't know what I'm talkin' about? Bet yer life I do."

"I should nach'ally hev thought you'd bin a rich man afore this, Jedge," said Bill Kinneman.

"Oh, you'd thought that, would you?" replied the judge. "I've heard you tell how to get rich, Kinneman, fur the las' ten years. Fact is, if every man was to get rich who believes he knows how, we'd have no paupers."

"Say, Jedge, we're goin' to hev hot winds, ain't we?" asked Dan

Spencer, grinning. "Thet's what you've bin preachin' fur the last three years, ain't it, boys?"

"Gee whillikens!" exclaimed the judge, "did you feel that? That's a hot wind, sure as you're born."

"Oh, no, Judge," said Captain Osborn, "that could hardly be called a hot wind. Still, it is rather warm."

"Gentlemen," said Major Hampton, as he moved along with the crowd on the sidewalk to a point somewhat sheltered from the wind, "if Judge Lynn is correct, and we do not have rain soon, the growing crops will be seriously injured."

Judge Linus Lynn walked on down to the corner of the building, where the wind was unobstructed, and, hastily returning, said, "The jig's up, boys, an' bets are all off. The hot winds of hell are sweepin' the plains; bet yer life they are. The wolves will sure'nuff scratch the varnish off the front door of the new town hall and dig holes in the public square this winter, if this dangnation holycaust of hot wind keeps on Mowin' very long. You bet I know a thing or two."

The hot wind began blowing a regular gale, and soon the crowd disappeared. All feeling of merriment gave way before the contemplation of the ravaging blast that was hourly doing irreparable damage to the growing crops. As the day advanced, the wind became hotter and hotter, until not a soul was visible on the streets of Meade. People hastened to their homes, offices, and stores for shelter, and shut themselves away from the intensely suffocating air. A few minutes' exposure would blister the face and hands of the hardiest farmer.

On rushed the scorching wave,—its wilting breath shriveling up every growing thing as effectually as a prairie fire,—everything excepting the native buffalo-grass, the cacti, and the sunflowers. The grass it cured, and made more sweet and fattening for the cattlemen's herds.

The thermometer registered 102 degrees in the shade. The following day it ran up to 108 degrees,—next day it registered 114 degrees, while on the fourth day of this terribly heated blast of parching, burning winds, the mercury reached 119 degrees in the shade.

It was a suffocation indescribable, dealing relentless death to the agricultural hopes of the great Southwest. It was like some intense heat driven from thousands of furnaces, where limitless quantities of anthracite burn with blue and forked flames, creating heat sufficient to change even the very rocks into liquid. For a hundred hours this stifling, burning breath belched forth from the jaws of calamitous destruction. Utter devastation followed.

On the first day, the fields of growing corn seemed to shrink in timidity; on the second day the proud plumage of tassels drooped on the stalks; on the third day the blades whitened and shriveled and became like some aged and decrepit thing; while on the fourth day the tassels, blades, and even the stalks were snapped off in their parched brittleness and scattered by the winds of this terrific tornado of heat.

The fields were swept of every vestige of growing grain. The entire country became a desolate waste. For a hundred miles in every direction no living vegetation, planted by the hand of man, survived. The hopes, the labors, and the achievements of years were alike swept into the vortex of absolute ruin; and these farmers in the Southwest beheld the Great American Desert, as depicted by the earlier geographers, in all its primitive awfulness.

Farmers became mendicants; business men, paupers; while notes and bonds in the bankers' hands turned into worthless assets. A cry went up from the starving thousands, and once more train-loads of provisions came from the East for the relief of the Kansas sufferers.

John B. Horton, the cattle king, caused hundreds of beeves to be brought in from the range, and he opened a free market on the public square of Meade, to feed the destitute and hungry.

CHAPTER XXVIII.

"THY WILL BE DONE"

AFEW days after the country had been devastated by the hot winds, Hugh met Major Hampton on the street.

"Come on," said the major, "I am going over to the *Patriot* office, and I want to have a talk with you."

"All right," replied Hugh; "financially, I am ruined; and I now have more time on my hands than anything else."

On reaching the major's den at the *Patriot* office, he turned to Hugh and said, "I can distinctly see, Mr. Stanton, that there's something on your mind. Perhaps you'd like to ask my advice. If so, you need not be backward."

Hugh laughed good-naturedly, as he puffed a ring of cigar smoke toward the ceiling. "Well," he replied, "bankruptcy stares us in the face. Our bank, in all probability, will have to close its doors. Is not that quite enough to have on one's mind?"

"Quite enough," replied the major, "but there is something else that is worrying you. Come, what is it?"

"I almost believe, Major, that you are a mind-reader," replied Hugh.

"Oh, I am a student," replied the major, "and it would be strange, indeed, if I had not made some progress in all my years of study."

"Well, I will ask you a question," said Hugh. "If something you coveted very much were within your grasp, and you should awaken to find that it really belonged to another—some one whom you believed unworthy of the prize—what would you do?"

The major lay back on the lounge, and, after deliberating for a moment, replied: "From a selfish standpoint, I would secure for myself that which I coveted; but from an altruistic standpoint, it would be mean, low, and contemptible to take an unfair advantage of one's equals, and much worse to take advantage of one's inferiors. Again, the prize coveted should not be made a football, to toss about for transitory pleasure. One becomes a social outcast when he loves himself better than he loves his neighbor."

The major's reply struck home, and Hugh was noticeably ill at ease. Presently he said, "Major, what is going to become of the Southwest? The crops are all burned up,—our bank securities are worthless. Financially, I am a ruined man."

"Help the poor," replied the major. "Personally I have laid something away that will help me to accomplish charitable purposes toward the ever increasing army of unfortunates. Next year the crops may be better. I believe it is in my power to put you in a way to retrieve some of your lost fortune, and at the same time enable you to benefit mankind."

"In what way?" asked Hugh, eagerly.

The major hesitated for a few moments, and then said: "I do not feel at liberty to explain just now, but I will think it over for a day or two, and if I can be of service to you, Stanton, you will find me a true friend. My keenest pleasure is in befriending those in need of help, and wreathing the face of pain and sorrow with smiles of gladness."

"Thank you, Major," replied Hugh, "It's very kind of you, I am sure, and I shall wait with impatience for any suggestions that you may have to offer."

That evening Hugh called at the major's house. He quite forgot his losses and the ruined condition of the country in the pleasant conversation with the major and his daughter. The music, which formed a feature of the evening, was concluded by Marie singing a selection from Tannhbuser.

As Hugh was getting ready to bid his host good night, the major said: "Stanton, I am exceedingly glad you came to-night; I feel ennobled,—feel that it is good to live and that my days have been lengthened. The true epicurean of rationalism teaches us that the good and bad in man are engaged in a constant combat, and even the bad can better enjoy occasional indulgence by permitting the good to rule most of the time." It struck Hugh as being an odd remark for the major to make.

After bidding them good night, he walked hurriedly along the street toward the hotel in a thoughtful mood. When he reached his room, he sat down by the open window, determined to reach a decision in regard to Ethel Horton.

He had now been in Meade a little over a year. His inheritance of fifty thousand dollars from his father's estate had been swept away by the hot winds, and the securities which he held, bearing a high rate of interest, were practically worthless. The cattlemen were the only people who had not suffered by the cancerous breath that had swept over the country.

Ethel had trusted him to decide a momentous question. If he decided one way, Ethel Horton would become his wife. A voice whispered to him from the night wind, "Do this, and you need not care for the fortune you have lost. Ethel is the only child and heiress to millions."

"No," shouted Hugh, vehemently, starting up as if combating with the tempter, "no, that is a contemptible, cowardly thought. It is true that to-day poverty with her sable robe envelops me, and that a fortune is mine if I will only reach out and take it—a fortune that will make me a Croesus, while a resigned and heart-broken woman is ready to lift up her fair white arms to me as her savior, if I—I, Hugh Stanton—am willing to place upon her lips the kiss of a Judas. Shall I do it?" Conscience pricked him to a decision, and he fairly shouted, "Never, never, so long as my soul is in partnership with God Almighty." His clenched fist struck the table. His victory was complete.

Seating himself at his desk, he hastily wrote the following letter:

"My dear Jack:—About a year ago I called on you and said

*good-bye. Forgive me for not writing before. Jack, this let-
ter must determine whether I ever again address you as a
friend. I have met Ethel Horton, and have learned—God
knows the price of the wisdom—that her heart is wholly
yours. Why have you trampled upon it? If you are an honorable man, as I have ever believed you to be, answer her
letter, or, better still, come to me at once. I regard her as one
of the noblest girls in the wide, wide world. If the love which
you whispered to her at Lake Geneva was not sincere, then I
am no longer your friend, but shall ever remain your enemy.*

"Awaiting an answer, I am

"Your friend,

"Hugh Stanton."

He enclosed this letter in an envelope and addressed it to Jack
Redfield. He then wrote the following:

*"My dear Ethel:—Only God knows how earnestly I have
deliberated and prayed over the question which you commis-
sioned me to decide. Since I saw you last, my thoughts have
been given to this one subject. I feel exalted to-night. My soul
has arisen from the mists of doubt and uncertainty,—and,
I hope, selfishness,—and the way seems clearer to me. My
regard for you remains unchanged, but I will not insist on
your becoming my wife. To do this would prove me cowardly, selfish, and unjust. To pursue the course I have marked
out, will, I trust, demonstrate ere long,—not only that I am
unselfish where you are concerned, but also that I am securing a greater happiness for you than you could possibly know
if our lives were more closely linked together. Do not think
that I have arrived at this conclusion hastily,—far from it. It
has cost me much suffering and many heartaches. You spoke*

*of a calamity,—be patient and wait; an avenue of escape,
bordered with fairest flowers, awaits you.*

"Affectionately your friend,

"Hugh,"

After this letter was written, sealed, and addressed to Ethel Horton, Hugh paced the room, weighing the justice of his conclusion. Yes, he believed he had acted honorably.

Notwithstanding the lateness of the hour, he went out and posted his letter to Jack Redfield; then, mounting his horse, he galloped away across the prairie toward Horton's Grove. As he neared the place, he met Mrs. Osborn's turnout, and he noticed, as it passed him, that Lord Avondale accompanied her. Dismounting and hitching his horse, he walked along the winding path, and was fortunate in meeting one of the servants. After securing her promise that the letter would be delivered at once to Miss Ethel, he dropped a coin into her hand and, turning back, was soon riding homeward.

When Ethel had broken the seal and read Hugh's letter, no tears came to her eyes, but, as she put it from her, a stony expression was on her face. "He has no use for the worm-eaten rose," said she to herself, "that's what his letter means. A girl's artificiality is forced upon her in this cold, scheming world. I long to get away from it all. Oh, Hugh, my fancied tower of strength,—you, too, are crumbling. The environments are closing around me. I presume resistance is almost useless. Nothing will satisfy them but a human sacrifice on the altar of a questionable nobility, and a repetition of the old fable of the earthen and iron pots drifting down the stream together."

Mrs. J. Bruce-Horton was looking out of her window and recognized Hugh Stanton as he came up the path. She surmised that he had brought some communication for Ethel, and she determined to make sure before retiring. She rapped at Ethel's door, and, without further announcement, made her appearance in her daughter's room.

"Why are n't you in bed, Ethel?" she asked, stroking the girl's heavy tresses affectionately. "I fear you are not getting sufficient sleep. You look pale, and there are dark circles under your eyes."

Ethel was indeed far from the rosy-cheeked girl of a few months before. She seemed listless and indifferent, as her mother went on. She spoke, in an incidental way at first and then with feverish enthusiasm, of Lord Avondale, and told Ethel how madly in love with her he was.

"Mamma, mamma, please don't!" cried Ethel, burying her face in her hands.

"Why, child, you must not take on so," said her mother, drawing near and attempting to take her in her arms. "Come, Ethel, you must be sensible about this. You should have confidence in my judgment. It is for your good,—really it is."

After a time, Ethel looked up at her mother. Her hot cheeks had dried the tears. Her voice sounded strangely harsh, as she said, "Very well, mamma, make yourself easy; I will do as you wish." There was a sad smile of resignation on the face of the girl as she spoke. She permitted her mother to take her in her arms, and she listened to her expressions of gratitude.

Ethel had surrendered to the wishes of an ambitious mother, whose respect for titled aristocracy exceeded her admiration for independent American womanhood.

The next morning a thin, misty rain began falling. A prayer of thanksgiving was in the hearts of the people. The rain gradually increased and continued a steady downpour all that day and night, and all of the following day. The earth was saturated with refreshing moisture. Then the sun came out, wreathed in smiling gladness. The browned landscape took on a new life. The buffalo-grass, within a few days, was a carpet of living green. The cacti put forth new shoots and spines, and their buds opened into beautiful flowers, as fragrant as the Cape jasmine. The sunflowers lifted their drooping leaves, and bulbs of promise swelled in triumph under the caressing rays of the wooing sun.

No wonder hope sprang up anew in the hearts of the farmers. True their crops were gone,—the country devastated,—but here was nature smiling with promise. To them it was the rainbow of hope, and they began making ready for another seed-time.

CHAPTER XXIX.

JACK REDFIELD ARRIVES

CATTLE Thieving and Its Punishment," was the headline of an editorial written by Maj. Buell Hampton for the *Patriot*. This editorial, perhaps, brought its writer more subscribers from the cattlemen than any other one editorial ever published in southwestern Kansas.

Notwithstanding this article and the wide notice it received, cattle thieving continued. John Horton estimated that he had lost, during the year, fully one hundred thousand dollars worth of beeves, while other cattlemen of less pretensions had also lost heavily.

With a view to popularizing the Barley Hullers, Major Hampton announced through the columns of his paper that he was preparing to issue a general order to all lodges of Barley Hullers bordering on No-Man's-Land, to resolve themselves into committees, and, by a concert of action, annihilate, root and branch, the cattle-thieving cancer that had fastened itself upon the frontier of the Southwest.

Since the country had been devastated by hot winds, cattle thieving had noticeably increased. Major Hampton's duties as district organizer of the Farmers' Alliance, also as a general lecturer of the Barley Hullers' organization, called him away from his home much of the time.

He was perhaps the most resourceful citizen of Meade, and, when not engaged in work that called him away from home, he was actively and energetically endeavoring to advance the interests of his town by advocating policies that he believed to be for the good of the people, and by secretly giving help to the needy. It was a noticeable feet that the farmers in their straitened circumstances, surrounded by ruin and want, became more active than ever in organizing Alliances. Overtaken by a great calamity, they seemed to believe that the laws of both state and nation were seriously at fault. They denounced the money-lender and the coupon-clipper in scathing terms. Day after day they brooded over their misfortunes, nursed their wrath, and swore vengeance against the loan companies and the capitalists to whom they had mortgaged their farms. They forgot that the merchant and the banker who had given them credit were also bankrupts.

In the meantime, the announcement of the betrothal of Ethel Horton to Lord Avondale was heralded throughout the country. Mrs. Osborn may have been responsible for its wide publicity. Hugh was greatly depressed by the turn affairs had taken.

One morning he received a letter from Jack Redfield, which briefly stated that his letter had been received and that he would leave Chicago for Meade the next day. Hugh wondered whether Jack's presence in the Southwest might not now complicate matters more than ever, but he concluded that its possible beneficial results were well worth the trial. "Ethel must be saved," said he; and conscience applauded the declaration. He knew her to be a proud and spirited girl, and, now that her betrothal to Lord Avondale had been announced, he feared she would be actuated by some fancied sense of duty.

That same evening, by invitation, Hugh called at the Osborns. The old captain was not a man easily discouraged. He told Hugh that they must keep the bank doors open at all hazards, and, if possible, never permit the word "failure" to cloud their name.

"We may lose our private fortunes, Hugh, my boy," said he, "but if you have the blood in your veins that your father had, you will care more about protecting your name, and having it said by the world that every depositor was paid in full, than you will for the fortune you have lost."

Mrs. Osborn seemed but little distressed by the captain's financial embarrassment. She was as animated and bewitching as ever in her conversation. Little Harry nestled in his father's arms, and seemed to realize, far more keenly than his mother, that the old captain was engulfed in a perilous position. Hugh wondered, as the conversation went on, if the captain knew what the daring tongue of gossip was saying about his wife and Lord Avondale; but he could not penetrate the calm exterior of his old friend, for nothing was to be read in his bronzed face.

"It may be that we shall have to call upon Lucy for a little money to help us out," said the captain, winking at Hugh.

"Captain," replied his wife, determinedly, "you have hinted several times about appropriating my private fortune to save yourself from bankruptcy, and I want you to understand distinctly that I object. You know I am going to England soon, and do not want to be bothered by having my private means interfered with."

"All right, Lucy, all right," replied the captain, but there was a look of genuine disappointment on his face as he spoke. "We will try to get along without calling on you. You see, Hugh, when Mrs. Osborn and I were married, I made her a present of a hundred thousand dollars in government bonds. I collect the interest and place it in her private account, and keep the bonds securely locked in a strong box in our vault."

"That reminds me, Captain," observed his wife, rather frigidly, "I wish to take my bonds with me when I start for England. I have concluded to deposit them in a New York bank." The captain made no reply.

"When do you expect to start on your European trip?" inquired Hugh.

"In six weeks," replied Mrs. Osborn. "You know Ethel is to be married on the first of September, and we shall start immediately after that notable event. You really must not ask me when I am going to return," she said, laughing coquettishly. "Lord Avondale has extended such a pressing invitation that I have at last yielded.

Mrs. Horton says we may not return for a year."

The next day Doctor Redfield came. His meeting with Hugh was at first a little strained, but soon mellowed into the old-time comradeship.

"Why the deuce, Hugh, didn't you tell me before leaving Chicago, that you were coming to this out-of-the-way frontier town of Meade?" asked Redfield, when they were comfortably seated in Hugh's room at the hotel.

"It certainly was very careless of me not to," replied Hugh, "and I was likewise very neglectful in not writing to you long before I did. You see, Jack, the frontier was like a new world to me—foil of excitement and money-getting. Why, at one time, before the hot winds came, I supposed that I had at least doubled my fortune, and now,—well, let us not talk about it,—it is practically all gone. I shall not care for the lost fortune, however, if I can only in some small way help to bring you and Ethel together. Ah, Jack, she is indeed a fine character."

Doctor Redfield paced the floor in silence for a few minutes. "I never knew the meaning of the word love, until I met Ethel Horton at Lake Geneva," he finally said. "My whole heart was, then and there, given to her. I have been waiting the longest year of my life for the letter that never came—a letter that would tell me to come. The destiny marked out for her by her ambitious mother, I fear, has proved stronger than her love. Really, Hugh, did you ever read a more cruel letter than the one Mrs. Horton wrote me?"

"Let me see it again," said Hugh. "I have a suspicion that Mrs. Horton never wrote that letter."

"What do you mean?" asked Jack, in astonishment, as he handed it to Hugh.

"Just this," replied Hugh, "I have an impression that it was written by Mrs. Osborn. I should like to show this handwriting to Captain Osborn."

"As you like," replied Jack. "But what am I to do? Here I am, within a half-hour's ride of Ethel; have come without her permission, only to learn of her approaching marriage to Lord Avondale. Was ever a man placed in such a trying position?"

"Cheer up, old fellow," said Hugh, good-naturedly. "Come, faint heart ne'er won fair lady—or anything else. We must prevent this widely-published marriage if possible."

"Easily enough said," replied Jack, dejectedly. "Of course," he went on, half jestingly, "we might raid her home some dark night and carry her off into captivity, and then take our chances on a reconciliation."

"Not a bad idea, after all," said Hugh, elevating his eyebrows, "and if we are pushed too closely by the enemy, we may consider the plan seriously. You see, Jack, I would not be quite frank with you did I not confess that at one time I asked Ethel Horton to become my wife." Jack looked at his friend in utter astonishment. "Yes," Hugh went on, "and that is the way I learned of her love for you—a love that you never need doubt. I was dumfounded, for how should I be expected to know that you had ever met her. I finally pulled myself together, however, and sent for you."

Jack took his friend's hand in both his own, and pressed it warmly. "Hugh," said he, "you are a good fellow. The fight is now on, and, with your help, I must and shall win."

They talked far into the night, but this did not deter them from arising early next morning and making ready for a horseback ride. Immediately after breakfast they set out for Martilla, a little village some fifteen miles to the northwest.

"I want to show you Kansas," said Hugh, "and there is no better way for you to meet the people and familiarize yourself with their customs. The recent heavy rain has made the country look habitable again. If the rains had only come before the hot winds, why—we would have had no hot winds, and plenty instead of poverty would now be the farmer's lot, to say nothing of my own condition."

The morning was an ideal one. There was an exhilarating tonic in the soft west winds. Vast herds dotted the prairie. The catde, in their lazy, contented way, went on biting shorter the short, green buffalo-grass.

A little way on, at the side of the road, lay a cowboy reading, while his bronco was near him, munching and browsing. As they drew near, Hugh exclaimed, "Why, it's Seaton Cornwall, my English friend!" They reined their horses and dismounted.

Seaton Cornwall arose from where he had been lying, laid aside his book and came toward them. After an introduction, Doctor Redfield observed: "I see you pass some of your time reading. An interesting novel, I suppose?"

"No, I was reading 'Plutarch's Lives,' replied Cornwall. Since leaving Oxford I have never been able to give up entirely my admiration for some of the old masters, and, notwithstanding my home is on a catde range, I still find great pleasure in keeping up my studies."

"Mr. Cornwall," interposed Hugh, "is one of my earliest acquaintances in Kansas, and, while he is of English birth and a lover of his native land, still, he admires America and American institutions."

"Yes," said Cornwall, "instead of hearing the music of 'God Save the Queen' out here, or even my 'My Country, 'T is of Thee,' I listen to the lowing of herds, the bawl of mavericks, the yelp of coyotes, and the howl of wolves. However, I am not lonely, for I have quite a number of books with me."

"I hope you like America?" Doctor Redfield interrogated.

"Very much, indeed," replied Cornwall. "There are opportunities here which England can never give to her people. I love the land of my birth, I love Englishmen and English ways,—I none the less, however, love democratic America and the opportunities that it affords. We are one race, anyway, speaking a common language and closely allied on all international subjects."

"England," he continued, "is seriously misunderstood by many in America. This misunderstanding is occasioned by adventurers with titles, questionable or otherwise, who do not represent the true sentiment of the mother country. Personally, I believe that a country which affords me a home and protection, and which I have adopted for my own, merits my loyalty and unswerving devotion; therefore, although not an American born, I am in sentiment American, in all that the term implies. Indeed, I have no patience with that class of my countrymen who omit no opportunity to impress upon the people of this country the superiority of England and her people. It is a cockney trait at the best, and does not represent the true sentiments of England toward her American cousins."

"I am delighted at your expressions," said Doctor Redfield.

"That which prejudices Americans against the English," continued Seaton Cornwall, "more than any other thing, is the delegation of adventurers who come to this country to barter their titles for American wealth. Fortunately, they deal with a class of Americans as foolish as they are themselves. Efforts in this direction, both on the part of my countrymen and on the part of Americans, are to be lamented. Indeed, in my opinion, this class of intermarriages engenders more criticism on the part of the masses than any other one thing in this generation, and if this selfish and ambitious, 'barter and sale' custom were abrogated, America and England would entertain still more friendly relations than they do to-day."

When Hugh and Doctor Redfield had taken their leave of Cornwall, the latter returned to his Plutarch. Hugh and Jack, as they rode on, mutually agreed that Cornwall entertained a most sensible view of the existing conditions, and both deplored the Anglomania of the age.

At midday Hugh drew rein and dismounted in front of a dugout home. It was a sample of hundreds in the Southwest, and from the outside had more the appearance of a cyclone cellar than a dwelling.

The owner came out and greeted them warmly, and, with usual western hospitality, insisted that they feed their jaded animals, and share with his family their noonday meal.

"I assure you," said Mr. Redner, "that such as we have you are most welcome to."

The Redner family consisted of Mr. Redner, his wife, a lovely daughter, Miss Lena, and a son whom they called Dick. Their dugout home was furnished with fragments of eastern elegance. A Chickering upright stood in one corner, strangely contrasting with the rude sideboard-table, which was supported by pins fastened in the wall.

The luncheon consisted of corn bread, potatoes, bacon, and coffee. No apology was offered for the meagre fare. It was the best they had.

The Redner family was a representative one. They had emigrated from the East to better their condition, if possible, in the great Southwest. The devastation of the hot winds had reduced them to direst want. Even the absolute necessities became luxuries. This frugality and scant provender was but a link in the great chain of experiences on the frontier. In all their suffering, these people were still happy in anticipation that after awhile the rain belt would creep westward, and that their homestead of 160 acres would yet bless them in their old age.

After luncheon, Hugh and Doctor Redfield bade adieu to the Redner family, and turned their ponies homeward by a circuitous route.

"We will return by a different route," said Hugh, "for it just occurs to me that I want you to see the flowing wells in the Crooked Valley north of Meade."

"This is a new life to me," said Jack,—"the frontier. It has a new meaning to me."

"Yes," replied Hugh, "and, strange as it may seem, I love the frontier. It is true the hot winds have swept away my fortune, and I am penniless. Still, on the frontier one is surrounded by friends different from those one makes in cities,—the great congested centres of our population."

"I deeply regret," replied Jack, "your having come into this inhospitable place. However, old fellow, your coming may be the means of my succeeding in restoring relations with Ethel."

"It must be the means," said Hugh, decidedly. "Really, Jack, I hardly believe you understand the depth and nobleness of Ethel's character."

"Well, Hugh," replied Jack, thoughtfully, "I know she appealed to me as no other woman ever has or ever will. You assure me that she still loves me. This fills me with a determination at least to let her know that my love is the one strong fiber of the fabric in my existence."

"You will not fail, Jack, but if you should—?"

"Ah! if I should," said Jack, energetically, as he looked far away across the prairie, "yes, that is a question to be considered. If Ethel, for any reason, objects to marrying me, excepting for the one reason that she does not love me, I will overcome every obstacle, and carry her away. If, contrary to your belief, her love has been given to another, or she no longer cares for me, I will return to Chicago and devote my life to my profession. True, my sad heart may be reflected in my countenance; but then, you know, a physician's life leads him into scenes of suffering, and it is not strange if sometimes one's surroundings are depicted in one's face, and my patients will interpret my sadness as sympathy rather than a broken heart. After all," mused Jack, "an elastic falsehood by inference is often more impressive than a cumbersome truth indifferently spoken."

For awhile they rode on in silence, when suddenly Jack, in some surprise, exclaimed, "Why, what is that over yonder?" pointing to an agile prairie-dog, and then another, and still another.

"They are prairie-dogs," laughingly replied Hugh. "There may be ten thousand dogs within a radius of half a mile."

"Well, what a novel sight!" exclaimed Doctor Redfield. "I should say there were rather more than ten thousand, than less, and every one of the little fellows sitting up on his haunches in such an observant way." With this, Jack put spurs to his horse, and made a dash toward the nearest prairie-dog, uttering a great whoop as he did so, when, instantly, this army of prairie-dogs disappeared as if by magic into their burrowed homes.

"Well, did you ever!" he ejaculated in wonder at the activity of these little animals.

"Yes," replied Hugh, "they really possess great caution. It is said they migrate in companies from one locality to another, and live principally on roots."

While they were yet talking, a myriad of heads protruded from the doorways of the underground ones, as if sentinels on the lookout for danger, with petite faces turned toward Jack and Hugh.

"Just look at the little fellows," cried Jack, enthusiastically, "hundreds of little heads, and double that number of spying eyes peeping at us in intense wonderment. How I should like to carry some of them back to Chicago with me."

"And deprive them of their liberty?" asked Hugh.

"I forgot," replied Jack, "that you are a sympathizer with the Humane Society."

"I certainly am," replied Hugh. "I would not purposely take the life of a worm. To me the freedom these little prairie-dogs enjoy in the companionship of their mates is very beautiful, and I should be grieved to see even one of them deprived of liberty. Then, too, they are the most hospitable creatures in the world. It is said that a prairie-dog town is the home of as many rattlesnakes and owls as of dogs, all occupying the same underground apartments. Whether they do so willingly or not, I am unable to say. I only know that such a condition prevails, and it is said that they live in perfect harmony."

Jack Redfield insisted upon riding clear through the dog town, and was greatly interested in chasing the dogs, watching their rapid disappearance and then reappearance and the blinking of their bright eyes.

The afternoon was well-spent before they reached Meade. On entering the town they came by the public school building. Through an open window the united melody of a hundred little voices rose and fell in their afternoon exercises before dismissal. They were singing:

"John Brown's body lies a-mouldering in the grave,
John Brown's body lies a-mouldering in the grave."

"Ah," said Jack, as he turned to Hugh, "there is indeed a patriotism peculiar to itself in the great Southwest. I have marveled at your love for the frontier, but why should I, when the very air is redolent with the songs of school children immortalizing the great emancipator, John Brown? I am beginning to have a profound respect for the Sunflower State myself."

"Yes," said Hugh, "it is the birthplace and home of Ethel Horton."

"Ah!" said Jack, looking up quickly, "what magic there is in that name. The good right arm of the breadwinner is strengthened more, my dear Hugh, by an unexpected caress or an encouraging word from loved ones than by all the roast beef in Christendom."

CHAPTER XXX.

THE QUARREL

MRS. HORTON was tireless in her devotion to Ethel. "The poor child," said she to Mrs. Osborn, "needs a change—salt breeze and good old English air again, and then the color will come back to her cheeks."

"How charming it will be," replied Mrs. Osborn, "to see jolly old England once more." She was a little nervous as she spoke, and seemed ill at ease.

She had called at the Hortons', accompanied by Lord Avondale. Ethel begged to be excused, pleading weariness, and remained in her room. The English lord seemed anything but dejected at Ethel's not wishing to see him, and, with his pipe, he strolled leisurely down the graveled walk toward the lake. A sense of proprietorship came to him as he walked back and forth in a contemplative mood. A wedding portion in good government bonds had already been formally agreed upon.

"By Jove! I wish the affair were coming off to-morrow," mused Avondale, as he knocked the ashes from his brier-root pipe and refilled and lighted it afresh. "Those beastly hot winds have left the landscape deucedly barren. The recent rains brightened it up a bit; otherwise it would be unendurable. It's a blooming country, I must say. This little lake and woods surrounding Ethel's home are about the only sights worth seeing." He laughed a little, and repeated the name of Ethel. "It sounds odd, quite odd,— and yet—" He did not audibly finish the sentence, but went on walking and smoking in a most self-satisfied way.

Ethel was in a listless mood. Her betrothal to Lord Avondale, however, while far from her own wish of making, was gradually becoming less terrible to contemplate. After all, it would be a change, and what did it matter? Jack had long ago forgotten her, while Hugh had deserted her at the first test.

In the meantime, a rather animated conversation was going on in the parlors below, between Ethel's mother and Lucy Osborn.

"There is another matter," Mrs. Osborn was saying, "that is unfortunate, to say the least. It has disturbed me quite a little."

"Nothing serious, I hope," exclaimed Mrs. Horton, as she looked anxiously into the pretty face opposite her.

"Not necessarily serious, but very annoying," replied Mrs. Osborn. "Now, don't let it worry you, Mrs. Horton, but Doctor Redfield is in Meade."

"Impossible!" exclaimed Mrs. Horton, in great astonishment.

"Yes, I saw him last evening while driving with Lord Avondale. He was walking down the street with Mr. Stanton. It is rather deplorable that he should have turned up just at this time. There is no mistaking his broad shoulders and blond mustache."

Mrs. Horton was seriously perplexed and noticeably agitated, while Lucy Osborn fidgeted about in her chair, as she remembered the part she had played in Ethel's correspondence. She secretly wondered if Doctor Redfield had preserved that letter written over Mrs. Horton's signature. It made her nervous to contemplate the possibly humiliating results of an investigation. Her almost reckless relations with Lord Avondale placed her in a position, however, that compelled her to go on doing his bidding, until the farce of his marriage to the American heiress was consummated. She was tired, alike, of the spiritless behavior of Ethel and the silly ambition of Mrs. Horton for an English alliance. True, it afforded Lucy Osborn a way of escape from the monotony of frontier life, and, at the same time, placed her on English soil with a firmer footing, she fancied, than ever before, and this thought was milk on which she fed her famishing ambition. That Ethel, in time, would become insanely jealous, or possibly would have ample reason to be so, if appearances counted for anything, she did not doubt. Her self-assurance, however, told her that she could easily call Lenox Avondale to her when his honeymoon with Ethel was over, and her beauty would compel him to be her champion. Another thought slipped in unbidden, and it made her shudder a little; the thought was this,—what would become of her when her beauty of face and figure was gone?

Mrs. Horton assured Lucy Osborn that she would not have a moment's peace until Dr. Jack Redfield had taken his departure.

"My dear Mrs. Horton, I shall be constantly on the watch. Should any letters come, they might seriously complicate our arrangements, unless you intercept them and bring them to me." Mrs. Horton blushed at the remembrance of her unworthy actions in regard to her daughter's letters, and said, "Why, Doctor Redfield has evidently heard before this of the betrothal of my daughter, and he certainly is too honorable to interfere."

When Mrs. Osborn and Lord Avondale were driving away from the Grove, he turned and asked her, rather brusquely, "Why did Miss Ethel refuse to see me?"

"Indeed, Lenox, I did not see her myself."

"I will teach her, after we are married, that it is contrary to the canons of good form to go moping about and wearing that bored expression." As he finished speaking, he gave the horse a stinging cut with his whip.

"Her actions are not very commendable,—in fact, rather disagreeable," replied Mrs. Osborn.

"Stop!" said Lord Avondale, bluntly; "please have the kindness to say nothing of a disparaging nature concerning the future Lady Avondale. I will not permit it. Ethel is a noble woman, with a virtuous and wholesome air of purity about her."

"Oh, how delicately considerate you are," replied Mrs. Osborn, piqued and stung by his brusque words and manner.

"Do you doubt my estimate of her?" asked Avondale.

"No, I do not," replied Mrs. Osborn, rather spiritedly, "but I certainly doubt your being worthy of her. In fact, I know you are not."

"Take care, don't go too far, Lucy!" exclaimed Lord Avondale, coloring with anger. "I do not claim to be a paragon of virtue, but you invited me to dishonor. You would make any man doubt the goodness of womankind."

"It is false!" cried Lucy Osborn, while a dangerous anger flashed from her eyes. "A man who has made vows to as many women as you have, hesitating until invited to dishonor! Bah! Lenox, you weary me with your mock piety. That you should turn against me, after all my sacrifices and devotion, now that you have secured the promise of Ethel Horton to become your wife, proves you to be a contemptible toward, and destitute of chivalry or any sense of gratitude."

"Come, come, my dear Lucy," said Avondale, in a conciliatory tone, "you are a very clever woman; indeed you are, and have been quite invaluable to me. Do not be so hasty as to accuse me of ingratitude. I fancy you are trying to quarrel with me now for a purpose."

"Indeed?" said Mrs. Osborn, haughtily. "Who commenced the quarrel, pray? And what object could I have in quarreling with you?" The carriage stopped before the Osborn home as she ceased speaking.

"I asked you this morning for an additional loan of a hundred pounds," said Lord Avondale, "but as yet I have not received the favor."

"And I am not at all sure that you will," replied Lucy Osborn, disdainfully, as he handed her from the carriage. Lord Avondale, lifting his hat, bowed low, while Mrs. Osborn turned stiffly away and disappeared through the doorway of her home.

CHAPTER XXXI.

THE PASSING OF LORD AVONDALE

REACHING the privacy of her room, Mrs. Osborn threw herself into a chair and cried. She felt relieved afterward and thought how foolish it was of her to have quarreled with Lord Avondale. Unlocking a small drawer of her writing-desk, she fondly scrutinized, with an absorbing and passionate glance, a late photograph of the blasi Englishman.

"Yes," she said aloud, "I was very rude to Lenox. But I will make amends. He shall come to-night, and we shall be friends again. Of course the dear fellow can have the money for which he asked."

Drawing some writing material toward her, she wrote the following letter:

"My own dear Lenox:—I am so sorry that we quarreled to-day. No, it was not your fault, but all my own. When I think of you, and how much we have been to each other, I wonder that I could ever have spoken so rudely to you. You will forgive me, will you not, dear?

"Oh, Lenox, I forget all else at times in trying to make you happy. You cannot know how much you are to me.

"Come to-night at eleven. I will admit you at the side door of my room. Will have the money you requested.

"With my heart's best love, I am, all your own, Lucy."

Laying the letter aside, she wrote a note to her husband, enclosing her personal check for five hundred dollars and requesting him to bring the currency that evening. Glancing at her watch, she saw that it was almost four o'clock. Addressing two envelopes, one to Lord Avondale and the other to her husband, she hastily enclosed the letters and rang for her maid, requesting her to deliver them at once.

"I want the captain's letter handed to him before the bank closes. Call at the bank first, and afterward on Lord Avondale at the hotel. If he is out, push it under the door of his room."

The maid hurried away, and Mrs. Osborn turned to her toilet, determined to surpass herself, in point of beauty and fascinating allurements, when Avondale should call that evening. It was a question whether it was adoration or adorers that she courted most.

It was scarcely four o'clock when one of the bank clerks informed Hugh that Captain Osborn wanted to see him in his private room. As Hugh entered the apartments of the president, he noticed that his old friend was under a strain of great excitement. His face was very white and his hands trembled.

"Close the door, Stanton," said Captain Osborn, with forced calmness. "Perhaps you had better turn the key. I have something of a very private nature to talk to you about."

Hugh complied with his requests, and, as he seated himself, Captain Osborn handed him his wife's letter. "You will observe," said he, "the envelope is addressed to me. Please read the letter carefully."

As Hugh perused the billet-doux, he discovered that clever Mrs. Osborn had at last entrapped herself, and, by mistake, had enclosed the letter for Avondale in the envelope addressed to her husband.

"My old friend," said Hugh, after he had read the letter to the end, "I am not only heartily sorry for you, but I stand ready to do your bidding in any way within my power." He held out his hand, which Captain Osborn grasped eagerly.

"Ah, Hugh," he replied, huskily, "there are many sorrows in life, but those which have to do with the heart cause the most suffering. Happiness at best, where a woman is concerned, is usually coextensive with our ignorance. Do not think that I have been entirely blind in the months past. We all have sorrows, but it really seems to me that I have had my heart-strings tugged at rather more than my share. I should have killed that scoundrel of a fortune-hunter months ago; I would have done so, had it not been for little Harry,—poor little chap, I love him so tenderly that I don't want the blot of murder on his family name,—it is not fair to bequeath dishonor to such a loving little fellow." Hugh hardly knew what to say, the captain seemed so noble, so deserving of respect and pity. Presently he said: "Had we not better secure the letter written by your wi—Mrs. Osborn to you? It might help us to act more intelligently."

"That's right, Hugh, do not speak of her as my wife," replied the captain. "I told you once that my wife could do no wrong; neither can she, for a woman ceases to be a wife when she dishonors her marriage vows. Go to the hotel and secure the other letter, if possible. I shall be very impatient for your return."

Hugh left Captain Osborn alone in his room, and half an hour later returned.

"I found this letter, Captain, pushed partly under Lord Avondale's door," said he.

"It is Mrs. Osborn's writing," said the captain, as he scrutinized the superscription. "A military necessity compels me to open it," he continued, and, after glancing it over, he handed it to Hugh. "Cash the check, and bring me the currency," he said.

When Hugh returned to the room, the captain placed the money in his pocket, and then enclosed the Englishman's letter in the envelope addressed to him, saying, "Seal it as carefully as you can, and push it under the door of his room at the hotel. I want the titled scoundrel to keep his appointment!"

It was after eleven o'clock that night when Captain Osborn, who had ever been most considerate and deferential to his wife, admitted himself with his private key to her boudoir, without ceremony. The pretty little room was brilliantly lighted. Mrs. Osborn and the Englishman occupied a dainty settee, a rare creation of a French upholsterer. Their faces were partially turned from the door through which the captain entered. Before them, on a small, richly-carved table, was a basket of fruit, some cake, and a bottle of wine.

"Pardon me for intruding," said the captain, in a cold, metallic voice. With one startled impulse they turned, and saw standing before them the wronged husband.

"What, you here, Captain!" exclaimed his wife, angrily, "and unannounced? Why, how dare you, sir; how dare—" She could not finish the sentence. Her eyes fell before the keen, stern look of the old veteran.

"Yes, strange as it may seem, I, your own husband, under his own roof, venture to visit you; a privilege you have not encouraged me in, I admit, but one I insist upon in this instance."

The captain spoke calmly, and, whatever internal emotion he might have felt was concealed behind a cold, gleaming smile of determination and sorrowful triumph.

Avondale permitted his eye-glass to fall from its accustomed place, and started to arise. "Ah, really, sir," said he, "I must be going. It is getting so late, I—"

"Remain where you are, sir!" said the captain, in deep, resolute tones. There was an iron ring in his voice that startled the Englishman. "Late as it may be," the captain went on, "you have been in this room less than fifteen minutes. Subterfuges are unavailing."

Lucy Osborn raised her queenly head, and, with one resentful glance at the old captain, hissed, "Spying on your wife is hardly in keeping with the dignity of a financier."

"I have surrendered dignity, Lucy, in the hope of saving you," replied the captain, calmly.

Her eyes flashed an angry glance at him. "What do you mean?" she stammered. "I don't quite—" She broke off in silence, as her eyes met his sorrowful and yet scornful glance. There was something in the searching gaze of her husband that seemed to read the very secrets of her soul. It stung her proud heart with remorse.

Turning to Avondale, the captain said: "I ought to have killed you long ago, before this liaison with Mrs. Osborn began. I should have shot you to death like some vile cur, d—— you, and would have done so but for my little son."

"I beg your pardon, sir," said Avondale, now thoroughly alarmed. "Really, sir, you are mis-tak—"

"Stop!" cried the captain, fiercely, "do not add to your dastardly crimes by lying. I know all. Give me the letter—the one which Mrs. Osborn wrote you this afternoon—in which she promised to give you some money."

Lord Avondale seemed to shrivel up before the captain's emphatic demand. He nervously fumbled the letter from his pocket. The captain unceremoniously took possession of it.

"Really, sir," stammered Avondale, "I am only a man, not a saint, you know, and these improprieties with Mrs. Osborn can hardly be considered as any fault of mine." Mrs. Osborn turned toward her paramour, and a look of disgust flitted across her face. It began to dawn upon her that he was an arrant coward.

"Adam attempted to lay the blame on the woman in the Garden of Eden," shouted the captain, in anger. "You, perhaps, are a gentleman by birth, but you are an infernal wretch by practice. Titled you may be, but at heart you are betrayer of the virtue of a weak woman. The nobility at your hands is a prostituted aristocracy; your admiration and attentions are an insult to all good women. Return to the shores whence you came, you contemptible scoundrel, and never again set foot on free America's soil. Your mission was one of adventure and fortune-hunting. Release that noble girl, Ethel Horton, from the promise of marriage which you and your coterie of damnable conspirators have forced and inveigled her into making, or, by the Eternal, your bones shall bleach in Dead Man's Hollow! Will you do this?"

"Yes, indeed—certainly," stammered Lord Avondale, who was shaking from head to foot in cowardly fright.

"Then go!" fairly yelled the captain, "cur that you are, and, if you value your worthless life, never let me look into your licentious face again. I will look for you to-morrow morning at sunrise, and if I find you in this part of the State, by the living God, your life or mine shall pay the penalty."

CHAPTER XXXII.

THE SILENCING OF GOSSIP

WHEN Lord Avondale had gone, Captain Osborn turned mechanically toward his wife. She stood before him, defiant and beautiful, like a tigress at bay, without defense or chance of escape. "Lucy," said he, in resolute and yet sorrowful tones, "my very soul revolts at you. A pretty-faced woman whose purity is questioned is like a rose broken from its stem. We cannot use the one as a decoration and dare not trust the other as a companion."

She started to speak, but he motioned her to silence.

"Explanations," he continued, "are unavailing. Should you attempt to explain, you would but stultify the wife that I once knew and loved, and sink yourself still deeper into the quagmires of shame and dishonor. I have not been ignorant of the fact that the wagging tongues of scandal have for months proclaimed the liaison of which you are guilty. Yes, I have been silent while brooding over your shame, and yet, Lucy, I have suffered the tortures of hell. For the sake of my son, I had hoped that you would leave the Southwest forever; and I had arranged that a letter should follow you to England, requesting you never to return to further disgrace my name. In that letter I had expected to express all that I am now saying. Your marriage vows at the holy altar have been made a football of convenience to shield your wickedness under the protection of my good name. You have brought disgrace not only upon your family, but even upon the very name of wifehood and womanhood."

The face of Lucy Osborn was indeed a study. Her haughtiness melted away before the ringing words of the old captain. She tried in vain to regain her self-control.

"Lyman, Lyman," she finally sobbed, clasping her jeweled hands together, "this chastisement is worse than death." She sank to the floor in humiliation. "Oh, that I were dead," she moaned. "Lyman, Lyman, what will become of me?"

The captain was visibly affected. A stifled sob seemed, for a moment, almost to shake his resolution.

"Lucy," said he, "you are true to your selfish instincts even in your utter wretchedness. Self-love prompts you to inquire as to your fate rather than to consider the effect that your tarnished name will have on our little son,—to say nothing of myself. I have a question to ask. Was that letter to Doctor Redfield sent at Mrs. Horton's request or with her knowledge?"

"No, no, she was quite ignorant of my having sent it." Mrs. Osborn arose from the floor, where she had thrown herself in anguish. Approaching her escritoire, she unlocked a small drawer, and, in a hopeless endeavor to mend the luster of a dimmed diamond, she handed the captain four letters,—one addressed to Doctor Redfield and three addressed to Ethel Horton. The captain put them in his pocket.

"You ask," said he, "in regard to your future. I have considered this question carefully since receiving that misdirected letter this afternoon. It is wonderful what painstaking consideration we can give some questions on a very few hours' notice. Written evidence of the black passionflower of your choice is now in my possession. I have but one course to suggest. Your friend, the adventurer, is such a contemptible coward that I doubt not he is already on nis way to Dodge City. You can easily overtake him in New York, by leaving Meade to-morrow. You have your own private fortune, well invested in government bonds. This fortune is quite ample—it is even princely. I will forward your securities to you immediately. To-morrow morning I shall hand you ten thousand dollars, which will be quite sufficient to provide you and also your friend, the adventurer, with the necessities if not indeed the luxuries of life until you receive your quarterly interest. Lucy, I have but one request; in memory of other, sweeter and holier days, give me your promise that after to-morrow we shall never meet again. Your love for Harry, even though you have none for me, now that the blighting sense of shame has swept over your weak and foolish heart, should prompt you to see the wisdom of this."

There was a cold, rasping ring in his voice, denoting unfaltering determination. The interview had evidently cost him great effort and much pain.

"Never, never!" she cried, with hysterical bitterness. "Oh, I loathe the very thought of that man; his name, even, has become a terrible nightmare to me. How could I have been so blind and wicked as to forget your strength and nobility! Lyman, oh, Lyman, my husband, is there no possible way to regain your pity, if not your love? Must I forever be separated from our little Harry? Yes, I shall go away from this home, if you insist, and shall never return, but for God's sake, Lyman, believe me, here on my bended knees before you and before God, when I say that I shall never again willingly look upon the face of Lenox Avondale. Should I meet him by chance, I would not even speak to him. Believe this of me, and all else shall be as you wish."

The captain looked into her tear-stained free, and he saw truth written thereon.

"Lucy, do not kneel to me: kneel to your God."

"God will forgive me," she sobbed, turning her eyes toward heaven, "but, Lyman, you will not."

She arose and came close to him, and gazed sorrowfully up into his face.

"You do not understand me," said the captain. "My pity you already have, although it is worth but little. Pity comes from the heart, and my heart has been made poor with long and bitter suffering."

"But, Lyman, have you no forgiveness for the penitent? Must I go out into the world alone, believing that you will never forgive my sins? I do not ask you to compromise yourself by forgetting them; but, oh, will you not tell me that you forgive them?"

Captain Osborn sighed, as if a scalding tear had fallen down into his withered heart. His eyes rested for a moment upon her, and then he walked thoughtfully back and forth. His just resentment struggled with his innate tenderness of soul. He returned to where she was standing and said, in a low, husky voice, "Lucy, you have sinned against yourself, against me, against our baby boy, and against God; but if your contrition can gain the forgiveness of the Infinite, it certainly should gain the forgiveness of a poor, finite being like myself." He turned away, and for a moment seemed to be struggling for mastery over himself. "Lucy," said he, "our paths from this night must lead in opposite directions; but as I, myself, hope to be forgiven in the world to come, where mortal souls are weighed in the unerring scales of justice, so I, in my poor, weak heart forgive you."

She sobbed aloud in fervent thanksgiving for her escape. "Oh, Lyman, Lyman, my tears are now of joy, rather than of sorrow! I feel regenerated and purified. Your mercy means more than you know." Her countenance grew strangely fair. A halo of light seemed to envelop her. A tear trembled on the cheek of the old veteran as he said, "Good night."

At an early hour of the following morning the muffled stroke of church bells sounded thirty-six times.

Lucy Osborn was dead. A council of physicians said that death had come to her through heart failure, caused by some great mental strain.

The clods that fell upon her coffin sounded a plaintive requiem over the remains of an erring woman. However, they stilled the tongue of gossip. The captain may have been weak in his great forgiveness, but his was a weakness tempered with much mercy.

CHAPTER XXXIII.

A RIDE AMONG SUNFLOWERS

WHEN Mrs. Horton learned of the flight of Lord Avondale and of the death of her friend, Lucy Osborn, she was prostrated with grief and chagrin. The Englishman had sent her a hastily-scrawled note, briefly stating that he released her daughter from their engagement, and that his immediate departure was of the greatest importance.

A few mornings after this, Ethel asked her father if she might go with him on a trip that he had planned to the Cimarron River. "I just feel, daddy," said she, "like taking a wild ride down the valley. It will do me good. Mamma is much improved, and I can go as well as not." The cattle king looked at his daughter with delighted astonishment. "Go? Of course you may," said he. "Why, Ethel, you are beginning to look like yourself again. It will seem like old times to have my little girl galloping over the range with me."

Soon they mounted their horses, and were off for an all-day jaunt. Ethel rode her horse with queenly grace, and, as they dashed along, the color came back into her velvet cheeks, and her face beamed once more with girlish delight. Occasionally a long-eared jack-rabbit would be startled from his cover, and go skipping away like a deer, while Ethel would rein her horse after him in a wild, mad gallop, not with any expectation of overtaking the rabbit, but simply in a spirit of frolicsome excitement.

"Look at the sunflowers, daddy!" exclaimed Ethel. "What a wonderful wealth of them!"

"Yes," replied her father, "the sunflower, you know, is the

emblem of our State. It grows here in generous profusion, and is certainly as emblematic of plenty, for the cattlemen at least, as the seeds of the pomegranate."

As they advanced toward the Cimarron River, the fields of sunflowers grew more plentiful, and finally they found themselves in a veritable wilderness of this Kansas emblem. Hundreds of acres stretched away, thickly peopled with these blazing sun-worshipers, ever turning and following with their queenly heads the course of the king of day. The darkened multitude of seeds, like black-eyed-susans, were encircled with bordering crowns of yellowest gold. The gentle wind stirred them into rythmic melody of motion. Every petal seemed to have caught the sunshine of heaven, and to hold within its gracefully nodding head a warmth of welcome to the visitor. The brown stalks were suggestive of brawny health and strength, while their fanlike leaves presented an unrivaled background to the golden grandeur of a waving sea of yellow. They resembled an army of officers with a burnished epaulet on every shoulder.

Then, too, there was a grace in their lithe and willowy undulations expressing a poetry unspoken, which charmed the visitors into admiration and reverence for this floral emblem. Mingled with the beauties of this yellow sheen and graceful harmony, there seemed to be a rare independence and stateliness. A music like the rippling of many waters was suggested by the gently clashing arms and leaves of this wilderness of sunflowers. It was also like an anthem of hope, with liberty as its deathless theme. The soulful music seemed to float lazily, and to rest like a benediction on the shadows beneath the leaves and golden coronets. There was an odor, too, like redolent, languorous ether distilled by the alchemy of Nature, wooing the visitors away from the cares, the trials, the heartaches and the regrets of the great, harsh world.

Here amid the stately sunflowers, bathed in their celestial beauty, with the radiance of the sun deftly gathered and crystallized into crowns of glory, like hammered gold, the vexations of life and its trials were forgotten. The onlookers were lifted into a realm of ecstasy where songs without words abound. O gorgeous sunflower, incomparable in thy beauty, unequaled in thy queenliness, surpassing in thy stateliness, glorious in thy radiance, emblematic of freedom, liberty, and deathless love of justice! Indeed thou art the worthy emblem of a land of freedom, of a commonwealth asserting and establishing "man's humanity to man." The rose has its beauty and transcendent fragrance, the hyacinth its charm of color, the columbine its mountain freshness, the lily its stateliness of poise, the dandelion its golden warmth, the daisy its modesty, the honeysuckle its vining tendrils of love; but amid all the realm of the flowery kingdom, thou alone hast robbed the sun of his prismatic rays, and heaven hath crowned thee with a golden sceptre of everlasting superiority and imperishable majesty.

"Oh, daddy," exclaimed Ethel, "what a gorgeous forest of flowers. I feel lost in admiration. I am prouder than ever, daddy, indeed I am, of being an American girl and a daughter of Kansas, that has the beautiful sunflower for its emblem."

It was past noon when they dismounted for dinner at one of Mr. Horton's ranch-houses on the banks of the river. They did not start on their return trip until late in the afternoon. When the sun had disappeared behind the horizon, they were still several miles down the valley from Horton's Grove. Their road lay along the banks of the Manaroya, whose cool, purling waters talked incessantly in their flight.

They had reined their horses into a walk.

Ethel had become communicative, and, as she talked and laughed, her father was delighted; indeed, the cattle king was in a humor to be pleased with whatever Ethel might do or say. He told himself that the day had been a treat such as he had not enjoyed since Ethel went away to school.

"Do you know, daddy," said she, "that I am really glad Lord Avondale has gone."

Mr. Horton had not expected that his daughter would refer to the painful subject. "Well, Ethel," said he, "I am glad to see that you are not cut up about it, although I expected you would be from what your mother said."

"Not a bit, daddy; I did not love him. Could you not see that I was unhappy? But it seemed that there was no escape. Don't look so scared, daddy, or I won't talk to you." Her silvery laugh floated away on the soft night winds, and John Horton tried to disguise his surprise.

"I don't say, Ethel," said he, "that it would not have been a great trial to me for you to have gone so far away. I thought it was your wish, however, and you know I am ready at all times to sacrifice all the beeves on the range to add to your happiness."

"I don't care to speak disrespectfully of any one, daddy, but I will say that mamma was not to blame as much as others, in this foolish ambition to have me wedded to a title. I am not the sort of American girl to value old English laces and bric-`-brac, simply because they are old."

"How about your brain-worker, Ethel, that you once told me of?" asked her father, timidly.

"That's just it, daddy, I love him and can't stop. I wrote him that you were on our side and told him to come, but he never answered my letter." She sighed wearily, and her voice was plaintively low. "Well, I've had a great day," she went on, "and here we are at home again."

As the father and daughter dismounted and walked up the terraced lawn toward the house, he said, "My little girl, you have made me very happy by giving me your confidence, and, under all circumstances, remember that I am, as you put it, always and forever on your side."

She pressed his hand affectionately. "All right, daddy," said she, "I may put your promise to a severe test before long."

As they mounted the steps that led to the wide veranda, they found Mrs. Horton comfortably seated in an easy chair, entertaining Hugh Stanton and another gentleman.

"Why, Mr. Stanton!" exclaimed Ethel, advancing and bidding

him welcome, "you are such a stranger at the Grove that I hardly knew you in this uncertain light."

Mr. Horton grasped Hugh's hand warmly. "At some other time," said he, "I shall insist on your giving an account of yourself, and explaining your long absence from our home."

The girl stood face to face with Hugh's friend.

"Ethel," said he, with trembling voice, "can you not bid me welcome?"

"Oh, Jack!" cried she, advancing and placing both her hands in his, "a thousand welcomes. How surprised and glad I am to see you."

The touch of her hands and the responsive message of love from her eyes were more than Dr. Jack Redfield could stand. He caught her quickly in his arms and tenderly kissed her willing lips. Mrs. Horton was engaged for the moment in a conversation with Hugh, and had not noticed Ethel's greeting of Doctor Redfield. Not so, however, with her father.

"Oh, daddy," said she, turning to him, "come and welcome Jack—I mean Doctor Redfield. He is my—my brain-worker; don't you remember?"

"Welcome, thrice welcome, Doctor Redfield," said Mr. Horton, cordially, as he extended his hand with all the warmth of greeting of a frontiersman.

That night when Hugh and Doctor Redfield were gone, Ethel excused herself and went to her room. She was humming an old love-song as she left the veranda, and seemed as lighthearted as some bird that had suddenly gained its freedom from a caged bondage.

"Ethel seems to be very contented and happy over her ride," observed Mrs. Horton.

"I fancy, my dear, that there are other reasons," replied her husband.

"Indeed, how is that?" asked his wife. John Horton replied by inquiring about Doctor Redfield.

"Oh," said Mrs. Horton, "Doctor Redfield is a Chicagoan. He

was my physician at Lake Geneva, and for awhile I feared that Ethel really cared for him."

"And if she had?" observed Mr. Horton, interrogatively.

"Oh, Doctor Redfield was recommended very highly, professionally and otherwise," replied his wife, "but you know,—well, Lucy and I had planned it differently." She spoke in a slow and hesitating manner. Mr. Horton made no reply. Presently she said, "The death of Mrs. Osborn has been a great shock to me. I cannot bring myself to believe those shameful rumors about her and Lord Avondale; I really can't."

"My dear wife," replied Mr. Horton, with more firmness than was usual with him, "it is proper to let the dead rest in peace. The atmosphere of strict propriety, as a matter of fact, bristled with interrogation points, though unknown to you. Mrs. Osborn's death, however, calmed all into silent and mute forgiveness. It is best that it should be so. I do not regard it as strange that you should have been deceived by the machinations of a clever woman and of a consummate scoundrel. Avondale was a mercenary adventurer, and used his newly acquired title as a social 'jimmy' to break into the sanctity of our home. Let us be truly grateful for Ethel's escape. That is one reason, I imagine, why she is so happy to-night."

"And pray, do you think there are other reasons?" asked Mrs. Horton, apprehensively.

"There is one other reason," replied her husband, "that I know of. Ethel is in love with Doctor Redfield. I have so much confidence in her judgment that I cannot question the wisdom of her choice. Her wishes and happiness, my dear, must be paramount to all else."

Mrs. Horton had never before heard her husband speak so decisively about Ethel, and it began to dawn upon her that she had been cruelly deceived by Mrs. Osborn and Lenox Avondale. Even Ethel had not confided in her as a daughter should. It was too much for Mrs. Horton, and genuine tears filled her eyes. In her ambition for her daughter's place in society, she felt she had been imposed upon, and it cut her deeply.

"Come, come, my dear," said her husband, observing her tears, "I am sure Ethel does not blame you. She thinks, and, I believe, rightly, that you have been imposed upon by those far more designing than it was possible for you to imagine."

A little later Mrs. Horton rapped at the door of her daughter's room. Ethel's face was flushed with the joy of her great love for Jack. He had given her the letters that had been intercepted by Mrs. Osborn, and also the letter purporting to have been written by her mother. She knew the handwriting, and imagined that her mother was ignorant of the intrigue that had kept Jack from her so long. As Mrs. Horton entered the room, Ethel saw traces of tears on her cheeks. The stately woman came close to her daughter and caressed and kissed her affectionately.

"Oh, Ethel, my child, why did n't you tell me that you cared so much for Doctor Redfield?" Ethel was astonished. She looked up at her mother and saw the old-time tenderness divested of all ambition. "Oh, mamma," she cried, resting her head gently upon her mother's breast, "I have so often wanted to, but you would n't let me. I can tell you to-night," she sobbed, "for you are again the mother I knew before I went away to that horrid London school."

Jack Redfield and Hugh were almost too happy for sleep, and talked far into the night, laying plans for Jack's future. It was a bright moonlit night, and Jack Redfield declared, with a lover's enthusiasm, that it was his reciprocated affection for Ethel that was turning the night into day,—a reflex glow of his deathless love lighting up the world.

The next morning when Hugh went to the bank he found Judge Lynn waiting for him. The latter pushed his hat well back on his head, as if in a sort of desperate and determined mood, and said: "Look 'e 'ere, Stanton, I want to borrow a thousand dollars. What's banks for, anyway? I am 'lowin' if you're doin' a bankin' business, you nachally want to loan money. Is n't that so?"

Hugh replied that it was if the bank had money to loan and the borrower had proper security.

"Well," said the judge, "I want to borrow a thousand dollars."

"What security have you to offer?" asked Hugh, looking up from his bank ledger.

"My own name, sir; jist the individual name of Linus Lynn," said the judge. "Speakin' deep down an' continuous-like, I am thinkin' my own personal'ty is good enough for a thousand any day; bet yer life."

Hugh looked up and saw that the judge was in earnest. After a moment he said, "Well, Judge, I am only the cashier of this banking-house, and I would rather refer important matters of this kind to the president. Now, if you had time to wait a little while, until Captain Osborn comes in, I will mention the matter to him. Understand, Judge, personally I would like very much to accommodate you. Can you wait?"

"Can I wait? Well, if you think I can't, you're strugglin' in the coils of error. I should say I could. Hav' n't a suit on the docket that's half as important as tendin' to this here little bankin' matter." With this, the judge tucked his thumbs in the arm-holes of his vest, crossed one foot over the other, and leaned his back against the railings of the bank—and waited.

Captain Osborn came in, and Hugh, giving him a knowing look, stated Judge Lynn's wishes.

"Well," said Captain Osborn, "I have no objections, personally, that I know of, but we usually have security."

"Now, look 'e 'ere, Captain," said the judge, "I'm assoomin' that a note with my name signed to it is jist 'bout as good as a gover'ment bond, and don't you furgit it. I've never borrowed a dollar in this 'ere bank in my life, and there is no use talkin', I have jist got to have the money or I'll be plumb locoed."

"Well, Judge," said the captain, laughing softly to himself, "if you can wait until we talk with Mr. Edward Doole, our vice-president, we will see what can be done for you. He will be here in a few minutes, and I would rather defer to his judgment in passing upon loans, once in awhile."

"All right, Captain," said the judge, "I'm 'lowin' I can wait jist as well as not,—bet yer life I can."

When the vice-president came in, Hugh, with a forewarning nod, explained to him Judge Lynn's wants.

"Well," said Mr. Doole, "you are the cashier and Captain Osborn is the president. I should think, if you do not wish to assume the responsibility of loaning the judge a thousand dollars on his individual name, that you had better refer it to the directors. I understand we are to have a directors' meeting this forenoon."

"Mr. Vice-President," said the judge, as he shut one eye and looked intently at Mr. Doole, "I'm not projectin' 'round here for fan, an' I'd like to ask, how do you feel person'ly 'bout lettin' me have the money? That's the question I'm hankerin' to have answered pow'rfal quick."

"Personally? Oh, personally," said Mr. Doole, hesitating a moment, and catching a mischievous twinkle in Captain Osborn's eye, "I would like to let you have it, of course."

"Very well," said the judge, with a flourish of his greasy coat-sleeve, "I'll jist wait till you-alls, as directors of this financial institootion, pass jedgment. Oh, I've got time to spread 'round profase-like; I'm in no hurry; bet yer life, I ain't."

The directors had been in session but a short time when Hugh Stanton was delegated to report adversely to Judge Lynn's application. Coming out of the directors' room, Hugh said, "Say, Judge, the directors have looked over the bank's business and have concluded that we are pretty well loaned up, and they do not care to increase our discounts, especially since the country has been burned up with the hot winds and collections are very hard to make. A little later—next week or next month, you know—things may be different. Well, good-day, Judge."

"Not quite so fast, Stanton," said Judge

Lynn, "I'm not stampedin' yit; I am sort of a stayer, I am, an' I'm assoomin' I'll not be satisfied till I speak jist a word an' onboosomin' myself like to the board of directors."

"All right," said Hugh, "step in," and, with this, Judge Lynn was ushered into the directors' room.

He struck an attitude of great dignity, thrusting one hand deep into his waistcoat, and, with the other resting upon his hip, he said, "Gentlemen, you-alls 'll pardon me, but I'm desirin' to jist ask two or three questions."

The directors nodded their heads, as much as to say, "Go on."

"Captain Osborn," said the judge, "did n't I onderstand you to say that person'ly you'd like to 'commodate me with the loan of a thousand dollars?"

"I believe I did," replied the captain.

"Mr. Vice-President," said the judge, turning to Mr. Doole, "did n't I onderstand you to say that person'ly you'd no objections to loanin' me the money?"

"I think I made such an observation,—yes!" replied Mr. Doole.

"Stanton," continued the judge, with awful seriousness, "is n't it a fact that you said you'd be glad to 'commodate me if it was a personal matter of your own?"

"Yes, I think I said something like that, Judge," replied Hugh.

"Well, gentlemen, person'ly each and every one of you would like to 'commodate me, but collectively you've turned me down; is n't that 'bout it?"

The directors nodded their heads.

"But you see—" said the captain.

"Never mind, Captain," interrupted the judge, "explainin' don't count. Here's what I want to say to you-alls. I jist want to say that person'ly I think you're a mighty nice lot o' fellers, but collectively I'm assoomin' you're the darndest lot of skates I ever run up agin'."

And, with this parting shot, the judge hastily left the room, muttering dire vengeance against bloated bondholders and coupon-clippers.

CHAPTER XXXIV.

THE PRAIRIE-FIRE

AKANSAS prairie is a veritable inland sea. From Meade to the northwest a broad expanse of buffalo-grass lands stretched away for many miles, almost as level as the top of a table, without even a single gully or rill to break its tiresome monotony. Often, at night, I have walked along some quiet roadway far into the country, listening to the silence that enveloped me. Sometimes the very air that, seemingly, pulsed with monotonous stillness, would be startled by the sharp, quick bark of a wolf in the distance. I have looked out across these flat table-lands, dimly lighted by the moon in its last quarter, and for hours watched half-formed shadows of passing clouds flit vaguely on across this vast sea of silence, while others followed in countless numbers, until vision became confused and imagination triumphed over knowledge. At such times, in fancy I stood on the beach of a mighty ocean, and each shadow was a sable-shrouded sail-boat carrying my hopes away to some unknown shore of mystery.

The hot winds had dried and browned the buffalo-grass. Then the rain came and freshened the landscape into a new life. Several weeks of warm, windy weather had now intervened. The country was becoming parched and dry again. The thick, matted buffalo-grass was cured as effectually as is the Eastern farmer's hay when it is cut into swaths and dried before it is bunched into windrows. It, however, retained its nutritiousness. Indeed, it was said to be more fattening for the vast herds of cattle than prior to the hot winds.

One afternoon a thin line of smoke was discernible afar in

the western horizon. It seemed like a black ribbon reaching from No-Man's-Land, on the south, to the sand-hills, a distance of almost a hundred miles to the north. These remarkable mounds of sand, in width from five to fifteen miles, border the Arkansas River on its south bank. They separate the river from the table-lands lying farther to the south. To the inexperienced observer, the dark border in the western horizon had more the appearance of dust-clouds, caused by innumerable whirlwinds, than of smoke, but the older frontiersmen recognized in the menacing dark border, a prairie-fire.

As Hugh Stanton was walking along the street, his attention was called to this distant cloud, by Judge Lynn.

"I say, Stanton," said he, "do you see that line of smoke? Onless I don't know a thing or two, the cattlemen will have to shift their herds to a new range. You bet yer life they will. Reckon I knows a thing or two."

"Why, is that smoke?" asked Hugh. "Looks like a whirlwind of dust to me."

"Yes, sirree, that's smoke, and one of the tarnallest, biggest prairie-fires is ragin' over there that ever scorched dry buffalo-grass. Things'll be sizzin' hot 'round here soon. You bet I know what I'm talkin' 'bout."

Hugh gazed intently while the Judge was speaking, and then observed, "Well, if it were n't so far away I should like to drive over and see a genuine prairie-fire."

"See a prairie-fire! Why, dang my buttons, man, I'm lowin' you 're liable to see enough prairie-fire afore mornin' to last you the rest of your nach'al days. You bet if it once gets started this way things'll be poppin' 'round here, an' the whole country will be locoed."

"Why, how so?" asked Hugh. "That dust line, or smoke, or whatever it is, must be fully a hundred miles away."

Lynn laughed in derision. "Gee, Stanton, not speakin' onfeelin' or careless-like, but you're tender. You're dead easy. 'Course it's a hundred miles away, maybe more, but if the wind gets a-comin' an' a-blowin' this way, you'll see the all-firedest time in these diggin's you ever heerd tell of, an' somethin' mighty thrillin' will happen. You bet I'm not 'round makin' a virtue out of duty, but, speakin' onrestrained-like, every able-bodied man'll have a duty to perform if that fire gets to racin' this way, an' I'm not assoomin' any spechul knowledge in sayin' it. I reckon I can tell a fire when I see smoke, an' there's no misonderstandin' 'bout that."

It was not long until several hundred townspeople were on the street, discussing the great prairie-fire that was raging in the western counties. Some of the more timid expressed alarm, but the majority had never experienced a Kansas prairie-fire, and even in the dullest soul there was a pronounced novelty in anticipation of so grand a sight.

The smoke-cloud grew blacker and thicker near the earth, and gradually rose higher and higher. A strong wind set in from the west, and, before five o'clock, the ominous-looking pillars of smoke had so dimmed the sun that it appeared like a great shield of bronze. The earth was overcast with a yellow, subdued light; and the winds in their onward sweeping seemed surcharged with presentiment—burdened with dread. To the onlookers it did not seem possible that danger to them lurked in this unchained fire demon, so far away. Some one suggested that it might be well to plow furrows around the western limits of the town, and back-fire, but he was quickly laughed into silence for his fears. The increasing throng seemed to enjoy a scene that all the while was growing plainer and grander in the western horizon.

It was perhaps eight o'clock that night when the residents of Meade discovered a thin glow of fire cutting the dark belt near the earth, like a blood-red sickle. The line reached for miles from north to south. The sight was novel and inspiring. The rapidly-moving smoke-clouds, in their spiral twistings, had floated far to the east, and they now presented an appearance as spectacular as an aurora borealis. Great, reddened banks of clouds mounted almost to the zenith, while on either side were interspersed columns of rolling smoke of inky blackness.

The people ceased jesting now, for the scene was awe-inspiring. A stillness fell over the assemblage. Presently the rumble of wagons was heard on the different country roads leading into Meade. The country folks had taken alarm, and, with well-filled wagons containing their more valuable belongings, were hastening away from their lonely dugouts to the protection of the town.

Some of the townspeople were inclined, at first, to jeer at the fears of the farmers and ranchmen; but beneath their jeering there had anchored a universal lodestone of depression and apprehension. Arrangements were hastily made to protect the town by back-firing, and by plowing furrows in the prairie sod on its western, southern, and northern limits. Hundreds of willing hands volunteered to do this work. The fireline grew plainer as it continued its eastward advance. The shifting banks of smoke now resembled a seething ocean of tumult. Some of the clouds were as yellow as molten gold, while others appeared blood-stained, and fearful to look upon. The entire western sky was aglow; and even high in the heavens were restless, shifting banks of rose-tinted clouds, that feathered and paled into a fringe of dissolving pink and white.

The streets were crowded with the inhabitants of the surrounding country. By midnight a quiver of fear had shot through every heart, and the weird light of the fire was casting a deathlike pallor over every face. A dull, threatening roar could be heard. The flames were leaping one upon another, like the incoming waves of the billowy deep, ever changing and seething like an army of hissing serpents. Their forked tongues shot high into the emblazoned clouds, fantastically lighting up the landscape.

The hoarse, doleful bellowing of cattle was heard in the distance. A smell of burning grass filled the air with stifling odor. The cattle came nearer, and the sound of their trampling hoofs resembled the sullen mutterings of thunder. A command was given to turn the herds from the principal streets, but it was unavailing. Before the people realized the danger, nearly a thousand beeves, bellowing in stampeded terror, rushed pell-mell through the streets of Meade, horning each other in their fury, and trampling to death any unfortunate who happened to get in their way. They finally corralled themselves in the public square.

Captain Osborn's sonorous voice was heard above the tumult, calling for additional volunteers to help fight the oncoming flames.

Horses were hastily hitched to wagons in which barrels of water were placed. Blankets, old coats, quilts, gunny-sacks, and every conceivable kind of cast-off garments were hastily secured and fastened to hoe and fork handles and poles, to be used by the brave men in fighting the fire. These recruits hastened to the limits of the town, and joined the fire-fighters, who were now begrimed with soot and smoke even beyond recognition. They continued back-firing, but it was practically unavailing. The fire would burn in the buffalo-grass only when going with the wind. The teams and breaking-plows were hastily transferred to a point nearer the town, and here wide, deep furrows were plowed. The firemen then burned the grass between these headlands, but their efforts were to prove futile in checking the sweeping flames.

Then a wildly novel scene occurred. Flocks of prairie-hens, quails, meadow-larks, and thrushes, all blinded, singed, and frightened, began flying against the buildings, many of them falling to the earth either crippled or dead. The entire town echoed with fluttering wings. Wolves, driven from their dens and haunts by the prostrating heat, rushed by the fire-fighters in frantic fright. Soon the town was fairly besieged by these frenzied animals. Their advent seemed to madden the already infuriated cattle, and a general mjlie and warfare to the death ensued. The yelps and barking cries of this bedlam were at once pitiful and terrible. Dozens of wolves were gored to death.

Hundreds of jack-rabbits, their long ears lying flat upon their backs, came bounding in from the burning prairie. The wolves had been intimidated by the sharp horns of the terrified cattle, but now they turned, with many a snarl and growl, upon the rabbits, and killed scores of these helpless habituis of the Great Southwest.

The people had taken refuge in the upper stories, and on the roofs of buildings, to protect themselves from the savage arena below. As the fire drew nearer, and the light and heat became more intensified, a spectral hue fell over the blanched faces of all.

A suffocating fear, far exceeding even that of the hot winds, enveloped the beleaguered town of Meade. The situation was desperate. The flames, in their maddened fury of triumph, were rushing on the wings of the wind toward their defenseless victims. The brave battalion of firefighters was forced to retire in haste before the stifling heat. The western fronts of the buildings were as light as noonday, while to the eastward the long shadows danced, grew less distinct, and then darkened, as the scarlet smoke rose and fell, producing strange and weird phantoms.

The rapidly-gliding columns of smoke, resting "one upon another—one upon another," seemed to have ignited and become a surging sea—a pyrotechnical display of fire waves. A few buildings on the outskirts caught fire from the great heat. Millions of flying sparks, as countless as the stars, filled the air, threatening complete annihilation. The menacing flames were advancing upon their helpless prey with a fierceness that seemed to partake of hellish glee. The cries of rabbits, the yelps of coyotes, the moaning howl of wolves, the frantic roarings of cattle, and the wail of hysterical and fainting women,—all produced the wildest pandemonium. Above this terrible tumult could be heard the hissing, crackling, seething laugh of the undulating, death-dealing labyrinth of flames,—on they rushed, in awful fury. Extinction seemed imminent. The burning buildings were already crumbling into charred ruins; while others were being enveloped with roaring, swirling sheets of fire. Like prophets, they seemed to be foretelling, by example, a certain destruction. The cattle, the wolves, the jack-rabbits and the people, were alike demoralized and stampeded by an overpowering fear.

The fire now advanced like a line of molten lava. On, on it came, to the very limits of Meade. Man and beast seemed about to be offered up on a fiery altar. The cattle moaned a sacrificial dirge. The smothering smoke crept stealthily down through the streets, and suffocation hushed the wail of the people. Like hordes of painted savages, the flames seemed to be brandishing bloody tomahawks, as they rushed at their victims with demoniacal shrieks of exultation.

Then, God smote the rock of deliverance,—a divine hand reached out in infinite compassion. The heavens opened, the rain descended in blinding torrents, the earth trembled with deafening peals of thunder, the lightning pierced the clouds in fearful grandeur, as if the Almighty, in His immeasurable goodness, were hurling an admonition at the flames.

Providence grappled the devouring demon by the throat, as he was in the very act of exulting over an almost certain victory. The fire-king of terror surrendered to an omnipotent decree. Its mighty strength was broken, and what a few moments before had seemed an irresistible artillery of power and defiance became a charnel-house, wrapped in the sable robes of its own defeat. Then there went up a cry from the people, "God lives! Our lives are spared! All praise to the Ruler of the universe!"

When the wreck and ruin had been surveyed in the gray dawn and morning of a new day, these loyal people, with a fortitude unequaled in the history of communities, returned to the burning embers of their dugout homes, and, forgetting the devastation of the hot winds and the calamity of the greatest prairie-fire that had ever swept over the Southwest, they went on loving Kansas,—the land of sunshine and of sunflowers.

CHAPTER XXXV.

A BUCKING BRONCO

THE great fire left nothing in its trail but ruin and hunger. The farmers were, indeed, in sad circumstances. Want and misery were in reality glaring at the people with gaunt and hollow eyes. The spring sunshine and rain had clothed the landscape in brilliant green; the hot winds had changed all, as if by magic, into a world of dullest brown; while the great fire had spread over the prairie a sable robe of ruin. Nor had the fire-king been entirely cheated of the sacrifice of flesh and blood. The brown prairie had been turned into a vast graveyard where suffocated men, horses, cattle, wild animals, and flying things had, alike, been offered up to the insatiable greed of the flames. Side by side lay these half-burned carcasses and bones, telling where the victims had fallen, vanquished in their race for life.

Time, however, would strangely change this field of desolation. Other seasons would come, and here, where blackened embers lay scattered for miles in every direction, new hopes would blossom. Springing up from among these very bones, and enriched by them, would grow the johnny-jump-ups, the daisies, and the dandelions. The plum bushes that grow in straggling bunches along the sand-dunes would again blossom and yield their plenteous offerings of scarlet-red sand-plums. A new carpet of growing green, interspersed with a myriad of rainbow-tinted flowers, would cover these barren plains with a mantle of renewed life and beauty. This hope stimulated the people and robbed their defeat of many remorseful stings.

Major Buell Hampton came to the rescue. In his usual

magnificent generosity, he announced through the *Patriot* that there would be ample assistance for the comfort of all. Arrangements were made for the farmers to drive their teams northward, along the old "Jones and Plummer" trail, to Dodge City, the nearest railroad point, and there load their wagons with provisions for man and beast. In a few days plenty once more blessed the impoverished people.

Major Hampton was ably seconded in his benevolence by John Horton, Captain Osborn, and others.

"I am of the opinion," said Major Hampton, when talking to Hugh Stanton, "that in the crucible of suffering, God separates the dross from the gold. It is necessary to jar men into a realization of 'man's dependence upon his brother man.'.rdquo;

"Every condition that arises, Major," replied Hugh, "brings to light a new phase of your character. You have donated thousands of dollars to these unfortunates, and you should be almost idolized by them for your rare generosity."

"My dear Stanton, let me say to you that praise, even though deserved, is, after all, only flattery. I am not entitled to your complimentary words. To feed the hungry, visit the sick, and clothe the naked is a command from the Supreme Ruler. The only real happiness in the world is in making others happy."

John Horton rode up the street while they were talking, and reported to Major Hampton that a hundred head of beeves would arrive that evening for distribution among the sufferers.

"Well, Stanton, my boy," said the major, "I am going into the country this afternoon, but shall try to see you to-morrow." With this he turned toward the *Patriot* office, leaving Hugh to marvel at this strange man whose liberality to the needy seemed limitless.

In the meantime Mrs. Horton had awakened to a realization that she had been unfairly influenced in many ways by the late Mrs. Osborn.

She now wondered why she had been so blinded. She was a woman of great nobility of heart and of excellent judgment in most matters, and she was beginning to acknowledge to herself that she had committed a great error in her foolish Anglomania ambitions. She seldom did things by halves. Discovering that Ethel was irrevocably in love with Doctor Redfield, she determined to make amends for the miserable daubs she had painted in the stage setting of an unsuccessful English comedy. She therefore wrote at once to Doctor Redfield, assuring him of her unqualified approval of his suit, and urging him to stop at the Grove, as their guest, as long as he remained in the Southwest. This urgent request was supplemented by the rugged and yet whole-souled invitation of the cattle king.

Accordingly, the doctor left Hugh Stanton's rooms at the hotel for the hospitality of Horton's Grove, where he might be with Ethel. Hugh was filled with a keen sense of loneliness when Jack drove away with his fiancie. Her tender eyes shone with a new light when in Jack Redfield's presence. She coaxingly told Hugh that he must come over to the Grove every day, and, if he did not, they would surely send for him.

When they were gone, Hugh turned back to his room, marveling at the transformation in Ethel. Her cheeks glowed with the pink tinge of ruddy health and her lips were like well-ripened cherries, while the whole expression of her youthful face was one of contentment and of hope. "Love is a wonderful thing," said he, as he stood by the window watching the carriage containing Jack and Ethel drive away toward the country. He sighed, muttered something to himself, and turned from the window.

"After all," said he, aloud, "marriage is a mystery, the prelude an illusion decked with ribbons of flattery, the awakening an introduction to the real, where the happiness of each hangs upon the caprice of both; while life, at best, is only a straw blown about on the surface of chance, with the devil ever standing near, beckoning us on to a labyrinth of confusion and misery." Then he thought of Ethel's fair hand, which he had so recently held in his own, and there crept into his soul, as the fanning breath of springtime, a feeling of reverence, loyalty and respect.

The next morning, as Hugh was walking down the street, he

met Marie Hampton. A rich color mounted her cheek at their meeting. "You are quite a stranger," said she, smiling pleasantly. "We have not seen you at our home for more than a week, and papa says you have ceased calling at the *Patriot* office, altogether."

"A friend has been visiting me," replied Hugh, "and I have given him considerable of my time, but that's over with now," said he, with a sigh, "and I shall hope to see more of you and your father, too."

"Oh, has he gone away so soon?" asked Marie.

"No," replied Hugh, moodily, "but he does not need me any longer."

"Indeed?" said Marie, and there was an interrogative accent in her voice.

"Yes," replied Hugh, nervously. "Come, I will walk with you and tell you a romance."

They turned down the street toward Major Hampton's home, and, as they walked along, Hugh told Marie of Jack Redfield's love affair.

"Oh, how romantic!" she exclaimed, when he had finished. "Just like a story in a novel. I am impatient to see Ethel and this hero of hers."

They had reached Marie's home, and she was standing on the veranda, leaning her pretty head, with its wealth of bronzed hair, against one of the supports. Her eyes were resting radiantly on Hugh's face.

"I doubt not," Hugh was saying, "that they are very happy, and I presume it is only a question of time until we shall lose Ethel."

"Papa says he fears you will also go away now that the hot winds have destroyed the crops and the big fire has generally devastated the country."

Hugh shrugged his shoulders. "The greater the pressure, the better the wine." He laughed a little and continued, "The test has been a crucial one. Perhaps I will be compelled to go. When one is conquered, the surrender should be unconditional."

"That might be true of a woman," said Marie, "but a man

should resist."

"And why of a woman more than of a man?" inquired Hugh.

"A man has greater strength," she replied. "A woman is all heart and sentiment, and, while her fortress is a strong one, yet she expects to be conquered, and once she surrenders, she loves no one more than her conqueror."

Hugh thought for a moment and then said, "Yes, I presume that is the rule."

"Not the rule, but the condition," replied Marie.

"But there are rules that govern lives," persisted Hugh. "Do you not think so?"

"Perhaps in a commercial sense, but not in love affairs," said Marie, laughing. "Now what sort of a rule could possibly have governed Ethel and her lover?"

"Certainly a poor one," replied Hugh.

"Are you quite sure, Mr. Stanton, that this Dr. Jack Redfield loves Ethel as a hero in a novel seems to love his fiancie?"

"The illusion seems to be perfect," replied Hugh, smiling.

"Do you believe in love, Mr. Stanton?" asked Marie, demurely.

"Yes, I presume there is such a sentiment," replied Hugh.

"And do you think," Marie went on, "that true love will endure any sort of a test?"

"I do not know, I'm sure," said Hugh.

"Well," persisted Marie, "what is the test of a man's love for a woman?"

"The test," replied Hugh, "of a man's love for a woman?" He looked afar across the valley as if meditatively weighing the question that has perplexed the sages of all centuries. Finally he said, "A man not infrequently lies with reckless prodigality to the woman he truly loves, while to those toward whom he entertains sentiments of indifference he will confess the truth without clothing it with sufficient covering to even hide its nakedness."

"I do not believe in your definition at all," said Marie, with heightened color, "and I look upon rules as the most worthless baggage with which a life can be encumbered. A principle may apply to all conditions, but a rule is narrow; while your idea of love's test is horrid."

Hugh smiled at her philosophy and looked at the blushing girl with increasing interest. "You are quite a reasoner, as well as a genius," said he, "even if you do not agree with my ideas of the test of man's love for woman. May I come tonight and hear you sing and play?"

"You may come," she replied, "and I will play for you a simple little melody,—one I have recently learned. You persist in saying I am a genius; if so, I must be eccentric, and one of my whims is simplicity."

"I like you all the better for your whims," said Hugh, gallantly, and, as he lifted his hat and turned away, he noticed that the compliment had deepened the color in Marie's face.

As he walked along the street, still thinking of his conversation with Marie, he met Bill Kinne-man, riding a bronco. Kinneman called out to him, "Look 'e 'ere, pardner, I thought you agreed not to browse on my range."

"What's the matter with you, Kinneman, anyway?" asked Hugh, angrily.

"Waal, I'll jist tell you what's a-chafin' me, an' makin' me feel a heap careless," replied the cowboy. "You want to keep away from Major Hampton's an' quit foolin' 'round Miss Marie, my wayfarin' friend, or you'll git into a whole lot o' trouble that'll result in yer nach'ally git-tin' uncorked and spilled."

"Oh, is that so?" replied Hugh, contemptuously.

"You bet yer life, it's so," replied Kinneman, "an' speakin' sort o' quick and hostile-like, you've bin stealin' my thunder, an' now you may nach'ally expect to git a dose o' my forked-tongued lightnin'."

"You may do your worst," said Hugh, angrily. "I shall call on Major Hampton and his daughter as often as I like, as long as it is agreeable to them. You are a contemptible whelp at best, and as far beneath Miss Hampton as hades is below heaven, and if she had the faintest suspicion that you aspired to her hand, she would be so incensed at your presumption that she would never speak to you again. Now go on about your business, if you have any, and never again dare speak to me."

Hugh turned on his heel and walked briskly away toward the bank, while Bill Kinneman rode his pony into a side street, muttering dire vengeance.

As Hugh neared the bank he saw John B. Horton riding madly down the street. His fiery bronco seemed to have gotten beyond his control. It reared, pitched, plunged forward, kicked viciously, and pawed the earth. The cattle king sat in his saddle like a born equestrian, but it was evident that he was pretty well exhausted.

Presently the pony started swiftly forward into a mad, breakneck run. When directly in front of Captain Osborn's bank, the mustang suddenly shied, reared into almost an upright position, and then, as its fore feet came down, it "bucked," made a wicked plunge, and kicked high in the air. The onlookers, though accustomed to bucking broncos, were beginning to be alarmed. Another mad plunge, and still another. Suddenly the saddle-girth broke, and Mr. Horton was thrown violently from the pony, his head striking against the curb of the sidewalk. By a strange coincidence, the ugly red scar that Hugh had noticed at their first meeting was cut open by the fall.

Captain Osborn rushed from the bank, and, with the assistance of Hugh and others, the bleeding man was carried into the captain's private room and a physician hastily summoned.

Before the physician could arrive, a report was circulating on the streets of Meade that John B. Horton, the cattle king, had been thrown from a bronco and killed.

CHAPTER XXXVI.

A STARTLING REVELATION

FAR into the night John Horton lay in an unconscious condition, between life and death. The physician characterized the wound as an ugly one, and expressed great doubt as to the outcome. Agreeable to his advice, it was thought best not to move the patient for a few hours at least; and a comfortable cot was provided, on which he lay moaning, tossing, and mumbling incoherently. By his side sat the grim-visaged Captain Osborn, whose heart was tender with sympathy and solicitude. Occasionally the captain would exchange a few words with Hugh Stanton, in subdued tones, regarding the doctor's orders and the ices that were to be kept constantly on the wound. The name "Ethel" escaped the patient's lips amidst his moaning, and again the words "little Hugh."

It was after midnight when he seemed to arouse from the unconscious condition in which he had lain, and began moaning again and pulling at the bandages on his wound. It required no little effort on the part of his attendants to prevent him from tearing the bandages entirely away. Presently he started up as if awakening from a troubled sleep. He opened his eyes and for a few minutes looked vacantly at Captain Osborn. Then, in a quick, nervous tone, he asked, "Where is my canteen and sword?"

"They are all right," replied the captain, soothingly, "don't think anything about them at present. What you need now is quiet and sleep."

"Where am I?" the wounded man next asked, and then, without waiting for a reply, he continued, "Did we whip them or did they whip us?"

"There, there," said the captain, gently, "you have a bad wound. Don't disturb yourself by trying to think. Go to sleep now, and I will tell you all about the affair in the morning."

"Very kind of you, stranger, I am sure," said Horton. "I have had all the sleep I care for. I must now join my regiment." As he said this he tried to arise from the cot. Both Hugh and Captain Osborn had all they could do to prevent him from doing so. They persuaded him to believe that the physician had forbidden undue exertion. The wounded man lay back on his cot, exhausted from his effort, and looked at his attendants in half anger, while his eyes lighted up with the fire of a soldier.

"My duty as a soldier," he protested, "outranks the order of the hospital physician. As civilians, you, perhaps, cannot understand this, but it is imperative that I join my regiment, the Twenty-ninth, immediately."

Hugh started to speak, but the old captain motioned him to silence. "He is badly out of his head," thought he, "and I must handle him by strategy." Perhaps Captain Osborn remembered the gallant services of the Twenty-ninth Massachusetts regiment, of which he had been the colonel, and was pardonably proud of his achievements while defending the flag during the war.

"The Twenty-ninth is all right, comrade," observed the captain. "Officers and men behaved like heroes."

"A glorious report!" cried the wounded man, enthusiastically. "That repays me for this painful wound on my head, and lying around in the hospital insensible for I know not how many hours. It was a grand charge our men made,—right in the face of bristling bayonets, shot and shell from the 'gray coats.' Our captain commanded the right wing, the second lieutenant the left, while I occupied the central position, and, in the doublequick charge that we were making, something struck me on the head, just as our boys crossed over a little brook, and then—well, I knew nothing more until just now, when I came to my senses in this improvised hospital." As he concluded, he let his eyes wander about the small, dimly-lighted room.

The captain looked at Hugh, and shook his head doubtfully.

"Perhaps you would like to send a report to the commander of your brigade, comrade?"

"Good idea," said Mr. Horton. "By the way, as we whipped the 'rebs,' communication with the North is still open, and I would like also to send a few lines to a noble little wife away up in Massachusetts."

"Let me be your amanuensis," said Hugh, drawing his chair to the captain's table, and arranging some writing material.

"Thank you, sir; are you ready?"

"Quite ready," replied Hugh.

> "*Hospital near Fortress Monroe.*
>
> "*To Captain Lyman Osborn, 29th Mass. Inf.:*
>
> "*Will join the company to-morrow. Am all right with the exception of a scalp wound, which is somewhat painful. Have had a good sleep and feel refreshed. Expect me by noon.*
>
> "*Your obedient servant,*
>
> "*Lieut. Hugh Stanton.*"

When the wounded man had finished dictating his report he uttered a moan, and pressed his hand against the painful wound on his head. Hugh lifted his eyes to Captain Osborn, and saw that the old veteran's face was ashen white. The startling revelation had also dawned upon Hugh, and nis hand trembled violently. Captain Osborn controlled his feelings, and, with iron-like firmness, remarked, "Excellent report, comrade, splendid! Now, suppose you dictate a short letter to your wife, and I will see that it is posted on the north-bound train that leaves here within an hour."

Mr. Horton was evidently in great pain. He lay with closed eyes for a few minutes, as if waiting for the throbbing of his head to cease, and then said: "Oh, I hope the garbled telegraph reports have not numbered me among the missing. It would break the little woman's heart to read such a report as that in the newspapers."

"I am ready," said Hugh, huskily.

"Very well; say Fortress Monroe—don't date it at the hospital; it would only cause her needless anxiety."

"All right, I will do as you request," replied Hugh.

> *"My dear wife Ethel:—Yesterday, June 10th, our company formed part of a detachment sent to dislodge the forces under General Magruder, which were stationed a few miles from here, in the vicinity of Bethel Church. The battle did not last long, but was quite severe. I was slightly wounded— nothing serious. Will report to my company for active service within a few hours. Have just learned that we completely routed the enemy, which was, of course, a most satisfactory termination of the engagement. Every man of the Twenty- ninth proved himself a hero, for, like myself, they were fight- ing for a great principle and for loved ones at home, and this made their services to their country a holy crusade.*
>
> *"When our little Hugh—God bless him!—is older, teach him that his father was a soldier and a defender of hearthstones and of the glorious old stars and stripes. The Bethel Church encounter will doubtless go down in history as one of the most spirited engagements of the war.*
>
> *"Affectionately your husband,*
>
> *"Hugh Stanton."*

It required no small effort on the part of Captain Osborn to control his agitation at this marvelous revelation. However, he hastily prepared an opiate that had been left by the physician, and gave it to the wounded man, who soon after fell into a peaceful slumber. Then he moved nervously from the side of the cot, and approached Hugh.

"My boy," said he, in a low, trembling voice, "what a revelation! Do you realize that this man is none other than your father?"

"I do," faltered Hugh.

"Yes, and by the eternal," the captain went on, "we will save him. To think I have failed to recognize my old lieutenant all these years is a piece of unpardonable stupidity on my part."

Hugh's head had been bowed in his hands, while his whole frame was convulsed with stifled sobs. When the captain ceased speaking, he stood up before him, and their hands closed in a fervent hand-clasp.

"God bless you, my old friend," said Hugh, "you have nothing to condemn yourself for, but together we are confronting a great problem. Will he awake from his present sleep as John Horton, the cattle king, or as Hugh Stanton, my father?"

CHAPTER XXXVII.

TRYING TO REMEMBER

CAPTAIN OSBORN had sent word to Mrs. Horton immediately after the accident, that her husband was detained on some business matters and would not return home until the following day. With the gray dawn of morning, he took counsel with Hugh whether it were better to keep up the deception or communicate with the family, and tell them of the accident and of Mr. Horton's real condition. It was finally decided that the deception was a necessity, and every effort should be made to keep the facts from Mrs. Horton. Accordingly, the captain wrote a hasty note to Mrs. Horton, saying that her husband had been detained on some important business affairs, and would probably not return home for several days. As it was nothing unusual for the cattle owner to be unexpectedly called away in looking after his various interests, his wife, on receipt of the captain's note, was not at all alarmed.

Captain Robert Painter, the commander of the local G. A. R. post, was quietly informed of the situation, and a report was promptly circulated on the streets of Meade that J. B. Horton had sustained no serious injuries from his fall. In the meantime, before the morning sun had climbed above the horizon, strong and willing hands of old comrades had tenderly carried the injured man, who was still under the influence of opiates, to Captain Osborn's home. Captain Painter secured four old veterans as assistants, and held them subject to orders in a room adjoining the one occupied by the patient. They conversed in whispers of the strange revelation, and shook their heads doubtfully, wondering if the sufferer would recover and be reconciled to the two lives he had lived.

Captain Osborn and Hugh were constantly by the patient's bedside. The physician arrived, and, after a careful examination, pronounced the symptoms favorable. The fever had been allayed, while the pulse and respiration were almost normal. When the effects of the opiates began to wear away, the patient became restless and presently opened his eyes. "Good morning, gentlemen," said he, as he glanced hastily from the face of Captain Osborn and then to Hugh. "I fear I have overslept," and he made a motion as if to arise from the bed.

"I don't consider it prudent," hastily interposed the physician, laying his hand gently on the patient's head, "I advise perfect quiet."

"Indeed!" said Mr. Horton, rather brusquely, pushing the physician's hand roughly away, "in the absence of the army surgeon I shall decide for myself."

"I beg of you, comrade," interposed the captain, "not to fatigue yourself, but rest quietly in bed. The colonel of the Twenty-ninth has been sent for, and will be here shortly."

"Where is your blue?" asked the patient, while his dark eyes sparkled with a trace of indignation. "If you are a comrade of mine, you should be wearing the colors. Perhaps, though, you are too old for service; you look decidedly grizzled."

"Very true, Lieutenant Stanton," replied the captain, "as you say, I am rather gray and grizzled; nevertheless, I am your comrade as far as the sentiments of loyalty for the old flag are concerned. Indeed, I am quite as ready to sacrifice my life in the defense of the stars and stripes as you have shown yourself to be."

"You exaggerate the severity of my wound. I assure you it is comparatively slight. By the way," he continued, turning toward Hugh, "did you send my letters?" Hugh nodded affirmatively. "Very well," he continued, addressing the captain, "if you are a comrade of mine you will permit me to dress and be ready to receive my captain." The physician caught Captain Osborn's eye, and made a sign that perhaps it would be best to humor the injured man's whim. The doctor and Hugh withdrew to an adjoining room, but Captain Osborn remained. The cattle owner assumed a sitting position on the side of the bed. His coat, vest, and trousers were resting on a chair near by, but he seemed in no hurry about dressing. "Well, comrade," said Captain Osborn, "perhaps, if you feel strong enough, you had better make haste and dress, as the captain of your company will arrive before long."

"Where are my clothes?" asked the lieutenant.

"Why, don't you see them on the chair before you?"

"What?" roared the injured man, "My uniform, my uniform, sir! Don't you understand? Do you think for a moment that I will tolerate the idea of wearing citizen's clothes,—and secondhand at that?" Whereupon he gave the chair a vigorous push with his foot, upsetting it, clothes and all. As he did so, a pocketbook slipped from his coat pocket and rested on the floor at his feet. Captain Osborn was momentarily at a loss to know what to do or say in the emergency. In the meantime, the cattle owner had reached for and picked up the pocketbook and some business cards that had fallen out of it. "Ho, ho! what's this?" said he, glancing at one of the cards. "'Hugh Stanton, Cashier Meade National Bank, Meade, Kansas.' It seems that I have a namesake in the banking business." As he opened the pocketbook to replace the cards, he read aloud the name stamped in gold on the russet leather lining, "'John B. Horton.' Horton, Horton," he repeated to himself, as he pressed his hand against his wound. "Where have I heard that name?" and he looked half vacantly at the old captain, who was watching him intently.

"Lieutenant Stanton," said the captain, coming closer to him and looking him squarely in the face, "this pocketbook belongs to the man whose name you have pronounced—John B. Horton— the cattle king of southwestern Kansas and No-Man's-Land, who is worth ten million dollars if he is worth a cent. His beautiful home is at Horton's Grove; he has a noble wife and a most lovely daughter, Ethel."

"Ethel, Ethel," repeated the injured man, "my wife's name."

"Not a vestige of remembrance," murmured the captain to himself, "this is, indeed, sad." Then nerving himself for the occasion, he said aloud and with marked firmness, "Lieutenant Stanton, dress yourself; put on your clothes, citizen's though they be, and I will undertake to clear up the mystery."

The wounded man stared vacantly at the captain for a moment, and then began mechanically to dress himself in silence, and, before Captain Osborn could intercept him, he approached a large French plate mirror.

"Hold on," cried the captain, but it was too late. The wounded man, with his bandaged head, had seen his reflection in the glass.

"Great God! What is this?" he exclaimed, starting back in amazement. "This beard streaked with gray. My God! What am I? Where am I?" and he sank back into a chair, overcome with confusion and mystery.

Captain Osborn hastily opened a drawer of a desk and took from it an old daguerreotype, and, approaching him, said, "Do you recognize this?"

"Oh, yes," said he, after a moment's scrutiny, "indeed, this is my captain, Captain Osborn of the Twenty-ninth, the warmest friend of my boyhood, and as brave a man as ever wore the blue."

"My dear Stanton," said the captain, "you are right in saying that it is a likeness of Captain Osborn; you are correct also in saying that he was your warmest friend; not only was, but is to this day. I am Captain Lyman Osborn."

"What!" shouted the wounded man, starting up. "No, no; impossible! You may be the captain's father or grandfather, but you're not the captain of my company."

"Yes, my dear friend," said Captain Osborn, laying a hand gently on either shoulder of the patient, who had risen from his chair, "the war has been over a long time—over twenty years. I am now an old man, and so are you." The captain's gentle embrace seemed to soothe and subdue the listener. "More than twenty-five years have intervened since that engagement at

Bethel Church, when you received that terrible wound on your head. You were captured by the enemy and nursed back to life among strangers, but the unnatural pressure of a misplaced bone disturbed your memory, leaving your previous life a blank. Your friends supposed you were dead, but I thank God you are not. You had forgotten your name, and in some way substituted the name of John B. Horton."

The rich cattle owner gazed speechlessly into the captain's face as he made this wonderful revelation. He glanced hastily over his shoulder at the mirror, and seemed to realize the truth of all that he had heard, and his hand unconsciously stole into the captain's.

"But my wife, Captain, my wife and little Hugh?" The captain was silent.

"Come, Captain Osborn, if it is really true as you state, don't trifle with me, don't keep me in suspense. My darling wife, my little boy,—tell me of them." He clasped the captain's hand in both his own, as if he were beginning to believe and trust him.

"My dear Hugh," replied the captain, "I know your love for Ethel was very great; then you were a young man, only twenty-five years old. You are more than fifty now, and many changes have come. Be brave and courageous. Ethel, your little wife, died a year after you were wounded, but little Hugh has grown to be a man much loved and respected by all. He is an honor to you."

"But, Captain," faltered Stanton, while tears sprang to his eyes, "where have I been all these years?"

"Not idle," replied the captain, "you are perhaps the richest man in southwestern Kansas; you are called John B. Horton, the cattle king, and, as I remarked awhile ago, you live at Horton's Grove, two miles from here, with your good wife and your lovely daughter, Ethel."

"Yes, yes," said he, clasping his hands to his head and sinking into a chair which the captain had pushed toward him. "Yes, yes, I am beginning to remember,—yes, beginning to remember." He finally grew silent and was lost in thought.

Captain Osborn paced patiently back and forth before the silent man. He felt sure that Hugh Stanton of his boyhood days and John B. Horton of the present were manfully struggling with the tangled thread of memory, for many years severed but now laboring to be reunited.

CHAPTER XXXVIII.

TRUTH STRANGER THAN FICTION

AFTER what seemed to Captain Osborn to be an interminable length of time, the wounded man arose from his chair and gazed long and earnestly at his reflection in the mirror; then, turning, he said:

"God be praised, Captain Osborn, I remember all. Yes," he went on, as the two men clasped hands, "I remember my two lives. I've lived them all over, even down to the time when I was thrown from the mustang in front of your bank. I must be known as John Bruce Horton, but, for God's sake, bring me my boy, my son, Hugh. No wonder I took such a strong fancy to him from the first day we met after his arrival in Meade."

The two men embraced, and then the captain, going to the adjoining room, beckoned to Hugh, who hastily approached. "He remembers all," said the captain, "both his lives. Go in to your father." Then, gently closing the door, Captain Osborn turned to the post commander, Captain Painter, and his associates, and explained to them in detail the marvelous story.

An hour later Hugh joined Captain Osborn and his associates. He was noticeably agitated, and his eyes were red with weeping. "Gentlemen," he said, "my tears have been those of joy at finding my father. I am going to Horton's Grove." Then, bidding them adieu, he hastily took his departure.

Arriving at the Grove, he found Mrs. Horton seated on the veranda. "Welcome, Mr. Stanton," said she, as Hugh, with flushed face, saluted her with more warmth than usual. Without wasting time, he hastily narrated to her all that had occurred.

Her expressions of distress and alarm, when told of the accident which had befallen her husband, and of amazement as Hugh's narrative proceeded, were indeed a study.

"Then you," she exclaimed, "you, Mr. Stanton, you are my husband's son, and I—I will be your mother, if you will let me, and you shall be my boy as well as his." She embraced him warmly, while tears dimmed her eyes. "Oh!" she exclaimed, "it is all so new—so sudden; I can hardly understand the unraveling of such a mystery. Before our marriage he told me that the beginning of all memory with him was his recovery from that ugly wound on his head."

"And now," asked Hugh, "where is Ethel—my sister?" Hardly had he asked the question when he heard her singing within.

"Go, Hugh, my son, and tell her all. I am so overcome; I must compose myself and prepare to set out immediately for your father."

As Hugh turned and walked briskly along the veranda, he saw Doctor Redfield disembarking from a boat-ride. Through the screen door he saw Ethel, whose tender brown eyes and marvelous beauty were daily growing more radiant under the expanding influence of an ennobling and reciprocal love. She was humming a love ditty to herself as Hugh pushed aside the screen and approached her.

"Welcome, my good friend," said she, looking up and extending her hand, "Jack and I were talking of you while taking our boat-ride, and had made up our minds to go and fetch you, had you not come of your own accord. Now then," said she, roguishly, "where are your excuses and explanations?"

"Ah, Ethel," said Hugh, as he still held her hand in his with tenderest loyalty and respect, "I have much to say." And then, controlling his excitement as much as possible, he hurriedly related all that had happened.

"Poor daddy," murmured Ethel, while tears trembled in her eyes as she followed the detail with closest attention.

"And have you told mamma?"

"All," replied Hugh.

"Then we must order the carriage and go at once for my darling father. Ah, Hugh, he is your father as well; and you—you are my brother!" A flood of recollections seemed suddenly to envelop both brother and sister, and for a moment they were stunned.

"Yes," said Hugh, "you are my sister," and, taking her in his strong arms, he embraced her fervently.

A moment later they were both startled at a footstep on the veranda, and, turning, they found themselves face to face with Doctor Redfield, who had observed their affectionate embrace.

"Pardon me," he said, stiffly, and with marked politeness, "I was not aware that our friend had arrived."

"Yes," stammered Ethel, while a smile played around her lips, "Hugh has given us quite a surprise, and you don't know how glad I am that he is here."

"Yes, I imagine that you are decidedly pleased," said Jack, in his most frigid tones, while he shot a glance at Hugh as much as to say, "An explanation is in order, sir; otherwise, coffee and pistols for two." In the meantime, Ethel had quite recovered herself.

"Why, Jack," said she, "you are usually so jolly; what makes you act so petulantly? I believe you are angry at something?"

"Me angry? Oh, no," said Jack, coldly; "possibly a little displeased with myself for having interrupted such a pleasant conversation." He tried to give an expression of indifference and half amusement to his face, but instead it was one of absolute vexation.

"Well, old fellow," said Hugh, "how are you, anyhow? I saw you getting out of your boat awhile ago, and intended coming down to the boat-house after you, but was detained. You know how fascinating Ethel is. She makes a foolish fellow like myself forget all about time and everything else."

"It is quite evident that you did not expect me at the house quite so soon," replied the doctor, quickly.

"To be candid," replied Hugh, "we did not. You, nevertheless, welcome. Can't you say as much to me?" There was a certain dangerous look of passion in Jack's eyes that filled them with a glowing, searching gaze, as he replied:

"I have never failed, sir, to welcome you at all times, because until now I believed you to be an honorable man."

Hugh laughed good-naturedly, and, leading Ethel, he went over to Jack, put one hand on his shoulder, and with the other arm he encircled Ethel's waist. "Now, Jack, old fellow, I know that 'love maketh a man mad,' but you surely would not suspect me of a dishonorable act, especially where your interests are concerned." There was a bewitching sweetness, mingled with amusement, hovering in Ethel's eyes, while Hugh was speaking.

"Well," said Jack, as he forced a little husky laugh, "I've always supposed you were my friend."

"Go on believing it," said Hugh, "and, when you and Ethel are married, remember that you will then become my brother, for this noble girl is my sister," and there, with one hand on Jack's shoulder, and an arm about Ethel, Hugh told him the strange story. When he had finished, Jack clasped his hand warmly, and said:

"Hugh, my dear fellow, accept my congratulations. Truly, facts are stranger than fiction. Thank God my confidence in your friendship is unshaken. Ethel, forgive me."

The Horton carriage was soon ready, and it was not long before John Horton was surrounded by his loved ones from the Grove. During the afternoon the patient was removed to his home. On returning to Meade, Hugh found Captain Osborn at the bank.

While they were talking, little Harry came in. His tiny arms were clasped about bunches of dandelions and wild flowers that he had gathered from the protected nooks and banks of the Manaroya. The captain opened the door of his private office and said, "Come in, Harry, come in here, you little rascal. Where have you been all day?"…..

The child, still holding the flowers in his chubby arms, climbed upon his father's knee. "I's been out to det the pretty posies, papa. I bringed 'ou ha'f of 'em, an' I left ha'f of 'em wiv mamma. I laid 'em down on dat little place, papa, and I whispered, 'Mamma, little Harry 'oves'ou, and papa 'oves 'ou, too.' I listened long time, papa, but I did n't hear nuffin. I 'spec mamma was asleep, but maybe she was 'way wiv the angels. Do you fink so, papa?"

The old captain held the boy to his great heart, while his eyes filled with tears.

"Yes, papa, I bringed 'ou ha'f of 'em, an' I give mamma ha'f of 'em. I put 'em all round dat little mound, papa, an' I stacked 'em up high, and when mamma turns back from visitin' the angels, she'll see 'em, won't she, papa? And I wrote her a great big letter and doubled it all up, and put on the outside—'

"To mamma from Harry.'.rdquo;"

CHAPTER XXXIX.

JUDGE LYNN HAS AN IDEA

AFEW days later Judge Linus Lynn called at the *Patriot* office, and Major Hampton looked up from a book he was intently reading as his study was invaded. "Come in, Lynn," said the major, "and be seated. How are you, anyway?"

"Comfortable, my dear Major, quite comfortable, I assure you," replied Lynn, as he helped himself to a cigar from an open box.

"That's right, Judge," said the major, observing his familiarity; "shall I help you to a light?"

"Thanks," said Judge Lynn, "I'm always provided with matches, or I'd have you gimme one. I regard it as mighty poor taste for an old smoker like me to always be browzin' 'round askin' his 'sociates for matches—therefore I'm always supplied."

"How thoughtful," observed the major, smiling sarcastically.

"Yes," replied Lynn, "I claim to be a thoughtful man,—the result of much thinkin'. Don't look soopercilious an' disbelievin', for it's a fac'. Now, Major, I have an idee."

"Indeed?" replied the major, as he picked up a pencil. "Let me record it; it is doubtless quite an affair, and should be captured before it gets away from you."

Judge Lynn appeared to take no notice of the major's irony, and said: "You see, Major, I'll onboosom myself enough to tell you that in my pinion honesty will soon be so condemned scarce in this 'ere mortgage-ridden Southwest, that a feller 'll have to use the article itself to deceive the deceivers. Now it's gettin' dangnation slow with me, an' while I'm mighty near worked to death in my office,—feet is, I'm 'lowin' I'll have the brain fag if

244

things don't let up,—yet it is bringin' me no ready cash. I'm jest whoopin' 'round doin' a credit bizness. Do you see?"

The major laughed outright. "Yes, I see, Judge, and I also know what an easy matter it is for some people to be overworked. The same class of men find a shady corner on a hot day almost irresistible."

"Don't laugh, Major," said Judge Lynn, with an injured look on his countenance, "you can bet it's no laughin' matter. Speakin' wide-open an' confidential-like, I'll say we're out o' flour down at my palace, an' my grocer has adopted a sort o' C. O. D. policy that is quite paralyzin', an' besides the rent is way past due, the landlord is screechin' 'round, an' I fear a successful suit of ejectment will soon be brought, bet yer life I do. The burnin' up of the country by hot winds an' the big prairie-fire nach'ally started litigation off on a canter all right 'nuff, but nobody has come projectin' 'round so far with money to pay court fees. I'd be all right if it had n't been for the trouble I got into with the attorney-gen'ral. That nach'ally locoed me good and plenty. You, perhaps, are rememberin' how I 'tempted to reverse a decision of the Supreme Court in regard to the foreclosure of a mortgage on a poor devil's farm, an' in turn they got malignant-like an' reversed me,—in short, turned me down, an' at the same time made things thrillin' by exhaustin' my ready cash and hypothecatin' all my credit an' anticipated earnin's for the next year, to keep me out of the clutches of what the aforesaid attorney-gen'ral calls law. I jist had all I could do to keep my han's away from my artillery. If the attorney-gen'ral'd come down 'ere there'd been obsequies."

"Yes, I remember," said the major, sighing; "you made a mistake, and yet your error was on the side of humanity. I forgive you and so does humanity. Take this," said he, reaching the judge a roll of bills, "with my forgiveness and this advice,— be careful not to exceed your authority again, for law, in the hands of Shylocks, is a relentless thing. Take this, Judge, and pay your debts."

"What, Major, a hundred dollars? Why, surely, sir, I'm already more deeply indebted to you than I can ever squar' up. This, I'm assoomin', is too much."

"My dear Lynn," said Major Hampton, throwing his head back in his own unique way, "my mission in life is to help the needy. More years of sorrow and suffering than you can comprehend have opened the doorway of my understanding. I was an old veteran in the cause of humanity when I helped in the crusade for liberty at Valley Forge; later I was at the Commune in Paris during the Reign of Terror, when it was demonstrated that man can endure the galling yoke of slavery and adversity easier than he can withstand prosperity or the tickled vanity of a new-found power. Later I was honored with the confidence of John Brown in his noble and heroic attempts to overthrow slavery; and still afterwards gave my advice to Lincoln, and at his solicitation helped formulate the Emancipation Proclamation. Yes, I've seen the black race freed from slavery, but the yoke was not destroyed, and in turn it has, like an octopus, fettered a race of white slaves. As a lover of mankind and a reformist, I am now building up the nucleus of a power in my organization, the Barley Hullers, that will not only free from bondage the white slaves of our land, but will also effectually destroy the yoke—the instrument of torture. This can be done only by an equal distribution of wealth. In giving you this money I am acting as an instrument of the Unseen, yet, nevertheless, potent force that will never rest until liberty liberates."

"Major Hampton," said Judge Lynn, rising and striking an attitude, and bringing the tips of his fingers and thumbs together, as was his wont in addressing a jury, "you sure do me an honor by givin' me such a plain, comprehensive statement, speakin' gay and genial-like, of your position and life's mission. I'm thrilled to overflowin' at your confidence in me. Think I don't know thoughts when I hear 'em rumblin' down all 'round me? Course I do! Speakin' of the Barley Hullers brings me face to face with the idee which I had in mind when I entered this room. In short, sir, I wish to jine the organ'zation, and to secure a place as lecturer, or somethin' of that sort, at some stipulated, but not exorbitant compensation. Do you see?"

"Pay your grocery-bill from the funds I have given you," said the major, with a wave of his hand. "Do your utmost to provide for your family by your own exertions; but, should you fail, come and see me again. I think I understand folly your ambition, and why you wish to join the Barley Hullers. I will consider it, but do not understand me, at all, to say that I favor your plans."

"By the great horn spoon, Major!" said Judge Lynn, lighting his cigar afresh, "I hope to be shot if I don't wish you were at the head of the gover'ment. You nach'ally would jist show 'em a legerdemain trick or two worth knowin', an' don't you furgit it You've got a sooperior quality of good jedgment an' a whole log-yard rail o' book learnin'. Oh, I know what I'm talkin' 'bout."

Major Hampton laughed good-naturedly at the judge's attempted compliment. "Thank you," said he, "my mission is not to rule, but to reform and to emancipate. However, if I had the reins of government in my hands, knowing as I do the poverty and sufferings of the masses, I should employ different methods than those often adopted for their relief. By the way," continued the major, "have you seen anything of Hugh Stanton?"

"No," replied the judge, "hain't seen him projectin' 'round lately, but I'm allowin' he's at the bank as usual. Speakin' ca'mly-like, that was a wonderful affair—John B. Horton cornin' to life, so to speak, and Hugh discoverin' him to be his father. Bet yer life it was a speshul chunk of good luck to Hugh."

"Yes, indeed," replied the major, "truly wonderful. I have felt a deep interest in the young man, especially since his reverses occasioned by the hot winds, but now that he is heir apparent to half of John B. Horton's enormous wealth, my plans will necessarily have to be changed. I have an impression," he went on, thoughtfully, "that Mr. Horton will find in Hugh a veritable watch-dog for his vast herds, and that cattle thieving as a science is liable to be reckoned among the lost arts."

"Don't suppose Hugh 'll get toomultuous-like an' troubled

with the swell-head, do you, now that he is financially loafin' 'round in sight of a mint?" inquired Lynn.

"Oh, no," replied the major, "he is too well-balanced,—he is too intelligent and sensible."

"Speakin' pretty p'lite-like, them's my sentiments to a nicety, Major. Now, there's no use denyin' I'm carryin' more wrinkles to-day than when I was a younger man, but I'm 'lowin' in my face there's a sign of much thinkin' and not decrepitood. Course it's different with women, for wrinkles in one o' these reg'lar high-steppin' women's faces are sort o' zither strings on which are played the death-knell of their noomerous conquests. Ancient hist'ry is suggested at onct, while poverty of looks, if not of purse, is an actooality. Person'ly, if I had a million to-morrow I'd actooally wear the same sized hat I do to-day, which I must admit is not a roarin' big one at best. Now, if you should git a hankerin', Major, to put me in the push as a sort of speshul deputy lecturer 'mong the Barley Hullers, it would n't loco me nor puff me up a mite; no, sir, bet yer life it would n't. I nach'ally have no ultra ambitions for absorbin' wealth in this 'ere world, an', when I die, a quiet funeral without flowers will be quite satisfact'ry."

Some one knocked at the door, and a moment later Dan Spencer came shuffling in. His short, sandy beard seemed redder than ever, while the freckles on his face gave him a leopard-like appearance. His immense feet and hands and slightly stooped shoulders made his gaunt figure look especially angular. His eyes were as restless as ever, while nis abnormal tooth seemed constantly saluting those with whom he conversed.

"How d' ye do, Major? Jist dropped in fur a minute. Did n't know you wuz here, Judge, though I'm proud to see you—always glad to see the court in a friendly way."

"Well, Spencer, what is it?" asked the major, looking at him intently.

"Nothin' much alarmin'," replied Spencer, "only me an' Kinneman jist got back from the Cimarron River, an' it's reported there wuz about two hundred head of fat beeves cut out uv Horton's herd and driv' off 'bout ten days ago."

"Infamous, infamous!" said the major, coming to his feet, and striking the table with his hand, as if to give emphasis to his feelings.

"Us fellers heerd," replied Dan,' "thet you wuz still 'way lecturin' to the Barley Hullers, else we'd come back sooner an' reported, an' thet's the truth."

"Another reason, Major," interposed Lynn, "speakin' on the spur of the minute like, why you should favorably consider my idee. You need a deputy—bet yer life you do, in this 'ere lecturin' business; then you could give yer time to runnin' down and locoin' the cattle thieves. I wear magnifyin' glasses, I do, when such swell opportunities as this 'ere comes slidin' 'round under my nose, bet yer life I do."

The major seemed lost in thought, and walked slowly back and forth, with his hands clasped behind him, paying no attention whatever to Judge Lynn's observations. Presently he said: "Very well, Spencer, I will see you and Kinne-man this evening, after the Barley Hullers' meeting. Call at my house about eleven o'clock."

"All right," replied Spencer, "jist as you say; you kin always count on Bill Kinneman and yours truly bein' punctu'l when you give the word," and with this Dan shuffled out of the room.

After he had gone, the major said: "This is a bad business, very bad. The *Patriot* comes out to-morrow, and I must write up this last outrage of the cattle thieves. It is simply incomprehensible how they can carry on this lawless work without being detected."

"My private opinion, Major, speakin' once-served-like," said Judge Lynn, "is that you're needed dangnation bad to sort o' look after these 'ere fellers, person'ly, an' you can't do it spendin' yer time away from home lecturin', bet yer life you can't."

The major scowled, and, seating himself at the table, commenced writing, and soon after Judge Lynn quietly took his departure, without again venturing to broach the subject of being made deputy lecturer.

About eight o'clock that evening Hugh called at

the *Patriot* office.

"Well, well!" exclaimed Major Hampton. "This is, indeed, a pleasing surprise,—a refreshing whiff of the unexpected."

"The pleasure is all mine, Major," replied Hugh, seating himself at the earnest solicitation of his old friend. "I have been trying," continued Hugh, "for several days to find time to call on you, but you know so much has happened."

"True," said the major, "much has occurred,—much that is marvelous, and yet in it all can be traced the hand of an all-wise Providence. Let me take this occasion, my dear Stanton, to tender my congratulations on your good fortune in discovering your long-lost father."

"Thank you," said Hugh. "It is all so new and strange that I can't realize the new relations."

"Stanton," said the major, turning to his writing-table, "I have just been preparing an article on cattle-thieving, and I am anxious to know how it will impress you." The old major threw his head back in a supreme way, and looked thoughtfully into a darkened corner of the room.

"You certainly know, Major," said Hugh, "that I am an admirer of your writings, it matters not on what subject."

"John Brown," said the major, without removing his eyes from the darkened corner, "was an emancipator, and his memory is revered, his name honored, and the personality of the man loved by thousands of people. Is not that so?" Hugh answered that it was. "Very well," said the major, while the deep wrinkles in his face began to grow more prominent, "what was John Brown but a law-breaker, a notorious thief, on a gigantic scale? What right had he to take slaves from their owners,—black men who were worth, in the market, a thousand dollars apiece, and help them to escape?"

"You must remember," said Hugh, "that time has covered any mistakes the great emancipator may have made with the veil of charity. The fact remains, of course, that he was a lawbreaker."

"That is just it," exclaimed the major. "He was a law-breaker,—

he violated the statutes,—and yet his name is honored by this generation, while others yet unborn will revere his memory and honor his name as one of earth's greatest."

"Yes; not because he was a law-breaker, Major, but because he led a crusade in behalf of the oppressed and the helpless."

"Ah!" said the major, leaning back in his chair, and taking his eyes away from the darkened corner, and beaming benignly at Hugh, "now you are uttering words of great wisdom. What a magnificent reformist you would make. I wanted you to give expression to that thought."

Hugh was noticeably complimented with the major's words, and finally stammered, "I am sure, Major, that Captain Osborn and others entertain similar views, and I am not entitled to any special credit for these sentiments."

Major Hampton let his eyes turn again toward the darkened corner of the room.

"Captain Osborn," he said, half to himself, "poor old Captain; I am sorry for him, indeed I am, and yet in one way he is to be congratulated, for sorrow is a torch that enlarges the scope of the understanding and softens the heart of the sufferer toward humanity. Yes, I feel sorry for the captain," he went on. "My regret, however, is not so much for the termination of the affair as it is that such an unequal marriage should have been made in the first place."

"Why do you call it unequal, Major? Of course, you understand that I readily admit there was a vast difference between Captain Osborn and Mrs. Osborn, but I interpret their differences as a lack of congeniality, rather than inequality."

"An equal marriage," said the old major, "is one where the infatuation or illusion goes on until the end; an unequal marriage is where one or the other has foiled to find that for which they sought. I know it is contrary to the canons of good society, but, nevertheless, my sympathies linger with the transgressor in these unequal marriages, rather than with the dolt of a man or woman who is satisfied with a monotonous existence instead of living in the exhilarating atmosphere of love's fullest intoxication. Lucy Osborn was never willing to trudge along, elbow to elbow with the captain, sympathetically sharing the poverty as well as the successes of life; she was brave in the latter and a coward in the former condition. Poor woman, probably this would never have occurred had their marriage been an equal one."

"I am glad, Major," said Hugh, "that you regard the memory of Mrs. Osborn with so much charity. Of course we cannot deny that she was, perhaps, indiscreet, but I cannot believe that she was wicked."

"The unforgivable sin," said the major, "with one's friends, is not to sin in silence—if one sins at all. It is not the part of honest charity to have even an opinion in regard to the truthfulness or untruthfulness of the rumors which connected her name with that of Lord Avondale. Lucy Osborn," continued Major Hampton, "belonged to a not uncommon class of women. In their youth they long with passionate impatience for an impetuous, strong, overpowering, consuming love, but when the semblance finally comes along,—like, for instance, the refined and exalted affection of a man like Captain Osborn,—they seize upon it like a famished tigress and then immediately cease suing the adorer for continued adoration, but sit idly down and satiate themselves with revels in supremest selfishness, prodigal indifference, and reckless abandonment of opportunities. Lucy Osborn even threw open the window of prudence, and something flew away, leaving emptiness and poverty of heart, where plenty should have reigned; indeed, her life's boudoir was stripped of its rich furnishings, leaving instead a tangled maze of regret to feed upon her famished and impoverished heart, driving her, perhaps, to play at lottery with her reputation, and, like any other gambler standing before the green cloth, the chances were ninety-nine to one that she would lose."

Just here they were interrupted by Judge Lynn, who came rushing in at the door, his tall hat well back on his small head and his coat sleeves pushed up, as if he were transacting all the business, worth mentioning, in the Great Southwest.

"Hello, Major; why, hello, Stanton; did n't know you had any one with you, Major."

The major nodded and motioned him to be seated, and, turning to Hugh, he went on talking. "It is a hard question, therefore, to determine, Stanton, and seemingly an unfair one to decide, whether or not Captain Osborn is not better off under the present conditions than he would have been had Mrs. Osborn lived. The infatuation of love is a peculiar sentiment; sages and poets have endeavored to describe it, from the beginning of the world to the present time, and they usually have written most volubly of it at that period of their lives when they knew the least about it. My long years of observation teach me that love is actuated either by sentiment, interest, or reason. The first has to do with a handsome face and a beautiful form; the second with a homely face, which certainly suggests sympathy; and the third with a woman virtuous in mind and body. Fortunate is the man who discovers a woman who excites in him the first and last of these motives. A womanly woman binds our hearts with ungalling chains on earth, and keeps our souls in tune and in communication with heaven."

"Excuse me, Major," said Judge Lynn, "for observin' that, in my jedgment, thar's a heap o' ig'nance 'round these diggin's 'bout the sentiment of love."

The old major smiled and looked compassionately at the judge. "What do you know, Judge, about love matters?" he asked, giving Hugh a knowing look.

"Well," said the judge, "thar ain't no use denyin' or contendin' but what there is a nach'al, inborn sort of a feelin' called love. I'm 'lowin' when a young feller an' a girl gits to cooin' 'round and locoed-like, and fin'ly git pot-hooked on the same laceratin' thorn, and survive, why, then they are usually reconciled to each other's short-comin's. Howsumever, speakin' prompt and cheerful-like, in my opinion love's a pipe dream that sure 'nuff ends, instead o' begins, when a feller gits married. In other words, when a feller takes a better half the toomultuous soap-bubble of illusion busts, and history begins with the hard scratchin' duties of makin' a livin'. Bet yer life, I 'low I know what I'm talkin' 'bout. I'm not peevish or complainin', but, gee, think what I've gone through, an' then bat yer eyes with thrillin' surprise."

At this the old major and Hugh laughed immoderately, while the judge looked on in blank astonishment, as if vexed and incensed at their hilarity.

CHAPTER XL.

THE CATTLE THIEF CAUGHT

AT Horton's Grove they were indulging in a family reunion and thanksgiving for all that had occurred. The cattle king had almost entirely recovered from the effects of his fall, and his wound was rapidly healing. Therefore, when Kinneman reported the last depredations of the cattle thieves, it threw no particular gloom over the household.

"We are too thankful, and our happiness is too great," said Ethel, "to care very much about a few hundred head of beeves."

"Quite true, daughter," observed Mrs. Horton; "nevertheless, the loss is considerable, and it is unfortunate that these marauders cannot be captured."

"With father's consent," said Hugh, "I shall undertake to help him in ferreting out this mystery, and in learning who the cattle thieves really are."

"It is truly comforting," observed Mr. Horton, "to know that I have some one on whom I can depend," and his eyes rested lovingly on Hugh. "After you have deliberated on the subject, I shall be glad of your advice and help."

"Has it ever occurred to you," asked Hugh, "that it might be a good idea to discharge your present force of cowboys, and employ others?"

"I hardly think that is necessary," replied Mr. Horton. "They are a fairly good lot of fellows; and, while it cannot be denied that they are careless at times, yet, as a rule, they take a deep interest in all that concerns me. I believe you had better arrange matters at the bank, my son, so you can be absent about two weeks, and we will take a trip along the Cimarron River and over into No-Man's-Land, and down into the Panhandle country, and you can, in this way, advise yourself as to the extent of our herds, and also become acquainted with the range bosses and their assistants."

"A good idea, father. When do you advise that we go?"

"Let me see; the round-up and maverick branding will commence in about ten days. Perhaps we had better arrange to start about that time. As you have never witnessed a round-up you will find it very interesting. Doctor Redfield might like to go with us. Roping and flanking calves has an interest peculiar to itself."

"I most certainly would," said Jack, looking up when his name was pronounced. "Ethel has just been telling me of the feats of horsemanship and lariat-throwing in which the cowboys indulge at these annual festivities on the range."

Accordingly it was arranged that Hugh and Jack should accompany the cattle king and witness these novel and interesting sights of range life.

Hugh had been installed at the Grove after discovering his father, and enjoyed, far more than words can express, the home life thus afforded him, and his daily horseback rides to and from the bank. During these days, Captain Osborn, with little Harry, was much at the Hortons', and together the captain and his lieutenant lived over again the pleasant times of their youth and of their early manhood, and the stirring events of army life.

Every one seemed greatly attached to the captain's little son, and, at Mrs. Horton's earnest solicitation, the little fellow remained with her for days at a time. The proud and ambitious wife of the cattle king seemed entirely changed. The Dr. Lenox Avondale and Lucy Osborn affair,—the flight of one and the unexpected death of the other,—the discovery that Ethel had more heart than foolish ambition, her husband's accident and its attendant revelations, and the finding in Hugh Stanton a son, had all exercised an influence that ennobled, subdued, and reconciled her to the sanctity of home and of family. With this awakening came a genuine sympathy and love for little Harry Osborn.

Dr. Jack Redfield managed to monopolize most of Ethel's time; Mr. Horton and Hugh were necessarily absent a great deal, and thus Mrs. Horton came to find much pleasure in the little fellow's society.

One evening, while they were gathered around the dinner-table, Hugh observed that in his new happiness and selfishness he had almost forgotten his promise to call on Major Hampton, and said that he would do so immediately.

"Ah, my brother," said Ethel, as she looked archly at him, "are you going to call on the major or the major's daughter? Come now, confess."

Hugh reddened noticeably, but insisted that it was the major, and soon after took his leave. On arriving at Major Buell Hampton's, Hugh was received into the library by Marie herself.

"You never were more welcome," said Marie, extending a plump, white hand, which Hugh pressed, perhaps, a little harder and held a little longer than the occasion seemed to warrant.

"Thank you," said he, bowing, and blushing like a schoolboy, "and I never was more delighted to see you; and permit me to say that you are looking extremely well."

Her eyes rested inquiringly on his face for a moment. The rays from the chandelier reflected a fascinating glow from her wealth of bronzed hair, and Hugh thought that she had never before looked so bewitchingly irresistible.

"You have come to see papa," said Marie, half inquiringly.

"No, I came expressly to see you."

He doubtless had forgotten, or else was indifferent to the denial that he had made at the dinner-table.

"Indeed, I am honored," replied Marie, smiling, while her cheeks flushed at Hugh's words. "I was about to send for you, and had quite made up my mind to do so. Your coming, therefore, is quite fortunate."

"Yours to command," said Hugh, gallantly; "in what way may I serve you?"

"Papa," she replied, half hesitatingly, "is very strict about his private affairs, but I feel sure that he will heartily approve of what I am about to do, which is nothing more nor less than to ask your advice regarding a note that was left for him by that detestable Kinneman. Somehow, I can't bear him at all. He requested me to give it to papa this evening, but, instead of coming home, papa sent me word by the office boy that he had been suddenly called away and would not return for perhaps a week. You know that he has much to do with the Barley Hullers, and his time is therefore hardly his own. Indeed, I remarked to him the other day that I was getting jealous, I see so little of him. I opened the letter left by Mr. Kinneman, and here it is. It seems to me of the utmost importance, and that is why I made up my mind to send for you."

"You certainly honor me," said Hugh, bowing deferentially, as he took the letter, "in thinking of sending for me in preference to any of your other friends."

Unfolding the letter, he read:

"Dear Major:—'Bout 300 head of beeves will be driv' 'cross the river at the ford close to the red bluffs between midnight and mornin'. Come at once to the old Dodson corral, four miles west of Englewood.

"Kinneman and Spencer."

"Yes," said Hugh, hastily arising, "this is, indeed, more important than any other business affair of which I can now conceive. The only regret I have is that your father is not at home to go with us, and share in the glory of making a capture that now seems certain. Through the columns of the *Patriot*, and otherwise, he has fought the cattle thieves with more determination than any other half-dozen men in the Southwest."

"Yes, papa insists that cattle stealing can be done away with only by the most vigorous punishment. I am so glad, Mr. Stanton, that you approve of my giving you this letter, and I am sure papa will commend me for doing so." Hugh glanced at his watch. "It is almost eight o'clock," he observed, "and while it is a ride of full thirty miles to the red bluffs on the Cimarron River, yet we can make it by midnight if we start at once. I sincerely regret," he continued extending his hand to Marie, "that my call has to terminate so suddenly, but, as Captain Osborn would say, it is a military necessity."

After bidding her adieu, he hastened down the steps, and was soon in his saddle galloping along the road toward Horton's Grove. He found Captain Osborn chatting pleasantly with his father and mother, and Dr. Jack Redfield employed in turning music for Ethel in the music-room.

"Boots and saddles!" he called out, as he came rushing in, and then he hurriedly explained the important news of which he was bearer, by reading the Kinneman and Spencer letter. Both Captain Osborn and Doctor Redfield insisted that they should accompany the cattle king and Hugh on their midnight *coup de main* undertaking.

"I don't quite understand," said Mr. Horton, "how my man Kinneman could be at Major Hampton's late this afternoon, as he started for the Cimarron River immediately after the noon lunch. Then again, he ought to have informed me, as well as Major Hampton, of the intended raid. I presume, however, he fancied that I was not strong enough for the excitement which the affair promises. But he is mistaken, for I never felt better in my life."

Within half an hour everything was in readiness, and the four horsemen, "armed to the teeth," started down the valley road, at a pellmell gait, bound for the red bluffs on the Cimarron. The moon was just showing itself above the eastern horizon, but it was veiled by scraggly clouds, and promised but little assistance. They were well mounted on strong ponies, and galloped easily along without engaging in any connected conversation. The patter of the hoofs of the four ponies was so uniform that it might have been taken for the galloping of a single horse. The cattle king and Captain Osborn rode in front, closely followed by

Hugh and Doctor Redfield. At the end of about two hours, Hugh called out to his father, asking him if he were sure of the road.

"Perfectly," replied Mr. Horton, "and, as we are going at a speed better than ten miles an hour, we shall easily reach the old Dodson corral by midnight. The last few miles of our journey the road will be somewhat broken, leading over numerous sand-dunes, as we descend into the Cimarron valley, and we will then necessarily have to lessen our speed."

Onward they dashed, over the smooth road, until finally they were forced to rein their ponies to a walk over rough places in the sand-hills. At last, a few minutes before midnight, they halted their tired horses at the corral, and quickly dismounted. Hugh immediately went on a tour of investigation of the old deserted cattle-shed, and found that the opening fronted the river only about a quarter of a mile above the ford. It was built on an abrupt hillside, and consisted of small trunks of trees firmly planted in the ground on the lower side, and cut off evenly at the top, six or seven feet from the ground. Branches of trees were then laid across from the top of this formidable wall to the abrupt bank, which formed the opposite side of the enclosure, the earthen floor having been leveled with spade and shovel.

The corral consisted of four rooms, connected with doorway openings sufficiently large for a horse to pass through. Returning from his reconnoiter he advised that their ponies be led into the back pen of the corral. The only ingress was through the south end of the enclosure. The suggestion was at once acted upon, and soon after the jaded animals were securely fastened within the inner pen. In the meantime, the clouds were clearing away, and the moon was shining forth in all its brilliancy.

"A good idea, Hugh, my son," observed Mr. Horton. "Now if any one chances along near the corral, he will not be frightened away by seeing our horses. We will keep ourselves in the shadow, our guns in our hands, and await developments."

They waited patiently for over an hour, but the silence was unbroken. Presently a rumbling sound, like distant thunder, was heard.

"Listen," said the cattle king, "a drove of cattle is headed this way."

Just then they heard the galloping of horses, and, as a matter of precaution, they hastily retreated into one of the back parts of the corral. Presently they heard voices without.

"Waal, I reckon we're sure here at last, an' thar' ain't no denyin' I'm tired a heap," said one of the horsemen, riding up and dismounting.

"Yes, and yonder comes the cattle," observed the other. "You are sure Kinneman is helping to drive?"

"Dead sure. Ain't no doubt of it. He'll be cavortin' 'round an' tidin' up here in a minute hisself."

A moment later a third horseman came galloping across the valley from the river ford.

"On time, as usual, Kinneman," said a voice that made the cattle king, Captain Osborn, and Hugh start with surprise.

"Thet's what I am; an' don't you-alls furgit I'm powerful nigh used up," growled the cowboy, in a surly tone.

Hugh started from his concealment, but Captain Osborn laid a restraining hand on his arm.

"You think, Dan, that we can handle them all right, do you?" asked the same rich voice that had spoken before.

"Bet yer life we kin," ejaculated Dan Spencer, "an' speakin' plenty perlite to you'ns, I'm cal-kalatin' in four days' time we'll have 'em in the St. Louis market, same as t'other time, an' we'll do it sure, or I'll git plenty hostile."

"Well, Kinneman," said the master voice, "as soon as the last steer is across the ford, order your assistants to return at once, and you go with them. To-morrow morning when it is discovered that some cattle have been stolen, select three tried and true assistants and start out as usual on a hunt for the cattle thieves. Of course you know how to manage the balance of it."

At this moment, four determined men, with leveled guns, advanced on the party.

"Throw up your hands," shouted Captain Osborn, in thundering tones, "or, by the Eternal, we'll shoot you down like dogs."

Both Dan Spencer and Bill Kinneman threw themselves into their saddles quick as lightning, and sinking their spurs deep into the sides of their ponies, bounded away like arrows from well-bent bows, covering their retreat with a cloud of dust. The other cattle thief stood perfectly still, resting an arm on his pony's neck, looking away toward the river, where Kinneman and Spencer were riding at breakneck speed. Four shots, from repeating carbines sang out on the night air, but they missed the fleeing men.

"Don't waste your ammunition, gentlemen, on mere helpers in the cattle-stealing business. I am the man you want, for I am the king of the cattle thieves," and, pulling away his bearded mask, Major Buell Hampton stood before John B. Horton and his associates, while the rays of the moon fell on a face that was contorted and ghastly to look upon.

CHAPTER XLI.

A ROSICRUCIAN

THE cattle king and his associates were shocked into silence by their discovery. That Major Buell Hampton, of all men in southwestern Kansas, should turn out to be the master spirit of the cattle thieves, was quite beyond their apprehension.

"Gentlemen," said the major, "I realize that the situation is an embarrassing one. I certainly had no idea of meeting you, and I am equally certain that you had no expectation of finding in me the cattle thief of the Southwest. I, perhaps, could explain, but it is useless. I certainly cannot deny that for the past three years I have been responsible for the so-called cattle outrages in this part of the country."

"Major Hampton," said Captain Osborn, "I am so surprised and stunned at this revelation, together with your confession, that I am at a loss for words. I would have doubted myself as quickly as you."

The major turned his blanched face toward the moon, and for a moment seemed lost in thought, as if he were communing with some invisible spirit. Finally he replied, "Captain Osborn, I know full well the humiliation of the moment, and the consequences of my capture. At this time I will say only that I have been ruled and guided by a higher power than is found in the laws of our country,—but, why discuss either the motive or the statutes? The former would be disbelieved, while the latter will be cheated by the Vigilantes. The doom of a cattle thief is so well known that it is useless to waste time in further discussion of a subject that is certainly no less distressing to you than it is embarrassing to me."

263

"Father," said Hugh, turning to Mr. Horton, "there must be some deep mystery here which we do not understand. There certainly is an explanation that will exonerate Major Hampton. Whatever we do, let us not act hastily. I cannot and will not believe that the major is in his right mind in making these damaging admissions."

Major Hampton turned his massive head and looked kindly at Hugh. "My dear Stanton," said he, "your trusting confidence in your friends is seemingly boundless. It is the nobility of your generous nature, which prompts you to attempt defense where no defense is possible. At present I have no apologies to offer, and but one request to make. I should sincerely appreciate your consideration if you would let me return to Meade immediately. I have a few business matters to adjust, and then I wish to bid my daughter adieu."

At Captain Osborn's request the major mounted his horse and permitted himself to be disarmed and thoroughly bound, hand and foot. A hasty consultation was held, and it was decided that Captain Osborn and Doctor Redfield should accompany the prisoner to Meade, while Mr. Horton and Hugh would turn the cattle back to the range camp, which was located a few miles to the west, after which they would, with all possible speed, hasten homeward.

Their plans were carried out satisfactorily, and a little after sunrise on the following morning the four horsemen with their prisoner dismounted in front of the grimy-looking county jail, and, soon after, Major Buell Hampton was securely lodged in prison. He had, with considerable emotion, requested Hugh, the last thing before the doors closed upon him, to keep the truth from Marie as long as possible, and to urge her to go at once to Horton's Grove.

A wave of strangely varying sentiments swept over the country in an astonishingly short time, and before noon from two to three hundred strangers were on the streets of Meade. They were principally cattlemen and cowboys, who had suffered more or less by reason of cattle thieving. By three o'clock the streets were jammed with cattlemen and farmers. They seemed to come from all directions, and the feeling was undoubtedly growing more dangerous every moment.

The cattlemen were distinguishable by their broad sombreros, high-topped boots, and Mexican spurs; the farmers by the disappointment which each wore indelibly impressed on his pinched and haggard face. Many of them supported boutonnihres of barley in the lapels of their ragged coats, thus denoting their affiliation with the Barley Hullers. It was a strange mixture of frontiersmen, with conflicting hopes and fears.

To have captured the ringleader of the cattle thieves would within itself have startled the people almost into an universal vigilance committee, but to learn that the leader of these lawless depredations was none other than Major Buell Hampton, so beloved by the masses for his generous deeds of charity, was a great shock. Many refused to believe that he was guilty, and declared with great emphasis that no harm should come to Major Hampton, and that no hasty action should be taken.

There were others who expressed great sorrow at the major's downfall, but nevertheless maintained that the evidence seemed absolute, while the major's own confession admitted of no argument. There was a dangerous note of warning, that could not be misunderstood, in all these expressions of regret.

It was perhaps five o'clock in the afternoon when the Horton turnout came dashing up to the county jail, which was well guarded by the sheriff and a score of deputies. Hugh Stanton was driving. In the carriage was Marie, accompanied by Mrs. Horton and Ethel. The women were dressed in black and were heavily veiled. As they drove along, Marie's stifled sobs were audible to those nearest the carriage.

The mob of people in the street gave way to the carriage, and a hushed silence fell over all. On alighting from the carriage, Marie was quickly admitted to her father's presence by an officer. She remained in the jail nearly an hour, and, on coming out, Hugh met her at the door and assisted her into the carriage. He then drove rapidly away toward the Grove.

As night came on, the throng of people increased, and the sheriff swore in more deputies. Captain Osborn and Mr. Horton were talking in subdued tones in the captain's private office at the bank.

"Things are looking ugly, and I fear mob violence," said the captain.

"Yes," said his companion, "but there are dozens for defense, where there is one for hanging. I had no idea of the extent of Hampton's friends. His sympathizers are legion."

"The result of his known and secret charities," replied the captain. "His hobby has ever been to 'clothe the naked and feed the hungry.' I now understand where his seemingly limitless means came from. His mania has been to take from those who have Abundance and give to the destitute. His theory of a more equal distribution of wealth has been carried into practice."

"What I most fear," said Mr. Horton, "is that summary justice will be meted out to him, and that we snail find ourselves in a position where we shall be helpless to prevent a brutal murder. Is there not some way to quiet and disperse the people?"

Before Captain Osborn could reply, Hugh and Doctor Redfield admitted themselves with a private key. Hugh's face was flushed with excitement. "Captain," said he, "they are preparing to hang Major Hampton. Something must be done, and quickly, or there will be bloodshed."

"But he has defenders among the people," said Mr. Horton.

"Very true," said Hugh, "and the result will be a riot, a pitched battle between the farmers and their sympathizers on the one side and the cattlemen and the cowboys on the other. A wholesale massacre will be the result. If the cowmen win, the major's life is not worth a penny."

Just then there came a loud knocking on the back door of the bank. Hugh hastened to the door and soon returned with a note which had been handed him by a deputy. It was from the major, and requested him to come immediately to the jail.

"Go at once, my son," said Mr. Horton, "and I will assist the captain in trying to quiet the mob. I think, Captain, you had better make them a speech."

Hugh hurried away to the jail, and was soon in the iron cage with the major. The latter greeted him warmly, and seemed so free from excitement that Hugh was astonished.

"Do you not know that they are planning to hang you?" asked Hugh, excitedly.

"My dear Stanton," replied the major, smiling, "I am protected, fully and absolutely; therefore give yourself no uneasiness on my account. By the way, have you an extra cigar with you?"

Hugh handed him a cigar, one of the major's favorite brand.

"Thank you," said he, with his old-time politeness.

"I must admit, Major, that you inspire me with a sense of security such as I have not before experienced to-day. The Barley Hullers are out *en masse*. They are the protection to which you refer, I presume. What we all fear is a riot. The cowboys, as you know, are veritable devils when they get into a row, and one of them can usually whip half a dozen farmers in a rough-and-tumble shooting scrape."

The major threw back his clustering iron-gray hair, and, with a smile, said: "Stanton, I have learned to love you, and therefore have concluded to tell you what no man living in America knows to-day."

He paused a moment, and lighted his cigar.

"Well?" said Hugh, as if impatiently asking a question.

"They cannot harm me," said he, jerking his thumb over his shoulder toward the howling mob, whose angry mutterings could be plainly heard. "But I will tell you what may happen."

He spoke slowly and seemed to Hugh to change for the moment from the Major Hampton he had admired so much into a patriarch with gullied furrows on his brow. Hugh concluded that his light remarks of a few moments before had been assumed, and intended simply to cover the deep emotion that he really felt.

"Captain Osborn will make a speech," the major continued, "and it will be an impassioned one, seasoned with the eloquence of rare power, inspired by his deep love of justice as well as of myself. The crowd will gradually disperse and wander across the bleak prairies to their miserable homes, furnished principally with poverty and hunger and deferred hopes. The Vigilantes, composed of cattlemen, will come back after midnight and probably select by ballot three of their number to kill me. I will be taken away from here, and will accompany the committee over into Dead Man's Hollow, where already a grave is being dug and a rough board coffin prepared. The sheriff will be bought with the promise of reelection; he will discharge his deputies and turn me over to these would-be murderers."

Hugh could hardly restrain himself while the major was thus slowly counting the steps leading up to his death. "But, Major, don't you think—" he began.

"I will tell you—not what I think, but what I know." His voice sank almost to a whisper as he continued. "They cannot hurt me, my boy; no, they cannot kill me, for I am a Rosicrucian and my talisman is the supposedly lost philosopher's stone. This rare and precious chemical element was crystallized about the middle of the seventeenth century, after almost fifty years of exhaustive research and scientific investigation by my brothers of the Rosy Cross. The philosopher's stone, however, is but one of the many secrets known to our order. Our home is in the Himalayas, in unknown vaults and caves, far above the Thibetan table-lands.

"I am, in the broadest sense, a missionary sent out by our mystic order, to lighten the burdens of humanity. Suffering among the poor, whose eyes are blinded with scalding tears, appeals to me with a strong and resistless force. For centuries I have been battling for humanity. I have renounced the world and yielded all that was demanded of me for the cheering song of one small feathered thing, that, like a tiny bird, is always singing in my soul. It is called Hope, and it still sings, and its sweet warbling notes fill me with the abiding belief that the millennium is coming, when altruism will rule the world, and selfishness shall be reckoned as one of the lost attributes of man.

"Among the many secrets of our brotherhood is the knowledge of renewing youth, the prolonging of life. Our lives are renewed only that we may complete our work. We are reformists, and seek to benefit the world, to check the greed of wealth and the tyranny and despotism of bigotry and oppression. I have suffered so much at the hands of greed and avarice that my heart has become a touchstone of generosity to the poor.

"It is true that I have taken from the rich and given to the needy, and thereby gladdened the hearts of many; and, no matter what may follow, I have had my reward in the knowledge that I have exercised the courage of my convictions and put into practice not only theories, but truths that are approved by the living God. I have been controlled by an influence leagues beyond the power of man; an influence that lays its strong hand on every deed we do, on every act of our lives, and weaves its unerring results into an iron tissue of destiny. Listen! The mob is growing more tumultuous,—it is clamoring for my blood.

"Before you go, Stanton, I must entrust you with a message to Marie. She is not my daughter. It will almost break her heart, poor girl, when this is told her. In my wandering over the earth, I found a poor, famished woman, sick and without food or shelter, in a little town in eastern Kentucky. In her arms she held a sweet-faced cherub of a babe. I took her to a private hospital and supplied means for her comfort, and, for a time, hoped that she might recover. But the sands of life were too nearly ebbed away, and she finally realized that a few days at best were all that were left to her. I saw that I could lighten her sorrow and gladden her heart by assuring her that her babe would find in me a father, and you can testify as to how well I have kept that promise. I had the consolation of seeing the mother made happy before her spirit was called away. Her real name is Marie Redfield. Her genealogy is in my safe at the *Patriot* office, and you can learn from it that she is none other than Doctor Redfield's cousin. Tell her, my boy, that no father's heart was ever more tender toward a daughter than is mine toward her. Say to her that I shall see her before many days, but until I come I shall leave her in your care." Turning, the major took up a large envelope with Hugh's name upon it, and, continuing, he said: "I have appointed you my executor and representative. Full instructions and explanations will be found in this envelope. To this part of the world I shall be, from this night on, as one dead. Now go, my boy, and tell your father and Captain Osborn and Doctor Redfield to join you in taking an active part with the Vigilantes, who are clamoring for my death."

CHAPTER XLII.

A NEW-MADE GRAVE

WHEN Hugh returned to the street, Captain Osborn was concluding one of the most eloquent speeches of his life. His appeal to the better nature of his hearers was having a noticeable effect. Indeed, the wild huzzas and shoutings, which the major had mistaken for the clamoring of the people for his heart's blood, were, in reality, cheers of approval at Captain Osborn's words. He admonished them to give up the idea of taking so-called justice into their hands, and to permit the law of the land to take its course. His hearers listened attentively, and, when he concluded his speech with a stirring and eloquent appeal to them, the comments on every side were those of approval. Soon after, the crowd began to disperse, and before midnight the streets were almost deserted.

Captain Osborn, with Doctor Redfield, Hugh, and his father, returned to the bank, where Hugh proceeded to give them a synopsis of his interview with the major. When he concluded his narrative, a profound silence followed.

Presently Captain Osborn said: "Stanton, what do you think of the major's mental condition?"

"I believe him to be as mad as a March hare," replied Hugh. "We all know that he is a great student, and, while his knowledge of occult science is certainly extensive, the idea of his claiming to be two or three centuries old, and of his possessing, as a talisman, the philosopher's stone, is too ridiculous for thoughtful consideration."

"There is one part of his story that is remarkably rational," said Doctor Redfield. "A younger brother of my father married a beautiful woman of rare musical gifts and culture. For some reason his family opposed the marriage. My uncle located in eastern Kentucky, and several years went by without our receiving any word from them. Finally my father went there on a visit, and found that his brother had been dead for several years and that his wife had attempted to support herself and child, and had succeeded in doing so until her health became broken and she was reduced to direst poverty. She was too proud to ask for help, and finally died in a private hospital. The matron of the institution told a similar story to the one narrated by Major Hampton. All trace of the child was lost, and, although my father spent years in trying to ferret out some clue that might enable him to find her, his efforts were unavailing." The doctor continued: "I agree with Hugh that Major Hampton is suffering with at least temporary aberration of the mind. It may not be permanent; and yet, on the other hand, his hallucination may be incurable."

"Hark!" exclaimed Mr. Horton, "I think some one is calling my name."

They listened in silence for a moment, and presently heard the cattle king's name called by some one without.

"Remain here," said Mr. Horton, "and I will see what is wanted."

"Remember, father," interposed Hugh, "that the major's last request was that we join with the Vigilantes in case they are determined to mete out summary justice."

"I believe," said Captain Osborn, after Mr. Horton had gone, "that the major, with all his insane ideas, expects us to control any vigilance committee that might seek his life, and to ward off danger. I have always regarded him as being a man of excellent judgment. The humiliation of being discovered as a cattle thief has undoubtedly dethroned his reason. From his rambling talk to Hugh there can be no doubt of this."

"I assure you, Captain," replied Hugh, "that his observations were far from rambling in any respect. Neither was he in the least excited, but went on telling me his marvelous story as if he fully expected me to believe every word that he uttered."

At this moment Mr. Horton called from the back door of the bank, requesting those within to join him at once. As they came out, he said: "They want to know if we desire to be present, or if we intend to oppose them. Remembering Hugh's instructions, I told them that we secretly were with the Vigilantes; therefore, there is nothing left but to join them and see what we can do. They are meeting down at Foster's livery barn."

Nothing further was said as the four men walked down the street. They were joined by figures coming out of dark alleys and unexpected places, until fully a score of them were in line by the time the barn was reached. They filed into a dark room, whose doors were immediately barricaded. Then a gruff voice called out: "Every man prepare a mask for his face. No one must know his neighbor. A candle will be lighted as soon as your masks are on."

It required no second invitation, for even the most desperate member of the Vigilantes is careful to conceal his identity from his associates in crime.

Presently the same gruff voice called out: "Are you ready?"

A chorus of affirmative answers came from every part of the room.

The candle was lighted, and, with the aid of a penknife, was fastened to one of the rough beams of the building. The fitful, sputtering tight threw weird shadows over the motley gathering of men, most of whom regarded cattle thieving as the greatest crime in the whole criminal calendar.

"Gentlemen," said the gruff-voiced man, "I've been selected as chairman of this meeting. For three years past we have pledged ourselves to exterminate a cattle thief as soon as caught, without waiting for the slow process of law, which frequently cheats justice and permits guilty men to escape. We have prepared as many ballots as there are men present. Three of these ballots have blood-red crosses in the centre. Form in line and march past, while I hold the hat, and let each man draw therefrom one ballot. The three receiving the ballots with the red cross will remain here. All those drawing blanks will quietly and quickly repair to their homes."

It was a strangely spectral sight to see more than a score of masked men filing past the speaker to draw from his hat the ratal ballots destined to decree the murderous judgment of the Vigilantes.

Soon the barricades were removed, and all but three of the crowd walked out into the street, but, instead of hastening to their homes, they quickly concealed themselves behind fences, sheds, and stables, waiting to see what would occur.

When all had gone excepting the three who had drawn the fatal ballots, the leader, addressing them, said: "Gentlemen, the Vigilantes have made a compact with the sheriff. You will please go to the jail and knock for admittance. You will have no trouble in securing possession of the prisoner. When he is once in your custody, follow the laws of the Vigilantes. The grave is prepared and the coffin is ready." Presently three dark figures wended their way toward the county jail. Later four men were seen going from the jail toward Dead Man's Hollow. No word was spoken until they reached a slight ridge just south of Meade, which separated the town from the spot selected for these executions. Here they paused in deep discussion. The scraggy clouds hurried through the heavens as if even they were fretful and restless, with strange forebodings of the dread event; while the moon, which was in its last quarter, seemed to be endeavoring to catch a glimpse of the tragedy about to be enacted, through broken rifts of the scurrying clouds.

Not only the score or more of men who had taken part in the counsels of the Vigilantes, but perhaps a hundred others were craning their necks from places of concealment, eagerly watching the figures on the crest of the hill. They saw the old major throw back his head in his own princely manner. Notwithstanding the distance, his words were borne distinctly to them on the night winds.

"My life," said he, "is a charmed one. I am a member of the Mystic Brotherhood, and it is not for you to teach me the sting of death." They disappeared from view, and a little later three gunshots rang out on the night air, startling the whippoorwills and thrushes. A neighs boring rooster crowed hoarsely the hour. The watchers knew that the death penalty had been paid.

Captain Osborn and his three friends returned to the bank, but they were silent in their sorrow. In the first place, the major's friends had not expected the treachery of the sheriff, and they felt sure, because of that official's promise to Captain Osborn, that it would be impossible for the Vigilantes to secure the prisoner. From the standpoint of the cattlemen Major Hampton had certainly merited death, but it seemed so terrible, so unexpected, so shocking, that no one of the four could reconcile himself to the belief that so monstrous a tragedy had really been enacted.

"Have you opened the letter yet?" inquired the captain.

"No," replied Hugh, "perhaps we might as well do it now as later."

The four men gathered around the table, and Hugh broke the seal. The letter read as follows:

> "My dear Stanton:—Enclosed herewith I hand you my last will and testament, bequeathing all my possessions to my beloved daughter, Marie Redfield Hampton. I also enclose the combination of my safe.
>
> "You will find, in looking over my private books, an accurate statement of all moneys received from the sale of stolen cattle. You will also find a report of distributions which I have made of the money. The credit balance is less than one thousand dollars; all but this has been given to the poor and needy.
>
> "Instead of experiencing any sentiment of regret, I find deep consolation in thinking of the misery that I have lessened

and the hearts that I have gladdened. My remembrance of the great Southwest will ever be a pleasant one. The friendship of yourself, your father, and Captain Osborn, and your many kindnesses, are things engraven on my memory that will bear a golden harvest of responding love for mankind, and greater deeds of charity from my hands, in the years that are to come. The unwritten law of humanity contains stronger covenants than may be found on the statute books of all the nations of the earth.

"It takes a high-souled man to be as 'brave as a Caesar and wise as a Plato' when confronted with the trying ordeal of friendship on the one hand and humanity on the other.

"As one of the Rosicrucians—a member of the Brotherhood of the Highest Himalayas—whose only mission on earth is to reform and equalize, to lift up the lowly, to change tears of adversity into smiles of gladness, to oppose plutocracy and greed, to abolish bigotry and selfishness, and to sow seeds of altruistic virtue, I cannot, in taking a farewell retrospective view, discover a single opportunity that I have not endeavored to improve.

"Tell your father that Kinneman and Spencer were but helpers—paid servants to do my bidding—and therefore they should not merit his anger.

"My pen drags a little as I write, for I am thinking of my daughter. I call her mine, although no common blood flows in our veins, for my love of her is very great. Indeed, it is the one tie that is hardest for me to sever. I am sure at your request that both Mrs. Horton and Ethel will comfort her and give her a home. Tell her that it will not be long until we are reunited. The end of our sojourn in the Southwest will be but the beginning of other happy days in a new country where I *shall take up my abode.*

"*Tell her for me, as Charles the Ninth said to the queen mother,—'Wait. All human wisdom is in this single word,—wait. The greatest, strongest, most skilled is he who knows how to wait, and wait patiently.' So say I to her,—wait.*

"*Tell her also that, notwithstanding I am rich with the accumulated wisdom of the centuries, yet, nevertheless, I am subject to the laws of the country in which I may be living, and I can but bow to the frenzy of the mob, and ask that they may be forgiven for they know not what they do. I came to emancipate, and now they seek my life. I came to alleviate their sufferings, and now they would bite the hand that has fed them.*

"*Impress upon her that no condition can arise in this crisis that is not fully provided for, and, instead of being the 'plaything of chance,' I am a Rosicrucian, and am not subject to that mysterious force which compels the children of men to obey its mandates.*

"*The hope of the age is progress, and 'the noble few will lose nothing when it overtakes them.'*

"*You must not suppose, because I enclose my will herewith, that my mission on earth is finished; but in the Great Southwest I shall from this night on be regarded as legally dead. My protection is nothing less than the invincible philosopher's stone, a talisman which will protect me far more securely than a coat of mail.*

"*Let me, in conclusion, admonish you to devote at least a part of the millions you will inherit to the sacred cause of humanity.*

"Until we meet again, adieu!

"Buell Hampton."

When Hugh had finished reading the letter, Captain Osborn arose from his chair and walked impatiently up and down the room, with his hands clasped behind him.

"Dastardly," he finally ejaculated, "yes, a most dastardly and outrageous murder has been committed. A maniac has been slaughtered in cold blood. It is a calamity to this part of the Sunflower State, not even exceeded by the hot winds of Hades."

Soon after, they started for their homes. Hugh excused himself, promising to come on a little later. The sun was just showing its golden dawn in the east. The town of Meade was wrapped in sleep.

Left alone, Hugh gave himself up to thought, as he walked toward the outskirts or the town, in the direction of Dead Man's Hollow. Arriving on the brow of the hill, his heart smote him, for there, locked in each other arms in deepest grief, were Marie Hampton and Ethel Horton. He remembered his first evening at Major Hampton's home, and he marveled at the great change that had been wrought. The innocent, light-hearted girl had awakened to a sorrow which words could not comfort, a grief that he himself shared.

Then came to him the memory of his dream, wherein he had seen Marie standing before him weeping bitterly, her fair cheeks and violet eyes all bathed in tears, while near her was Ethel endeavoring to speak words of consolation. Between them was a mound of earth, and, looking closer, he saw that it was a new-made grave.

CHAPTER XLIII.

UNDER THE QUIET STARS

THE story of the midnight murder of Maj. Buell Hampton at the hands of the Vigilantes traveled swiftly from door to door across the bleak Kansas prairies.

Again the people thronged the streets of Meade. The lamentations of bronzed men and emaciated women, with pale-faced babes clinging to their breasts, was a scene never to be forgotten. These were the ones who had received charities from this man of complex destiny.

No broad-brimmed sombreros and Mexican spurs were observable among the people. The cattlemen were conspicuous only by their absence.

The sudden and startling discovery of Maj. Buell Hampton's misdeeds on the day before had intimidated many into partial inaction. Twenty-four hours had changed all this, however, and a love for their idol, the man of gentle manners and of generous acts, rose up before them like a spirit from the martyr's grave. The eyes of the gaunt and half-famished women were red with weeping, while mutterings of vengeance were heard on every side from the lips of disappointed and restless men.

Some few seemed inclined to blame Captain Osborn for his assurance of the prisoner's safety, in his speech of the night before.

A part of the men went in search of the sheriff, only to find that he had taken an early train for Kansas City. Captain Osborn's high standing and known friendship for Major Hampton, however, protected him from general censure, but the sheriff was branded as a Judas and a traitor.

279

Judge Linus Lynn, during the afternoon, climbed on top of a dry-goods box in the middle of the public square, and made a speech. The people were quite ready to listen to eulogies pronounced in behalf of their lost benefactor, and Judge Lynn made Major Hampton's charities and nobleness of heart his theme. He promised them that the *Patriot* should be issued on the following day under his management, and that he would map out and publish a plan looking toward disinterring the body of Major Hampton from Dead Man's Hollow and giving it a decent Christian burial in Graceland Cemetery. The people contented themselves with this arrangement, and returned to their homes.

The next day was Thursday, and, when the *Patriot* made its appearance, half the population of the surrounding country was waiting for a copy. Judge Lynn was the hero of the hour. His editorial, entitled "The Death of a Martyr," was, indeed, an able and forceful presentation of facts from the farmers' and Barley Hullers' point of view. The plan suggested by Judge Lynn was that the people should assemble *en masse* the following Saturday and give a proper burial to the remains of the founder of the Barley Hullers, and that the ceremonies should be conducted under the auspices of that order.

The suggestions were at once approved, and on the following Saturday there assembled on the streets of Meade such a gathering of people as had never before been seen on the frontier of the Great Southwest. The Barley Hullers from all over the district, wearing sprigs of barley as boutonnihres, occupied the places of honor next to Mr. Horton's carriage, in which were Marie, Hugh, Mrs. Horton, and Ethel. They were escorted to Dead Man's Hollow by the village band, which played a funeral march. In all the vast concourse of people that followed, there was not one but cherished tender memories for Buell Hampton.

On arriving at the new-made grave, willing hands commenced removing the soft earth. Presently their shovels struck against the rough-board coffin. A little later it was lifted to view, and a wailing sob went up from the people. Conscience smote their hearts, while charity and mercy blotted out all memory of Major Hampton, save his generosity to the poor and his goodness of heart.

The Barley Hullers formed in procession, and six pall-bearers lifted the coffin preparatory to the march to Graceland Cemetery. At this critical moment, destiny, by the hidden hand of her jester, loosened a buckle in the belt of fate. The wooden bottom of the coffin gave way, and several bushels of earth fell to the ground. The dirge-like music played by the band ceased abruptly. A hushed, death-like silence fell over the multitude. An awful suspense trembled in the balance of uncertainty, until the stupefied throng saw something white flutter and fall at their feet—it was Truth.

Then, as if by magic, it dawned upon them that the Vigilantes had been cheated and that Maj. Buell Hampton was not dead. A spontaneous yell of triumph rent the air. Women screamed in hysterical and tearful exultation. Men shouted, hugged each other, and wept like children. There were acclamations of joy on every hand, and the air became rent with a deafening clamor of happiness. Hugh could hardly control his team in the wild demonstrations of enthusiasm. Marie laughed and cried alternately, and finally fainted in the arms of Mrs. Horton and Ethel. Wild pandemonium of joy reigned. The people were transported with startling excitement and exalting surprise into a happiness that nothing but yells, hugs, and tears could express.

When the tumult had quieted a little, and Marie had partially recovered, Hugh managed to escape from the crush of excited people, and drove rapidly homeward.

The crowd, now thoroughly good-natured, drifted back into the streets of Meade, and then celebrated, in various ways, the noted event. Every man in the vast throng inquired of his neighbor, over and over, where he supposed Major Hampton was.

When the cattlemen learned of the deception that had been practised upon them by the committee of three selected by the council of the Vigilantes, they were greatly surprised but, strange as it may appear, they were neither sorry nor angry. The pendulum of public opinion had swung back, and influenced their better judgment. Indeed, they were already beginning to regret their hasty action, and they experienced a sense of relief when it was discovered that their chosen committee had proved treacherous and that Maj. Buell Hampton's blood was not on their heads.

How a just and learned judge would have looked upon their "intentions," had they been tried for manslaughter, did not enter into their contemplations. Even the council that had decreed Major Hampton's death had no means of knowing the personnel of the committee of three; evidently, however, they were friends of the condemned man.

Within a week the excitement of the strange incident had practically subsided, but interest and diligent inquiry as to Major Hampton's whereabouts were still active. The mystery of Major Hampton's escape was no greater surprise than had been the discovery that he was the master spirit of the cattle thieves of Southwestern Kansas. His crime was of such a nature that no self-respecting, law-abiding citizen could countenance it, and even sympathy from the better class would certainly have been withheld had developments not indicated so plainly that his reason was dethroned.

Marie soon recovered from the severe shock occasioned by the supposed death of her father, and anxiously awaited his return. The fact that he still lived acted as a tonic to her shattered nerves.

Her genealogy, found among the major's private papers, fully established her kinship to Dr. Jack Redfield. It was a joyful discovery to each of them, and the doctor never tired of answering the questions about the Redfield family, which were put to him by his pretty cousin.

"Just think, Marie," said Ethel, enthusiastically, "I shall soon— very soon—be your cousin, and you shall come and live with me in Chicago."

"No, Ethel," replied Marie, "I must wait for papa. I know he says that I am not his daughter, but my heart goes out to him just as much as if I were. Indeed, since I have learned the truth, it seems to me that I love him more than ever. His kindness to my mother, his loyalty, his generosity and love during all these many years, doubly endear him to me."

Hugh exhibited an increased consideration for Marie. He told Captain Osborn that it was because the major had requested him to look after her interests until he returned. The captain laughed good-naturedly, and Hugh looked embarrassed.

"But what will happen," asked Captain Osborn, in a bantering tone, "if the major never returns?"

"Your question," replied Hugh, in half-irritation, "is untenable, because it is not supposable. Major Hampton has promised to return, and he was never known to break his word in keeping an engagement."

In the solitude of his room, Hugh confessed to himself that at last he was face to face with love itself; and just at a time, too, when Marie appeared indifferent. Perhaps her seeming indifference had aroused him into action.

"I have always been willing to look at a difficulty and to go around it heretofore," he mused, "but in this case I will jump over every obstacle that stands between my foolish self and Marie Hampton."

Generous, noble-hearted Hugh Stanton was, indeed, awakened to his first great passion of absorbing love. Heretofore he had been influenced by cold judgment, seasoned by his high sense of honor; now, however, a new condition confronted him. His heart was speaking wildly, and it jealously bid defiance to judgment and to reason. He thought how blind he had been in not understanding his heart long before. Once he fancied that his interest in Marie was inspired by her musical gifts. Now he knew differently, and marveled at his stupidity in not recognizing, in the bud, the full-blown rose. It was no longer the jewels in the casket, but the wondrous casket itself.

The dinner-bell sounded, and, after an extra adjustment of his necktie, and a special brushing of his hair, he went down to the dining-room.

He was confused when Ethel spoke to him, and made unintelligible answers. Dr. Jack Redfield laughingly accused him of being absent-minded. The cattle king said that he had been working too hard, while Mrs. Horton insisted that Hugh, poor boy, must take a vacation and a rest from the severe nervous strain that he had been under.

A sense of guilt crept into Hugh's heart, for he knew a secret which he believed none of them guessed. Presently he discovered that he had no appetite. He raised his eyes like a blushing schoolboy to Marie's sweet face, and she was laughing a wicked, mischievous laugh. It was more than he could endure. He gulped rather than drank a swallow of coffee.

"I beg pardon, Miss Marie; you seem amused."

"Yes," said she, still laughing; "I know what is the matter with you, but seemingly the others do not."

Hugh's face was now on fire. He imagined that she at last knew the secret of his heart, and he feared that she would reveal it before the entire household.

Was ever a girl more beautiful, bewitching, and tantalizing than Marie!

Hastily arising from the table, he asked to be excused, and bolted like an awkward overgrown boy from the room.

Mrs. Horton looked distressed, and at once inquired of Marie what she fancied was troubling: Hugh.

"Why, Mrs. Horton," replied Marie, "could you not see that his collar was so tight that his face was fairly crimson?"

"Hey?" interposed Mr. Horton. "Collar too tight, you say? Then he must have been wearing the same sized collar for the last ten days. I have noticed a wonderful change in him for the past week or so."

Dr. Jack Redfield smiled and made a sign to Ethel, who in turn nodded her knowing head toward Marie.

In the meantime, Hugh put on his hat and walked down the

winding path to the lake. He bared his head and let the cool night winds fan his fevered brow. The moon in all its grandeur was climbing the eastern sky. Turning aside to a little summer-house, he seated himself and looked through the checkered openings at the twining tendrils of a honeysuckle. The moon's rays fell aslant on the earthen floor, which was cut into squares by the shadow. He soon grew restless and sauntered out along a path into the thickest part of the grove. The great trees seemed to him to be a battalion of giant soldiers in repose. The winds stirred the limbs, and, as they swayed up and down, moaning in half-stifled sobs, breaking off dry twigs and withered leaves, he fancied that they were "cracking their knuckles at him" in fiendish glee, and, while they pretended to sympathize, they were in fact only laughing at his rejected love. Yes, Marie had laughed at him, thereby confessing a knowledge of his great love, and at the same time trampling it cruelly beneath her feet.

After walking for an hour through the woods, he returned somewhat calmed, but filled with a determination to tell Marie at once that life to him was worthless without her reciprocal love. He came to the lake and paused a moment to watch the rippling waves, so beautifully yellowed by the moon's soft rays that they seemed like liquid gold. He turned, and then stopped suddenly. Immediately in front of him, and standing in the doorway of the summer-house, was Marie. She came toward him, and in solicitous tones inquired if he were ill. Her foot caught on a vine of honeysuckle, and she nearly fell. Hugh caught her in his strong arms and held her passionately to his breast.

"Marie, Marie, my darling," he whispered. "I love you—yes, love you better than life. Can you not see that this great love is driving me desperate and setting my blood on fire? Can you not, will you not, give me a word, a single word of hope?"

She struggled to free herself from his fervid embrace, trembling like a captured bird, but her struggles only caused him to press her closer to his beating heart.

He knew that the one woman in all the wide world, to whom

he had given his all-absorbing, blind affection, was resting in his arms.

She ceased struggling, and looked up into his face as if mutely appealing to him.

"Oh, my darling, my beloved Marie," he continued, "can you not tell me that you love me?"

His hot breath was on her cheeks.

"Pray do not be angry with me," he went on, wildly; "my heart is sobbing a prayer for your forgiveness; kiss me, dearest, and I shall know that I am forgiven and loved."

For a moment she hesitated, and then, timidly reaching up her plump, white arms, she clasped them about his neck and pressed her lips—soft as the velvet petals of a rose—to his own. It was a clinging, soulful kiss of an innocent girl given with the wealth of her whole heart to the man she loved.

It seemed that heaven enveloped them for a moment with its dazzling splendor.

"Ah, my darling," he murmured, "you forgive me, and love me. Complete my happiness by telling me in words."

Her countenance brightened with a smile of almost heavenly radiance, and, drawing him still closer, she whispered: "Do I love you, Hugh? Why, I loved you from the beginning."

Retreating within the summer-house, they seated themselves on a rustic seat and began telling over the sacred story that has been whispered by passionate lovers all round the world rom the beginning of time.

The checkered rays of the moon lay like a carpet at their feet, while all the light of starry heaven seemed to fall and rest upon them in glorious benediction.

A shadow fell across the doorway. It was Maj. Buell Hampton who stood before them. With a wild cry of joy and thanksgiving, Marie threw herself into his arms. After tenderly embracing her, he turned slowly toward Hugh, and, extending his hand in greeting, supported the sobbing girl with his other arm.

"My dear Stanton," said he, in his rich, full voice, "I am indeed delighted to see you. I am going to a new country, and shall begin again my labors for the lowly and suffering humanity. My home shall be somewhere amid the mighty canons and cliffs of rugged mountains. There is no lasting pleasure in living, unless we may do good to our fellow men. Years upon years of earnest labor have taught me that we can secure the blessings of a peaceful death and of a rich reward in the world beyond only by being steadfast in our labor of love while in the vineyards of earth."

Marie was sobbing as if her heart would break.

"Do not grieve, my little girl, at my going. We shall meet again. I leave you sheltered and protected by the love of a noble man. My blessing is upon you and on him. Remember, my daughter, that the crowning glory of wifehood is motherhood. Let your devotion to your husband and to the children that may bless your fireside be an untarnished shield, protecting your journey through life, and blessing you in old age.

"Hugh, my son, remember that partings are brief—it is possible that we shall meet again. Into your care and keeping I give this noble girl. Heretofore her innocence has been her safeguard. In the future you must be responsible for her happiness."

He lifted one of Marie's fair hands to his lips, and then placed it in Hugh's.

"My children, I can pronounce no richer eulogy than to say that I believe as firmly as I believe in doing good to suffering humanity, that you are each worthy of the other. Adieu, my daughter. Farewell, my son."

He went out under the quiet stars, and, like a spirit, disappeared in the deep shadows of the woods, and was seen no more by those who marveled at this supposed Rosicrucian, or by the multitudes who had learned to love him on the cattle range of the Great Southwest.